THE CURSE OF THE WENDIGO

2

Also by Rick Yancey

THE MONSTRUMOLOGIST
THE ISLE OF BLOOD

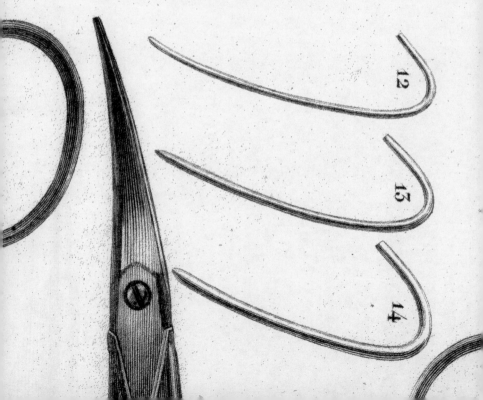

THE MONSTRUMOLOGIST

THE CURSE OF THE WENDIGO

WILLIAM JAMES HENRY

Edited by Rick Yancey

SIMON & SCHUSTER BFYR
NEW YORK LONDON TORONTO SYDNEY

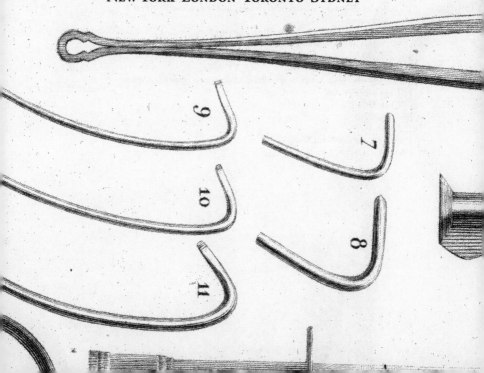

SIMON & SCHUSTER BFYR

An imprint of Simon & Schuster Children's Publishing Division

1230 Avenue of the Americas, New York, New York 10020

For information about special discounts for bulk purchases, please contact Simon & Schuster Special Sales at 1-866-506-1949 or business@simonandschuster.com.

The Simon & Schuster Speakers Bureau can bring authors to your live event. For more information or to book an event, contact the Simon & Schuster Speakers Bureau at 1-866-248-3049 or visit our website at www.simonspeakers.com.

Also available in a SIMON & SCHUSTER BFYR hardcover edition

Book design by Lucy Ruth Cummins

The text for this book is set in Adobe Jensen Pro.

Manufactured in the United States of America

First SIMON & SCHUSTER BFYR paperback edition September 2011

10 9 8 7 6 5 4 3 2 1

The Library of Congress has cataloged the hardcover edition as follows:

Yancey, Richard.

The curse of the Wendigo / William James Henry ; edited by Rick Yancey.—1st ed.

p. cm.—(Monstrumologist ; 2)

Summary: In 1888, twelve-year-old Will Henry chronicles his apprenticeship with Dr. Warthrop, a New England scientist who hunts and studies real-life monsters, as they discover and attempt to destroy the Wendigo, a creature that starves even as it gorges itself on human flesh.

ISBN 978-1-4169-8450-4 (hc)

[1. Monsters—Fiction. 2. Supernatural—Fiction. 3. Apprentices—Fiction. 4. Orphans—Fiction. 5. Horror stories.] I. Title.

PZ7.Y19197Cu 2010

[Fic]—dc22

2010019233

ISBN 978-1-4169-8451-1 (pbk)

ISBN 978-1-4169-8973-8 (eBook)

For Sandy, my light in the darkness

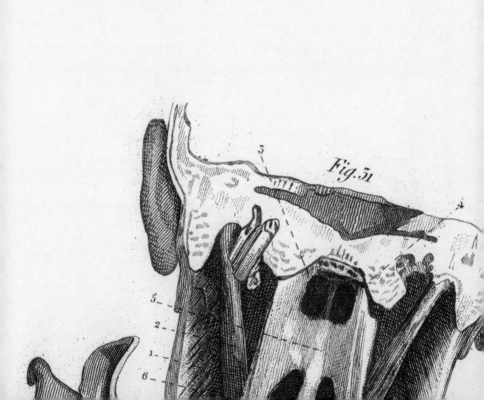

Fig. 31

ACKNOWLEDGMENTS

Editing this second set of Will Henry's journals proved a more daunting task than the first. Historical references abound throughout the folios, all of which had to be checked for accuracy. I am indebted to Jonathan DiGiovanni and copy editor Bara McNeill for their careful and thorough fact-checking of the manuscript.

For their generous help in vetting the languages spoken in the book, thanks to Dr. Sylvie Blum-Reid, Dr. Hana Filip, and Linda Kittendorf.

As with the first volume of *The Monstrumologist*, Dr. Jeffrey Wilt provided insight into the workings of human anatomy. His unfailing patience and good cheer in the face of a layman's barely articulate questions were truly invaluable.

My agent, Brian DeFiore, whose enthusiasm for this project seems to have no bounds, was an early reader of the manuscript. Throughout the editing process he offered suggestions for further research and provided guidance when certain avenues of inquiry came to an abrupt dead end. I am lucky to have him as an agent and proud to call him a friend.

I cannot thank my family enough for their amazing patience, understanding and support while I worked on this book. My sons have always been my biggest fans. Thanks, guys.

I owe the most by far to my wife, Sandy, to whom this book is dedicated. Without her love and fierce loyalty, her unflagging devotion and uncompromising honesty, I would be truly lost. She is my best friend.

Horrible Indian Murder.

WINNIPEG, Dec. 14.—Indian Agent Short has arrived here from Berens River, with particulars of a horrible murder which occurred eight miles west of Berens River Reserve. An Indian woman suffering from typhoid fever became delirious. Her husband thought she had become a "wendigo," and decided she must be killed in order to prevent her from eating other members of her band. He twisted her head until her neck was broken. The Indian was taken into custody on a charge of murder.

—*The New York Times*, December 15, 1897

SHOT THE CHIEF ON HIS ORDER.

WINNIPEG, Manitoba, Oct. 27.—R. G. Chamberlain of the Dominion police, Ottawa, and B. J. Bannalatyne, Indian Agent at Lacseul, arrived to-day with three Indians in their custody. Two of the Indians are charged with shooting their chief last Winter at Cat Lake, about 350 miles northeast of Dinordwic. The story told by the two prisoners is substantially as follows:

The chief of the Cat Lake Indians called Ah-Wah-Sa-Keh-Mig, became a "wendigo," or insane, and ordered the prisoners to shoot him. A counsel of the tribe was called, and they discussed the matter for two days, when they arrived at the conclusion that the chief's orders would have to be obeyed. The "wendigo" lay down in his wigwam and indicated with his hand where they were to shoot him.

After he was dead, wood was heaped upon his body, and the fire was kept going for two days, thereby, according to the belief of the Indians, thoroughly destroying the evil spirit of the chief. The matter was reported to Mr. Bannalatyne, but as the Cat Lake Tribe are non-treaty Indians, special legislation was passed to cover the case.

Constable Chamberlain went to Lacseul, where Mr. Bannalatyne and two guides joined him, and they made the 700-mile journey in twenty days. The arrest of the two Indians was effected, and they reached here to-day for trial.

PROLOGUE

September 2009:
"Cuttings"

The reader was a retired middle school English teacher whose mother had come to live at the facility in 2001. Every week for the next five years, the reader made the thirty-minute drive from Alachua to Gainesville to visit her mother. In clement weather they sat in the same cobblestoned courtyard, nestled between the two main residential buildings of the retirement home, where she now sat with me. A fountain gurgled in the center of the courtyard, ringed on three sides by bistro-style tables that had been painted and repainted to stay the corrosive effects of Florida's tropical climate. Even now, in late September, the air was thick with moisture and the temperature hovered near ninety—and that was in the shade.

Her mother had passed away in '06, but the reader still

returned each week as a volunteer to read to the residents who either had no family or had family who rarely, if ever, visited. The director of the facility had given me her name and phone number. No, he had told me, to his knowledge the man calling himself William James Henry had not been close to any resident. The only visitor he had had was the volunteer who sat across from me, sipping iced tea from a tall glass in which no ice remained. Perhaps she could help me, the director had said.

"I can't help you," the reader told me now.

"He never said anything?" I asked.

"Just his name and the year he was born."

"1876."

She nodded. "I'd tease him. I'd say, 'Now, William, that can't be the year you were born.' He would nod—and then he'd say it again."

"What would he do when you read to him?"

"Stare off into space. Sometimes he'd fall asleep."

"Did you ever have the impression he was actually listening?"

"That wasn't the point," she told me.

"What was the point, then?"

"Companionship. He had no one. Except every Tuesday at two o'clock, when he had me."

She sipped her tea. The fountain gurgled. The water in its basin dripped off one edge and spattered onto the stones. The fountain had settled several inches on one side into the soft, sandy soil. On the other side of the courtyard, two residents, a man and a woman, sat at another table holding hands, watching—or appearing to watch—the play of light in the cascading water. She nodded in their direction.

"Well, for a while he had her, too."

"'Had' her? Who is she?"

"Her name is Lillian. She was William's girlfriend."

"His girlfriend?"

"Not just his. Since I've been coming here, she's had about twelve boyfriends." The reader gave a little laugh. "She has Alzheimer's, the poor thing, goes from man to man, sticks to them like glue for a few weeks, and then she loses interest and 'picks up' somebody else. The staff calls her 'the Heartbreaker.' Some of the residents take it very hard when she moves on."

"Did William?"

She shook her head. "It's hard to say. William was . . ." She searched for the word. "Well, sometimes I thought he might be autistic. That it wasn't dementia at all but something he had been suffering from his entire life."

"He wasn't autistic."

She looked away from Lillian and Lillian's companion to study me, arching an eyebrow. "Oh?"

"After he died, they found some old notebooks hidden under his bed. A kind of diary or memoir that he must have written before he came here."

"Really? Then you know more about him than I do."

"I know what he wrote about himself, but I don't know anything about *him*," I said carefully. "I've only read the first three notebooks, and it's . . . well, pretty far out there." Her stare was making me uncomfortable. I shifted in my chair and looked across the courtyard at Lillian. "Would she remember him?" I wondered aloud.

"I doubt it."

"I guess I should ask," I said without much enthusiasm.

"They would sit together for hours," the reader said. "Not talking. Just holding hands and staring off into space. It was sweet in a way, if you didn't think about the inevitable."

"The inevitable?" I assumed she was talking about death.

"The next one catching her eye. That one she's sitting with now? His name is Kenneth, and she's been with him about a month. I give it another week, and poor Kenneth will be all alone again."

"How did Will take it—when she dumped him?"

The reader shrugged. "I didn't notice it affecting him in any way."

I continued to watch Lillian and her beau for another minute.

"Doesn't mean it didn't," I said.

"No," she said. "It doesn't."

That same afternoon I met with Will Henry's attending physician, the man who had declared him dead on the night of June 14, 2007. He had treated Will since his arrival at the facility.

"You know," he said with a twinkle in his eye, "he claimed he was born in 1876."

"So I've heard," I said. "How old do you think he actually was?"

"Hard to say. Mid- to late nineties. In excellent shape, though, for someone his age."

"Except the dementia."

"Well, dementia is inevitable, if you live long enough."

"What was the cause of death?"

"Old age."

"Heart attack? Stroke?"

"One of the two, most likely. Hard to tell without an autopsy. But he passed his last physical with flying colors."

"Did you ever find . . . Was there any indication of . . . maybe something odd about his . . . Can you tell me if you ever took a blood sample?"

"Of course. It was part of the physical."

"And did you ever find anything . . . unusual?"

The doctor cocked his head quizzically, and I had the impression he was fighting back a smile.

"As in?"

I cleared my throat. Spoken aloud, the idea seemed even more ridiculous. "In the journals, Will Henry talks about being, uh, infected by some kind of parasite when he was around eleven or twelve. An invertebrate like a tapeworm, only much smaller, that somehow gives people unnaturally long life."

The doctor was nodding. For a split second I misinterpreted the nod as an assent, an indication that he had heard of such a symbiotic creature. And, if that portion of Will Henry's fantastic life story were true, what else might be? Could it be that there was such a discipline as monstrumology practiced in the late nineteenth century by men such as his guardian, the brilliant and enigmatic Pellinore Warthrop? Was it possible that I had in my possession not a work of fiction but a memoir of a truly extraordinary life that spanned more than a century? The central question, the thing that woke me in the dead of night shivering in a cold sweat, the notion that haunted me as I fought to go back to sleep . . . Could monsters be *real*?

My hope—if what I was feeling could be called that—was short-lived. The doctor's nod was not to signify recognition; it was his way of being polite.

"Wouldn't that be nice?" he asked rhetorically. "But no, his blood was perfectly normal. A bit high on the bad cholesterol. Other than that . . ." He shrugged.

"What about a CT scan or an MRI?"

"What about them?"

"Did you ever give him one?"

"The state won't fund unnecessary procedures in a case like Mr. Henry's. My job was to make his last days as comfortable as possible, and that's what I did. Do you mind if I ask you a question? Where are you going with this?"

"You mean why does it matter?"

"Yes. Why?"

"I'm not sure. I guess part of it is the mystery. Who was this guy? Where did he come from, and how did he end up in that culvert? And why did he write that journal or novel or whatever it is? I guess the main reason, though, has to do with a promise I made."

"To Will Henry?"

I hesitated. "I was talking about the director. He gave me the journals and asked me to read them, to see if there might be clues that will help us find his relatives. Somewhere there must be someone who knew him before he came here. Everyone has someone."

The doctor was smiling. He got it. "And for now you're the only someone he has."

I dropped the notes of my interviews with the reader and the doctor into the ever-expanding file I was keeping on Will Henry, and then I dropped the file into a drawer with yet another promise to myself that I wasn't going to obsess; I would work on it as my schedule permitted. I had a deadline on a book, familial obligations, worries of my own. The old leather-bound books with their cracked hides and yellowing pages remained undisturbed in a stack beside my desk. I was publishing the first three under the title of *The Monstrumologist* the following year in the hopes that some reader somewhere might recognize something familiar in them.

It was a long shot. For legal reasons the notebooks would

have to be presented as fiction. Even if someone recognized the name of William James Henry, it would be taken as a coincidence, but something in his tale might spark a memory; perhaps he had thrilled his children or grandchildren with the story of the bizarre and horrifying creatures called *Anthropophagi*. He had obviously been an educated man. Perhaps at some point in the distant past he had even published something, maybe not under his own name—if, that is, William James Henry *was* his name. After he'd been discovered in the drainage ditch, the police had run his fingerprints. The person claiming to be William James Henry had never been arrested, had never served in the military, and had never held any job where registering his fingertips was required by law.

I thought, if those first three notebooks were a work of fiction—and, given the subject matter, they would have to be—then the author, in his demented state, might have come to identify so closely with his protagonist that he *became* Will Henry. Odder things have happened to flaky writers.

I had spent the entire summer trolling the Internet, making calls, interviewing everyone I could think of who might have that one special nugget of information, that heretofore undiscovered key that would unlock the truth from the stubborn confines of the past.

Late in September, while I sat at my desk suffering from yet another severe case of writer's block, my eye wandered to the journals. Impulsively I pulled out the fourth volume and flipped it open to a random page. To my astonishment, a newspaper clipping slipped onto the desktop.* My heart racing with excitement, I thumbed through the entire volume, finding other scraps of paper tucked between the pages, as if the journal had served a dual purpose as Will Henry's diary and as his scrapbook.

Over the next three days I found more memorabilia tucked between the pages of the remaining journals. I began a new file, which I labeled "Cuttings," organized by their location in the journals (in other words, by volume and page number), with notes outlining possible avenues for more research. While I can vouch for the authenticity of some of them (the *New York Times* articles, for example), others, like the calling card of Abram von Helrung, have yet to be fully vetted. I cannot say with 100 percent certainty that they are not forgeries or part of some very weird creative exercise on the part of the journals' author.

R.Y.
Gainesville, Florida
September 2009

*Reproduced in the front matter of this book.

Fig. 2

"Logic sometimes breeds monsters."
—Henri Poincaré

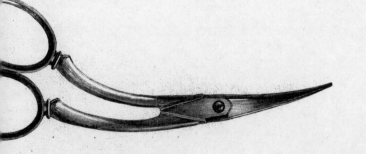

FOLIO IV
Desolation

"FOR THE PANIC OF THE WILDERNESS HAD CALLED TO HIM IN
THAT FAR VOICE—THE POWER OF UNTAMED DISTANCE—
THE ENTICEMENT OF THE DESOLATION THAT DESTROYS."
—ALGERNON BLACKWOOD

ONE

"What Am I, Will Henry?"

I do not wish to remember these things.

I wish to be rid of them, to be rid of *him*. I set down the pen nearly a year ago, swearing I would never pick it up again. Let it die with me, I thought. I am an old man. I owe the future nothing.

Soon I will fall asleep and I will wake from this terrible dream. The endless night will fall, and I will rise.

I long for that night. I do not fear it.

I have had my fill of fear. I have stared too long into the abyss, and now the abyss stares back at me.

Between the sleeping and the waking, it is there.

Between the rising and the resting, it is there.

It is always there.

It gnaws my heart. It chews my soul.

I turn aside and see it. I stop my ears and hear it. I cover myself and feel it.

There are no human words for what I mean.

It is the language of the bare bough and the cold stone, pronounced in the fell wind's sullen whisper and the metronomic *drip-drip* of the rain. It is the song the falling snow sings and the discordant clamor of sunlight ripped apart by the canopy and miserly filtered down.

It is what the unseeing eye sees. It is what the deaf ear hears.

It is the romantic ballad of death's embrace; the solemn hymn of offal dripping from bloody teeth; the lamentation of the bloated corpse rotting in the sun; and the graceful ballet of maggots twisting in the ruins of God's temple.

Here in this gray land, we have no name. We are the carcasses reflected in the yellow eye.

Our bones are bleached within our skin; our empty sockets regard the hungry crow.

Here in this shadow country, our tinny voices scratch like a fly's wing against unmoving air.

Ours is the language of imbeciles, the gibberish of idiots. The root and the vine have more to say than us.

I want to show you something. There is no name for it; it has no human symbol. It is old and its memory is long. It knew the world before we named it.

It knows everything. It knows me and it knows you.

And I will show it to you.

I will show you.

Let us go then, you and I, like Alice down the rabbit hole, to a time when there still were dark places in the world, and there were men who dared to delve into them.

An old man, I am a boy again.

And dead, the monstrumologist lives.

He was a solitary man, a dweller in silences, a genius enslaved to his own despotic thought, meticulous in his work, careless in his appearance, given to bouts of debilitating melancholia and driven by demons as formidable as the physical monstrosities he pursued.

He was a hard man, obstinate, cold to the point of cruelty, with impenetrable motives and rigid expectations, a strict taskmaster and an exacting teacher when he didn't ignore me altogether. Days would pass with but a word or two between us. I might have been another stick of dusty furniture in a forgotten room of his ancestral home. If I had fled, I do not doubt weeks would have passed before he would have noticed. Then, without warning, I would find myself the sole focus of his attention, a singularly unpleasant phenomenon that produced an effect not unlike the sensation of drowning or being crushed by a thousand-pound rock. Those dark, strangely backlit eyes would turn upon me, the brow would furrow, the lips tighten and grow white, the same expression of intense concentration I had seen a hundred times at the necropsy table as he flayed open some nameless thing to explore its innards. A look from him could lay me bare. I spent many a useless hour debating with myself which was worse, being ignored by him or being acknowledged.

But I remained. He was all I had, and I do not flatter myself when I say I was all that he had. The fact is, to his death, I was his sole companion.

That had not always been the case.

He was a solitary man, but he was no hermit. In those waning days of the century, the monstrumologist was much in demand. Letters and telegrams arrived daily from all over the world seeking his advice, inviting him to speak, appealing to him for this or that service. He preferred the field to the laboratory and would drop everything at a moment's notice to investigate a sighting of some rare species; he always kept a packed suitcase and a field kit in his closet.

He looked forward to the colloquium of the Monstrumologist Society held annually in New York City, where for two weeks scientists of the same philosophical bent met to present papers, exchange ideas, share discoveries, and, as was their counterintuitive wont, close down every bar and saloon on the island of Manhattan. Perhaps this was not so incongruous, though. These were men who pursued things from which the vast majority of their fellows would run as fast as their legs would carry them. The hardships they endured in this pursuit almost necessitated some kind of Dionysian release. Warthrop was the exception. He never touched alcohol or tobacco or any mind-altering drug. He sneered at those he considered slaves to their vices, but he was no different—only his vice was. In fact, one might argue his was the more dangerous by far. It was not the fruit of the vine that killed Narcissus, after all.

The letter that arrived late in the spring of 1888 was just one of many received that day—an alarming missive that, upon coming into his possession, quickly came to possess him.

Postmarked in New York City, it read:

My Dear Dr. Warthrop,

I have it upon good authority that his Hon. Pres. von Helrung intends to present the enclosed Proposal at the annual Congress in New York this November instant. That he is the author of this outrageous proposition, I have no doubt, and I would not trouble you if I possessed so much as a scintilla of uncertainty.

The man has clearly gone mad. I care as little about that as I care for the man, but my fear is not unjustified, I think. I consider his insidious argument a genuine threat to the legitimacy of our vocation, with the potential to doom our work to oblivion or—worse—to doom us to sharing space in the public mind with the

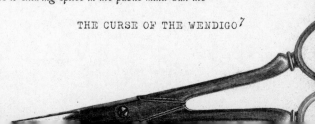

charlatan and the quack. Thus, I vouch it is no hyperbole to aver that the very future of our discipline is at stake.

Once you have read this offensive tripe, I am certain you will agree that our only hope lies in delivering a _forceful_ Reply upon the completion of his Presentation. And I can think of no better man to contest our esteemed president's alarming and dangerous disquisitions than you, Dr. Warthrop, the leading Philosopher of Aberrant Natural History of his generation.

I remain, as always, etc., etc.,

Your Obt. Servant,

A Concerned Colleague

A single reading of the enclosed monograph of Abram von Helrung convinced the doctor that his correspondent was correct in at least one regard. The proposal did indeed pose a threat to the legitimacy of his beloved profession. That he was the best—and obvious—choice to refute the claims of the most renowned monstrumologist in the world required no convincing on anyone's part. Pellinore Warthrop's genius included the profound insight that he happened to be one.

So everything was put aside. Visitors were turned away. Letters went unanswered. All invitations were declined. His studies were abandoned. Sleep and sustenance were reduced to the barest minimum. His thirty-seven-page monograph, with the rather unwieldy title, *Shall We Doom the Natural Philosophy of Monstrumology to the Dustbin of History? A Reply to the Hon. President Dr. Abram von Helrung upon His*

Proposal to Investigate and Consider as Possible Inclusions into the Catalogue of Aberrant Species Certain Heretofore Mythical Creatures of Supernatural Origin at the One Hundred Tenth Congress of the Society for the Advancement of the Science of Monstrumology, went through multiple revisions and refinements over that frantic summer.

He enlisted me in the cause, naturally, as his research assistant, in addition to my duties as cook, maid, manservant, laundryman, and errand boy. I fetched books, took dictation, and played audience to his stiff, overly formal, sometimes ludicrously awkward presentation. He would stand ramrod straight with his lanky arms folded stiffly behind his back, eyes focused unerringly upon the floor, chin tilted downward so that his otherwise compellingly dark features were lost in shadow.

He refused to read directly from his paper, so he often "went up" in the parlance of the theater, completely losing track of his argument, thrashing like King Pellinore, his namesake, in the dense thicket of his thoughts in search of the elusive Questing Beast of his reasoning.

At other times he fell into rambling asides that took the audience from the birth of monstrumology in the early eighteenth century (beginning with Bacqueville de la Potherie, the acknowledged father of this most curious of esoteric disciplines) to the present day, with references to obscure personages whose voices had long been stifled in the Dark Angel's smothering embrace.

"Now, where was I, Will Henry?" he would ask after one

of these extended extemporaneities. It never failed that this question came at the precise moment when my mind had wandered to more interesting matters, more often than not to the current weather conditions or the menu for our long-overdue supper.

Unwilling to incur his inestimable ire, I would fumble a reply, blurting the best guess I had, which usually included somewhere in the sentence the name of Darwin, Warthrop's personal hero.

The ploy did not always work.

"Darwin!" the monstrumologist cried once in reply, striking his fist into his palm in agitation. "Darwin! Really, Will Henry, what does Darwin have to do with the native folklore of the Carpathians? Or the mythos of Homer? Or Norse cosmology? Have I not impressed upon you the importance of this endeavor? If I should fail in this, the seminal moment of my career, not only will I go down in humiliation and disrepute, but the entire house will fall! The end of monstrumology, the immediate and irrevocable loss of nearly two hundred years of unselfish devotion by men who *dwarf* all those who came after them, myself included. Even me, Will Henry. Think of that!"

"I think it was . . . You were talking about the Carpathians, I think . . ."

"Dear Lord! I *know* that, Will Henry. And the only reason *you* know that is I just said it!"

As hard as he threw himself into the task of his oral presentation, more assiduously still did he labor over his written reply, composing at least twelve drafts, each of them in his nearly illegible scrawl, and all of which fell to me to transcribe into readable form, for, if the reply had been delivered to the printer's in its original state, it would undoubtedly have been wadded up and hurled at my head.

Upon the conclusion of my hours of toil, hunching over my desk like a medieval monk with aching ink-stained fingers and itching, burning eyes, the monstrumologist would snatch the product from my quivering grip and compare it to the original, hunting for the slightest error, which, of course, he would invariably find.

At the end of this Herculean effort, after the printer delivered the finished product and there was little left to do (and little left of the monstrumologist, for he must have lost more than fifteen pounds since the project had begun) but wait for that fall's convocation, he fell into a profound depression. The monstrumologist retreated to his shuttered study, where he brooded in a gloom both actual and metaphysical, refusing to even acknowledge my halfhearted attempts to alleviate his suffering. I brought him raspberry scones (his favorite) from the baker's. I shared with him the latest gossip gleaned from the society pages (he held a strange fascination for them) and the local doings of our little hamlet of New Jerusalem. He would not be comforted. He even lost interest in the mail, which I arranged for him, unread, upon his desk, until the desk's surface was covered as thickly as the forest floor by the leaves of autumn.

Near the end of August, a large package arrived from Menlo Park, and for a few moments he was his old self again, delighting in the gift from his friend. Enclosed with it was a brief note: *All my thanks for your help with the design, Thos. A. Edison.* He played with the phonograph for the space of an hour, and then touched it no more. It sat upon the table beside him like a silent rebuke. Here was the dream made real of Thomas Edison, a man who was destined to be lauded as one of the greatest minds of his generation, if not in all history, a true man of science whose world would be forever changed for his having lived in it.

"What am I, Will Henry?" the doctor asked abruptly one rainy afternoon.

I answered with the literalness of a child, which, of course, at the time I was.

"You're a monstrumologist, sir."

"I am a mote of dust," he said. "Who will remember me when I am gone?"

I glanced at the mountain of letters upon his desk. What did he mean? It seemed he knew everyone. Just that morning a letter had arrived from the Royal Society of London. Sensing he meant something deeper, I answered intuitively, "I will, sir. I will remember you."

"You! Well, I suppose you won't have much choice in the matter." His eyes wandered to the phonograph. "Do you know it was not always my desire to be a scientist? When I was much younger, my great ambition was to be a poet."

If he had stated that his brain were made of Swiss cheese, I would not have been more flabbergasted.

"A poet, Dr. Warthrop?"

"Oh, yes. The desire is gone, but the temperament, you may have noticed, still lingers. I was quite the romantic, Will Henry, if you can imagine it."

"What happened?" I asked.

"I grew up."

He placed one of his thin, delicate fingers upon the ceresin cylinder, running the tip along the pits and grooves like a blind man reading braille.

"There is no future in it, Will Henry," he said pensively. "The future belongs to science. The fate of our species will be determined by the likes of Edison and Tesla, not Wordsworth or Whitman. The poets will lie upon the shores of Babylon and weep, poisoned by the fruit that grows from the ground where the Muses' corpses rot. The poets' voices will be drowned out by the gears of progress. I foresee the day when all sentiment is reduced to a chemical equation in our brains—hope, faith, even love—their exact locations pinned down and mapped out, so we may point to it and say, 'Here, in this region of our cerebral cortex, lies the soul.'"

"I like poetry," I said.

"Yes, and some like to whittle, Will Henry, so they will always find trees."

"Have you kept any of your poems, Doctor?"

"No, I have not, for which you should be grateful. I was horrible."

"What did you write about?"

"What every poet writes about. I fail to understand it, Will Henry, your uncanny gift for seizing upon the most tangential aspect of the issue and drubbing it to death."

To prove him wrong, I said, "I will never forget you, sir. Ever. And neither will the whole world. You'll be more famous than Edison and Bell and all the rest put together. I'll make sure of it."

"I will pass into oblivion, to the vile dust from whence I sprung, unwept, unhonored, and unsung. . . . That is poetry, in case you're wondering. Sir Walter Scott."

He stood up, and now his countenance shone with the profundity of his passion, at once terrifying and strangely beautiful, the look of the mystic or the saint, transported from the constraints of ego and all fleshy desires.

"But I am nothing. My memory is nothing. The work is everything, and I will not see it mocked. Though the cost be my very life, I will not let it pass, Will Henry. If von Helrung should succeed—if we allow our noble cause to be reduced to the study of the silly superstitions of the masses—so that we jibber-jabber on about the nature of the vampire or the zombie as if they sat at the same table as the manticore and the *Anthropophagus*, then monstrumology is as dead as alchemy, as ridiculous as astrology, as serious as one of Mr. Barnum's sideshow freaks!

"Grown men, educated men, men of the highest sophistication and social refinement, cross themselves like the most ignorant peasant when they pass this house. 'What queer and unnatural goings-on in there, the house of Warthrop!' When you yourself can attest that there is nothing queer or unnatural about it, that what I deal in is altogether natural, that if it weren't for me and men like me, these fools might find themselves choking on their own entrails or being digested in the belly of some beast no more queer than the lowly housefly!"

He drew a breath deeply, the pause before the start of the next movement in his symphony, then suddenly he became very still, head cocked slightly to one side. I listened, but heard nothing but the rain's gentle kiss upon the window and the metronomic *tick-tick* of the mantel clock.

"Someone is here," he said. He turned and peered through the blinds. I could see nothing but the reflection of his angular face. How hollow his cheeks! How pale his flesh! He had spoken boldly of his ultimate fate—did he know how close he seemed to that vile dust from whence he came?

"Quickly, to the door, Will Henry. Whoever it is, remember I am indisposed and can't receive visitors. Well, what are you waiting for? Snap to, Will Henry, snap to!"

A moment later the bell rang. He closed the study door behind me. I lit the jets in the front hall to chase away the preternatural shadows lying thick in the entryway, and threw wide the door to behold the most beautiful woman I have ever seen in all the years of my exceedingly long life.

TWO

"There Is Nothing I Can Do for You"

"Why, hello there," she said with a puzzled smile. "I'm afraid I may be lost. I am looking for the house of Pellinore Warthrop."

"This is Dr. Warthrop's house," I returned, in a voice only moderately steady. More stunning than her extraordinary looks was her very presence upon our doorstep. In all the time I had lived with him, the doctor had never received a lady caller. It simply did not happen. The doorstep of 425 Harrington Lane was not the sort of place upon which a proper lady appeared.

"Oh, good. I thought I might have come to the wrong place."

She stepped into the vestibule without my asking, removed her gray traveling cloak, and adjusted her hat. A strand of her auburn hair had escaped from its pin and now clung, dripping, to her graceful neck. Her face was radiant in the glow of the lamps, rain-moist and without defect—unless the fine spray of freckles across her nose and cheeks might be called thus—though I will admit it may not have been the lighting that painted her with perfection.

It is exceedingly strange to me that I, who have no difficulty in describing the multifarious manifestations of the doctor's gruesome craft, the foul denizens of the dark in all their grotesque aspects to the smallest detail, now struggle with the lexicon, reaching for words as ephemeral as the will-o'-the-wisp to do justice to the woman I met that summer afternoon seventy years ago. I might speak of the way the light played along her glittering tresses—but what of that? I might go on about her hazel eyes flecked with flashing bits of brighter green—but still fall short. There are things that are too terrible to remember, and there are things that are almost too wonderful to recall.

"Could you tell him that Mrs. Chanler is here to speak with him?" she asked. She was smiling warmly at me.

I stammered something completely unintelligible, which did nothing to diminish her smile.

"He is here, isn't he?"

"No, ma'am," I managed. "I mean, yes, he is, but he is not. . . . The doctor is indisposed."

"Well, perhaps if you told him I'm here, he might be disposed to make an exception."

"Yes, ma'am," I said, and then quickly added, "He is very busy, so—"

"Oh, he is always *busy*," she said with a delighted little laugh. "I've never known him not to be. But where are my manners? We haven't been properly introduced." She offered her hand. I took it, only later wondering if her intent had been for me to kiss it. I was woefully ignorant in the social graces. I was being raised, after all, by Pellinore Warthrop.

"My name is Muriel," she said.

"I'm William James Henry," I responded with awkward formality.

"Henry! So *that's* who you are. I should have realized. You're James Henry's son." She placed her cool hand upon my arm. "I am terribly sorry for your loss, Will. And you are here because . . . ?"

"The doctor took me in."

"Did he? How extraordinarily uncharacteristic of him. Are you certain we're speaking of the same doctor?"

Behind me the study door came open and I heard the monstrumologist say, "Will Henry, who was—" I turned to discover a look of profound shock upon his face, though that was quickly replaced by a mask of icy indifference.

"Pellinore," Muriel Chanler said softly.

The doctor spoke to me, though his eyes did not abandon her. "Will Henry, I thought my instructions were unambiguous."

"You mustn't blame William," she said with a note of playfulness. "He took pity upon me, standing on your stoop like a wet cat. Are you ill?" she asked suddenly. "You look as if you might have a fever."

"I have never been better," returned the doctor. "I can complain of nothing."

"That's more—or less—than I might say. I am soaked to the skin! Do you suppose I might have a cup of hot cider or tea before you toss me out the door? I did come a very long way to see you."

"New York is not that far," Warthrop replied. "Unless you came on foot."

"Is that a no, then?" she asked.

"Saying no would be foolish on my part, wouldn't it? No one says no to Muriel Barnes."

"Chanler," she corrected him.

"Of course. Thank you. I believe I remember who you are. Will Henry, show Mrs. *Chanler*"—he spat out the name—"to the parlor and put on a pot of tea. I'm sorry, Mrs. *Chanler*, but we've no cider. It isn't in season."

Returning from the kitchen with the serving tray a few minutes later, I paused outside the parlor, for within I could hear a vehement discussion in progress, the doctor's voice high-pitched and tight, our guest's quieter but no less urgent.

"Even if I accepted it on its face," he was saying, "even if I believed such claptrap . . . no, even if it existed regardless of my belief . . . there are a dozen men to whom you could turn for help."

"That may be," she allowed. "But there is only one Pellinore Warthrop."

"Flattery? I am astounded, Muriel."

"A measure of my desperation, Pellinore. Believe me, if I thought anyone else could help me, I would not ask you."

"Ever the diplomat."

"Ever the realist—unlike you."

"I am a scientist, and therefore an absolute realist."

"I understand that you're bitter—"

"To assume I am bitter proves your lack of understanding. It assumes I harbor some residuum of affection, which I assure you I do not."

"Can you not put aside who asks for help and consider the one who needs it? You loved him once."

"Whom I have loved is none of your business."

"True. My business is with whom *I* love."

"Then why don't you find him yourself? Why have you come all this way to bother me with it?"

Straining forward in my eagerness to eavesdrop, I lost my balance and nearly dropped the tray, stumbling into the doorway like a drunkard, while the tea sloshed from the spout and the cups rattled in their saucers. I discovered the doctor standing by the fireplace. Muriel sat stiffly in the chair a few feet from him, a piece of stationery clutched in her hand.

The doctor clucked his disapproval at me, then stepped forward and snatched the letter from her hand. I placed the tray on the table beside her.

"Your tea, Mrs. Chanler," I said.

"Thank you, Will," she said.

"Yes, leave us," the doctor said, his nose stuck in the letter.

"Is there anything else I can get for you, ma'am?" I asked. "We have some fresh scones—"

"Do *not*," growled the doctor from behind the paper, "bring out the scones!"

He snorted and tossed the letter upon the floor. I snatched up the letter and, forgotten for a moment in the heat of their tête-à-tête, read it through.

Dear Missus John,
You forgive my English, its not goodly done. Got back to RP this morning came straightaway to post this. There is no good way to say this, I am sorry. Mister John—he gone. It called to him and the thing done carried him off. I tell Jack Fiddler and he will keep the lookout for him but its got him and even ol Jack Fiddler cant get him back now. I told him not to go, but it called him night and day, so's he went. Mister John he rides the high wind now and the Mossmouth not going to let him go. I'm sorry, missus.
P. Larose

"Will Henry," the doctor snapped. "What are you doing? Give me that!" He snatched the letter from my hand. "Who is Larose?" he asked Mrs. Chanler.

"Pierre Larose—John's guide."

"And this Jack Fiddler he mentions?"

She shook her head. "I've never heard the name before."

"'He rides the high wind now,'" the doctor read, "'and the Mossmouth not going to let him go.' I suppose not!" He laughed humorlessly. "I assume you've notified the proper authorities."

"Yes, of course. The search party returned to Rat Portage two days ago. . . ." She shook her head, unable to go on.

"Then I fail to see how I can help," said Warthrop. "Except to state my opinion that this is no matter for monstrumology. Whatever bore your husband away on the 'high wind' was no 'Mossmouth,' though I find the imagery oddly compelling. I'd never heard the sobriquet applied to a *Lepto lurconis*. It must be an invention of the good Monsieur Larose and not, I suspect, the only one. It would not be the first time a death in the wilderness has been attributed to the Wendigo."

"You think he's lying?"

"I think he is being false—intentionally or not, I cannot say. *Lepto lurconis* is a myth, Muriel, no more real than the tooth fairy—which is the strangest aspect of this whole affair. Why was John searching for something that does not exist?"

"He was . . . encouraged to go."

"Ah." The monstrumologist was nodding. "It was von Helrung, wasn't it? Von Helrung told him to go—"

"He suggested it."

"And being the good little lapdog that he is, John went."

She stiffened. "I am wasting my time, aren't I?" she asked.

"That *is* the issue, Muriel. How long has he been missing?"

"Almost three months."

"Then, yes, you are wasting your time here. There is nothing I can do for you—or for John. Your husband is dead."

Though tears shone in her eyes, she did not break. Though every fiber of her being bespoke her desperation, she held firm in the face of his bald assertion. Men might be the stronger sex, but women are made of much sterner stuff!

"I refuse to believe that."

"Your faith is misplaced."

"No, Pellinore, not my faith. My hope that the one man I thought I could turn to . . . whom John could turn to—"

Warthrop nodded. He turned his gaze from her lovely upturned face and spoke in that dry, lecturing manner I had often heard. "Once, in the Andes, at base camp on the slopes of Mount Chimborazo, I came face-to-face with a mature male *Astomi*, a creature with the disconcerting ability to scream at decibel levels loud enough to shatter the eardrum; I have seen men's brains literally leaking from their ears after an encounter with one. He had stumbled upon our camp in the dead of night and was as surprised as I at our meeting. For a moment we just stared at each other, our faces no more than a foot apart.

I had my revolver; he had his mouth; and at any time we both had the opportunity to use them. We held this way for several tense minutes, until finally I said to him, 'Well, my friend, I will agree to hold my fire if you will agree to hold your tongue!'"

The lesson of this impromptu parable was not lost on her. She nodded slowly, set down her cup, and rose from the chair. Though she made no move toward either of us, the monstrumologist and I drew back. There is beauty that soothes like the warm kiss of the spring sun upon the cheek, and then there is beauty that terrifies, like the cry of Ozymandias, inviting despair.

"I am a fool," she said. "You will never change."

"If that was your hope, then, yes, you are quite foolish."

"I am not the only one. I pity you, Pellinore Warthrop. Do you know that? I pity you. The most intelligent man I have ever met, and also the most vain and vindictive. You have always been a little in love with death. That's the surprising thing. I should think you'd leap at the chance to see it again face-to-face. It's the only reason you chose your repulsive 'profession.'"

She whirled away and hurried from the room, a hand pressed against her mouth as if to stop up what else might come out.

I glanced at the doctor, but he had turned away; his face was half in shadow, half in light. I hurried after Muriel Chanler and helped her with her wrap. A gust of wind blew through the door when I opened it, and rain spattered and popped upon the vestibule floor. At the curb, through the gray curtain of the storm, I could see the shining black hansom, the driver hunched in his seat, the withers of the great dray horse glittering with the watery sheen.

"It was a pleasure to meet you, Will," she said before she stepped out. A hand rested briefly upon my shoulder. "I will pray for you."

In the parlor the doctor had not moved, nor did he upon my return. I stood for several awful moments in silence, not knowing what to say.

"Yes?" he said softly.

"Mrs. Chanler has left, sir."

He made no reply. He remained still. I picked up the tray, went back to the kitchen, washed up the china, and placed it in the rack to dry. When I returned, the doctor still had not moved an inch. I'd seen it dozens of times before: Warthrop's reticence solidified in direct proportion to the intensity of his feelings. The more powerful the emotion, the less he revealed. His face was as tranquil—and blank—as a death mask.

"Yes? What is it now, Will Henry?"

"Would you like something for dinner, sir?"

He made no reply. He remained where he was, and I remained where I was.

"What are you doing now?" he asked.

"Nothing, sir."

"Forgive me, but isn't that something you could do practically anywhere?"

"Yes, sir. I'll . . . I will do that, sir."

"What? What will you do?"

"Nothing . . . I will do nothing somewhere else."

THREE

"It Is a Patient Hunter"

The shout came a little after four the following morning, and, of course, I answered. I found him in his room, shivering uncontrollably beneath the covers, as if gripped by a fever. His face was corpse white. Sweat shone upon his forehead and glistened on his upper lip.

"Will Henry," he croaked. "Why aren't you in bed?"

"You called me, sir."

"Did I? I don't remember. What time is it?"

"After four, sir."

"Four—in the morning?"

"Yes, sir."

"It feels much earlier than that. Are you sure?"

I said I was, and sank into the chair at his bedside. We sat in silence for a moment, he, shivering; I, yawning.

"I fear I may have caught a cold," he said.

"Shall I fetch the doctor, sir?"

"Or the duck. How old was that duck, Will Henry? Perhaps it was bad."

"I don't think so, sir. I had some too, and I'm not sick."

"But you are a child. Children have stronger stomachs. That is a known fact, Will Henry."

"I thought the duck was very good, sir."

"Yes, I could tell. The way you stuffed yourself, one might think you hadn't eaten for a week. I've told you many times, Will Henry, either a man controls his appetites or his appetites control him. You do know Dante devoted more than one circle of hell to the unregulated desires. For your transgressions of the flesh, you would be consigned to the third circle, where you would lie in total darkness while shit rained down upon you from the sky."

I nodded. "Yes, sir."

"'Yes, sir.' . . . Do you find it a pleasant prospect, Will Henry? Shit raining down upon you for all eternity?"

"No, sir."

"But that is not what you said. You said, 'yes, sir,' as if you might find it agreeable."

"I was agreeing with *you*, Dr. Warthrop, not the idea of shit."

"'The idea of shit.' . . . Will Henry, I am beginning to believe you are far too obsequious for your own good—and certainly for *my* own good. Flattery lands you in the eighth circle, where you wallow in a river of the selfsame excrement."

"Then there doesn't seem to be much hope for me, sir."

He grunted. "Not much, no."

I fought back a yawn.

"Am I keeping you awake, Will Henry?"

"Yes, sir. No, sir. I'm sorry, sir."

"For what?"

"For . . . I don't remember."

"You are sorry for something you've forgotten?"

"No, sir. I've forgotten what I'm sorry for."

"You're giving me a headache, Will Henry. A conversation with you is like negotiating Minos's labyrinth."

"Yes, sir."

"'Yes, sir! Yes, sir!'" he mocked me, his voice rising an octave. "If I said pixies danced jigs upon the hearth, you would answer, 'Yes, sir; yes, sir!' If the house were on fire and I told you to throw gasoline upon it to quench the flames, you would cry, 'Yes, sir! Yes, sir!' and blow us both to kingdom come! You have a mind, do you not, William James Henry? You were born with that indispensable appendage, were you not?"

The words were upon my lips—"Yes, sir!"—and in the nick of time I bit them back. He took no notice, however. The monstrumologist was on a tear.

"Have all my efforts been for naught?" he cried to the ceiling, striking a fist against his pillow. "The sacrifices of time and privacy, the patient instruction and guidance, the special consideration I showed in honor of your father's service to me—all for nothing? Really, what dividends have my efforts earned, Will Henry? For almost two years you've been with me, and when put to the test, your reply is the obsequious echo I might expect from the lowliest liveryman. So I shall ask it again: Do you have a brain?"

"Y-yes, sir," I stammered.

"Oh, for the love of God, there you say it again!" he roared.

"Of course I do!" I hollered back. I had finally reached the end of my endurance. This was not the first time I had been summoned by the shrill cry of *Will Henreeeeeee!* to the bedside of a self-absorbed lunatic who barely seemed to tolerate my existence. What did he want from me? Was I merely his whipping boy, a convenient dog to kick when frustration and childish angst overwhelmed him? Dark demons possessed him, I would never deny that, but they were not *my* demons.

"The thing I said about appetite," he said deliberately, clearly taken aback by my reaction, "applies to the emotions as well, Will Henry. There is no need to lose your temper."

"You lost yours," I pointed out.

"I had cause," he returned, implying that I'd had none. "And at any rate, I would not advise you to follow my example in all things. Well, in hardly anything." He laughed dryly. "Take the study of monstrumology . . ."

I would rather not, thought I, but held my tongue.

"I believe I've told you, Will Henry, that there is no university that offers instruction in the science of monstrumology—not yet, at any rate. Instead we receive our instruction from an acknowledged master. Though my own studies began under my father, in his day a monstrumologist of extraordinary gifts, they were finished under Abram von Helrung, the president of our Society and the author of that unfortunate treatise that seems to have sent John Chanler to his doom. For nearly six years I studied under von Helrung, even lived with him for a time—we both did, John and I. And since my relations with my father were strained, to put it mildly, it was not long before von Helrung became as a father to me, filling that paternal void as I fully believe I fulfilled the filial one."

He sighed. Even in the warm glow of the lamp, his face appeared deathly pale. His cheeks were shadow-filled hollows, and his eyes receded far into their sockets and were lined in charcoal gray.

"It is a grievous loss, Will Henry—and not just to monstrumology," he went on. I assumed he was talking about John Chanler, his fellow monstrumologist, whom Muriel had claimed he loved. He was not.

"In astronomy, botany, psychology, physics—if anyone might be called the Leonardo da Vinci of his time, his name would be von Helrung. His parlor on Fifth Avenue has been home to one of the preeminent scientific salons in North America, graced by the likes of Edison and Tesla, Kelvin and Pasteur. He was a special adviser to the court of Czar Alexander and an honorary fellow of the Royal Society in London. His oratorical gifts rivaled those of Cicero. Why, I remember his presentation on the anatomical variances of the six species of the genus *Ingenus* during the congress of '79, holding the hall spellbound for three solid hours— one of the most intellectually exhilarating experiences of my life, Will Henry. And now . . . *this*. How a scientist of John Chanler's acumen could fall under the spell of such palpable nonsense is beyond all comprehension. I daresay even a child of average intelligence could refute it. Even *you* could, Will Henry, which is not meant to cast aspersions upon your intellect, but to point out the obvious parallel to that classic tale of the naked king."

"Naked king, sir?"

"Yes, yes, you know the one," he said testily. "There's no need to patronize me, you know. While the masses clapped and cheered for his fine regalia, a little child called out from the crowd, 'But he's wearing no clothes!' Just so, Chanler was always in awe of von Helrung—though not the only one, by any means. There has been more than one congress in which his remarks have been received by grown men as Moses cowering before the burning bush. No doubt Chanler raced off to Rat Portage to provide his beloved mentor with proof of his dubious proposition—a specimen of *Lepto lurconis*."

"What is a *Lepto lurconis*, Dr. Warthrop?" I asked.

"I have told you, a myth."

"Yes, sir. But what kind of creature is it exactly?"

"You really must brush up on your classical languages, Will Henry," he chided me. "Its formal name is *Lepto lurconis semihominis americanus*. '*Lepto*' is from the Greek. It means 'gaunt' or 'abnormally thin'—emaciated. '*Lurconis*' is Latin for 'glutton.' Thus: 'the starving glutton.' The rest, '*semihominis americanus*,' I trust you can decipher for yourself."

"Yes, sir," I said. "But what *is* it exactly?"

He said nothing for a moment. He sighed deeply. He ran a hand through his bedraggled hair.

"The hunger," he breathed.

"Hunger?"

"*The* hunger, Will Henry. The kind that is never satisfied."

"What kind of hunger is never satisfied?" I wondered.

"It rides on the wind," the monstrumologist said, a far-away look in his dark eyes. "In the absolute dark of the wilderness, a fell voice calls your name, the voice of damnation's desire, from the desolation that destroys . . ."

I shivered. He did not sound like himself at all. I watched as his eyes darted back and forth, his gaze flitting over the ceiling, seeing something there that was beyond my power to see.

"It is called *Atcen . . . Djenu . . . Outiko . . . Vindiko*. It has a dozen names in a dozen lands, and it is older than the hills, Will Henry. It feeds, and the more it feeds, the hungrier it becomes. It starves even as it gorges. It is the hunger that cannot be satisfied. In the Algonquin tongue its name literally means 'the one who devours all mankind.'

"You are young," the monstrumologist said. "You have yet to hear it call your name. But from the moment it knows you, you are doomed. Doomed, Will Henry! There is no escaping it. It is a patient hunter and will endure all hardship, waiting to strike when you least expect it, and once you are in its icy grip, there is no hope of rescue. It bears you to unimaginable heights and plunges you to unfathomable depths. It crushes your soul; it breaks your breath in half. And, *even as it eats you*, you share in the feast. Yes! As you rise to the very gates of heaven, as you fall to the innermost circle of hell, you rejoice in the misery it brings—you *become* the hunger. Flying, you fall. Gorging, you starve. . . ."

The doctor breathed deeply. Hard though it might be to accept, it seemed Pellinore Warthrop had run out of words. I waited for him to go on, puzzling over his cryptic dissertation upon the nature of the beast. In one breath he'd called it a myth and in the next had spoken of it as if it were entirely real. *You are young. You have yet to hear it call your name.* What did this mean? What had yet to call my name?

The room was stuffy and warm—the doctor refused, even on the hottest of nights, to sleep with the windows open, a habit that was most likely common among monstrumologists— and under my nightshirt I had begun to sweat. Though his eyes remained fixed upon the ceiling, I had the discomforting sensation of being watched. The hairs on the back of my neck rose, and my heart quickened. Something was there, just outside my range of vision, incorporeal and ravenously hungry.

"She is right, you know," he said softly. "I am vain and vindictive, and I have always been a little in love with death. Perhaps I lost her because it was the one thing she could not give me. I had not thought of that. It is hard, Will Henry, very hard, to think about those things that we do not think about. One day you will understand that."

He rolled over onto his side, turning his back to me.

"Now put out the light and go to bed. We leave for Rat Portage in the morning."

I retired to my little loft, where I tossed and turned for another hour or more, unable to fall into anything deeper than a fitful, transient doze. I could not shake the feeling that something lurked just outside the periphery of my vision, that the shadows held something, and that something knew my name.

I saw Muriel standing in the rain, a vision rising from fecund memory, her gray shawl glistening with water, the light skittering along her wet lashes, the parting of her lips when she saw me standing in the doorway, and I am filled with astonishment and dismay.

Suddenly she is gone and I am at my mother's bedside, where I sit at her feet and watch her comb her long hair, and somewhere in the room is my father, but I cannot see him, and the golden light shimmers in my mother's auburn hair. Her feet are bare and her wrists are thin and delicate, and the hypnotic rhythm of the brush coaxes the light to recline in perfect rows. And the light is golden all around her.

The doctor called out from his room below, and I jerked upright, gasping like a drowning man breaking the surface. I started down the ladder, for his cries were loud and desperate and not totally unexpected, but I stopped at the bottom rung, for he was not calling for me. It was someone's name, though it was not my own.

FOUR

"He Was My Best Friend, and How I Hated Him!"

We embarked upon our impromptu rescue mission the following morning—to a place that has now vanished from the earth.

Seventeen years after our expedition to that rough-and-tumble outpost on Canada's western frontier, the town of Rat Portage merged with two sister settlements named Keewatin and Norman, each lending the first two letters of its name to the new incorporation: Ke-No-Ra. The change was brought about by the refusal of the Maple Leaf Flour Company to build in Rat Portage, fearing that the word "rat" on its bags might depress sales.

Situated on the north shore of Lake of the Woods near the border of Ontario and Manitoba, the area around modern-day Kenora was known in the native tongue as

Wauzhushk Onigum—literally the "portage to the country of the muskrat," from which Rat Portage derived its name. Today the town is a mecca for sportsmen; in 1888, the hunting was of a different sort entirely. Gold had been discovered ten years before, transforming the sleepy little village into a bustling boomtown of swindlers and speculators, starry-eyed fortune seekers, and desperadoes of every stripe, with the occasional bandit, cutthroat, and scallywag thrown into the mix. Even the ladies of the town, it was said, dared not venture onto the boardwalk unarmed.

Thank goodness for the gold, though! If it had not been discovered, our journey to the edge of the vast Canadian wilderness would have taken weeks. As it was, by the time of our expedition, the gold had transformed Rat Portage into a major distribution and supply hub of the Canadian Pacific Railway. Our journey took only three days, and those were spent in luxury aboard a well-appointed Pullman sleeper.

The doctor, expecting no end of hardship at the journey's end, spared no comfort during the journey itself. Three copious meals each day, a pot of tea and a platter of scones in the afternoons, and between times candies and mints and all the salted peanuts he could eat, and Warthrop could eat quite a lot of them. He slept more soundly than I had ever witnessed at Harrington Lane. In fact, the teeth-jarring resonance of his snoring kept me up most nights well into the indecent hours.

But I hardly minded. For the first time in my life, I had

left behind the quaint confines of the Massachusetts country-side on an adventure of wondrous promise. What boy my age didn't dream of fleeing the well-tended lawn and lamp-lit street for the untamed wilderness, where grand adventure awaited on the other side of the horizon, where the stars burned undimmed in the velvet sky above his head and the virgin ground lay untrodden beneath his feet? It called to me with thrice the urgency of a thousand "snap to!"s in a language unspoken by any human tongue but apprehended by every human heart. It made all things bearable, even the monstrumologist's insistence that we dress each night for dinner, and the globs upon globs of philocome he applied to my hair in a vain attempt to plaster my multitudinous cowlicks.

It was the first time I had witnessed him take the slight-est care in his appearance. Even to this day, when he has been forty years in the grave, when I picture the monstrumologist, I see him in that tattered old smock smeared with the blood and dried viscera of his latest "curiosity," his hair swirled into tempestuous confusion, his cheeks dotted with three-day-old stubble, his nails cracked and encrusted with gore. It was startling and oddly disconcerting to see him wearing a high collar and a fashionable cravat, freshly shaven and washed, his nails neatly trimmed, his black hair glistening, its waves tamed and swept back from his strong brow.

I was not the only one who took note of this remarkable transformation. At dinner service I saw women glance at him or offer a smile as we made our way to the table. This was every bit as vexing as his transformation. Women were fascinated by—nay, one might even say *attracted to*—Pellinore Warthrop! Some would even blush or—more horrifying still—smile and attempt to flirt with him. Flirt—with the monstrumologist!

Of course Warthrop, being Warthrop, ignored these coquettish advances, or rather, he seemed oblivious to them, which, naturally, made him all the more intriguing. I'd always thought him more cold stone than flesh and blood, and these shy smiles, these glancing looks, these blushing cheeks—I simply did not know what to make of them.

"The conclusion is unavoidable. After three months, he must be dead," the doctor opined abruptly while we enjoyed the final evening service, his face turned toward the large window beside our table. Night had fallen, and the landscape was obscured by our reflections; I could not tell if he was looking beyond his own face in the glass. "More a recovery than a rescue, and there's small hope of even that, since the failure of professionals practically ensures our own."

"Then, why are we going?" I asked.

He turned from the window and stared at me for a long, uncomfortable moment.

"Because he was my friend."

Later that evening, as we lay in our bunks and the train's lulling motion and the lullaby of her wheels eased us toward slumber, he spoke up suddenly, as if no time had passed since the onset of the conversation.

"I was an only child like you, Will Henry, but in John Chanler I found the closest thing I would ever have to a brother. We lived together for six years under the tutelage of von Helrung, sharing the same room, eating the same meals, reading the same books—but in nearly every other aspect we were complete opposites. Where I was retiring and somewhat sickly, John was outgoing and quite the athlete— an accomplished boxer with whom I made the mistake of picking a fight; he broke my nose and fractured my left cheek before *Meister* Abram pulled us apart.

"We came to monstrumology by different routes. He loved the sport of it, the thrill of the chase, whereas I was drawn to it for more complicated reasons, many of which you already know. John's father was no scientist and was appalled when he applied to apprentice under von Helrung. The Chanlers are one of the wealthiest families on the East Coast, his father a friend to presidents and men such as Vanderbilt, Morgan, and Astor. John was expected to fol-low in his father's footsteps, and, to my knowledge, he has never been forgiven for his recalcitrance. I don't know for certain, but I believe his father may have disowned him. Not that John cared. He seemed to delight in defying the expec-tations of others."

He fell silent. After a time I thought he must have fallen asleep, and then suddenly he spoke again.

"He loved practical jokes, particularly at my expense. You may be surprised to hear this, but the Warthrops have always been known for their lack of humor; it's a sort of congenital defect. In his lifetime I heard my father laugh only once, and that politely. It delighted John to short-sheet my bed or dip my hand in warm water as I slept. Once he drained the blood from the carcass of a Tanzanian *Ngoloko* we were to dissect the next day and placed the pail on top of the door going into our room. Well, you can guess what happened. He put sealing wax in the earpieces of my stethoscope; he mixed dried feces in my tooth powder; and, in one memorably unfortunate incident, right before I was to take my final exams before the entire governing board of the Society, he laced my tea with an extract of dried beans heavy in oligosaccharides, a sugar that most human beings—including me—cannot digest, causing excessive bloating and, at least in my case, explosive gas. I literally farted my way through the entire dissertation, and the tears that flowed from every eye had little to do with the profundity of my presentation. The hall seemed larger than the Metropolitan Opera house when I entered. By the time I left, it seemed as cramped as a water closet, and was just as odiferous. . . . What is that sound, Will Henry? Are you laughing?"

"No, sir," I managed to gasp.

"I hated John Chanler," he said. "He was my best friend, and how I hated him!"

We arrived in Rat Portage the next morning under a cloudless sapphire sky, with a biting north wind at our backs that ruffled the surface of Lake of the Woods like the invisible hand of a giant baby splashing its bathwater. Fishing boats bobbed upon the chop, loons dove and splashed in their wake, and I spied a steamboat chugging along the far southern shore, a bald eagle soaring high above its billowing stacks.

A wiry lad of native descent wearing a buckskin jacket and beaver hat popped out from the milling crowd and offered in broken English to tote our bags to the hotel for twenty-five cents. His offer inaugurated a prolonged negotiation. Like many of substantial means, Warthrop was tighter than a clam. I had witnessed him dicker for an hour to save a penny on a two-day-old loaf of bread. Add to this his native distrust of his fellow man's honesty—he never could shake the suspicion that he was being cheated—and a simple transaction that should have lasted no more than a minute could stretch out to seventy times that. By the end of their prolonged dickering—offer and counteroffer and counter-counteroffer—both the doctor and our porter seemed dissatisfied with the outcome; each felt a little had by the other.

My master's mood did not improve upon our arrival at the Russell House. Our room was small, containing a washstand, a dresser that looked as though it had been cobbled together by a blind man, and a single equally rickety bed. Warthrop was forced to rent a cot from the proprietor for an extra ten cents a night, a fee he likened to highway robbery.

We tarried only long enough to drop our bags and find something to eat at a smoke-clogged restaurant across the street, where men spat mouthfuls of oily tobacco juice into battered brass spittoons and eyed our eastern clothing with frank suspicion. We then set about to find Muriel's correspondent, a task that proved more frustrating than the doctor had anticipated.

From the hotel clerk who checked us in: "Larose? Yes, I know him. He's a popular guide; few know the backwoods better than Larose. Haven't seen him in over a month, I'd say. Don't know where he's gone to, but let me know if you find him, Dr. Warthrop. He owes me money."

From the Rat Portage postmaster: "Yes, I know Larose. Nice enough fellow when he isn't three sheets to the wind. Can't remember the last time I saw him. . . ."

"He posted a letter from here sometime in late July," the monstrumologist said.

"Yes, that would be about right. I remember that. Falling down drunk. He'd just come in from the bush, he said. Seemed out of sorts, not his usual self. He wouldn't say any more about it. If you can't find him, I'd say he's back in the woods, maybe up Sandy Lake way, but he'll be back. He always comes back."

"He has a family?"

"Not that I know of. He comes back for the liquor and the gambling. Which reminds me, if you see him, tell him I haven't forgotten about the money he owes me."

From the storekeepers along Main Street, to the dock-workers on the wharf, from the gambling halls and crowded halfpenny beer dives, from the offices of the Hudson's Bay Company, to the deafening interior of sawmills choked in swirling wood chips, it seemed the entire town knew Pierre Larose, or at least knew of him, but no one knew where he might be. All agreed he had not been seen for some time, and he owed all, it seemed, for one debt or another. The consensus was that he either had picked up stakes and returned to his native Quebec or had fled into the wilderness to escape his burgeoning debt. The few who claimed to have seen him around the time he'd posted the letter to Muriel Chanler whispered of a man who had lost his mind, who had stumbled about the streets lost in a besotted fog, "spitting and frothing at the mouth like a mad dog," slapping at his ears until they bled, whimpering and moaning and muttering on and on about a voice only he seemed able to hear.

Before that, Chanler had been seen with Larose at the chief outfitting shop on Main Street. (The clerk recognized Warthrop's description of his colleague.) Chanler had paid for their supplies—ammunition, a tent, bedding, and the like—and when asked what was their game, Larose had winked and cagily replied, "We be goin' after the Old One of the Woods."

The clerk chuckled now, and added, "I knew what he was about with that, and sure enough, next he asks if we've got any silver bullets! 'For what do you need silver bullets?' I ask, but I know why he's askin'. . . . Say, that Chanler—is he the one they was looking for couple weeks back? Whole troop of the NWMP were through here looking for some big shot that got lost in the bush, I recall."

On the boardwalk outside, Warthrop shook his head ruefully.

"I am a fool, Will Henry. The NWMP is the first place we should have asked."

He obtained directions from a man loitering outside the blacksmith shop, and we dashed across the dusty thoroughfare, dodging dray and carriage, to the other side, where the long shadows of late afternoon lay. We hopped over the steaming mounds of horse manure and slid through a small knot of miners standing in front of the tavern, fresh in town from their subterranean digs, their faces as black as players in a minstrel show, the whites of their eyes startlingly bright, each wearing a gun strapped to his waist. From the open door tinny music floated onto the street, faint and ethereal, unnervingly cheery, interrupted suddenly by what sounded to my anxious ears like a gunshot, only to resume again to the accompaniment of raucous laughter.

We ducked into the offices of the North-West Mounted Police, the precursor to the Royal Canadian Mounties. A strapping young sergeant dressed in a crisp red uniform rose from his desk.

"May I help you gentlemen?"

"I sincerely hope so," replied the doctor. "I am looking

for an American by the name of Dr. John Chanler. I understand you've been advised of his disappearance."

The sergeant nodded, and his eyes narrowed slightly. "Are you a friend of Dr. Chanler?"

"I am. His wife asked that I look into the matter."

"Well," the man said with a careless shrug of his broad shoulders, "you are free to look, Mr.—"

"*Doctor* Warthrop."

The Mountie's eyes widened in astonishment. "Not the same Warthrop who's the monster hunter?"

"I am a scientist in the natural philosophy of aberrant biology," the doctor corrected him stiffly.

"Right—you hunt monsters! I've heard of you."

"I'd no idea my reputation had preceded me so far north," replied Warthrop dryly.

"Oh, my mother used to tell us children tales of your exploits—and I always thought it was to get us to mind!"

"Your mother? Then they were not my exploits. She must have been speaking of my father."

"Well, whoever's they were, they frightened the pants off us! But this Chanler—was he a monster hunter too?"

"His wife did not tell you?"

The man shook his head. "She said he'd come for the moose. He and his guide went in, and only the guide came out."

"Pierre Larose."

"Yes, that's his name. Only he's gone missing too, is my understanding."

"So you were not able to question him?"

"Be the one I'd most like to lay my hands on, Dr. Warthrop, if I only knew where to put them. He's the key to this whole riddle—last to see the man alive and then gone into thin air without even reporting it to us. We spent nearly a month in the bush trying to pick up their trail, all the way up to Sandy Lake and the Suckers encampment—"

"The Suckers?"

"Right. Jack Fiddler's people."

"Fiddler. I've heard that name before."

"I'll wager you have! He's no doctor of monster philosophy, but he hunts them just the same. He's a shaman, too—a medicine man—and fairly civilized for a savage. Speaks passing English. Used to work down here on the boats. Makes fiddles, that's how he got his name."

"And you questioned him about Chanler and Larose?"

"And got nothing from him—nothing of any use anyway. Told us the same thing Larose told Chanler's poor wife—"

"*Lepto lurconis*," murmured the doctor.

"*Lepto* what?"

He sighed. "The Wendigo."

The sergeant nodded slowly, and then the connection dawned on him. His voice shook with wonder as he said, "You don't mean to say—I never put any stock in those stories. Is *that* why you've come? It's *real*?"

"Of course it isn't real," the doctor said irritably. "It's a convenience, like the stories your mother told to frighten you into submission."

"You mean those weren't real either?"

"No, those probably were. It's an entirely different species."

"The Wendigo?"

"The *stories*. My good man, I understand Chanler is missing, but I'd hoped I might be able to dredge up information on Larose's whereabouts . . ."

"You and half the town of Rat Portage. The man's melted away like a puff of smoke."

"It has been my experience that men do not simply 'melt away,' Sergeant. But it seems to me the best place to start is the last person to see both men alive."

"You mean Jack Fiddler, but I told you I've already talked to him and he claims to know nothing about it."

"Perhaps he will be more convivial with someone of the same spiritual inclinations."

"I beg your pardon, Doctor?"

"A fellow monster hunter."

FIVE

"You Will Live to Regret It"

When the monstrumologist asked where he might find the best man to guide us to Sandy Lake, the young sergeant, whose name was Jonathan Hawk, eagerly volunteered his services.

"There's no one knows these woods better than me, Dr. Warthrop. I've wandered them since I was no bigger than your boy here. Why, I used to hunt the very same creatures my mother told me *you* hunted—all in play, you understand, and it's surely a comfort to know none of them were real! My relief arrives from Ottawa this evening, so we can set out tomorrow at first light."

The doctor was delighted, saying later we could not have procured a more ideal guide than a member of the North-West Mounted Police. Hawk then inquired as to what kind of gear we had brought along for the expedition. Our passage would be a hard one through dense boreal forest, a hike of more than four hundred miles round-trip. Warthrop admitted we'd brought little but our resolve, just some warm clothes and, he added darkly, as if to make an impression, his revolver, at which point the sergeant laughed.

"Might do you some good against the muskrats or a beaver, maybe—not much else. There're grizzlies and wildcat and of course the wolves, but I'll find you a rifle. As for the rest, leave it to me. I will tell you, Doctor, I had a funny feeling when I spoke to Fiddler—like he wasn't telling all he knew. But his kind don't trust us—the police, I mean—and maybe you're right; he'll talk to a brother monster hunter."

They parted for the time being, each with the highest estimation of the other, though Hawk was clearly the more impressed. He seemed positively starstruck, unable to grasp that the hero of his childhood fantasies was the elder Warthrop and not my master.

The doctor, his spirits buoyed by this serendipitous turn of events, made straight for the telegraph office, where he fired off a telegram to Muriel Chanler in New York:

```
ARRIVED RAT PORTAGE THIS
MORNING STOP LAROSE HAS
DISAPPEARED STOP LEAVING AT
DAWN FOR SANDY LAKE WITH SGT
HAWK STOP WILL ADVISE
```

"I can't imagine her reaction when she receives the telegram," he confided over our supper. His face fairly glowed with the thought. "Surprised, I would guess, but not shocked. I probably should keep mum till I have a definitive answer—I don't want to get her hopes up. The odds that the poor fool is alive are practically nil, but I fear she might take it into her head to come look for him herself. It would be just like her. Muriel is a woman of remarkable—some might say damnable—stubbornness. She will not believe he is gone until she lays her hands on his lifeless corpse."

So expansive was his mood, I decided to step foot into the no-man's-land of his past and risk getting my head blown off.

"What happened, sir?"

He frowned. "What do you mean?"

"Between you and Muriel—Mrs. Chanler, I mean."

"Weren't you there? I distinctly remember it, though I also distinctly remember telling you to leave."

"I'm sorry, sir. I meant before . . ."

"Why do you presume anything at all happened?"

My face grew hot. I looked away. "Some things that she said . . . and that you said, afterward, when you couldn't sleep. I—I heard you calling out her name."

"I'm certain you heard nothing of the kind. May I give a piece of advice, Will Henry? In everyone's life, as the apostle said, there comes a time to put away childish things. What happened between Muriel and me is one of those things."

On the night she had arrived at our house, it seemed to me he had put nothing away, childish or otherwise. He might have told himself so—even believed it to be so—but that did not make it so. Even the hardest cynic is gullible to his own lies.

"So you've known each other since you were children?" I asked.

"It is an expression that refers to the thing, Will Henry, not the person. I was not a child when we met."

"She was married to Mr. Chanler?"

"No. I introduced them. Well, in a manner of speaking. It was because of me that they met."

I waited for him to go on. He picked at his venison, sipped his tea, stared at a spot just over my right shoulder.

"There was an accident. I fell off a bridge."

"You fell off a bridge?"

"Yes, I fell off a bridge," he said testily. "Why is that surprising?"

"Why did you fall off a bridge?"

"For the same reason as Newton's apple. Anyway, I wasn't injured, but it was February and the river was cold. I became quite ill with a fever and was laid up for several days in the hospital, and that's how they met, more *over* me than *through* me, I guess you could say."

"Over you?"

"Over my bed."

"Was she your nurse?"

"No, she wasn't my nurse. Dear God! She was—we were engaged, if you must know."

I was stunned. The thought of the monstrumologist betrothed to anyone was beyond my poor power to comprehend.

"Why are you looking at me like that?" he demanded. "It was a fortuitous fall into that river. Barring it, in all likelihood I would have married her and suffered much more than the discomfort of a fever. I am not constitutionally suited for it, Will Henry. Think of it—a man like me, married! Think of the poor woman *in* it. I am not opposed to marriage in principle—it is, at least in our culture, necessary for the survival of the species—only as the institution relates to monstrumology. Which is why I told both of them not to do it."

"Not to do what?"

"Get married! 'You will live to regret it,' I told her. 'He will never be home. He may never *come* home.' Obviously, neither listened to me. Love has a way of making us stupid, Will Henry. It blinds us to certain blatant realities, in this case the spectacularly high mortality rate among monstrumologists. Rarely do we live past forty—my father and von Helrung being the exceptions. And now time has proven me right."

He leaned forward, bringing the full force of his formidable personality to bear upon me. Involuntarily, I shrunk back, slipping down in my chair to make myself the smallest possible target.

"Never fall in love, Will Henry. *Never.* Regardless of whether you follow in my footsteps, falling in love, marriage, family, it would be disastrous. The organism that infects you—if the population remains stable and you do not suffer the fate of your father—will grant you unnaturally long life, long enough to see your children's children pass into oblivion. Everyone you love you are doomed to see die before you. They will go, and you will go on. Like the sibyl cursed, you will go on."

Sergeant Hawk was waiting for us in the lobby the next morning. We shared a hearty breakfast—our last proper meal for many days to come—and then stepped outside under a sky blanketed with clouds, into a brisk artic wind, reminders that the brutal Canadian winter was fast approaching. Our gear lay piled beside a hitching post: two bulging rucksacks, each festooned with tools and implements—shovels, hatchets, pots and pans, and the like; a smaller bag containing our provisions; and a pair of Winchester rifles.

"Traveling light, Doctor," our guide said brightly. "Make the best time that way."

The rifles reminded Warthrop he had left his revolver in our room, and he ordered me to fetch it for him.

He dropped it into the pocket of his duster and said, "Shall we snap to, then, Hawk? I'll take the rucksack and a rifle. Will Henry can port the rations."

Startled, Jonathan Hawk said to him, "Your boy is coming with us?"

"He is not my 'boy,' and, yes, he is."

The young policeman frowned. "It's none of my business, of course—"

"Of course it is not."

"He could wait for us here."

"Will Henry is my assistant, Sergeant Hawk; his services are indispensable to me."

"What kind of services might those be?" He was having some difficulty picturing it.

"Of the indispensable variety."

"He'll slow us down."

"No more than standing on a sidewalk holding a pointless debate, Sergeant. I guarantee you that he is more useful than he looks."

Hawk considered my "looks" dubiously for a moment.

"I'll take your word for that, Doctor, but he strikes me as a little on the delicate side. You're not in New England anymore; this is the backcountry we're talking about."

Sergeant Hawk turned to me. "There are no monsters in the bush, Mr. Will Henry, but there are other things just as eager to eat you. Are you sure you want to come?"

"My place is with the doctor," I said, trying to sound resolute.

He gave up after that. With a shrug of his broad shoulders and a lopsided grin, he slung his rifle over his back and bade us follow. He was a tall man, and his stride was long; he was used to hiking long distances over difficult terrain; and in the days to come the doctor and I would be taxed to our limits, both physically and psychologically, for he was right. We were not in New England anymore.

SIX

"A Different Species Altogether"

We made camp that first night on the northern shore of a vast lake, after a hike of nearly twenty miles along a fairly well-trod path. Canoes had been left on each side of the lake, a courtesy for local hunters and the native peoples who used the trail as a trade route to Rat Portage. The lake crossing took the better part of two hours, so vast was the water's expanse and so deliberate was our passage, for with the three of us and all our gear on board, the little canoe rode alarmingly low in the water. While Warthrop helped Hawk pitch the tent—he had packed only one, not expecting a party of three—I was dispatched into the surrounding woods to gather kindling for our fire. In the twilight shadows I thought I heard the rustle of some large creature slinking, and I cannot say if that was truly the case, only that the fruitfulness of my imagination seemed to grow exponentially as the daylight faded.

Night had not fully come on, however, before Sergeant Hawk had a merry fire going and a pan of fresh venison sausages frying, and he was happily chattering on like an excited schoolboy on the eve of the summer holiday.

"Now you must tell me something about this monstrumology business, Doctor," he said. "I've seen some pretty strange things in the bush, but they can't be nothing to what you've seen in your travels! Why, if half the things my mother said are true . . ."

"Not knowing what she told you, I cannot speak to your mother's truthfulness," replied the doctor.

"What about vampires—have you ever hunted one of those?"

"I have not. It would be extraordinarily difficult to do."

"Why? Because they're hard to catch?"

"They are impossible to catch."

"Not if you find one in his coffin, I hear."

"Sergeant, I do not hunt them because, like the Wendigo, they do not exist."

"What about the werewolf? Ever hunt one of them?"

"Never."

"Don't exist either?"

"I'm afraid not."

"What about—"

"I hope you aren't about to say 'zombie.'"

The man's mouth closed. He stared into the fire for a few moments, stirring the flickering embers with the end of a stick. He seemed somewhat crestfallen.

"Well, if you don't hunt any of them, what kind of things *do* you hunt?"

"In the main, I do not. I have devoted myself to the study of them. Capturing or killing them is something I try to avoid."

"Doesn't sound as fun."

"I suppose that depends upon your definition of 'fun.'"

"Well, if monstrumology ain't about those things, why'd your friend Chanler come up here looking for the Wendigo?"

"I can't be entirely sure. I would say, though, it was *not* to prove their nonexistence, since failing to find one would demonstrate only that one was not found. My suspicion is that he *hoped* to find one, or at least irrefutable evidence of one. You see, there is a movement afoot to expand the scope of our inquiries to include these very creatures of which you spoke—vampires, werewolves, and the like—a movement to which I am very much opposed."

"And why's that?"

Warthrop tried very hard to remain calm. "Because, my good Sergeant Hawk, as I've said, they do not exist."

"But you also said *not* finding one don't prove they don't exist."

"I may say with near absolute certainty that they do not, and I need venture no further than my own thought to prove it. Let's take the Wendigo as an example. What are its characteristics?"

"Characteristics?"

"Yes. What makes it different from, say, a wolf or a bear? How would you define it?"

Hawk closed his eyes, as if to better picture the subject in his mind's eye.

"Well, they're big. Over fifteen feet tall, they say, and thin, so thin that when they turn sideways, they disappear."

The doctor was smiling. "Yes. Go on."

"He's a shape-changer. Sometimes he's just like a wolf or bear, and he's always hungry and he don't eat anything but people, and the more he eats, the hungrier he gets and the thinner he gets, so he has to keep hunting; he can't stop. He travels through the forest jumping from treetop to treetop, or some say he spreads out his long arms and glides on the wind. He always comes after you at night, and once he finds you, you're a goner; there's nothing you can do. He'll track you for days, calling your name, and something in his voice makes you want to go.

"A bullet can't take him down, unless it's made of silver. Anything silver can kill him, but it's the only thing that can, but even then you have to cut out his heart and chop off his head, and then burn the body."

He took a deep breath and glanced at my master with a chagrined expression.

"So we have covered most of the physical attributes," the

doctor said in the manner of a headmaster leading a class. "Humanoid in appearance, very tall, more than twice the size of a grown man, extremely thin, so thin, you say, as to defy physics and become invisible upon turning sideways. One thing you failed to mention is that the heart of *Lepto lurconis* is made of ice. The Wendigo's diet consists of human beings—and, interestingly, certain species of moss, if I may append—and it has the ability to fly. Another attribute you failed to mention is its method of propagation."

"Its what?"

"Every species on the planet must have some way of producing the next generation, Sergeant. Every schoolboy knows that. So tell me, how does the Wendigo make little Wendigos? Being a hominid, it is a higher order of mammal—putting aside the issue of how a heart made of ice can pump blood—so it is not asexual. What can you tell me about its courtship rituals? Do Wendigos date? Do they fall in love? Are they monogamous, or do they take multiple mates?"

Our guide laughed in spite of himself. The absurdity of the thing had become too much for him.

"Maybe they do fall in love, Doctor. It's nice to think we're not the only ones who can."

"One must be careful not to anthropomorphize nature, Sergeant. Though, we must leave room for love in the lower orders—I am not inside Mr. Beaver's head; perhaps he loves Mrs. Beaver with all his heart. But to return to my question about the Wendigo: Are they immortal—unlike every other organism on earth—and therefore have no need to reproduce?"

"They take us and turn us into them."

"But I thought you said they *ate* us."

"Well, I can't say exactly how it happens. Stories come out of the bush, a hunter or trapper or, more often, an Indian 'goes Wendigo.'"

"Ah, so it's like the vampire or werewolf. We are its food as well as its progeny." The doctor was nodding with mock gravity. "The case is nearly unassailable, isn't it? Much more likely than the alternative, that the Wendigo is a metaphor for famine and the taboo of cannibalism in times of starvation, or a boogeyman to frighten children into obeying their parents."

Neither spoke for a few minutes. The fire crackled and popped; shadows danced and whirled about our little camp; the lake shimmered in the moonlight, its waves sensually licking the shore; and the woods reverberated with the song of crickets and the occasional snap of a twig underfoot of some woodland creature.

"Well, Dr. Warthrop, I'm almost sorry I asked about monstrumology," said Hawk wistfully. "You've darn near taken all the fun out of it."

The men flipped a coin to see who would take the first watch. Though we were but a day's hike from civilization, we were already well within wolf and bear country, and someone would need to keep the fire going throughout the night. Warthrop lost—he would have to be the last to sleep—but seemed pleased with the outcome. It would give him, he said, time to think, a statement that struck me as rich with irony. It was my impression he did little else with his time.

The burly Sergeant Hawk crawled into the tent and threw himself onto the ground next to me; so small were our quarters that his shoulder rubbed against mine.

"Sort of a queer fellow your boss is, Will," he said quietly, lest Warthrop hear him. I could see the doctor's silhouette through the open flap, hunched before the orange glow of the fire, the Winchester propped against his thigh. "Polite but not very friendly. Kind of coldlike. But he must have a good heart to come all this way after his friend."

"I'm not sure if all of it's about his friend," I said.

"No?"

"He thinks Dr. Chanler is dead."

"Well, that's my thought too, and why we called off the search. But it's like this Wendigo. Odds are your boss ain't going to find him—and that won't prove he is or isn't dead."

"I'm not sure it's even about finding him," I confessed.

"Then, what the devil *is* it about?"

"I think it's mostly about her."

"Who?"

"Mrs. Chanler."

"Mrs. Chanler!" Sergeant Hawk whispered. "What do you—Oh. Oh! Is that what—Well, you don't say!" He chuckled sleepily. "Not so coldlike after all, eh?"

He rolled onto his side, and within a few seconds the sides of the tent began to vibrate from the potency of his snores. I lay sleepless for a long time, not kept awake by his snoring so much as by the disorienting lightness of being, the sense of being very small in a vast, empty space, far from all that was familiar, adrift in a strange and indifferent sea. I watched through half-closed eyes the shape of my master outside; it comforted me somehow. I fell asleep holding close that unexpected balm, drawing it into me or allowing it to draw me into it—the conceit of the monstrumologist watching over me.

The unease I suffered that first night in the bush—made all the more distressing after the keen anticipation I had felt on the outset of the journey—persisted in the days that followed, an odd mixture of boredom and anxiety, for as hour followed monotonous hour, the woods took on a dreadful sameness, each turn of the path bringing more of the same, mere distinctions with no difference. At times the trees suddenly parted, like a curtain being whipped aside, and we'd stumble from the forest's perpetual gloom into the sudden sunlight of a clearing. Huge boulders thrust their heads from the earth, stony leviathans breaking the surface of the glen, their craggy faces sporting shaggy beards of lichen.

We crossed innumerable streams and creeks, some too wide to jump across; we'd no choice but to ford their icy waters on foot. We scrambled over washouts and through deep ravines where the shadows pooled thickly even at midday. Ruined landscapes that Hawk called *brûlé* rose up to meet us, where the charred bones of silver birch and maple, spruce and hemlock, marched to the horizon, victims of the spring fires that had raged for weeks, creating an apocalyptic vista stretching as far as the eye could see, where the restless wind whipped the inch-deep ash underfoot into a choking fog. In the midst of this desolation, I looked up and saw high above a black shape against the featureless gray, an eagle or some other great bird of prey, and for a shuddering moment I saw us through its eyes—pitifully small, wholly insignificant nomads, interlopers in this lifeless land.

Sergeant Hawk tried to halt each day's march at some open spot in the bush, but sunset often caught us deep in the forest's belly, forcing us to make camp in a blackness as profound as the grave's, where, if not for the campfire, you could not see your hand an inch from your face.

Our guide's good nature helped too in relieving the insistent dark. He told stories and jokes—some, if not most, on the bawdy side—and, possessing a fairly decent voice, sang the old songs of the French voyageurs, tilting his chin slightly as if to offer his song to some nameless forest god:

> *J'ai fait une mâtresse y a pas longtemps.*
> *J'irai la voir dimanche, ah oui, j'irai!*

"Do you know that one, Doctor?" he teased my master. "'*Le Coeur de Ma Bien-aimée*'—'*The Heart of My Well-Beloved*'?'A gentle lady charmed me, not long ago . . .' Reminds me of a girl I knew in Keewatin. Can't recall her name now, but by God I was damn near to marrying that one! Are you married, Doctor?"

"No."

"Ever been?"

"I have not," replied the monstrumologist.

"Been damn near ready, though?"

"Never."

"What, don't you like women?" he ribbed, giving me a wink.

The doctor pursed his lips sourly. "As a man of science, I have often thought that, for the sake of accuracy, they should be classified as a different species altogether—*Homo enigma*, perhaps, or *Homo mortalis*."

"Well, I don't know much about your science, Dr. Warthrop. I reckon a monster hunter looks at things a little differently than most, always with the eye turned to the dark and ugly, but all the more appreciative of the bright and fair when it comes along, or so I'd guess. I'll take your word for it, though."

He sang softly, "*La demande à m'amie je lui ferai . . .*"

Warthrop pushed himself to his feet with a snarl. "Please, would you cease with that infernal singing!"

He stomped away into the thick underbrush, stopping

where the light of the campfire met the dark of the forest. His lean frame seemed to writhe as though he were in the superheated air above the fire.

Hawk was unperturbed. He poked me in the side and pointed at the doctor. "Seems to me he's the kind who hates what he loves, Will," he opined. "And the other way around!"

"I heard that, Sergeant!" snapped Warthrop over his shoulder.

"I was speaking to your indispensable servant, Doctor!" Hawk called back jovially.

The doctor lowered his head slightly. He held up his hand. His fingertips twitched; otherwise, he was motionless, as inflexible as a post driven into the ground. He seemed to be listening to something. Hawk turned to me, grinning foolishly, and started to speak, but his words died on his tongue when I scrambled to my feet. I knew my master; my instinct reacted to his.

A gust of wind stirred the monstrumologist's hair and excited the flames of our fire; sparks jigged and spun; the sides of the tent fluttered. Hawk called softly the doctor's name, but the monstrumologist gave no reply. He was peering into the dark woods, as if he had cat's eyes that could penetrate the murk.

Hawk looked at me quizzically. "What is it, Will?"

The doctor plunged into the brush, disappearing into the trees in a wink, swallowed whole by the leviathan dark. So quickly did it happen that it looked as if something had reached out of the woods and snatched him. I rushed forward; Hawk grabbed me by the collar and yanked me back.

"Hold now, Will!" he cried. "Quick, there's a couple of lamps in my rucksack."

Within the woods we could hear the doctor crashing and stomping about, the sound fading as he drew farther and farther away. I lit the lamps with a brand from the fire and handed one to Hawk, and we charged into the bush after my wayward mentor. Though our lights barely dinted the dark, Warthrop's trail was not hard for Hawk to follow. His expert eye picked out every broken twig, every bit of disturbed earth. Sight was all he could rely upon, for the night had gone deathly quiet. There was no sound but that of our own passage through the dense foliage. Vine and branch tugged upon us as if the forest itself were trying to slow us down, as if some primal spirit were saying, *Stay. Stay, you do not wish to see.*

The ground rose. The trees thinned. We stumbled into a clearing radiant in starlight, in the center of which stood the shattered trunk of a young hemlock, snapped off eight feet from the ground, and around its base were scattered the broken bones of its branches. It looked as if some giant had reached down from the star-encrusted heavens and snapped it in two like a toothpick.

Standing a few feet from the tree was the monstrumologist, head cocked slightly to one side, arms folded over his chest, like a connoisseur at a gallery regarding a particularly interesting piece of art.

A human being was impaled upon the splintered hemlock, the pole protruding from a spot just below its sternum,
the body at the level of Warthrop's eye—arms and legs outstretched, head thrown back, mouth agape, depthless shadows pooling there and in its eyeless sockets.

The body had been stripped bare. There were no clothes
and, except for on the face, there was no skin; the body had
been flayed of both. The underlying sinew and muscle glim-
mered wetly in the silver light.

The cold stars spun to the ancient rhythm, the august
march of an everlasting symphony.

They are old, the stars, and their memory is long.

SEVEN

"There Is Nothing to Fear"

"Holy Mother of God," the sergeant whispered. He crossed himself. He looked at the empty oracular cavities, the mouth frozen wide in a voiceless scream.

"You know who this is?" asked the monstrumologist, then answered his own question: "It is Pierre Larose."

Hawk wet his lips, nodded, turned away from the skewered corpse and scanned the clearing with a quick and frightened eye, finger quivering on the trigger of his rifle. He muttered darkly under his breath.

"Will Henry," the doctor said, "run back to camp and fetch the hatchet."

"The hatchet?" Hawk repeated.

"We can't leave him stuck here like a pig on a stick," Warthrop replied. "Snap to, Will Henry."

I returned to find the doctor in that same attitude of quiet regard, pensively stroking his whiskered chin, while Hawk crashed and blundered in the brush on the far side of the clearing, his lamp bobbing between the trees like a massive firefly. I handed the axe to Warthrop, who approached the victim gingerly, as if being careful not to disturb the well-earned rest of a weary traveler. He motioned for me to bring the light closer. At that moment Hawk rejoined us, huffing for breath, twigs and shards of dead leaves clinging to his hair, the color high in his cheeks.

"Nothing," he said. "Can't see anything in this blasted dark. We'll have to wait for daylight . . . but what are you doing?"

"I am removing the victim from this tree," the doctor replied.

He slammed the sharp blade into the torso. Shards of stringy muscle landed on Hawk's cheek. The poor man, unaccustomed to the methods of the monstrumologist, gave a dismayed cry and slapped the bit of meat from his face.

"Cut down the *tree*, God damn it—not *him!*" he shouted. "What is wrong with you, Warthrop?"

The doctor grunted, reared back, and swung again. The second blow ripped all the way to the wood; the body slid an inch or two, and then, in grotesque, heartrending slowness, the body pulled free and flipped, landing facedown at the base of the hemlock. The sickening thud as it hit the ground sounded very loud in the cold air. Though the body fell nowhere near him, Hawk recoiled.

"Come along, Will Henry," said the doctor grimly, handing the bloody axe back to me.

I stepped up to the body, holding the light low. Warthrop knelt down, grunted, and observed dispassionately, "The upper dermis has been stripped from the posterior as well," as if we were not deep in the wilderness but in the bowels of his laboratory on Harrington Lane. "Light closer, please, Will Henry. Some laceration of the underlying tissue. No evidence of serration. Whatever they used, it was very sharp, though here and there there is some indication of tearing." He pressed his fingertips into the latissimus dorsi. A viscous puddle rose up, the blood closer to black than crimson. "Will Henry, try to hold the light still, will you? You're throwing shadows everywhere."

He dropped to his hands and knees and brought his eyes to within an inch of the corpse, moving his head back and forth, up and down, peering, prodding, poking—then sniffing, the tip of his nose practically touching the putrefying flesh.

It was too much for Hawk, who let loose a string of expletives and commenced to stomp in a furious ever widening circle behind us. In the space of a few moments their roles had been reversed. We had passed from the bucolic backcountry of Hawk's youth into the land of blood and umbrage, the territory of monstrumology.

"What the bloody hell are you doing, Warthrop?" His panicky cry echoed in the indifferent air. "We shouldn't be out here like this. We don't know if . . ." He let the thought die unfinished. His voice betrayed how closely he teetered upon the edge. It was as if the world had lost all familiarity; he was the aboriginal man, alone in an alien landscape. "Let's get him back to camp, and there you can sniff him to your heart's content!"

The doctor assented to the wisdom of the suggestion. I led the way, the doctor and Hawk bearing our gruesome find behind me. The fire had burned down to a few ash-covered embers in our absence, and I used the hatchet to cut up some more wood. Hawk was dissatisfied with my efforts; he added two more armfuls of fuel, and soon the fire was blazing four feet into the air.

"You're quite right, Sergeant," Warthrop said, kneeling beside the corpse, as a penitent before a patron saint. "This is much better." He cupped the head gently in his hands and pulled the chin back. The empty eye sockets rolled toward the canopy. "Look closely now. Are you quite certain it's Larose?"

"Yes. It's him. It's Larose." Hawk dug into his rucksack and removed a silver flask, unscrewed the top with shaking fingers, gulped down a few swallows, and shuddered violently. "I recognize the red hair."

"Hmm. It *is* quite red, isn't it? Curious how the face has been left untouched, except for the eyes."

"Why did they cut out his eyes?"

"I am not certain anyone did." The doctor brought his

face close. "My guess would be carrion, but I can't make out any marks in this light. We'll have to wait for morning."

"All right, but what about the skin? No animal strips off the skin and leaves the rest—and where the hell are his clothes?"

"No, whatever flayed him was no animal," the doctor said. "At least, not of the four-legged variety. The skin has been sliced off, with something extremely sharp, a hunting knife or . . ." He stopped, hovering over a large hole that yawned in the middle of the man's chest, the only obvious wound visible other than the spot lower down where he had been impaled, and then hacked free from the hemlock. The monstrumologist laughed under his breath and shook his head ruefully. "Ah, my kingdom for some real light! We could wait, but . . . Will Henry, fetch my instrument case."

I scooted around our consternated guide and retrieved the doctor's soft canvas field case. He tugged free the leather ties, flipped it open, and pulled out the desired instrument, holding it up for Hawk to see.

"Or a scalpel, Sergeant. Will Henry, I'll need more light here—no, take the opposite side and hold the lamp low. That's it."

"What are you doing?" demanded Hawk. He drew closer, curiosity getting the better of his revulsion.

"There is something very peculiar. . . ." The monstrumologist's hand disappeared inside the hole. Operating by sense of touch and his knowledge of anatomy, he made several quick slices with the scalpel, then handed the instrument to me.

"What is?" asked Hawk. "What's peculiar?"

"Ack!" the doctor groaned. "I can't do both. . . . Will Henry, set down the lamp a moment and pull this apart. No, deeper; you'll have to get hold of the ribs. Pull *hard*, Will Henry. Harder!"

I felt someone's breath upon my cheek—Hawk's. He was staring at me.

"Indispensable," he whispered. "*Now* I understand!"

The doctor's hands disappeared between mine. Then, with a dramatic flourish, the monstrumologist hauled out the severed heart, cradling it in his hands and holding it high like a bloody offering. I plopped onto my backside, the muscles of my forearms singing with pain. Warthrop turned toward the fire and allowed the light to play over the organ. As he pressed on the pericardium, thick curds of arterial blood dribbled over the severed lip of the pulmonary artery and fell into the fire, where it popped and bubbled, steaming in the intense heat.

"Most peculiar . . . There appears to be denticulated trauma to the right ventricle."

"What?" Hawk fairly shouted. "What to the what?"

"Teeth marks, Sergeant. Something bored a hole through his chest and took a bite out of his heart."

There would be no sleep that night for the monstrumologist. Around three in the morning he shooed me to bed—"You'll

be no use to me in the morning otherwise, Will Henry"—
and urged Hawk to get some rest as well. He would take
both watches. Our shaken escort did not take kindly to the
suggestion.

"What if you fall asleep?" he asked. "If that fire goes
out . . . the smell of . . . It will draw all sorts of things. . . ." He
was hugging his rifle as a child might his favorite blanket.
"Not to mention whoever did this is still out there. They
could be watching us right now, waiting for us to fall asleep."

"I assure you, Sergeant, I will not doze off, and I shall
keep my rifle close. There is nothing to fear."

Hawk would have none of it. He did not know the doctor as I did. When the hunt was on, he could stay awake for
days. Now Warthrop's eyes were bright, and all fatigue had
fled. He was in his element now.

"Nothing to fear! Sweet Mary and Joseph, listen to the
man!"

"Yes, I would beg that you do, Sergeant. Now is not
the time to lose our heads and submit to our baser instinct.
How far are we from the Sucker encampment?"

"A day . . . a day and a half."

"Good. We are of the same mind here. The quicker we
reach our destination, the better. You know these people,
Sergeant. Have you ever heard of anything like this?" He
nodded toward the body, its arms outstretched as if waiting
for a hug. "Is there anything in their culture to suggest such
desecration, perhaps for shamanistic reasons?"

"You're asking if they'd ever skin a man and eat his heart?"

The doctor smiled wanly. "There are certain indigenous beliefs about taking on the spirit of what one consumes."

"Well, I don't know about that, Mr. Monstrumologist, but I've never heard of the Cree doing anything like what was done to poor Larose here. They say they'll chop off the head sometimes—chop off the head, cut out the heart, and burn the body to keep it from coming back."

"To keep what from coming back?"

"The *Outiko*—the Wendigo!"

"Ah. Yes, of course. Well, whatever snacked on Monsieur Larose's heart was no Cree—or anyone of any color for that matter. The bite radius is too large, for one thing, and every cut is jagged—an indication that the mouth that bit him lacked incisors."

"Lacked . . . ?"

"The cutting teeth. These here." The doctor tapped his front teeth with a blood-encrusted fingernail. "In other words, whatever bit him had a mouth full of fangs."

The night wore on, and Hawk wore down, at last throwing himself upon the ground beside me with an agonized moan. Warthrop remained outside the tent, keeping watch over his special charge while keeping the fire stoked. If not in actuality, at least the fire gave off the illusion of defense against whatever might lurk just beyond the range of its beneficent light.

Soon my tent mate's moans were replaced by the pleasant drone of his humming, perhaps to comfort himself in the way a man might whistle in a graveyard, the same haunting voyageur song he had sung before:

J'ai fait une mâtresse y a pas longtemps.
J'irai la voir dimanche, ah oui, j'irai!

A gentle lady charmed me, not long ago . . .
I'll visit her on Sunday, it shall be so!

I was roused from my restless slumber by something tugging upon my boot. I sat up with a small cry.

"Easy, Will Henry; it's only me," the monstrumologist said. He was smiling. His face had taken on the same feverish glow I had seen a hundred times before. He gestured for me to join him outside. The cold, moist air made my lungs ache, but my heart sang with the shimmering bars of golden light streaming through the welcoming arms of the trees. The fire had all but died, and now in its smoldering ruin sat the coffeepot, steam rising languorously from its spout. The doctor gave a soft clap of his hands and desultorily asked how I had slept.

"Very well, sir," I said.

"Why do you lie, Will Henry? Have you never heard that a person who will lie about the smallest of things will have no compunction when it comes to the largest?"

"Yes, sir," I said.

"'Yes, sir.' Again with the 'yes, sir.' What have I told you about that?"

"Yes . . ." I hesitated, but now I was somewhat committed. ". . . sir."

"Come, I've found a suitable spot."

A suitable spot for *what?* I followed him a few yards into the trees, where I found a shallow trench; the camp shovel lay abandoned beside it.

"Finish up and be quick about it, Will Henry. You may break your fast afterward. If Sergeant Hawk is correct and not indulging in some wishful thinking, we may reach Sandy Lake before sundown."

"We're going to bury him?"

"We can't very well bring him with us, and it wouldn't do to leave him here exposed to the elements." He sighed. His steamy breath roiled in the cold air. "I had hoped the morning light would reveal more clues as to what happened to him, but there's little else I can do without the proper equipment."

"What did happen to him, sir?"

"It appears from the evidence that someone impaled him upon the broken trunk of a hemlock tree, Will Henry," he said dryly. "Snap to now! Remember, he that would have fruit must climb the tree."

And many hands make light work, I thought as I snapped to with the shovel. The handle was half the length of a proper shovel's, the ground was rocky and unyielding, and blisters soon formed on my hands and a dull ache set in between my shoulders. From the campsite I heard my companions arguing—Hawk must have gotten up—their disembodied voices sounding ethereal and tinny in the labyrinthine halls of the arboreal cathedral.

Presently I spied them stumbling along the crooked path toward me, bearing between them the body of poor Larose, the sergeant holding the upper half, Warthrop the legs. Hawk, who was forced by the narrowness of the passage to walk backward with the load, lost his balance on the dew-slick ground and fell, pulling the body sideways and down as the doctor remained upright. The gash inflicted by Warthrop the night before split wide with a sickening crunch, and the corpse broke completely in two. The top half came to rest in Hawk's lap, the head with its shock of red hair nestled in the crook of Hawk's neck, the open mouth pressed under the sergeant's jaw in an obscene mockery of a kiss. Hawk dropped the torso, scrambled to his feet, and cursed Warthrop roundly for his failure to "go down" with him.

As the possessor of the sole shovel, the honors of the dead guide's internment fell to me. Hawk grew impatient; he seemed nearly mad with the desire to quit this part of the forest. He fell to his knees beside the grave, dragging handfuls of earth into the hole, all the while muttering obscenities under his breath. Then he collapsed against a tree trunk, his gasps all out of proportion to the difficulty of his efforts.

"Someone should say something," he said. "Do we have anything to say?"

Apparently we did not. The doctor absently wiped bits and pieces of tacky viscera from his duster. I twirled the tip of the shovel in the dirt.

Wearily, with words that struck me as hollowed out of all import, Hawk recited the Hail Mary prayer:

"Hail Mary, full of grace, the Lord is with thee. . . ."

Something stirred in the bush. A large crow, its ebony body as shiny as obsidian, its black eyes brightly inquisitive, was watching us.

"Blessed is the fruit of thy womb. . . ."

Another crow hopped out from the shadows. Then another. And another. They stood, motionless, balanced upon their skeletal legs, four pairs of depthless black and soulless eyes, watching us. More appeared from the tangle of vine and scrub; I counted a baker's dozen of crows, a mute congregation, a deputation of the desolation, come to pay their respects.

"Holy Mary, Mother of God, pray for us sinners, now and at the hour of our death."

Overcome, Hawk began to weep. The monstrumologist— and the crows—did not. The birds commandeered the rite when we left. I looked back and saw them hopping about the makeshift grave, pecking at the offal Warthrop had flicked from his coat.

After a hurried breakfast of dried biscuit and bitter coffee, we broke camp. Though both men were anxious to finish the final leg to Sandy Lake, they recognized the necessity of exploring the clearing and its environs in the daylight, and so for an hour we tramped the grounds, looking for any evidence that might help solve the riddle of our macabre discovery the night before. We found nothing—no tracks, no scrap of clothing, no personal belongings or trace of anything human. It was as if Pierre Larose had dropped from the sky to land in an extremely infelicitous spot.

"It's not possible," mused our guide, standing before the broken spine of the hemlock tree.

"It happened, so it must be possible," replied the monstrumologist.

"But how? How did he heft the body eight feet off the ground like that—unless he stood on something—and if he did, where is it? I'd say there were at least two, maybe more. Hard to imagine a single author to this story. But the more bothersome is not *how* it was done but *why* was it done? If I were to murder a man, I would not go to all the trouble of skinning him and heaving him onto a pike. What is the point of *that?*"

"There seems to be a ritualistic aspect to it," said Warthrop. "The author, as you call him, might have been getting at something symbolic."

Hawk nodded thoughtfully. "Larose was in debt to half the town. I've dealt with more than one complaint of his swindling."

"Ah. So perhaps an angry creditor kidnaps him, hauls him miles into the wilderness, skins him—how poetic!—then takes a bite out of his heart."

Hawk chuckled in spite of himself. "I like it better than the alternative, Doctor. I suspect our friend Jack Fiddler would say the Old One of the Woods got a little clumsy and dropped him from on high!"

The monstrumologist nodded grimly.

"I am very interested in what our friend Jack Fiddler has to say."

EIGHT

"I Have Come for My Friend"

His real name was Zhauwuno-geezhigo-gaubow—"He Who Stands in the Southern Sky"—or, according to records of the Hudson's Bay Company, with whom he traded, Maisaninnine or Mesnawetheno, Cree for "a stylish person."

He was the son of the chief, Peemeecheekag ("Porcupine Standing Sideways"), and he was the tribe's *ogimaa*, or shaman, respected to the point of fear by his clansmen for his skill and power, particularly over the evil spirit that possessed his kinsmen in times of famine. He claimed in his lifetime to have killed fourteen of these creatures that "devour all mankind," the last in 1906—Wahsakapeequay, the daughter-in-law of his brother, Joseph. His reward for this selfless act of altruism was his arrest by the Canadian authorities the following year.

After being convicted of murder and sentenced to death, Jack Fiddler escaped—from prison and from the indignity of the white man's justice. He carried out the sentence himself. The day following his escape they found him hanging from a tree.

He was a bit shy of his fiftieth year when he met his spiritual brother—Dr. Pellinore Warthrop, expert in the natural philosophy of aberrant species—though in appearance he seemed far older. Season after season in the brutal cold, and the unimaginable hardship and deprivation of the harsh subarctic wilderness, had taken its toll; he appeared closer to seventy than fifty, his skin cracked and laced with deep wrinkles, his face as dark and worn as old shoe leather, in which the eyes dominated, dark, deep set, intense but kind. His were the eyes of one who has seen too much suffering to take suffering too seriously.

As night fell, we reached Jack Fiddler's primitive kingdom hacked out of the Canadian bush on the shores of Sandy Lake, after the most grueling day of our long trek from Rat Portage, pushed by Warthrop's eagerness and Hawk's unease to the limit of our endurance. The latter's agitation grew as the day aged, his eyes flitting back and forth along the trail, seeing menace in every shadow, bad omens in even the most minor of delays.

"Have you noticed, Doctor," he said when we halted briefly for lunch, "that we haven't seen a single animal since leaving Rat Portage? Not a moose or a deer or a fox or anything.

Nothing but birds and insects, but I don't count them. I've never been up in these woods without seeing *something*. Even the squirrels—this is the busiest time of year for the squirrels—but not even a squirrel!"

Warthrop grunted. "We haven't exactly been as quiet as church mice, Sergeant. Still, I agree it is unusual. They say the animals of the island rushed pell-mell into the sea just before Krakatoa blew."

"What do you mean?"

The monstrumologist was smiling. "Perhaps a great disaster is upon the horizon and we are the only animals stupid enough to remain."

"Are you saying a moose is smarter than us?"

"I am saying a larger brain comes with a price. Our better instincts are oft put down by our reason."

"Well, I don't know about that. But there *is* something odd about it. Now, a single wolf will clear the woods for miles—but what is there that will chase a wolf away?"

If the doctor had an answer to that, he kept it to himself.

As the sun sank into the dark waters of the lake, painting the surface with fiery bars of expiring light, a group of elders appeared at the shore to meet us. Our arrival, it appeared, was not unexpected. We were greeted with great solemnity and were offered fresh fish and cured venison, which we gratefully accepted, supping by the roaring fire a stone's throw from the lakeshore, with the gift of warm blankets thrown over our laps, for the temperature plunged dramatically with the quitting of the sun. The entire village turned out for the meal—though we were the only ones eating. The villagers stared with intense, if mute, curiosity. White people were a highly uncommon sight this deep in the backcountry, Hawk explained; even the missionaries rarely visited here, and the few that did left heavyhearted. It seemed the Sucker people had no worries about the fate of their immortal souls.

They knew Sergeant Hawk and spoke to him in their tongue. I could make out hardly any of it, of course, except the words "Warthrop," "Chanler," and "*Outiko.*" The adults kept a respectable distance, but the children gave in to their fascination, easing closer and closer until they had clustered around us, and one by one they reached out with hesitant fingers and stroked my white skin and felt the coarse wool of my jacket. An elderly woman rebuked them, and they scampered away.

Another, much younger, woman—one of the shaman's wives, I later learned—escorted us to the wigwam of our host, a dome-shaped structure composed of woven mats and birch bark. The shaman was alone, sitting upon a mat near the small fire in the wigwam's center, wearing a wide-brimmed hat, and draped in a ceremonial blanket.

"*Tansi*, Jonathan Hawk," he greeted the sergeant. "*Tansi, tansi,*" he said to Warthrop, and waved us to sit beside him. Our sudden appearance in his village did not seem to faze him in the least, and he regarded the doctor and me with mild curiosity and little else. Unlike many of their displaced, hounded, and murdered brethren, the Sucker clan had been, but for the occasional visit from the well-meaning but misguided missionary, left alone by the European conquerors.

"I heard of your coming," he said to Hawk, who translated for our benefit. "But I did not expect you to return so soon, Jonathan Hawk."

"Dr. Warthrop is a friend of Chanler's," said Hawk. "He is *ogimaa* too, *Okimahkan*. Very strong, very powerful *ogimaa*. He's killed many *Outiko*, like you."

"I have done no such thing," protested the doctor, deeply offended.

Jack Fiddler seemed bemused. "But he is not *Iyiniwok*," he said to Hawk. "He is white."

"In his tribe, he is called 'monstrumologist.' All evil spirits fear him."

Fiddler squinted in the smoky light at my master. "I do not see it. His *atca'k* is hidden from me."

His fathomless dark eyes lighted upon me, and I squirmed under their quiet power.

"But this one—his *atca'k* is bright. It soars high like the hawk and sees the earth. But there is something . . ." He leaned toward me, studying my face intently. "Something heavy he carries. A great burden. Too great for one so young . . . and so old. As old and young as *misi-manito*, the Great Spirit. What is your name?"

I glanced at Warthrop, who nodded impatiently. He

seemed annoyed that the renowned medicine man had taken an interest in me.

"Will Henry," I answered.

"You are blessed by *misi-manito*, Will Henry," he said. "And a heavy burden is this blessing. Do you understand?"

"Don't you dare say no," the doctor whispered ominously in my ear. "I didn't come two thousand miles to discuss your *atca'k*, Will Henry."

I nodded my counterfeit assent to the old *Iyiniwok*.

"What he loves does not know him, and what he knows cannot love," said the *ogimaa*. "*Eha*, like *misi-manito*—that which loves, which love knows not . . . I like this Will Henry."

"I understand it's a nearly inexhaustible topic, but if we are quite finished singing Will Henry's praises, can we get to the point, Sergeant?" asked the doctor. He turned to Jack Fiddler. "Pierre Larose is dead."

Fiddler's expression did not change. "I know this."

"That is not what you told me, *Okimahkan*," said Hawk, startled by the admission. "You told me you didn't know where Larose was."

"For I did not know. We found him after you left us, Jonathan Hawk."

"What happened to him?" Warthrop demanded.

"The Old One called to him—*Wi-htikow*."

The doctor groaned softly. "I understand, but my question is why was he mutilated and left for carrion? Is this the way of your people, Jack Fiddler?"

"As we found him, so we left him."

"Why?"

"He does not belong to us. He belongs to *Outiko*."

"*Outiko* killed him."

"*Eha.*"

"Flayed the skin from his bones, impaled him upon a tree, and did *this*." The monstrumologist dug into his rucksack and removed the organ that had once animated Pierre Larose. Sergeant Hawk gasped; he didn't know Warthrop had kept it. Calmly our host accepted the macabre offering, cradling it in his gnarled hands as he studied it in the firelight.

"You should not have done this," he chided Warthrop. "*Wi-htikow* will be angry."

"I don't give a tinker's damn if he's angry," said the doctor. He gestured impatiently to Hawk, who had hesitated to translate the remark. Then he continued in a voice tight with indignation. "It is none of my concern what really happened to Pierre Larose. That is a matter for Sergeant Hawk and his superiors. I have come for my friend. Larose took him into the bush, and only Larose came out again."

"We do not take what belongs to *Wi-htikow*," said the shaman. "Did you leave the rest for him?"

"No," replied Hawk. "We buried the rest."

Fiddler shook his head, dismayed. "*Namoya*, say you did not."

"Where is John Chanler?" persisted my master. "Does he belong to *Wi-htikow* as well?"

"I am *ogimaa*. If you are *ogimaa*, as Jonathan Hawk has told me, you understand. I must protect my people."

"Then, you do know where he is?"

"I will tell you, monstrumologist Warthrop. Larose, he brings your friend to me. 'He hunts *Outiko*,' he says. And I tell your friend, '*Outiko* is not hunted; *Outiko* hunts. Do not look into the Yellow Eye, for if you look into the Yellow Eye, the Yellow Eye looks back at you.' Your friend does not listen to my words. His *atca'k* is bent; it is crooked; it does not flow cleanly to *misi-manito*. They go anyway. They call to *Outiko*, but you do not call *Outiko*. *Outiko* calls *you*.

"I have seen this. I am *ogimaa*; I protect my people from the Yellow Eye. Your friend is not *Iyiniwok*. Do you understand, *ogimaa* Warthrop? Do my words reach your ears? In truth, I ask you: Does the fox raise the bear cub, or the caribou suckle the gray wolf?

"*Outiko* is old, as old as the bones of the earth; *Outiko* was before the first word was spoken. He has no name like Zhauwuno-geezhigo-gaubow or Warthrop; '*Outiko*' we have named him. His ways are not our ways. But our doom is his and his is ours, for when you wake on the morrow, will you say, 'Since I have eaten last night, I need eat no more'? No! His hunger is our hunger, the hunger that is never satisfied."

"Then, why leave him Larose to snack upon?" the doctor asked, and then he waved away his own question. "With all respect, *Okimahkan*, I have no desire to discuss the subtleties of your people's animistic cosmology. My desire is far simpler. You either know what happened to John Chanler or you do not. If you do, I hope in the name of all human decency that you will share that information with me. If not, my business here is done."

The *ogimaa* of the Sucker clan looked down at the lifeless heart in his hands.

"I will protect my people," he said in English.

"Ah," the monstrumologist said. He looked at Hawk. "I see."

We were shown to a wigwam several hundred paces from Fiddler's, a guesthouse of sorts—and a mansion compared to our quarters for the past two weeks, large enough for all three of us to sleep under one roof without rubbing against one another. The beds were made with fresh balsam boughs, and I swear no feather mattress could feel as soft or as comfortable after one has been marching double time through the wilderness; I was sorer and more tired than the most tender of tenderfoots. I fell upon my bower with a satisfied moan.

The doctor did not go to bed, but sat in the open doorway, hugging his knees and staring across the compound at the glow from our host's abode.

"Do you think he's lying?" asked Hawk, trying to draw Warthrop from his reverie.

"I think he isn't telling everything he knows."

"I could arrest him."

"For what?"

"Suspicion of murder, Doctor."

"What is your evidence?"

"You've been carrying it around in your rucksack."

"He denies having anything to do with that, and neither the body nor the scene yielded anything to incriminate him."

"Well, *somebody* killed the poor bastard. Within a day's hike of this village, and in a way that no white man might do it."

"Really, Sergeant? If you believe that, then you do not spend enough time around white men. I have found there is very little they're incapable of."

"You don't understand, Dr. Warthrop. These people are savages. A man who boasts of killing his own people—*boasts* of it! Kills them to *save* them! Tell me what sort of person does that?"

"Well, Sergeant, the God of the Bible leaps immediately to mind. But I shan't argue the point. What you do about Jack Fiddler is your business. Mine is discovering what happened to my friend."

"He's dead."

"I've never had much doubt about that," said Warthrop. "Still, our interview with the *Okimahkan* has raised the possibility . . ." He shook his head as if to chase away the thought.

"What? That Jack knows where he is?"

"Correct me if I'm mistaken, but isn't it the practice of the *ogimaa* to isolate the victim of the Wendigo's attack in the hope of 'curing' him? Are there not certain spells that must be recited, prayers and rituals and the like, before all hope is abandoned and the victim sacrificed?"

Hawk snorted. "Seems to me you're clutching at straws, Doctor. He said it himself—he doesn't care what happens to us. We're not *Iyiniwok.*" He sneered the word.

"He would care if one of us endangered his tribe."

"Right! So he strips off our skin and chops up our heart and sticks us on a pole in the middle of nowhere. No more troubles for the tribe. Larose is all the proof we need that Chanler's dead."

He threw himself onto the bed beside me. "Turn down your *atca'k,* Will," he teased me. "It's shining right in my eyes." He glanced over at the doctor, who had not budged from his post.

"I'm quitting this godforsaken place at first light, Doctor, with or without you."

Warthrop smiled wearily. "Then you had better get some rest, Sergeant."

"You should too, sir," I piped up. He looked twice as tired as I felt.

The monstrumologist nodded toward the orange glow flickering in the *ogimaa*'s wigwam.

"I'll rest when he does," he said softly.

NINE

"I Shall Carry Him"

I was awakened by someone roughly shaking my leg.

"Will Henry!" the doctor urgently whispered. "Snap to, Will Henry!"

I jerked upright, catching him unawares. Our foreheads smacked against each other in the dark, and he gave a soft involuntary cry of pain.

"I'm sorry, sir," I muttered, but he had already turned away to roust Hawk, who lay snoring lustily beside me.

"Hawk! Sergeant! Get up!" Over his shoulder he growled, "Grab that rucksack, Will Henry, and the rifle. Hurry!"

"What happened?" I wondered aloud, but received no answer. Warthrop was busy trying to rouse our groggy companion. Through the doorway I saw a sliver of violet sky and the insubstantial gray landscape of dawn.

The doctor shoved a rifle into Hawk's chest.

"What you are doing?" Hawk murmured.

"Clutching at straws, Sergeant. You said you wanted to leave at first light. I suggest you do so if you wish to remain in one piece," Warthrop returned grimly. He threw Hawk's rucksack at him and ducked out of the wigwam.

We scrambled outside. The doctor was already several feet ahead, trotting toward the water's edge. A row of canoes lined the bank. Warthrop pulled the heavy rucksack from my hands and tossed it into the middle of a canoe, where it landed beside the prone body of a man, wrapped up in one of the clan's blankets. Warthrop snatched the rifle from my hand and jabbed a finger toward the forward seat—*Get in!* Then he gave Hawk an impatient jab between the shoulders.

"*Quickly*, Sergeant!"

He waited until Hawk had plopped down before he pushed off, splashing for several lunging strides through the icy water before heaving himself on board. He dug in with his paddle. Hawk quickly followed suit, and soon we were sliding through the water with barely a sound. A loon exploded before the bow with an angry cry and took off across the lake, its wing tips caressing the glassy surface.

I looked down at the man whose head lay at my feet. Even in the dim light, I saw a face deathly pale and painfully thin. His eyes jerked beneath the closed lids, as if he were gripped by a feverish dream. I looked up at the doctor, who was looking past me toward our destination, the southern shore of Sandy Lake.

We had not reached the halfway point when our theft was discovered. Several men carrying what appeared to be rifles rushed to the water's edge and leapt into canoes to give chase. Warthrop called for Hawk to quicken the pace, but the man needed no urging. He paddled furiously, glancing occasionally over his shoulder at our pursuers, who seemed to gain upon us with every expert stroke of their oars, their boats slicing through the water with the speed of downhill skaters, ghostlike in the thick morning mist. The doctor yanked the revolver from the pocket of his duster and tossed it into my lap, with the admonition that if I was forced to defend myself, I should make every effort not to shoot him in the head.

"We won't make it," gasped Hawk after a few frantic minutes. "Let's turn here and make our stand."

"I'd rather make it on a more substantial surface, Sergeant," returned the doctor, pulling hard for air.

"They won't dare hurt *me*. I'm a police officer, a duly deputized representative of the province! The whole village would hang."

"Yes, I'm sure you'll point that out to them right before they sink your bullet-ridden corpse to the bottom of the lake!"

The fog swirled around us, a gray shroud draped over the world, obliterating the canoes in our wake. To our left the rising sun was the palest of washed-out yellows. With no point of reference it was impossible to tell our speed or how far we had to go. The effect was unnerving to say the least—worse than hell, for even the souls in Charon's boat could see the opposite shore!

"Please drop the barrel of that gun, Will Henry," the doctor admonished. It was pointed directly at his chest. "And try to keep in mind that if we can't see them, they cannot see us. They're as blind in this soup as we are."

"No, I'm a bit blinder, Doctor," puffed Hawk. "*They* know what you're up to."

Warthrop did not respond. His gaze remained fixed over my shoulder, as if by virtue of the intensity of his stare he could part the mist and sight his goal.

We reached that goal finally—not touching the bank but slamming into it with enough force to send me flying backward over the edge of the canoe and into the shallow water. Warthrop yanked me to my feet and hurled my sopping wet carcass onto the muddy shore. Coughing and spitting, I sat up in time to see Hawk and the doctor pulling our unconscious cargo from the boat's belly. They carried him several feet into the trees before easing him to the ground and returning for our gear. At that moment three canoes bearing six armed men emerged from the fog, the men's black eyes glittering dangerously under their dark brows. Warthrop raised his hand, and Hawk raised his rifle.

"Tell them we intend no harm," the doctor instructed him.

Hawk barked a little laugh. "I'm more worried about *their* intent, Doctor!" Then he said something in their tongue. The tallest of the six, a young man close to Hawk's age, spoke quietly and without inflection, and pointed at Warthrop.

"He wants you to return what you've taken," Hawk said.

"Tell him I am merely recovering what they have taken."

Their leader spoke again, his manner one of utter earnestness laced with a touch of condescension; clearly Warthrop did not understand the consequences of his actions.

"Well?" the doctor snapped. "What does he say?"

"He says if you insist on taking him, you must kill him. The *Outiko* is with him."

"*With* him?"

"Or *in* him, it means the same thing."

"If he wants him dead, he'll have to kill me," Warthrop said, his eyes flashing dangerously. "All of us. The boy, too. Is he willing to do that? Ask him!"

Hardly were the words out of Hawk's mouth when six rifles rose as one. Instinctively I brought up the revolver. Warthrop, however, made no move with his weapon.

"No need to translate, Hawk," the doctor said.

"He is *Outiko's* now," the brave said in English. "We take him."

"Dear God, how much of this superstitious folderol must I bear?" Warthrop cried. He flung his rifle to the ground, grabbed the gun from my hand, and slung it toward the trees. Then, before Hawk could react, Warthrop ripped his rifle away and threw that down too. He opened his long arms wide and thrust out his chest, offering himself to their bullets.

"Go on and do it, then, damn you! Shoot us all in cold blood and take your precious *Outiko!*"

For an agonized moment I believed they would do just that. Their rifles remained unwaveringly upon us. I heard Hawk mutter, "Warthrop, I would have liked to have been included in this decision." Otherwise, all was quiet—that awful pregnant stillness before the clang and clatter of battle.

Their leader spoke, and his men slowly lowered their weapons. He said something to Warthrop.

"Well?" the doctor asked Hawk.

"He said, 'You are a fool.'" The sergeant took a deep breath. "And I think I agree with him."

Hawk's opinion mattered to the doctor as much as anyone else's—that is, hardly at all. He waited until our pursuers had turned their boats around and the mist had swallowed them up, before he hurried to the side of his fallen friend, snapping his fingers at me to grab his rucksack and join him. The sergeant lingered between the line of trees and the shore, standing watch in case the *Iyiniwok* changed their minds.

Warthrop knelt beside the unconscious victim and pulled back his eyelids to examine his eyes. They were bloodshot and slightly yellow, restless in their sockets, the pupils contracting and expanding in a pulsating rhythm, like tiny black hearts. In the gray forest light his face seemed devoid of all pigmentation, as white as paper and just as thin, stretched taut over his cheeks and forehead, the bones of his jaw protruding like large knuckles pushing insistently against the flesh. The lips were swollen and bright red, an obscenely comical juxtaposition against his pale skin, and they were laced with hairline cracks that oozed milky yellow pus.

The doctor ran his fingers through the thick sandy-blond hair. Fluffy tufts of it pulled free at his touch. The breeze caught some errant strands and sent them twirling like dandelion seeds into the deep forest gloom.

Grunting with effort, the monstrumologist freed the man from the cocoon of the old blanket. He had been stripped to his underclothes; they hung limply about his emaciated frame, but I could clearly see the ribs poking into the material. Warthrop lifted one bony arm and pressed his fingers against the wrist. The impressions from the pressure remained after the doctor removed his fingers, like footprints in wet sand.

"Severe dehydration," he observed quietly. "Fetch the canteen—but first I'll take the stethoscope."

He pushed the thin undershirt to the man's chin and listened for several minutes to the heartbeat. I could actually *see* its exhilarated pumping beneath the attenuated skin. When I returned with the water, the doctor was running his hands up and down the man's bony-kneed stork-thin legs, and then up to the torso, where he pressed gently. Everywhere he touched, his fingers left indentations in the pale skin.

He pressed the mouth of the canteen to the bloated lips, and rivulets of that life-giving liquid rolled out from either side of the gurgling mouth. Warthrop heaved the man's head onto his lap and bent low, cradling him like a child, one hand cupping his chin while he poured a thin stream through the half-opened lips. His oversize Adam's apple jerked as each swallow was forced down. The doctor breathed a sigh, and said softly, "John. John."

And then louder, his voice ringing in the trees, "John! John Chanler! Can you hear me?"

Sergeant Hawk appeared, his rifle resting in the crook of his arm. He regarded this tableau for a moment, and said, "So, this is Chanler?"

"No, Sergeant, this is Grover Cleveland," the doctor answered sardonically. With uncharacteristic gentleness the monstrumologist pulled the blanket back over Chanler.

"He's severely dehydrated and malnourished," Warthrop told Hawk. "And jaundiced; his liver may be shutting down. I can't find any external injuries beyond bedsores, which is to be expected, and internally there are no abnormalities or injuries, though it's difficult under these conditions to tell for certain. He has a mild fever but doesn't seem to be suffering from dysentery or anything else that might kill him before we can get him back."

Hawk glanced nervously around us, stroking the rifle's trigger, as if he expected marauders to burst from the bush at any second.

"Well, I'm all for that now that we've got him!"

"Me too, Sergeant. We've only to wait until he's ambulatory—"

"What do you mean 'ambulatory'? You mean wait till he can walk?" He squinted down at the comatose man at his feet. "How long?"

"Hard to say. His muscles are atrophied, his vigor sapped by the ordeal. It could be as long as a week or two."

"A week or two! No. No." Hawk was shaking his head violently. "That won't do, Doctor. We can't spend two weeks in the bush. There's our supplies, and then there's the weather. We'll get the first real snow of the season before two weeks are out."

"I am open to suggestions, Sergeant. You have eyes as well as I. You can observe the poor man's condition for yourself."

"We'll carry him out. Good God, he can't weigh more than Will here."

"To do so over this terrain could prove fatal."

"Walking across the street on a Sunday afternoon could prove fatal, Warthrop. If Will can take my rifle and rucksack, I could carry him."

He bent to scoop Chanler from the forest floor and was stopped by Warthrop's hand against his chest.

"I am willing to risk the elements, Sergeant," the doctor said stiffly.

"Well, guess what? I'm not. I don't know what it is about you and this monstrumology business, but it's like bear shit on your boots—follows you every step and is as hard as hell to get rid of."

He jabbed a finger into my master's chest.

"I'm getting the hell out of here, Doc. You're welcome to come with me, or you can try your luck finding the way out yourself."

For a moment neither man moved, locked in a test of wills—a test that Warthrop failed. He ran a hand through his thick hair and sighed loudly. He looked at Chanler; he looked at me. He considered the sliver of gray sky sliced off by the canopy.

"Very well," he said, "but it is my burden."

He slid his arms beneath the fragile form, and rose unsteadily with the wasted body. Chanler's forehead pressed against the base of Warthrop's neck.

"I shall carry him," the doctor said.

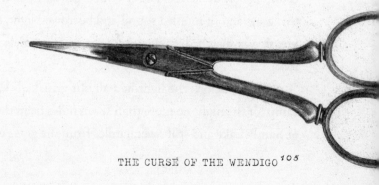

TEN

"It Can Break a Man's Mind in Half"

Our flight to Rat Portage was painfully slow. Warthrop called for many halts to check Chanler's vital signs and to attempt getting more water into him. Slowing the pace too was Sergeant Hawk—or rather Sergeant Hawk's finding his bearings in the fog. It thickened as the day wore on, a colorless miasma that obscured the trail and peopled the forest with looming shadows and flitting apparitions upon which the imagination seized and ascribed portents of doom. In this gray land of muffled sound and borrowed light, our very breath was snatched from our mouths and trammeled underfoot.

By four o'clock the light had all but vanished. We made camp for the night no more than seven miles from the shores of Sandy Lake and still several miles from the grave of Pierre

Larose. The doctor eased his load onto the ground and collapsed against a tree. His respite lasted only a minute or two; soon he was up again fussing over Chanler, wiping his brow, raising his head to force a bit more water down his throat, calling to him in a loud voice—but Chanler would not be roused. I gathered wood for our fire before the last of the light was snuffed out. Hawk inventoried our meager supplies, reckoning we had enough to last another five days. After that, we would have to live off the land.

"I'd planned on resupplying at Sandy Lake," he said defensively when the doctor raised an eyebrow at this bit of bad news. "You didn't tell me there'd be a kidnapping."

The sergeant did not seem himself. His eyes would not stay still; they shifted right and left and back again restlessly, and he could not seem to stop wetting his lips.

"How did you manage to find him?" he asked.

"Fiddler. I thought if John was alive, Fiddler might check on him, and the odds were he would not risk it while we were awake. And my guess was right. At a little after two he came out of his wigwam, and I followed him. They had put John in a wigwam on the northern edge of the village, far removed from the others, as one might expect. It is common practice among indigenous peoples to construct a 'sick house' to isolate infectious members from the rest of the tribe.

"After that, it was only a matter of time and preparation. No guard was posted. I merely had to wait for Fiddler to go to bed."

"What happened, do you think?" Hawk was staring at the opening of the tent wherein Chanler lay, the white of the blanket barely visible in the firelight.

"I can only guess," answered the doctor wearily. "Either he stumbled into their camp or someone found him and brought him there. He was probably lost, separated from Larose—the man admitted as much in his letter to Muriel—and it nearly got the better of him."

"It will, if you don't know what you're about," agreed Hawk. His eyes cut toward the doctor. "Muriel . . . is that the missus?"

"Yes."

"Hmm."

"What?"

The sergeant glanced my way. "Nothing," he said.

"Clearly it was not."

"Just clearing my throat."

"You did not clear your throat. You said, 'hmm,' like that. I would like to know what you meant."

"I didn't mean anything. Hmm. That's all it was, Doctor. Just hmm."

Warthrop snorted. He threw the dregs of his tea into the shadows and ducked into the tent to be with his patient. Hawk looked at me again, a crooked smile playing on his lips.

"*J'ai fait une mâtresse y a pas longtemps*," he sang softly.

"And cease that infernal singing!" the doctor shouted.

The sergeant complied with Warthrop's brusque request, and would not sing again for the remainder of our flight back to civilization. I call it 'flight,' for that is what it was, torturously slow though it proved to be. We were fleeing something—and we were bringing what we fled with us.

We woke on the next morning beneath an ominous gray sky. By noon a light snow had begun to fall, carpeting the trail with dusty powder that quickly grew slick; more than once the doctor nearly went down with his precious cargo. The sergeant would offer to spell him, each time rebuffed by Warthrop. The doctor seemed jealous of his burden.

It was cold and still; not a breath of wind stirred; and the snow, like the fog, deadened sound. We marched through vaulted chambers of brown and white, down desolate halls devoid of color, bereft of life. The nights fell with crushing suddenness. The daylight seemed not so much to fade as to vanish. Darkness was the true face of the desolation, its elemental substance.

More than the monotonous scenery or the miles of rough trail that crawled underfoot, that dark weighed upon us. It numbed our souls to senselessness as the cold numbed our fingertips and toes, a pitch-black tactile dark that mocked our feeble attempts to drive it away, a darkness that pressed down with suffocating force. I began to envy John Chanler and the feverish oblivion in which he dwelled.

And I worried about the doctor. Even on his worst days back at Harrington Lane, when he retreated to his bed and remained there for hours, refusing all sleep and sustenance, lost in a melancholy so profound all he could do was breathe, even those days seemed as bright as springtime compared to what he endured now. And he endured it for someone other than himself, a stunning revelation for me, who up to that point had thought him the most self-absorbed man on the continent. His face grew gaunt, his eyes receded into their sockets, his duster hung upon him like an empty garment upon a hanger. He was coming to resemble the man he was carrying.

I urged him to eat and rest, scolding him like a parent and reminding him he was no good to his friend if he succumbed to the same fate. He endured my chiding and rarely lost his temper, except on one memorable occasion when he dressed me down for more than a quarter of an hour. It might have gone on longer, but Hawk informed him that if he didn't shut up, the sergeant was going to put a bullet through the back of his head.

After the last morsel of hardtack and cured bacon had been consumed, the sergeant shouldered his rifle and tramped into the woods, disappearing for the rest of the afternoon. We made no progress that day. Near dusk Hawk returned, empty-handed. He dropped the weapon to the ground and collapsed before the fire, muttering under his breath, swiping his mouth with the back of his hand incessantly and wetting his lips.

"Nothing," he murmured. "Nothing. I've never seen anything like it. Nothing for miles."

He lifted his eyes to the sky. "Not even a bird. Nothing. Nothing."

"Well, we still have each other," said the doctor consolingly, trying to lift his spirits. "You know, the Donner Party option."

Hawk stared at him without expression, his mouth hanging open, and I thought the doctor, who knew so well his own limitations, must have been really out of sorts to even attempt humor. It was ludicrous, like a man trying to fly by flapping his arms.

Hunger became the newest member of our company, far stronger and far more resilient than the rest of us, and we were the dried bones upon which it chewed. There was no real resting when we stopped. Hawk and I would push our way into the bush, plucking berries, digging up edible roots such as Indian potatoes and toothwort, pinching the heads from puffball mushrooms, stripping bark from hickory trees, which we boiled, to soften it. (This "bark stew" was also beneficial for the digestion, the sergeant informed me, and was a native treatment for diarrhea and venereal disease.) We also gathered wolf's claw, an evergreen moss that grew in abundance on the forest floor, with dense needlelike leaves that Hawk boiled to make a kind of herbal tea. The taste was pungent and bitter—the doctor spat out his first sip—yet Hawk kept harvesting it. The spores were highly flammable, and he delighted in tossing them into the fire and watching the subsequent flash of hot white light.

We rose each day a little weaker than the day before, and halted each night a little hungrier. Our eyes took on the haunted, vacant look of slow starvation, and our voices were lean in the breathless air. We stumbled clumsily down trail and through dead meadow, and crossed the desolate miles of *brûlé*, the trackless snowbound desert, with the gray dome of the sky upheld by the blackened pillars of branchless trees. It was here that we spied the first sign of life since our escape from Sandy Lake. I tugged on Hawk's coat and pointed to them, lazily circling overhead on immobile wings, riding the high wind directly above us. He nodded and quickly looked away.

"Buteos," he said. "Buzzards."

The doctor's toe caught on a fallen branch. He pitched forward, twisting around just before he landed, to avoid crushing his precious cargo beneath him.

"I'm all right; I'm fine," he snarled at Hawk, who had reached down to help him up. He slapped away the offered hand.

"Let me carry him awhile, Doc," said the sergeant reasonably. "You look all done for."

"Do not touch him. Do you understand? I'll shoot you if you touch him. No one touches him but me!"

"I meant no offense," replied Hawk. "Just trying to help."

"This is mine," the doctor gasped. "Mine!" He slipped his arms beneath Chanler's body and struggled to his feet, where he stood swaying for an awful moment before falling again, landing this time with a muffled thump upon his backside. His friend's head lolled against his chest.

"God damn you to hell," the doctor whimpered to Chanler, the words smashed to nothing by the emptiness that engulfed him. "Why did you come here? What did you think you would find? You idiot . . . you imbecilic fool . . . *What did you think you would find?*"

He stroked the soft feathery hair. He pressed his cheek against the top of John Chanler's head.

"Ah, come on now, Doc," Hawk urged him. "It's not as bad as all that." He stepped toward him, and the doctor leveled his revolver at Hawk's forehead.

"You could have prevented this!" he cried. "You were here a month ago. He was a stone's throw from you and you left him. You *left* him!"

"Now, Doc, I told you what Fiddler said. . . ."

"The same thing he said to me, and did I listen? Did I take him at his word? Did I allow him to take me for a fool?"

"Well," answered Hawk tensely, "maybe you're just smarter than I am."

"That is no compliment."

With those words all passion drained from the doctor; his eyes glazed over; the hand holding the gun dropped to his side. His listlessness returned, the same curious apathy that had infected Hawk and me as well. Desolation's progeny—the lifeless living, every word pointless, every gesture useless, every hope vain.

I cannot say what day it was—it may have been the tenth or eleventh since our escape from the Sucker camp—when Hawk pulled my master aside, telling me, "Stay with Chanler, Will. I need a word with your boss." They walked several yards up the path, and I followed—which is completely understandable, I'm sure. I eased up behind them to eavesdrop on their hurried and anxious conversation.

"Are you certain?" the doctor was saying. He sounded worried but dubious.

Hawk nodded, wetting his lips. "At first I thought my mind was playing tricks on me. It happens in the bush. So I didn't say anything, but there's no mistaking it, Doctor. I'm sure of it."

"Since . . . ?"

"First heard it yesterday morning. Nothing on the watch last night, then off and on today."

"The *Iyiniwok?*"

Hawk shrugged. He wet his lips. "*Something.* I suppose it *could* be a wolf, though not a bear, nothing that big. It's . . . strange."

"If Fiddler's men were responsible for Larose . . . ," Warthrop began.

"Then it could be whoever filleted him," Hawk finished, nodding. Again, his tongue swiped across his chapped lips. "Thought you should know."

"Thank you, Sergeant," the doctor said. "Perhaps we should force a confrontation?"

Hawk shook his head. "Just two of us—and God knows how many of them. Plus, there's Chanler and Will to think about."

I returned to Chanler, my mind racing. Beneath the blackened lids Chanler's eyes roamed the darkness. Encompassing us, the mute forest brooded, shrouded in winter white.

The gray land was deceptively still. It kept its secrets.

Something was following us.

That night I saw the yellow eyes for the first time. I attributed it to my fevered imagination, overheated by the conversation earlier in the day—a trick of the firelight, I thought. Perhaps the reflection off a moth's wing or some shiny bit of fungus. The trees were festooned with all types of it. No sooner had I noticed them than they were gone. A moment later they returned, deep in the woods and this time farther to my left, hovering several feet above the ground, almond-shaped, glowing like twin beacons.

I grabbed Sergeant Hawk's forearm—the doctor had already crawled into the tent to lie with Chanler—and pointed. By the time he turned to look, the eyes had vanished again.

"What is it, Will?" he whispered.

"Eyes," I whispered back. "Over there."

For an eternity we waited, barely drawing breath, scanning the dark, but they did not reappear.

The eyes returned the following night. Warthrop saw them first, and rose silently to his feet, staring into the bush with a look of almost comical astonishment.

"Did you see that?" he asked us. "My eyes are probably playing tricks on me, but—"

"If it was eyes you saw, Will here saw them too—last night," Hawk said. He slung his rifle around; he kept it on his person at all times, even when he slept.

"Look!" I said, raising my voice in excitement. "There they are again—over there!"

And gone again in the time it took Sergeant Hawk to whip the barrel round. He kept the stock against his shoulder and swung the weapon slowly back and forth.

"A bear?" wondered the doctor.

"A bear, could be," breathed Hawk. "If he's strolling about on his hind legs. Those eyes were near ten feet off the ground, Doctor."

The seconds spun out, turned to minutes. A strange gurgling sound commenced behind us, and the sergeant whirled around to face the tent. Warthrop pushed down the barrel of the rifle and snapped, "It's Chanler," and rushed through the opening. "Will Henry!" he called. "Bring me some light!"

Within, the doctor was leaning over his patient, while the man's mouth opened and closed spasmodically, like a landed fish's, with burbling deep in his throat. Warthrop rolled him onto his side and lightly patted him in the small of the back. The body convulsed, and greenish-yellow bile erupted from his open mouth, soaking the doctor's shirt and trousers and filling the tent with an unearthly noxious odor. I pinched shut my nose and fought the urge to vomit. Warthrop wiped Chanler's mouth with his filthy handkerchief, and then looked up at me.

"Some water, Will Henry."

Chanler moaned, and Warthrop reacted as if he had sat up and said his name. The doctor's face fairly glowed with elation.

"Is he waking up?" I asked.

"John!" Warthrop shouted. "John Chanler! Can you hear me?"

If he could, he gave no reply. He went limp. We waited, but he had left again. Wherever he had been, he had gone back.

We did not see the yellow eyes for several nights thereafter, but their absence did little to relieve our unease. Hawk in particular seemed affected. He often lagged behind even the doctor, who was not walking so much as sliding, shuffling mechanically along the trail slick with the damp, dead leaves of autumn. Hawk would stop and turn around, rifle at the ready, and stare down the boreal tunnel in which we marched, every muscle tense, every sinew and nerve stretched, his head cocked to one side, listening. Listening to what, I cannot say, for neither the doctor nor I heard anything but our own ragged breath and the *scratch-scratch* of our boots along the ground. When we rested, the sergeant roamed the woods in all directions, and his angry muttering carried in the thin air like shards of conversations from splintered memory, bereft of meaning.

He grew sullen and taciturn, obsessively wiping his raw lips, sleeping for only a few minutes at a time and then starting awake with a growl, throwing more wood onto the fire or cursing when there was none left to throw. The fire could never be big enough for him. I think he would have burnt the entire forest if he could have. This man who had spent his entire life in these woods now seemed wholly at odds with them, distrusting and hating them with all the fury of a lover betrayed. What he loved did not love him. Indeed, it seemed bent on killing him.

Distracted though the doctor was by the condition of his patient, our guide's condition did not go unnoticed. The monstrumologist drew me aside and said, "I'm concerned about the sergeant, Will Henry. God help us if my concern is well founded! Here, take this; put it in your pocket." He pressed the revolver into my hand.

He must have noticed the question contained in my stunned expression.

"It can break a man's mind in half," he said. He did not define "it." I do not think he felt it was necessary. "I have seen it."

The sergeant broke the next day. We had stopped to rest, and no sooner had we eased our aching bodies down than he was up again and traipsing through the brush; I could see his hat, shimmering with dew, darting between the glistening ebony bodies of the trees.

"All right, damn you, all right!" he bellowed. "I hear you over there! You might as well come out where I can see you!"

I started to get up, and the doctor waved me back down. He picked up his rifle.

"I'll shoot you. Do you want that?" yelled Hawk toward the vacant trees. "I'll drop you like the miserable dog you are. Do you hear me?"

I jerked reflexively as the gunshot reverberated throughout the forest. Again I began to get up and the doctor pushed me gently down.

At that moment Hawk let loose with a banshee scream and raced away, crashing pell-mell through the undergrowth, firing wildly as he ran, his screams more like the high-pitched yelps of a wounded animal than those of a man.

"Stay with Chanler, Will Henry!"

With that the monstrumologist raced into the bush after him. I scooted closer to John Chanler, clutching the revolver in both hands, unsure what I should be more afraid of—the thing that might be following us or our deranged guide. Presently the snap and pop of the pursuit, the explosions of gunfire, and the hysterical screams faded. The quiet of the primeval forest returned, a preternatural stillness that was, if possible, even more unnerving than the noise.

I felt something stir beside me. I heard something moan. I smelled the breath of something foul. Then I looked down and saw that something looking back at me.

ELEVEN

"In My Rising, I Fell"

The skeletal hand grabbed my arm. The bulbous head lifted a few inches from the carpet of pine needles, the eyes wide open and swimming in a noisome yellow soup, the lips crimson with fresh blood framing the yawning mouth from which issued the foul stench of corruption and decay, and John Chanler spoke to me in a guttural gibberish, words I did not understand. With a viselike grip he pulled with surprising strength upon my arm. I think I screamed the doctor's name; I cannot remember. I saw the thick scum-covered tongue push angrily against the front teeth, and I watched those teeth slip loose of their moorings and fall straight back into the stygian blackness of his throat. He gagged; his body heaved. Without thinking, I dropped the gun into my lap and rammed my fingers into his mouth to dislodge the broken teeth. Instantly his mouth snapped shut and he bit down hard. The pain was explosive. I am sure I screamed then, though I have no clear memory of it. My mind was overcome by the pain and the horrible, vacant look in those yellow eyes, the animal panic replaced by cool, detached alertness, at once bestial and human, when his tongue was kissed by my blood.

I slammed my free hand into his hollow chest and yanked my other hand with all my might, stripping off the skin from my knuckles down to my nails. My hand popped free, coated in gore and yellow sputum. I could hear my blood bubbling in his throat, and then he swallowed, his grotesquely large Adam's apple jerking madly.

He reached for me. I scrambled away, my wounded hand tucked under my arm, the other clutching the doctor's revolver, though even in my panic I could not bring myself to point it at him.

He fell back; his back arched; he lifted his cadaverous face to the indifferent heavens. His bony hands clawed impotently at the air.

"Will Henry?" I heard behind me.

The doctor rushed past and threw himself beside Chanler. He cupped the man's face in his hands, called loudly his name, but the eyes had fluttered closed again, the sound had died on his suppurating lips. I turned and saw Hawk standing a few feet away, his face flushed, bits of twig and moss hanging from his hair.

"Are you all right?" he asked me.

I nodded. "What was it?" I asked.

"Nothing," he said. "Nothing."

He did not sound relieved.

There wasn't anything, it seemed, that could bring Hawk relief. To ward off the dark he built a roaring fire, feeding its rapacious gut with branch after branch until the heat scorched his face and singed the hair of his beard. The fire was against the cold, but he shivered nevertheless. It was against the faceless thing following us, though that thing already gripped him.

He could not turn to his remedy of choice. The doctor had used the last bit of the sergeant's whiskey to wash my wounds—a necessitous act, Warthrop tried to reassure him, to no avail. Hawk exploded into a tantrum worthy of the most infuriated two-year-old, stomping about the littered detritus of rotting leaves and dry crumbs of the earth's ancient bones, boxing the air with red-knuckled fists, spittle flying from his chapped lips.

"You had no right!" he shouted in the doctor's face, waving the empty flask. "This is mine! Mine! A man has a right to what belongs to him!"

"I had no choice, Sergeant," said Warthrop in the tone of a parent to a child. "I will buy you a whole case of it once we reach civilization."

"Civilization? Civilization!" Hawk laughed hysterically. "What is *that*?"

The forest returned his words in a mocking echo: *Civilization . . . What is that?*

"Can you show it to me, Warthrop? Can you point it out for me, because I'm having some trouble seeing it! There is nothing left—nothing, nothing, nothing."

"I can't show it to you," replied the monstrumologist calmly. "I am not the guide."

"What does that mean? What are you saying? Are you suggesting something, Warthrop?"

"I'm merely pointing out a fact, Sergeant."

"That I've gotten us lost in these damnable woods."

"I never said that, Jonathan. I wasn't even suggesting it."

"It isn't my fault. *That* isn't my fault." He gestured wildly at the still form of John Chanler inside the tent. "That was *your* doing, and this is where it's brought us!"

The doctor was nodding thoughtfully; I'd seen the expression a hundred times before, the same look of intense concentration as when he was studying some singular specimen of his bizarre discipline.

"How far is it to Rat Portage?" he asked quietly. "How many more days, Jonathan?"

"Do you think I'm going to fall for that? You must think I'm a complete idiot, Warthrop. I know what you're up to. I know what this is. I am doing the best I can. *None of this is my fault!*"

He kicked a burning stick, launching it into the undergrowth. Flame licked and spat in the dry tinder, and I raced to the spot to stamp it out. Behind me Sergeant Hawk laughed derisively.

"Let it burn, Will! Let the whole thing burn, and then let's see where it hides! Can't hide from me then, can you, you son of a bitch!"

"Sergeant," Warthrop said, "there is nothing hiding—"

"What are you, *dead*? I hear it every hour of the day and smell it every hour of the night. I smell it now—the stench of rot, the smell of putrefying filth! It's all over us; it's soaked into our clothes; we've bathed in it till it's in our *skin*; it comes out when we *breathe*."

He pointed a crooked finger toward the tent.

"You think any of this is new to me? I've been a hundred times in the bush after a lost tenderfoot looking for a trophy, some rich bastard without the good sense God gave him to not go where he don't belong! I know, I know . . ." He gave his mouth a hard swipe with the back of his hand, and his bottom lip split open. He turned his head and spat blood into the fire.

"Couple years ago I brought one out, and he went home without a face. A big grizzly hooked him in the eye sockets, punched out both his eyes with his claws, and *ripped* his whole face off. Just tore it completely off, the stupid blind bastard. I hiked back to Rat Portage with his God damn face in my pocket! How's *that* for your trophy, you rich, stupid, blind, faceless bastard!"

He laughed again, spat again. Glimmering specks of

blood and spittle clung to his whiskers. He threw his wide shoulders back and flexed his powerful chest toward the doctor.

"I'll get you out, Dr. Monstrumologist. One way or the other—even if it means I point the way with my cold, dead finger—I'll get you out."

Later I joined the doctor inside the tent, balancing my elbow on my upraised knee to elevate my hand; the wound throbbed horribly. We could see Hawk's hunkered silhouette through the open flap.

"Are we lost?" I whispered. My uninjured hand slowly caressed my aching belly. Hunger had become a knotted, twisting fist buried deep in my core.

The doctor did not answer at first.

"If we lose him, we are," he said. He meant "lose" in every sense of the word.

His hand reached out in the darkness. I felt his warmth against my cheek. I flinched: I was not used to the doctor touching me.

"No fever," he said quickly, removing his hand. "Good."

Exhausted, I fell into a doze. I awakened to find him curled against me, Chanler against him, and Pellinore Warthrop's hand was wrapped around my arm. He had reached for me in his sleep—me the buoy to keep him afloat, or he the weight to keep me from flying away.

When I opened my eyes, his were looking back at me—not the doctor's, Chanler's—and those eyes were a curious polished yellow, like marbles, splintered by arterial red fissures, as if some great force had squeezed them until they cracked. I lay close enough to see my reflection in the sightless pupils. For an instant I was certain he had passed away during the night. Then I heard his breath rattling, deep in his narrow chest, and I let out my own breath in relief. What a terrible thing it would have been, to have traveled so far and endured so much, only to have him die so close to deliverance! Remembering the last time our eyes had met, I scooted backward to place some distance between us, and when I did, the eyes did not follow but remained fixed upon the spot I had occupied. The cadaverous mouth moved; no sound emerged. Perhaps he was beyond breath for words.

I rolled out of the tent and stood blinking stupidly, for my mind rebelled against the sight. The camp was deserted. The smoke of the expired campfire lingered lazily in the cold morning air. That was the only movement I saw. Gone were the doctor and Hawk, and gone were their rifles.

Softly I called their names. My voice sounded small and muffled, like the cry of a wounded forest animal, and so I called out in a loud voice, "Dr. Warthrop! Sergeant Hawk! Hello! Hello!" My calls seemed to travel no farther than a foot from my mouth, slapped down by the malicious hand of the brooding trees, the syllables smashed to bits by the oppressive atmosphere. I shut my mouth, heart rocketing in my chest, abashed, thinking, *I'm sorry, I'm sorry*, for I had offended something; my cries were an affront to the malignant animus of the wilderness.

I heard someone speak directly behind me. I turned. Guttural and gurgling with phlegm, Chanler's voice floated in the frigid air, as ephemeral as the smoke rising from the smoldering brands. Not words belonging to any human tongue, nor mindless blather, more like the gibbering of a toddler mimicking speech, struggling to make concrete the abstract, the thoughts we think before we have words to think them.

I poked my head into the tent opening. The man had not moved. He lay curled upon his side, hands drawn to his chest, lips shining with spittle, the thick, yellowish tongue wrestling with words he knew but could not enunciate.

"*Gudsnuth nesht! Gebgung grojpech chrishunct. Cankah!*"

I flopped onto the ground with my back to the tent, fighting the mindless terror that now threatened to overwhelm me. Where had they gone? And why had they left without telling me? Surely the doctor at least would have awakened me before he left.

Unless he couldn't. Unless something had snatched him in the night, seized both him and Hawk. Unless . . . I recalled the hysterical laughter of our distressed guide, the red flush of his unshaven cheek, the blood flying from his lips. . . . What if his mind had finally given way and he had done something to the doctor, and was now disposing of his body, in this gray land that never gives up its secrets?

I patted my pockets, unable to remember if I had returned the doctor's revolver. Evidently I had.

What should I do? Should I go looking for my missing companions? What if they were not missing at all but had decided to investigate something one had seen or heard—or had merely gone out to hunt for game, to return at any moment? And what would the doctor say if and when I ever stumbled back into camp—what measure of wrath would come down upon my foolish head for wandering off alone into the bush, abandoning the sole reason we had come here? So I wondered, trying to arrange the deck chairs of my pitching and yawing faculties, buffeted by the maddening nonsense inside the tent and the panic bubbling up inside me.

He could be hurt, I thought. *Lying out there, unable to call for help. I might be able to save him, but who will save me?*

Any action at all is better than paralyzed dread, so I forced myself up with a *Snap to, Will Henry!* and quickly surveyed the ground, looking for footprints or any other sign that might shed light on what had happened. I detected no scuff marks or wounded soil, nothing to indicate a struggle. I did not know whether to be relieved or further perturbed. While I was thus employed, I heard something coming toward me, the crunch and snap of undergrowth announcing its approach. I turned on my heel and raced back to camp, to what real purpose I cannot say, for I was just as vulnerable there as here, with no means of defending myself, except the steaming broken branch I plucked from the ashes of the fire and swung before me as I backed toward the tent.

"Watch out!" I cried. "I have a weapon!"

"Will Henry, what the devil are you doing?"

He stepped into the clearing, the rifle resting in the crook of his arm, his clothes speckled with moisture, his dark eyes ringed in black and sunk deep in his pale whiskered face. I dropped my "weapon" and ran to him, overcome with relief. My first instinct was to throw my arms around his waist in thanksgiving, but something in his expression stopped me. With the acute intuition possessed by all children, I knew what that expression meant.

"Where's Sergeant Hawk?" I asked.

"That is indeed the pertinent question, Will Henry, but what is that sound?"

"It's Dr. Chanler, sir. He—"

He brushed me aside and hurried into the tent. I heard Warthrop call his friend's name, only to be answered by the same incoherent babble. The doctor came out again after a few minutes, dug into his duster pocket, said "Here," and dropped the revolver into my hands.

"Where is Sergeant Hawk?" I asked again.

"I was in a deep sleep," the doctor began, "when something woke me around dawn. I don't know what it was, but when I stepped outside, the sergeant was gone. I've been bumping about in those blasted woods for more than an hour and can find neither hide nor hair of the fool. Where he went and *why* he went, without a word to anyone, I do not know." He tapped with the tip of his boot the stick I had dropped. "What were you going to do with this, Will Henry?"

"Hit you with it, sir."

"Hit me?"

"I didn't have the gun."

"So if you'd had the gun, you would have shot me?"

"Yes, sir. No, sir! I would never shoot you, sir. Not on purpose anyway."

"Perhaps you should give it back to me. Your answer—or *answers*—have not served to put me entirely at ease, Will Henry."

He looked past me, into the abysmal shadows ringing the little clearing.

"A troubling development, given the apparent flimsiness of the sergeant's mental condition," he mused dispassionately, as if we were sitting comfortably in his study discussing the latest Jules Verne novel. "No sign of a struggle, no cry in the night to wake either of us, no note or explanation given."

He looked down at me. "How long has John been awake?"

"I don't know. He was staring . . . looking at me when I woke up, and the talking—or whatever it is—began a few minutes ago."

"I don't think he was looking at you, Will Henry—or at

anything else. He is still . . . not wholly with us."

He fell silent for a moment, deep in thought, and then nodded his head curtly.

"We shall cling to hope. Pointless to break camp on our own and wander about the woods looking for a way out. Equally fruitless to search for him. Only by dumb luck would we find him, and we haven't had too much of that—dumb or any other kind! The rest will also do John some good—us, too, Will Henry. We will wait."

It was a decision that feigned as action, but the alternatives were unthinkable to us both. I scavenged about the immediate vicinity for more kindling and anything the miserly forest might offer up by way of victuals, while the doctor crouched in the tent with Chanler, trying to coax from him something a bit more intelligible than *gebgung grojpech* and *cankah!*

Dr. Warthrop gave up after an hour and joined me by the resurrected fire, where we spoke little and kept our eyes forward and our hands on our weapons, starting at every crack of a twig or stir of a dry leaf, while low-hanging clouds scudded across the sky, diluting the light to an exhausted gray, the cover pushed along by a high wind that shunned the sullen earth.

The air about us was motionless, an acrid shroud of rotting vegetation laced with the faintest tincture of death, the palpable tartness of decay. *The stench of rot, the smell of putrefying filth!* Hawk had called it. It suffused the campsite. I smelled it rising from my clothes. We have gone far in our public places to push death aside, to consign it to a dusty corner, but in the wilderness it is ever present. It is the lover who makes life. The sensuous, entwined limbs of predator and prey, the orgasmic death cry, the final spasmodic rush of blood, and even the soundless insemination of the earth by the fallen tree and crumbling leaf; these are the caresses of life's beloved, the indispensable other.

Dusk crept over the land, and still there was no sign of the missing sergeant. Warthrop wore a path between the tent and the fire, fetching water and bits of forage for John Chanler. The water he managed to get into him, but the food Chanler refused, letting the morsels fall from his mouth with a gagging cry of revulsion. The eyes remained open, fixed, incognizant.

My uneasiness grew as the light faded. The likelihood of there being an innocent explanation for the sergeant's absence diminished with each passing hour. If he had gone ahead to scout the trail or had ventured into the bush for some much-needed animal protein, he would have returned by now. The viable explanations remaining were not pleasant to contemplate—especially for a twelve-year-old boy who up to that voyage had not journeyed more than twenty miles from his front doorstep. Forgetting for a moment with whom he kept company, that boy turned to the sole source of comfort available to him. Unfortunately for him, that happened to be Dr. Pellinore Warthrop.

"What do you think has happened to him?" I asked.

"How am I to answer that, Will Henry?" he asked in turn, stuffing a piece of hickory bark into his mouth. Chewing it helped tamp down the gnawing aches in our bellies. "We may speculate until the sun comes up, and that's all it would be. In the morning . . ." He did not finish the thought. He fondled the polished stock of the rifle lying across his lap, an effort to ease another gnawing ache. "I suspect he heard—or *thought* he heard—something in the bush and like a fool took off after it. Perhaps he has decided 'to hell' with us and now is seated comfortably by his hearth in Rat Portage. Though I doubt it."

"Why?"

"He left his rucksack. And his canteen. He intended to return."

Unless he did not leave of his own accord. That possibility the doctor did not give voice to. He chewed thoughtfully upon the wood; the firelight flickered in his eyes.

"We are lost," he said matter-of-factly. "That is the only explanation. You observed his reaction to the suggestion yesterday. So at first light he struck out to pick up the trail again. Darkness caught him in the bush, and he's waiting for daylight to come back for us."

"What if he doesn't?"

The doctor frowned. "Why wouldn't he?"

"He's afraid." I remembered the wild look in his eyes, the spittle flying from his chapped and swollen lips. I did not offer the other reason—that he wouldn't return because he *couldn't*. I thought of Pierre Larose, impaled upon a tree.

"All the more reason to find his way back," argued the doctor. Then, as if he had read my thoughts, he said, "I wouldn't choose solitude in these circumstances, and I am one who chooses it in nearly *every* circumstance!" His jaw worked the shavings incessantly; his eyes shone. "Secrets," he murmured.

"Secrets, sir?"

"The reason I became a monstrumologist, Will Henry." He lowered his voice, now whispery warm, as intimate as a lover's. "She cloaks herself in mystery. She hides her true face. I would unmask her. I would strip her bare. I would see her as she is."

He lifted his face toward the veiled heavens. He considered the treetops genuflecting to the high wind. "'The wind bloweth where it listeth, and thou hearest the sound thereof, but canst not tell whence it cometh.' . . . She is fickle and jealous and completely indifferent—and therefore completely irresistible. What mortal woman can approach her? What earthly maiden possesses her eternal youth or can inspire such rapture—and despair? There is something profoundly terrifying about her, Will Henry, and utterly seductive. In my lust to master her, I became her slave. In my rising, I fell. I fell . . . very far."

Though I sat three feet from the fire, I shivered. I wondered if, like Sergeant Hawk, the doctor was coming down with a case of "bush fever." If so—if I lost him, too—what would become of me?

He looked at me, shook his head, and laughed softly. "I warned you. I wanted to be a poet."

"Was that a poem?"

"No, of course not."

"It didn't sound like any poem I've ever read."

"You are a clever boy, Will Henry. That could be both a compliment *and* an insult."

He pulled the gnarled bit of wood from his mouth and tossed it into the fire.

"Terrible! Like chewing on a chair leg. But it's what we have. And we must learn to be satisfied with what we have, no matter how bland or bitter the taste."

We were quiet for a moment. The fire cracked and popped. The wind whistled in the bowed heads of the spruce and pine. Behind us John Chanler moaned in gentle harmony.

"Did he feel the same as you, Doctor?" I asked. "About . . . her?"

"John has more the soul of a boxer than a poet. He never quite grew up, in my opinion. Monstrumology is a sport to him, like hunting fox or playing cricket."

"He thought it was *fun?*" The idea that anyone could find the doctor's business enjoyable was bizarre.

"Oh, he thought it was great fun."

"What *part?*"

"Usually the part that brought him closest to the edge of ruin." He laughed morbidly. "Got a little too close to that edge this time."

"Mr. Larose went right over it," I said. I could not chase the image of his skinless corpse from my mind.

"An interesting extension of the metaphor, Will Henry. Perhaps this affair has more to do with monstrumology than we first assumed."

I was shocked. "You mean you've changed your mind? You think it could be . . ."

"Real? Oh, no. Not in the sense that you mean. Perhaps there is an organism native to this environment—something altogether natural—that gave rise to the myth. A bipedal predator with some of the Wendigo's traits—cannibalistic, humanoid, able to scale these trees and traverse vast distances quickly. John was not the first monstrumologist to come here searching for the inspiration of the legend. I even found some references to it in my father's papers—probably how the sergeant's mother knew the name."

"So there . . . there could be *something*. . . ."

"Oh, Will Henry, you've been with me long enough to know there is always *something*."

TWELVE

"The One Useful Thing You Could Do"

He had spoken of it as one speaks of a lover. The eternally young, fertile bride; the ancient, barren spinster; the siren; the sibyl—she was all these things, all at once, his beloved, the one for whom he denied himself the companionship of mere mortal company, against whom even the breathtaking Muriel Chanler paled. His beloved called that night, but she did not call to him.

Her voice—the voice of the untamed wilderness, the secret voice that rides the high wind, the voice of abundant desolation and exhilarating despair, the voice the *Iyiniwok* had named *Outiko*—called that night, and John Chanler answered.

I felt his presence before I saw him. The hairs on the back of my neck stood up. I had the distinctly uncomfortable feeling of being watched. I looked over my shoulder. My breath caught in my throat. I touched the doctor's arm, and he followed my gaze, both of us frozen for an instant in utter amazement at the sight.

John Chanler was standing at the tent's mouth, his spindly bare legs spread wide, his scrawny arms hanging loosely by his sides, the yellow eyes that dominated his skeletal face seeming to burn with their own inner fire, and in those eyes there was the shock of recognition—not in him, but in me, for I had seen a pair just like them, floating in the forest gloom.

His mouth hung open, the lips swollen and shining with blood, ripped open by his incessantly gnashing teeth. The front of his undershirt was wet with it. It hung in tear-shaped droplets from his beard.

Warthrop jumped to his feet with a startled cry. His rifle fell, forgotten, to the ground. He took a small, hesitant step toward his friend.

"John?"

Chanler did not respond. He did not move. He seemed to be regarding something high in the trees. His head, so disproportionately large next to his emaciated frame, was cocked to one side, as if he were listening for something— or *to* something. From his throat issued a noisome gurgling, like some foul spring bubbling up from the rancid depths.

Then this poor creature, who had for days barely clung to life, who was so weak my master had been forced to carry him like a newborn babe, who had eaten nothing for two weeks, suddenly exploded into flight, hurling himself past us with astonishing speed, a grotesquely hilarious whir of pumping arms and churning legs, leaping three feet over the fire and crashing into the bush with a bestial squeal. The doctor raced after him, calling frantically over his shoulder, "Will *Henry!*" I snatched up the rifle and followed a few paces behind.

Warthrop caught his maddened quarry by the scruff of the neck, his grip instantly broken by Chanler's arm as he twisted around. The monstrumologist wrapped his arms around the narrow waist and pulled him into his chest. Chanler responded by whipping his head from side to side, his broken teeth uselessly snapping, his legs scissoring back and forth, seeking a foothold in the slick cover of rotting leaves. He seized Warthrop's forearm and pulled it to his mouth.

The doctor cried out and stumbled backward. Chanler took off again, and Warthrop launched himself at his knees. The two men tumbled to the ground, the monstrumologist bringing his hands up to ward off the furious blows of his friend, whose goal, it now appeared, was to gouge out my master's eyes. His long, crooked fingers clawed at Warthrop's face. I rushed to the doctor's side and brought the heavy butt of the rifle over Chanler's exposed scalp.

"No, Will Henry!" Warthrop cried. He managed to grab hold of Chanler's wrists and, pushing with his legs, gained the advantage over his undersized opponent. Warthrop forced Chanler onto his back and threw his body over his friend's writhing form.

"It's me, John," the monstrumologist gasped. "Pellinore. It's me. Pellinore. Pellinore!"

"*No!*" Chanler groaned back. His thick tongue struggled to fashion the words. "Must go. . . . Must . . . *answer.*"

The afflicted man was staring toward the sky, where the treetops brushed the underbellies of the stately advancing clouds. The high wind sung.

And John Chanler in answer wept. His tears were yellow, streaked with red. He curled into a miserable ball and keened, his gnarled fingers scratching fretfully in the undergrowth.

The doctor sat back upon his heels and lifted his smudged face toward mine. "Well, he's regained some of his strength, at least."

He went rag-doll-limp in the doctor's arms, with not so much as a groan of protest while my master carried him back to the tent. Warthrop eased him down, covered him with the blanket, and washed his face with a handkerchief dampened with drinking water. Given the extremity of Chanler's condition, it was a pathetic gesture, bringing no succor to his suffering, but it was not for the patient. Washing the detritus from his friend's face, the last vestige, it seemed, of the wasted man's humanity, brought some small measure of comfort to the monstrumologist.

I held the lamp while he gently rubbed the edge of the cloth around the suppurating lips, then paused to examine the half-opened mouth. He pressed the bloodstained handkerchief into my free hand and slipped his fingers inside Chanler's mouth. I stiffened, expecting the jaws to snap shut as they had when I'd placed my fingers inside. Warthrop pulled a large wad of half-masticated greenery past the drooling lips—wolf's claw that Chanler must have stuffed into his mouth as he lay upon the forest floor. The little tent filled with its loamy aroma and the smell of Chanler's putrid saliva. The monstrumologist muttered the word "Mossmouth," and I remembered the letter from Pierre Larose. *The Mossmouth not going to let him go.*

"The fire, Will Henry," the doctor said wearily. "We mustn't let it go out."

I set down the lamp and hurried outside, relieved to make my escape from that claustrophobic space. The hungry embers chomped at the fresh wood; the flames reached with supplicating hands toward the sky. All was hunger, I thought. All was longing. After a moment the doctor dropped beside me and wrapped his arms around his upraised knees.

"Is he—?"

Warthrop nodded. "Asleep—or unconscious. He has to be exhausted. I don't think he'll get up again."

"But why did he—"

"Delirium, Will Henry. Obviously."

He absently picked the needles of wolf's claw that had

adhered to his palm and flicked them into the fire, where they sparked for an instant and died. As bright as stars, then gone.

"We'll wait an hour more after sunrise," he said. "Then we'll press on. If we are doomed to perish here, I would rather die looking for the way home than sit here like rabbits paralyzed with fear."

"Yes, sir."

Over the comforting crackle of our fire, the wind whistled, a melancholy sigh, a song of lamentation.

The doctor lifted his face and said, "There is a storm coming."

It arrived just before dawn. The wind dove down, driving ahead of it the first heavy snowfall of the season. By eight o'clock, when we broke camp, two inches of fresh powder lay upon the ground. It continued throughout that day, and we shunned the clearings, for our protection lay under the arms of the forest. In the open spaces the snow furiously swirled into blinding white maelstroms in which we were no more substantial than ghosts. By two o'clock more than a foot had fallen, and there was no sign of the snow abating. We stumbled over buried root and bumped into each other in the murk, trudging through a trackless maze. Too cold and too numb to speak, we lowered our heads against the freezing wind, and stopped only to relieve ourselves and fill our canteens with snow. I now carried both rucksacks and Hawk's rifle. Our provision bag had long ago been discarded.

My mind darkened with the day. By four, the storm had all but murdered the light, but the doctor pushed on, saying, "A little farther, a little farther."

With light nearly gone, all at once we happened upon some half-obscured tracks cutting across our path—human footprints—and immediately my fatigue melted away, replaced by unutterable joy. Fresh prints! The world had not swallowed up all humanity; here was proof we were not alone in the vastness. They snaked across our path, going from right to left, two pairs, one noticeably smaller than the other, small enough to be the footprints of a child. The significance of this hit the doctor first.

"Oh, no, Will Henry. No!"

He fell against a tree. Ice had formed in his whiskers; snow frosted his eyebrows. Other than his rosy cheeks and bright red nose, his face was horribly drawn and pale, the wrinkles in his forehead cavernously deep.

"They're ours," he murmured. "We have been walking in circles, Will Henry."

He slowly slid to the ground, cradling his charge in his lap. I stood next to him, buried to my ankles in snow, and so great was the loss in his eyes that I turned away. Around us the forest had been blasted white, and the snow continued to fall, flakes the size of quarters, a heartbreakingly beautiful landscape. Suddenly my eyes welled with tears—not tears of sorrow or despair but tears of hatred, of rage, of a loathing that rose from the very depths of my soul. The doctor had been wrong. His true love was not indifferent. She rejoiced in the brutality of her nature. She savored our slow, torturous death. There was no mercy, no justice, not even a purpose. She was killing us simply because she could.

"It's all right, sir," I said through my chattering teeth. "It's all right. We'll set up camp here. I'll make the fire now, sir."

He gave no reply. I might as well have tried to console the tree. I found my own consolation, however, in the task itself, the mindlessness of gathering the kindling for the fire (a chore that proved more challenging than usual in the three-foot drifts), clearing a spot well away from any tree, piling up the damp wood. The wind worked against me, the wind and the wet wood, for barely had I lit the match when it was a smoldering, impotent wick. Warthrop appeared beside me, jerking his head toward Chanler. "I'll do it; watch him."

"I can do it, sir," I said stubbornly. "I know how."

"Do as I say!" He grabbed at the box, and it flipped out of his fingers as I pulled back. The matchsticks cascaded onto the snow, and the monstrumologist cursed loudly, his voice strangely muffled, stamped down by the wind.

"Now see what you've done!" he cried. "Go! Fetch the tinderbox from the sergeant's rucksack. Snap to, Will Henry!"

I found no tinderbox in Hawk's gear. I turned over the contents of the doctor's rucksack next. Nothing. My heart sped up. What had happened to it? When was the last time

I'd seen it? Was it the night the sergeant disappeared? Had Hawk taken the tinderbox with him, and if so, why?

I felt someone come up behind me. Crouching in the snow, I craned my neck around. The doctor had stopped a few feet away. I could barely see him in the glimmering twilight.

"Well, Will Henry?"

"I can't find it, sir."

"It must be there."

"I thought so too, sir, but it isn't. You can look for yourself if you like."

"I would not." I could not see his face. I could not read his tone. Somehow that made it worse.

"If we had a knife," I began, "we could whittle a stick and—"

"If we had a knife, I would cut your throat with it."

"It isn't my fault, sir. The wind . . ."

"I left it to you. I thought such a simple thing as lighting a campfire would not be beyond even your limited capacity."

"You dropped the matches," I pointed out, trying to keep my voice level.

"And you lost our tinderbox!" he roared.

"I didn't lose it!"

"Then it hopped out of the rucksack and took off into the woods on its own little legs!"

"You're the one who decided to break camp in this!" I hollered back. "We should have stayed where we were!

Now we're lost and we're going to freeze to death."

He was upon me in two strides. His hand went back. I tensed myself to receive the blow. I did not flee. I did not cower. I froze, and waited for him to hit me.

The hand dropped to his side.

"You disgust me," he said. He turned on his heel and strode to the pitiful pile of sticks. He sent them flying with a violent kick.

"You *disgust* me!" he repeated. "Only the intelligent can afford to be so judgmental. Who are *you* to question my decisions? You thickheaded sycophantic piece of snot. I've dissected worms with larger brains than yours! You've been nothing but a burden to me, an albatross around my neck. . . . God damn your parents for dying and foisting your despicable carcass upon me. 'It's all right, sir! I'll make the fire now, sir.' You make me sick. Everything about you is repulsive, you nauseating, worthless mealymouthed half-wit!"

Now he was but a lighter shadow among darker ones, a maddened wraith.

"The only use left for you . . . the one useful thing you could do is *die*. We could live a week off your miserable hide, couldn't we, John? You would like that, wouldn't you, Chanler? Tastier than moss. It's what you really crave, isn't it? The *Outiko* has called you. The *Outiko* has you now. Isn't that so? Will Henry, be a dear and give him another taste!"

He fell down. One moment he was standing, railing as

loudly as the wind that whipped his long, unkempt hair. The next he was on his knees in the snow. His voice fell with him.

"Snap to now, Will Henry. Snap to."

I did—with the tent. I drove the stakes, tied off the lines, flung the weathered canvas over the poles. Then I dragged Chanler inside while the monstrumologist wallowed in his own malaise, in the spot where he'd collapsed. It was slow work in the dark—and absolute was that dark—slow work with senseless hands and freezing feet. Chanler was so still that I placed my hand beneath his nose to make sure he breathed. I remained inside the tent with him for some time, shivering uncontrollably, huddled against his filthy and stinking blanket, breathing shallowly the foul atmosphere of a dying man. I must have dozed off, for the next thing I knew Warthrop was sitting beside me. I kept my eyes closed, pretending to sleep. I was not afraid of him. I was too hungry, too cold, too empty to feel anything. Terror had given way to a soul-numbing lassitude. I felt nothing—nothing at all.

Gently he pulled my hands into his. His warm lips touched my knuckles. He blew onto my dead flesh. He vigorously rubbed my naked hand between his. Feeling began to return, and with it a measure of pain, the proof of life. He crossed my hands over my chest and pushed his body against mine, wrapping his long arms around me. I felt the delicious warmth of his breath against my neck.

He's just using you, I told myself. *He's just using you to keep from freezing.*

My parents had died in a fire. They had burned alive. Now I would die of cold. They by fire, I by ice. In the arms of the man who was responsible for both. A man to whom I was nothing but a burden.

You are young, he had told me. *You have yet to hear it call your name.*

I think now he was wrong. I think it had already called my name.

And now it lay with its arms enfolding me.

THIRTEEN

"The Real Danger"

We awoke to a world of dazzling white. The clouds that had lingered for untold days were torn away by the relentless wind, and dawn arrived on the wings of a sapphire sky. Our few fitful hours of rest had done little to relieve our exhaustion; we stumbled from the tent and surveyed this new world with dead expressions, like scarecrows contemplating the immense autumnal firmament.

Warthrop pointed off to his left. "Do you know what that is, Will Henry?" he asked in a raw voice.

I squinted along the line of his finger. "What?"

"Unless I am very much mistaken, that is what men call the sun. Which rises in the east, Will Henry, which means *that* way is west, *that* north, and *that* south!"

He clapped his hands. The sound was very loud in

the sanctuary stillness of the forest.

"Here we go! It's much colder, but much brighter, isn't it? We'll make good time now, and no going in circles this day! Snap to and let's pack up, Will Henry." He noticed my staring at him. "What is it? What's the matter? Don't you see? We're going to make it!"

"We're still lost," I pointed out.

"No, we are not," he insisted. "We've merely *misplaced* ourselves!" He forced himself to laugh—a ludicrous mimic of a laugh. "I don't see you smiling. It is so rare that I attempt witticism, Will Henry—smiling might encourage it."

"I don't want to encourage it," I replied. I kneeled to pull a stake from the ground.

"I see. You're still smarting from last night. You know I don't really mean those things I said. I have always attested to your usefulness, Will Henry. You have ever been indispensable to me."

"It's what I live for, sir."

"Now you are being facetious."

I shook my head. I was sincere.

It was not the carefree stroll the monstrumologist had envisioned. The snow was piled five feet deep in places, drifts as high as my head, into which I would drop to my waist, and I'd be forced to wait helplessly for the doctor to set down Chanler and pull me out. We stopped at midday, shoveling handfuls of snow into our parched mouths, and I endured twenty minutes of Warthrop whining on about snowshoes, wondering if, without doing anything about it, we might be able to fashion some from sticks. The sunlight hardly alleviated the cold; the deep snow made every step more a matter of willpower than strength. We were headed in the right direction, but could still have been scores of miles from civilization. I stopped caring. By midafternoon an enormous lethargy overwhelmed me. All I wanted to do was curl up and go to sleep. I even stopped feeling cold. Indeed, I began to sweat beneath my layers.

I was considering pulling off my heavy wool overcoat when Warthrop called to me, "Look over there, Will Henry."

Several black specks floated high over the treetops, rotating majestically on the updrafts. *Buteos*, Sergeant Hawk had called them.

"Snap to now!" said the doctor, making straight for them. "Where there are scavengers, there is carrion, Will Henry, or soon-to-be carrion! We may dine like kings tonight if we hurry!"

And hurry we did, pushing our way through the stubborn snow, our protesting muscles fighting against the creepers and scrub that lay buried beneath the snowpack. We were out of breath and near the end of all endurance when we reached the spot over which the scavengers patrolled—a towering white pine, upon whose upper branches several of their fellows perched, as serene as church deacons clustered about their afternoon repast.

Their meal hung tangled in the uppermost branches. His arms were outstretched and his legs together, like Christ crucified, and his head rested on one shoulder, the eyeless sockets looking toward the indiscernible horizon. He looked very small from our vantage point forty feet below, no larger than I. He looked like a child who had in fun climbed a tree and gotten stuck near the top, able to climb no higher and too fearful to scamper down.

I could see the shiny brass buttons of his open coat, his shredded shirt fluttering in the high wind, and the ropy snarl of his frozen intestines, glittering in the sunlight. While I watched, a buzzard turned its tonsured head toward the man's face, cocking it in that curiously obscene gesture of scavengers, and tore the tongue from his open mouth.

We had found our lost guide.

"Can you do it, Will Henry?" the doctor asked.

"I think so, sir."

"No. Not 'think so.' *Can you do it?*"

I nodded, feigning confidence. "Yes, sir."

"Good boy."

I slung the coil of rope over my shoulder and began the arduous climb. The skin of the pine was slick, the branches thick toward the bottom but tapering as I rose.

"Get to one side, Will Henry, not below him. He's bound to be frozen stiff, so it won't be easy. . . . Careful there! Watch what you're doing, boy. That branch is cracked—I can see it from here! Carefully, Will Henry, carefully!"

The wind tugged at my shoulders; it sliced at my cheeks; it sang in my ears. I kept my eyes on my quarry; I did not look down. I paused to rest with my head level with the bottom of his boots, arms aching, with feet too numb to feel the slender branch beneath them.

"Higher, Will Henry," the monstrumologist called up. "And to the *side*. He'll come down right on top of you from there!"

I nodded, though I doubted he could see my assent. Three feet more, and now I was level with the torso. His entire chest cavity had been opened up. Ice crystals glittered like jewels festooning his ribs, lining the walls of his ripped-open stomach; his lungs looked like two enormous multi-faceted diamonds; his frozen viscera shone as brightly as wet marble. It was terrible. And it was beautiful.

I climbed higher. With his outstretched arm brushing the top of my head, I looked up into the face of Jonathan Hawk—or what was left of it. How much does our expression rely upon our eyes! Without them, can one tell fear from wonder, joy from sorrow? His nose had been torn off—like his tongue, digesting in the bellies of the birds who had returned to the cloudless sky, with not so much as a protesting squawk at my intrusion. They were patient; the meat wasn't going anywhere, or if it did, there would be more meat somewhere else. There was always meat.

"No, no, no!" The doctor's voice floated up to me, puny

and feeble in the thin air, competing with the singing wind. "Not around his waist, Will Henry! Throw the loop around his neck!"

With one hand clinging to a branch that bowed dangerously low, I reached up with the rope and dropped the hastily fashioned noose over Sergeant Hawk's head.

The buteo had not gotten all of his tongue. A sliver the size of my little finger hung over the lower lip, still attached at the root. This the shredded tongue that had sung the words "*J'ai fait une mâtresse y a pas longtemps.*" These the frozen lungs that had given the words breath. This the icy heart that had given them meaning.

"Will Henry, what the devil are you doing up there? Come down at once. Snap to, Will Henry. Snap *to.*"

I dropped the rope down to him. Arduously slow was my descent to earth. The sergeant's was much faster—a hard yank on the rope, and the body dropped, as fixed as a statue, to land faceup with a muffled *whump!* in the snow. The doctor went to his knees beside the fallen man. He wanted to examine the body before the light failed. He may have been looking for similarities between Hawk's injuries and those of Pierre Larose. I cannot say for certain, for he did not communicate his intent to me. He may have simply been curious in the professional sense. I'd seen enough, so I did not watch. High in the tree, I had also seen something else, something that was almost as exhilarating to me as a corpse was to a monstrumologist.

I had turned my head to follow Hawk's "gaze" and had seen it, painted a glimmering gold by the dying sun—a broad lake in the distance and, upon its far shore, *Wauzhushk Onigum*, the town of Rat Portage.

He had kept his promise, high in the tree that the Haudenosaunee tribe called the Tree of Great Peace. He had shown us the way home.

It was our last night in the wilderness and it was our worst night in the wilderness. The temperature plunged with the sun; it could not have been much higher than zero, and we had no means to make a fire. We piled snow around the tent to help insulate it before crawling inside, though the doctor left me for a while alone with Chanler, whose condition deteriorated with each passing hour. His face had turned the color of ash, and the only signs of life were the tiny explosions of breath condensing in the frigid air. I feared all our hardships had been for naught. I feared John Chanler would not live out the night.

Warthrop had told me to stay with him. That order I disobeyed. The doctor was gone too long. After all, *something* had killed Pierre Larose and Jonathan Hawk.

I found him standing ankle-deep in the snow, contemplating the staggering profusion of stars, their gift a silvery infusion of light, transforming the forest into a glittering jewel.

"Yes," he said softly. "What is it?"

"I didn't know what happened to you, sir."

"Hmm? Nothing happened to me, Will Henry."

Sergeant Hawk lay where he had landed, with arms out-stretched, as if he had frozen while making a snow angel.

"Except that somewhere along the trail I misplaced my good sense," the doctor continued. "Why didn't I think to climb a tree to have a look around?"

"Is that what you think happened?"

"Well, he didn't fly up there, I'm nearly certain of that."

"But why didn't he come down again?"

He shook his head. He pointed at the sky. "See there? Orion, the hunter. Always has been my favorite. . . . Something prevented him, obviously. Perhaps some predator. He ran off without his rifle, the fool. Or perhaps he was afraid of heights, and froze in terror. 'Froze.' Well. That's a poor choice of words."

"But what could have torn him open like that?"

"Postmortem injuries, Will Henry. From the buzzards."

I took a moment to think—always the best course when talking with Pellinore Warthrop. He made you pay when you didn't.

"But he wasn't holding on to anything. He was facing *out*, and his arms were out, like this, like he had been . . . hung there."

"What are you suggesting, Will Henry?"

"I'm not, sir. I was asking. . . ."

"Forgive me. It is quite cold, and sound carries differently in the cold, but I did not hear you ask anything."

"It's nothing, sir."

"I suppose you meant to observe that his position does not fit the premise that he climbed the tree, for whatever purpose. I would argue the observation is irrelevant, since the *only* way he could have gotten up there is to have climbed. I was right all along. He left our camp looking for the way out—and found it. Just in time for us—and too late for him.

"The more important question is what killed him. The damage from the scavengers makes that question a bit difficult to answer, so for now my guess would be exposure. Sergeant Hawk froze to death."

I bit my lip. No living man would have turned around like that. None but a madman would have hung himself in such a manner forty feet from the ground. And that observation seemed entirely relevant to me.

That was the night it came for us, for we had offended it. We had taken what it had claimed for itself.

It came for us, the one who came before words, the Nameless One given countless names.

The monstrumologist was the first to hear it. He nudged me awake, and pressed a hand over my mouth. "There is something outside," he whispered, his lips brushing my ear.

He released me and slid toward the opening of the tent. I saw him crouching a foot away, and I saw the shape of the rifle in his hand. I heard nothing at first, only the far-winding lamentation of the wind high in the trees. Then I heard it, the distinct sound of something large crunching through the frosted snowpack.

It could be a bear, I thought. *Or even a moose.* It sounded much too large to be a man. I leaned forward, trying to locate the sound's origin. It seemed close at first, perhaps no farther than a few feet in front of us, and then I thought, *No, it is way off in the trees behind us.*

The monstrumologist motioned for me to come closer. "It appears our yellowed-eyed friend has returned, Will Henry," he whispered. "Stay here with John."

"You're going out there?" I was appalled.

He was gone before the question was done. I scooted into the spot he'd vacated and watched him ease carefully toward the trees, the outline of his form exquisitely distinct against the pristine snowbound backdrop. Now the only sound was the doctor's boots, breaking through the thin upper crust of the snow. That and the excited respirations of John Chanler behind me, like a man after a long uphill trek. I squinted into the silvery light, scanning the woods for the yellow eyes. So complete was my concentration, so utterly focused was I upon the task that I thought nothing when Chanler began to mutter in his delirium the same nonsense he'd been droning off and on for days. "*Gudsnuth nesht! Gebgung grojpech!*" My heart quickened, for the doctor had drifted completely out of sight, leaving me with only the sound of Chanler's gurgling drivel for company. If he would only be quiet, then perhaps I could at least *hear* the doctor! I glanced behind me.

He was sitting up, the top half of the old blanket pooled in his lap. His gray flesh, slick with sweat, shone in the semi-darkness. The eyes were open—grotesquely oversize in his emaciated face, and bright yellow, the pupils as small as pinpricks—from which dribbled ocherous tears the consistency of curd.

My first instinct, rooted in our recent past—the outcome the last time our eyes had met—was to run, to put as much distance between us as possible, certainly a response the doctor would not have approved of, given the circumstances. What I might have been running *toward* might have been far worse than what I ran *from*.

He was panting; I could see the tip of his gray tongue. Spittle ran over the enflamed lower lip and dripped into the sparse whiskers on his chin. By a trick of the insubstantial light, his teeth seemed exceptionally large.

Steady, steady, steady, I told myself. *He isn't a monster. He's a man. He's the doctor's friend.*

I gave him what I hoped was a reassuring smile.

His reaction was instantaneous. With an explosive leap—too fast for the eye to follow—he rocketed into me, his bony shoulder slamming into my chin with the force of a battering ram. I fell back, black stars blooming before my eyes. A hand clamped over my nose and mouth. The other hand ripped my shirtfront, shredding the material with its splintered nails, slicing open the tender skin beneath. The hot breath reeking of decay first, then the scaly, pustulant lips pressing against the flesh directly over my throbbing heart.

Then the teeth.

It is called Atcen . . . Djenu . . . Outiko . . . Vindiko, the monstrumologist had said. *It has a dozen names in a dozen lands, and it is older than the hills, Will Henry.*

I kicked my legs, and sucked uselessly upon the palm pressed hard against my open mouth. My head lay outside the tent, and my vision was clouded with the numberless stars sparking cold fire, shimmering like the crystalline ice inside the desecrated temple of Jonathan Hawk's remains. *Orion, the hunter. My favorite.*

Blood roared in my ears. My chest ached. My heart leapt; it pushed against my ribs, as if anxious for Chanler to ravish it. His mouth worked upon my burning chest; I felt the teeth scouring my corruption, desperate for the pure center.

It feeds, and the more it feeds, the hungrier it becomes. It starves even as it gorges. It is the hunger that cannot be satisfied.

In the ruined sanctuary, the bleating of the sacrificial goat. In the sepulchral silence, the calling of my name.

In its icy grip there is no hope of rescue.

Someone was sobbing; it could not have been me. Chanler wept into the wounds he'd created. He consumed flesh and tears.

In the deepest of pits, my mother combs out her hair. The light is golden. Her wrists are delicate. I remember the way she smelled.

One by one the stars begin to loose from heaven's grip; they fall into the golden light where my mother sits.

How could one so frail be so strong? My hands flailed uselessly at my sides. My heels dug feebly in the earth. I could feel myself flowing into him.

I am almost there, Mother. Through him I come to you, borne by the ark of his kiss.

In the blasted wasteland we hold our heads, confounded. We lift our eyeless sockets to the incurious moon. On the high wind rides the voice that calls our name.

The golden light is warm. It rushes into my eyes and fills me, and I am no longer afraid.

The butt of the Winchester smashed into the base of Chanler's skull. The spindly neck snapped back. Warthrop hit him again with all his force. He dropped the rifle, grabbed him by the shoulders, and hurled him off. Chanler leapt; the doctor met the lunge with his fist, slamming it into the side of his friend's head. Chanler collapsed across my jerking legs, his face wearing an obscenely painted mask of mucus and blood.

The doctor knelt beside me; his dark eyes replaced the stars in my sight.

"Will Henry?" he murmured.

He bent to examine the wound. I heard him hiss sharply through his teeth.

"Deep, but not too deep," he muttered. "The real danger is infection."

"The real danger . . . ," I echoed weakly.

With a thunderous wallop and a riot of riven canvas and shattered wood entangled with skeins of frozen rope, the tent blew apart, its remains hurtling into the trees, as if driven by a gale. The doctor fell over me—and a shadow fell over us. It blotted out the stars. Its stench engulfed the cosmos. Pale yellow shone its malevolent eye. I looked into that eye, and that eye looked back at me.

I have no memory of the next few moments. There was the yellow eye . . . and then trees, brambles, rotting logs, the perplexities of knotted vine and shallow half-frozen streams, the crackle of breaking snow, the dervish of the maddened stars, as we ran through the forest, I in my weakened state following in the footsteps stamped into the snow by the weight of two men—the doctor and the unconscious John Chanler, whom Warthrop had slung over his shoulder. We abandoned everything—rucksacks, canteens, medical kit—even the rifles. They were useless against the thing that pursued us.

Outiko *is not hunted*; Outiko *hunts*, the *ogimaa* had said. *You do not call* Outiko. Outiko *calls* you.

The wind no longer sang high in the trees. It screeched. It keened. It wailed. The ground shook beneath our feet. The forest echoed with a rhythmic pulse, an ear-shattering pounding, the primal beat of Gaia's heart.

I fell farther and farther behind. I couldn't see them anymore, just their footprints zigzagging through the primeval morass. Behind me, uprooted trees toppled with snow-muffled thunderclaps, the high-pitched snapping of their boughs pitiful accompaniment to the bawling wind and the teeth-rattling cannonade of the thing's pursuit. My stride became the stumbling semi-falling of a drunk; I went to my knees. Then up for a few yards, only to fall again. *Let it take me,* I thought. *You can't outrun it. You can't hide from it.* Kneeling, I covered my head with my hands and waited for the Old One to take me.

"Get up! Get up, Will Henry, *get up!*"

The monstrumologist hauled me to my feet and shoved me forward.

"You fall again and I'll *kick* you there," he shouted. "Do you understand?"

I nodded—and collapsed anyway. With a howl of rage the doctor yanked me back up, wrapped his free arm around my waist, and pushed forward, Chanler dangling over one shoulder, his recalcitrant ward hanging beneath the other. Thus borne down on one side with the burden he'd chosen and on the other with the one he'd inherited, Pellinore Warthrop carried on through the desolation.

FOLIO V
Abundance

"MEN ARE PROBABLY NEARER THE ESSENTIAL TRUTH IN
THEIR SUPERSTITIONS THAN IN THEIR SCIENCE."
—HENRY DAVID THOREAU

FOURTEEN

"The One Who Brought You Out"

At first I thought I was dreaming. The room was at once foreign and familiar, as in a dream—the chipped bowl upon the washstand, the rickety dresser, the narrow window with the dingy white curtains, the lumpy mattress on which I lay. Either I'm dreaming or I'm dead, I thought, though I'd never pictured heaven as so depressingly shoddy. Still, it was the first bed I'd lain in for . . . how long? It seemed longer than a lifetime.

"Well, finally you're up." The old floorboards creaked; a tall shadow approached. Then the meager light fell upon his face. Gone were the grit and grime of the forest, the whiskers, the old duster and filthy breeches. His hair was freshly trimmed. I detected a hint of talcum.

"Dr. Warthrop," I croaked. "Where am I?"

"Our old digs at the Russell House. I'm surprise you do not recognize the rustic charm."

"How long have I . . ."

"This is the morning of the third day," he said.

"Dr. Chanler . . . ?"

"He departs this afternoon for New York."

"He's alive?"

"I will forgive that question, Will Henry, as you've been out of sorts. But really."

He was smiling. He dropped his hand casually upon my forehead, and quickly removed it.

"You've been running a bit of a fever, but it's gone now."

My hand went up to my chest. I felt the gauze of the bandage.

"You'll have some scarring—something to impress the ladies when you're older. Nothing more serious than that."

I nodded, still unable to absorb all of it. It still felt dreamlike to me.

"We got out," I said hesitantly, seeking reassurance.

He nodded. "Yes, Will Henry. We got out."

The subject was dropped for the moment; he laid out my clothes and stood at the bedside impatiently while I struggled to dress. Every joint ached, every muscle quivered with fatigue, and my chest burned horribly with the slightest movement. When I sat up, the room spun around, and I gathered the sheets into my fists to ballast myself against the waves of nausea smashing against the brow of my enfeebled constitution. The shirt I managed to put on without aid, but when I lowered my head to slip on the pants, I toppled over—the doctor stepping forward to catch me before I smacked face-first onto the floor.

"Here, Will Henry," he said gruffly. "Come now. Lean against me."

He pulled up my pants, cinched the belt tight.

"There. Now, I trust you've too much pride to suffer the indignity of me carrying you downstairs. Here, hold on to my arm."

Thus we proceeded to the lobby restaurant, where the doctor ordered a pot of tea and instructed our waiter (who also happened to be the bartender and the cook) to "unload the larder." In good time I was stuffing my mouth with biscuits and venison gravy, pancakes glistening in maple syrup, fresh sausages and bacon, eggs, fried potatoes, hominy, and breaded trout filets. Warthrop cautioned me to slow down, but his warning went unheeded in the hurly-burly of my frontier bacchanal. It was as if I had never tasted food before, and the more I ate, the more exquisite became my appetite.

"You're going to make yourself sick," the monstrumologist said.

"Yes, sir," I muttered around a mouthful of biscuit.

He rolled his eyes, sipped his tea, and looked out the window to Main Street, drumming his fingers on the tabletop.

"Did you get a good look at it, sir?" I asked.

"A good look at what?"

"The . . . thing that was chasing us."

He turned back to me. His expression was unreadable.

"There was no 'thing' chasing us, Will Henry."

"But the eyes . . . you saw them."

"Did I?"

"*I* did."

"With the eyes of one suffering from dehydration, sleep deprivation, hunger, physical trauma, exhaustion, exposure, and extreme fear—not unlike my eyes at the time."

"What about the tent? Something tore it right out of—"

"Wind shear."

He smiled condescendingly at my baffled expression. "A freak meteorological phenomenon. Rare, but not unheard of."

"But I *heard* it, sir. Coming after us . . . It was *huge*."

"You heard nothing of the sort. As I've told you before, fear murders our reason. I should never have panicked, but I was, like you, in a state of heightened emotional distress. In my right mind I would have realized the best course of action would have been to stay where we were, as far from the trees as possible."

"Far from the trees?"

"The preferable place to be in an earthquake."

"An earthquake," I echoed disbelievingly. He was nodding. "It was an earthquake?"

"Well, what else could it have been?" he asked crossly. "Really, Will Henry, the alternative you're suggesting is absurd, and you know it."

I set down my fork. Suddenly I wasn't hungry anymore.

Indeed, I felt full to my ears, bloated and slightly nauseated. I looked down at my plate. The dead eye of the trout stared blankly back at me. Shards of white flesh clung to the delicate translucent bone. *I would strip her bare. I would see her as she is.* I thought of Pierre Larose. And then of Sergeant Hawk, his arms flung wide as if to embrace the limitless sky, his eyeless sockets regarding something we who retained our eyes could not see.

"If you are finished gorging yourself," the doctor said, consulting his watch, "we are late for our appointment."

"Appointment, sir?"

"They won't allow us to leave until they speak to you, and I am anxious to quit this charming little backcountry outpost as soon as possible."

"They" turned out to be two detectives with the North-West Mounted Police. The doctor had reported the deaths of Larose and Sergeant Hawk immediately, and Hawk's body had been quickly recovered where we had abandoned it, less than ten miles from the northern shore of the Lake of the Woods. A party had been dispatched to locate Larose's makeshift grave with the aid of a crude map sketched by Warthrop. He wasn't sure of the precise location, he told his interrogators, but he knew it was off the main trail about a day's hike from the Sucker camp at Sandy Lake.

The doctor was accustomed to dealing with all varieties of law enforcement; it was an inherent part of his work, since monstrumology was, in a way, the study of the criminal side of nature. He answered their questions forthrightly, his responses becoming vague only to the questions about the purpose of John Chanler's journey.

"Research," he replied cagily.

"Research of what, Dr. Warthrop?" the detectives asked.

"Of certain indigenous belief systems."

"Could you be more specific?"

"Well, he certainly didn't consult me about it," Warthrop said, a bit testily. "If you'd like to know more, I suggest you ask Dr. Chanler."

"We have. He claims to remember nothing."

"I've no doubt he's telling the truth. He has been through a terrible ordeal."

"Making out a little better than his guide, though."

"If you are suggesting he had something to do with Larose's murder, you are sadly mistaken, Detective Sergeant. I am not telling you how to execute your duties, but the person you should be asking these questions is Jack Fiddler."

"Oh, we'll be talking to Mr. Jack Fiddler. We've had reports about the strange goings-on up there at Sandy Lake."

Then it was my turn. The detectives politely asked the doctor to leave. He staunchly refused. They asked again with noticeably less politeness, and he, seeing that further recalcitrance would serve only to delay our departure, reluctantly agreed.

For the next hour they walked me through the story,

from first day to terrifying last, and I answered their questions as thoroughly as I could, omitting only those things the doctor had told me were borne of "dehydration, sleep deprivation, hunger, physical trauma, exhaustion, exposure, and extreme fear"—everything, that is, that smacked of *Outiko*.

"Do *you* know what Chanler went up there for?" they asked me.

"I think it was research."

"Research, yes, yes; we've heard that." Then, abruptly, they shifted gears. "What kind of doctor is he?"

"Dr. Chanler?"

"Dr. Warthrop."

"He is a . . . natural philosopher."

"Philosopher?"

"A scientist."

"What does he study?"

"N-natural things," I stuttered.

"And Dr. Chanler, he's the same kind of philosopher?"

"Yes."

"And what are you? Are you a philosopher too?"

"I'm an assistant."

"You're an assistant philosopher?"

"I provide services to the doctor."

"What kind of services?"

"Services of the . . . indispensable kind. Is the doctor in trouble?" I asked, hoping to change the subject.

"A sergeant of the NWMP is dead, boy. *Somebody* is going to be in trouble."

"But I told you—*he* left *us*. He disappeared one night and he was dead when we found him."

"Bush fever—climbed a tree and froze to death. A local boy who grew up in those woods, who hunted in them and fished in them, who's hiked them from here to the arctic circle. Just runs off, hauls himself up a tree in the middle of the first big storm of the season . . . You see how it doesn't add up, Will."

"Well, that's what happened."

I was practically giddy with relief when they escorted us outside without metal bracelets adorning our wrists.

"We shall be in touch, Dr. Warthrop," said they, rather ominously.

Having just survived my first interrogation as a detained foot soldier in the service of science, I was subjected to another by my master, who demanded to know every question and hear every answer.

"'Assistant philosopher'! What the devil is *that*, Will Henry?"

"The best I could come up with, sir."

We were walking toward the waterfront, away from our hotel.

"Where are we going?" I asked.

"Chanler," replied the monstrumologist curtly. "For some unfathomable reason, he's gotten it into his head he owes you a word of gratitude."

He was recuperating in the private residence of the town's apothecary and sole dentist. The residence was located on the second story directly above the business establishment, in a precarious-looking structure across the street from the wharf.

I will confess my ascent to John Chanler's room was fraught with no small measure of apprehension. Perhaps sensing my distress, the doctor drew me aside before we entered.

"He remembers nothing, Will Henry. His physical recovery has been nothing short of remarkable, but mentally . . . At any rate, try to control your tongue, and remember he has suffered more than either of us."

John Chanler was sitting in a rocking chair by the window. The late afternoon sun bathed his face with a kind of washed-out radiance, as sometimes the dead will seem to glow in their coffin. I noticed first that he, like the doctor, had had a shave and a trim. The fullness of his face made his eyes appear smaller, more in proportion with the rest. Of course, he was still horribly thin. His head seemed to be balanced precariously upon his spindly neck.

"Well, hullo there!" he called softly, motioning me closer with a freshly manicured claw. "And you must be Pellinore's Will Henry! I don't believe we've been properly introduced."

His hand was icy cold, though his grip was hard.

"I am John," he said. "I am so glad to meet you, Will—

and I'm delighted to see you up and about. Pellinore told me you've been under the weather."

"Yes, sir," I replied.

"And now you're feeling much better."

"Yes, sir."

"Glad to hear it!" His eyes had lost their yellow hue. The last time I had looked into those eyes, they'd seemed to burn with golden fire.

"You look just like him," Chanler said softly. "Your father. The resemblance is remarkable."

"You knew my father?" I asked.

"Oh, everyone knew James Henry. He was practically attached to Warthrop's hip. A terrible loss, Will. I am sorry."

In the awkward silence that ensued, we stared at each other across a space that felt far greater than the few feet that separated us. There was an odd blankness about him, a flatness to his inflection, like a poor actor reading from a script, or like the parroting of words in a language he did not comprehend.

"Will Henry," the doctor said. "John wanted to thank you."

"Yes! Pellinore tells me your services were indispensable to my rescue."

"It was Dr. Warthrop," I said quickly. "He rescued you from Jack Fiddler and he carried you, sir; he carried you all the way. For miles and miles he carried you—"

"Will Henry," the doctor said. He shook his head slightly and mouthed the word "no."

"Well! You *are* your father's son, William James Henry! Glad to be of service, honored to be in his august company, et cetera, et cetera." He turned to my master. "What is this magic you work on underlings, Pellinore? Why can't they see you for the irascible old mossback you are?"

"Perhaps it has something to do with the fact that my company happens to *be* august."

Chanler laughed, producing a rattle deep in his chest. He wiped the resulting spittle from his chin with the back of his hand.

"That was my chief mistake," he said. "I should have brought you with me on the expedition, Pellinore."

"I would have refused."

"Even for old times' sake?"

"Even for that, John."

"It doesn't matter that I failed, you know. The old man won't give it up."

"I'm prepared to deal with von Helrung."

"You know who's to blame for all this, don't you? That damned Irishman Stokely."

"Stokely? Who is he?"

"Or Stockman . . . Stickler . . . Stoker . . . Stocker? Oh, I don't know what's the matter; got moss on the brain or something. His first name is Abraham, but he doesn't go by that."

"I've never heard the name—or any variant of it. Is he a monstrumologist?"

"Good God, no. He's in the theater. The theater, Pellinore! Met the old man through his patron, that British actor—Harold Lerner—is that it?"

Warthrop was shaking his head. "I've no idea, John."

"He's very famous. Been knighted by the queen and everything. Over here on a tour last year and . . . Henry! That's the first name. Sir Henry—"

"Irving?"

"That's it! Sir Henry Irving. Stickman is his personal clerk or something. Sir Henry introduced him to von Helrung, and ever since the two have been as thick as two peas in a pod."

"Thieves," the doctor said. "The expression is as 'thick as thieves.'"

"Yes, I know that." Chanler's face darkened. "I misspoke, professor. Thank you so much for correcting me, though." He looked at me. "He does it to you, too; you don't have to tell me."

"So this personal secretary of Sir Henry convinced von Helrung of the Wendigo's existence?" Warthrop seemed dubious.

"Did I say that? You aren't listening to me. A vain man has no room in his head for the thoughts of others—remember that, little Bill! No, I don't think Stockman knows a Wendigo from a Welshman—but he's positively obsessed with all things monstrumological—even wants to write a book about it!"

The doctor's eyebrow rose. "A book?"

"He's an aspiring novelist, too. Fixated on the occult, native superstitions, that sort of thing."

"None of which has anything to do with monstrumology."

"That's what I told the old man! But he's slowing down; you know he's been slipping over the past couple of years. And this Stroker won't leave him in peace. Back in England now and writing letter after letter, forwarding von Helrung what he called 'eyewitness accounts,' excerpts from personal diaries and such, some of which von Helrung showed me. I told him, 'You can't trust this man. He's in the *theater*. He's a *writer*. He's making it up.' Well, the old man won't listen. Goes off and writes this damn paper to present to the congress and asks me to head up here—because proof of *one* lends credence to the existence of the *other*."

"The other," echoed the doctor.

"Nosferatu. The vampire. That damned Irishman's pet project."

"So *Meister* Abram sends you to bag its North American equivalent," Warthrop said. "Utter folly, John. Why did you agree to it?"

Chanler looked away. He did not answer for a moment. When he did, it was with a voice so soft I could hardly hear him.

"That is none of your business."

"You could have turned him down without hurting him."

The bulbous head whipped toward him; veins popped in the spindly neck; and John Chanler's eyes burned with anger.

"Don't preach to me about *hurt*, Pellinore Warthrop.

You have no concept of the word. What did you ever care about his feelings—or anyone's? When did you *ever* shed a tear for another human being? I challenge you to name one time in your miserable little life when you gave a damn about anyone but yourself."

"I shouldn't have to," returned my master calmly. He did not appear fazed by this vehement outburst. "Least of all with you, John."

"Oh, *that*. What a hypocrite you are, Warthrop. You must be a hypocrite; you're too intelligent for any other explanation. Throwing yourself into that river was the ultimate act of vanity and self-centeredness. 'Woe is me, poor tragic Pellinore!' Pitiful! I wish you had drowned."

The doctor refused to rise to the bait. "You have been through a terrible ordeal," he said gently. "I understand you are not yourself, but I pray in time you'll see your anger is misdirected, John. I am not the one who sent you here; I am the one who brought you out."

I thought of him crashing to the frozen ground, Chanler cradled in his arms, and the wild look in his eyes when Hawk tried to help him with his burden—the revolver inches from Hawk's face—and his broken cry so pitiably small in the unforgiving desolation: *No one touches him but me!*

"One and the same," whispered his friend cryptically. "One and the same."

Before Warthrop could ask the meaning of this remark, a knock came upon the door. The doctor stiffened at the sound and briefly closed his eyes, breathing to himself, "We have stayed too long."

Muriel Chanler stepped into the room, seeing Warthrop first and saying to him, "Where is John?"

Then she saw him, huddled in the little chair, a man who appeared twice as old as when she'd seen him last, pale and shriveled, ground down by the wilderness and the exorbitant cost of desire. She gave an involuntary gasp; her eyes welled with tears.

Chanler tried to rise, failed, tried again. He rocked unsteadily upon his feet. He seemed taller than I remembered.

"Here I am," he croaked.

She hurried toward him, slowed, stopped. She touched his cheek tenderly. The moment was heartrending and intensely private. I looked away—toward the author of the play, who had endured the unendurable so he might stage this scene—the woman he loved in the arms of another man.

"John?" she asked, as if she could not quite believe it.

"Yes," he lied. "It's me."

FIFTEEN

"We Should Be Honest with Each Other"

We saw them to the depot. As the porter was helping her husband board their private car, Muriel laid her hand upon the doctor's arm.

"Thank you," she said.

He eased his arm away. "It was for John," he said.

"You thought he was dead."

"Yes. You were right and I was wrong, Muriel. See to it he's looked after; he is far from recovered."

"Of course I will." Her eyes flashed. "I have every hope in *his* recovery."

She bade me good-bye. "I kept my promise, Will."

"Promise, ma'am?"

"I prayed for you." She glanced at the doctor. "*Half* of it was answered, at least—you're not dead."

"Not yet," said Warthrop. "Give it time."

I wasn't sure, but it appeared she was fighting back a smile.

"Will I see you in New York?" she asked him.

"I will be in New York," he said.

Now she did laugh, and it was like rain after a long, dry season.

The locomotive's whistle shrieked. Black smoke belched from the stack.

"Your train is leaving," the monstrumologist pointed out.

We remained on the empty platform until the train was well out of sight. The first stars were coming out. A loon cried mournfully against the dying of the light. The onset of darkness made me shiver more than the cold. Though miles from it, I was still very close to that spot where a man lay broken in half beneath the frozen ground.

"When will we be going home, sir?" I asked.

"Tomorrow," he answered.

I'd never been so happy to see that old house on Harrington Lane. I fairly bounded from our hansom when we pulled up, and kneeling to kiss the doormat would not have been out of keeping with my joy upon finding myself there. It seemed nothing short of miraculous. How I had hated that house—and now how I loved every single creaky old inch of it! Nothing makes us love something more than the loss of it—I think the monstrumologist would have agreed with that.

I would have never left it again, but the packing began first thing the following morning. In the afternoon there were errands to run—to the post office, the Western Union office, the laundry shop, the tailor's, and last, but certainly not least, the baker's for a basket of raspberry scones. The doctor, it appeared, had missed his scones the most. He worked late into the evening practicing his presentation, assuming—he was Pellinore Warthrop, after all—the absolute worst case. Despite his lack of an actual physical specimen, von Helrung would proceed to argue for the inclusion of *Lepto lurconis* and its myriad mythological cousins in the monstrumological canon.

The night before our departure for New York, a very odd thing happened—practically the oddest thing to happen between us up to that point. I was drifting off to sleep when his head popped through the little trapdoor to my alcove and, with an uncharacteristic chagrined expression, he softly asked if I was awake.

"Yes, sir," I replied. I sat up and lit the lamp beside the bed. In its glow the doctor's face seemed to float against the backdrop of profound darkness. I was a bit unnerved, to be honest, for in our history he had never come to my bedside in the middle of the night. It was always I who was summoned to his.

"Can't sleep either, then?" He sat at the foot of the bed. He looked about the tiny space, as if he, who had grown up in this house, had never seen it before. "You know, you might consider moving into one of the bedrooms on the second floor, Will Henry."

"I like it up here, sir."

"Do you? Why?"

"I don't know. I guess I feel more . . . safe here."

"Safe? Safe from what?"

He looked away. He did not seem to be waiting for an answer to his question, though he did seem to be waiting for something. What was it? Why had he come like this? It was not in his character.

"I spent many hours in this room when I was a child," he said, gently breaking the silence. "Our past dictates our perceptions, Will Henry. I could never associate this room with safety."

"Why?"

"I was quite sickly as a child—one of the reasons, though not the chief reason, my father sent me away. To 'toughen you up a bit,' were his words. Every time I fell ill, and that was often, I was banished to this attic, lest my contagion run through the entire household. . . ." He was staring through the little window over my head, to the glistening stars beyond.

"My mother died when I was ten; I believe I have told you that. Consumption. My father, though he never said it outright, blamed me. From the hour of her death, my days in this house were numbered. He withdrew from me and, although we shared the same rooms and supped at the same table, I was abandoned—as he was—both of us wrapped within the cocoon of our grief. He threw himself into his work—and threw me onto a boat to England. I would not see him again for almost fifteen years."

I tried to think of something that would comfort him. "I'm sorry, sir" was the best I could muster.

He frowned. "I am not seeking pity, Will Henry. I was discussing how our perceptions are shaped by our individual experience, thus calling into question the whole notion of objective truth. We cannot trust our perceptions—that is my point."

He abruptly cut short the lecture, looking away again, considering, by all appearances, the blank wall opposite the bed.

"I spent untold days up here, wracked with fevers and coughs, while upon the street below I could hear the laughter of the neighborhood children, their joy a cruelty I could hardly bear."

He shook his head sharply, as if to rid himself of the memory.

"The other difficulty with our perceptions," he continued at length in that maddeningly dry lecturing tone he often put on with me, "is our tendency to project them upon others. This room has unpleasant connotations for me and so I attribute the feeling to the room itself and am puzzled when you do not feel the same way."

"Yes, sir," I said.

"What have I told you about the incessant 'yes, sir's, Will Henry? It is sycophantic and demeaning to both of us."

"Yes, sir," I replied cheekily.

"I have been giving some thought to our . . ." He searched for the best word to describe it. "Arrangement, Will Henry. You have been with me almost two years now, and of course your services have tended to be, on the whole, more indispensable than not; still, your case is unusual in that you came to be here as a result of your parents' untimely demise, not by any desire on your part—or on mine, in all honesty. Unfortunate circumstances forced us together, but that does not mean we are entirely helpless. As a scientist, I do not truck much in free will, but neither do I subscribe to silly superstitions of predestination or fate. My perception may be entirely true that you have been indispensable to me. It does not follow, however, that you share the same perception when it comes to me."

He paused, waiting to hear my thoughts on the matter. When I didn't answer, he shrugged and said, "You are nearly thirteen, the age of majority in some cultures." He cleared his throat. "And you have demonstrated minor alacrity in lucid thought—sporadically at least," he added. It was a particular talent of the monstrumologist, the ability to insult and praise in the same breath. "Perfectly capable of making decisions."

"You're sending me away." My heart began to race. "You don't want me here anymore."

"Did I say that? Where do you wander off to, Will

Henry? What pleasant meadows do you frolic in while I'm talking? I said you are not entirely helpless. You can make a choice and, more important, I will honor that choice. I am not a fool. It has not escaped my notice that I can be difficult to live with."

He hesitated as if waiting for a rebuttal. When none was forthcoming, he hurried abashedly on. "I have certain idiosyncrasies. Some deficiencies in human . . . in relating to . . . What I mean to say is that perhaps I am the sort of man who lives best alone." He frowned. "What is this? Are those tears?"

"No, sir."

"Don't exacerbate the matter by lying, Will Henry."

"No, sir."

"And then there is the issue of my profession. It is a dangerous business, our recent difficulties in Rat Portage being a perfect case in point. I'm sure it has occurred to you that associating with a monstrumologist can be hazardous to one's health."

I touched the still-tender wound upon my chest.

"I've no intention of simply putting you out on the streets, if that's what is worrying you," he continued. "I would find a good place for you."

"This is my place. With you, sir."

"I'm flattered by your devotion, Will Henry, but—"

"If I left, how would you get along? There is no one to—"

He waved his hand impatiently. "I can always hire a cook and a maid, Will Henry, and you know every week there are applications to apprentice under me, from *serious* scholars who are actually interested in the craft."

These words stung. I lowered my head and said nothing.

He snorted softly. "How true that honesty is its own reward. More often than not, its *only* reward! We should be honest with each other, Will Henry. Your motives for staying here are no more pure than mine for allowing you to."

"Please, sir, I want to stay."

He stared intently at me for several long, uncomfortable moments. Was that his game? I wondered. To gauge the depths of my commitment to him? Or were his motives purer than that? Was he concerned for my safety, or troubled by his friend's demand—*I challenge you to name one time in your miserable little life when you gave a damn about anyone but yourself*—and this was his way of answering it? What did the monstrumologist really want from me? And what in the name of all that's holy did *I* want from *him*? Did either of us know?

"It is a terrible thing, Will Henry," he said at last. "To lose a friend."

SIXTEEN

"I Am Pleased to Find You Here"

A man of enormous proportions was waiting for us when we arrived at Grand Central Depot the following afternoon. At well over six feet, he towered above the crowd, wide-shouldered, thick-chested, with an untrimmed tangled mass of black hair obscuring the lower half of his large pock-marked face, his bowler hat pulled low, the brim resting just above his bushy eyebrows.

He bowed low to the doctor, an exaggerated show of subservience that struck me as slightly affected, a parody of deep respect, and he greeted the monstrumologist in a thick Slavic accent.

"Dr. Warthrop, I am Augustin Skala."

He gave Warthrop a card, which the doctor barely glanced at before pressing into my hand.

DR. A. VON HELRUNG

"Herr Doctor von Helrung welcomes you back to New York and requests that you accept my services."

"And what, precisely, might those services be, Mr. Skala?" inquired the doctor stiffly.

"To arrive you to hotel, sir." English clearly was not the Bohemian's first language.

"Our luggage—" began Warthrop.

"To be arrived by separate coach. All taken care of. No worries for the Dr. Warthrop."

Like the great ice-breaking prow of an arctic vessel, Augustin Skala plowed a path through the crowd as it bottlenecked before the Forty-second Street doors. We followed him to a black hansom cab hitched to an ebony behemoth of a horse. After opening the curbside door for us, Skala, with exaggerated formality and painfully ludicrous solemnity, dug into his jacket pocket and produced an envelope, which he offered, with equivalent obsequiousness, to my master. Warthrop accepted it without a word and slid into the cab, leaving me for the briefest moment alone with the Bohemian, my senses a bit overwhelmed by the intensity with which he stared down at me from so great a height, with dark, expressionless eyes and the malodorous aroma of sweat, tobacco, and stale beer that orbited his Jovian mass.

"You are who?" he asked.

"My name is Will Henry," I answered, my voice sounding small to me. "I serve the doctor."

"We are fellows," he intoned in his guttural accent. "I serve too." He dropped a huge paw upon my shoulder, lowering his face until it filled my entire field of vision. "I gladly die for *Meister* Abram."

"Will Henry!" Warthrop called from within the hansom. "Snap to!"

Never had my snapping to been happier. I fairly leapt inside, the door swung shut, and the entire rig bounced and shook as Skala took his seat above us.

The whip wickedly popped, and we swung on a single wheel—or so it felt—onto the street, barely missing a policeman and forcing his bicycle directly into the path of an advancing dray loaded with dry goods. The policeman's shrill whistle was swallowed quickly by the din of the depot—the *clop-clop* of the carriages and the cries of the vendors and the throaty notes of the six thirty express arriving from Philadelphia. The early evening traffic was heavy, the street clogged with carriages and bicycles, none of which seemed to concern our driver, who drove as one fleeing a fire, all the while cracking his whip and hurling obscenities in his native tongue at any and all with the temerity to cross his path.

Many years have passed since that day, my first in that city of cities, that crowning jewel in America's financial and cultural coronet, the living symbol of her abundance.

The picture is perfectly preserved in my memory. Look—there he goes now, rounding the corner onto Sixth Avenue! Little William James Henry all the way from his tiny New England hamlet, leaning out the window of that jostling taxi with his little mouth agape, as goggle-eyed as the most buffle-headed bumpkin fresh from the sticks, marveling with bald astonishment at the architectural triumphs of the avenue that dwarfed anything he had ever seen in the confines of the Massachusetts countryside, taller than the tallest church steeple.

See him now, his face lit up with delight at the parade advancing on every side, of cart and carriage, delivery truck and spacious brougham, of ladies in their colorful crinoline and dandies dandier than the foppish fop astride boneshaker bicycles weaving between the vendors' carts as expertly as rodeo barrel racers. Sunset was still almost two hours hence, but the buildings on the western side cast long engulfing shadows, between which the granite pavement glowed honey gold in smoky shafts of slanting light, the light painting the facades along the eastern side the same Hyblaean hue.

Thus it seemed to this twelve-year-old boy from the country that he had arrived, by means of the oddest and most terrible of circumstances, in a city made of gold, where wonders awaited him around every corner, and where, like the tens of thousands of immigrants who came before and after him, he might shrug off his dolorous past and don the bright and brilliant coat of endless possibility. Do you hear it—I certainly do—his barely suppressed giggles behind that silly grin?

But listen, William James Henry, your joy will be fleeting. This feast of eye and ear will soon be snatched from your table.

The golden light will die, and the plunge into darkness will be swift and unstoppable.

Beside me, the monstrumologist did not share an iota of my joy; he was absorbed in the letter handed to him by the Bohemian. He read it through several times before passing it to me with a pensive sigh. It read:

My Dear Warthrop,

Old friend, I open with the sincerest of apologies—forgive me! I would have met your train in person, but much demands my attention and I cannot get away. Herr Skala is an excellent man, and you may, as I do, trust to him the slightest detail. If he disappoints, tell me and it shall be dealt with!

Words fail to express my eagerness to see you again,

for it has been too long, old friend, and there is much that has happened—much that will in the coming days—but that is not to be written, and we have much to discuss.

I regret I cannot greet you properly tonight at the soiree— there are more pressing matters that demand my attention—but as recompense for my disgracious absence, I pray you will accept my invitation to dine tomorrow. Herr Skala will meet you at your hotel a quarter past seven.

I beg to remain,

Your Obt Svt,

A. von Helrung

"I suspect my old master would not be so eager to see me if he knew our plans, Will Henry!" he muttered.

Hardly had the words escaped his lips when the hansom jerked to a violent stop, snapping my head forward with such force that my hat was flung to the floorboards. As I bent to pick it up, the doctor jumped onto the sidewalk, striding away without a backward glance, the breeze whipping his dark cloak about him in a zephyrous dance.

I hopped from the cab, only to be confronted in my egress, as in my ingress, by the large slit-eyed servant of von Helrung. He said nothing at first; he only stared, but it was a stare curiously lacking in curiosity. He simply fixed his black eyes upon me as a man might regard a common insect that had crossed his path. He afforded me a smile noticeably deficient in teeth.

"You sleep goodly enough tonight, Mr. Will Henry," he said, with a slight emphasis on *tonight*, implying my subsequent rest might not be so 'goodly.'

I nodded and mumbled my gratitude. Then I fairly sprinted to the doctor's side.

We were met inside the lobby by what appeared to be the entire staff of the Plaza Hotel, from manager to lowly bellhop, a half dozen in all, who descended upon Warthrop as if he were the prodigal son. It was not any largess on the doctor's part that excited them—the doctor had stayed here before, and his parsimony was well known—but his reputation as one of the preeminent natural philosophers of his day. In short, and much to my surprise, the doctor was something of a celebrity, a fact that, given his particular and peculiar field of expertise, seemed counterintuitive, to say the least.

Warthrop, for his part, seemed nothing but annoyed by all the fawning and scraping, further evidence of his distress over the looming battle with von Helrung. Under normal circumstances he would have basked in the glow of their adoration for however long it shone.

So he cut short their slavish greetings, curtly informing the manager that he was tired and wished to be shown directly to his room.

There followed many repetitions of "Yes, Dr. Warthrop" and "Right this way, Dr. Warthrop!" And in a thrice I was aboard the first elevator in which I had ever ridden, operated by a boy not much older than myself, who was wearing a bright red jacket and a pillbox hat.

Our digs, a spacious suite on the eighth floor, with magnificent views of Central Park and Fifth Avenue, were lavishly appointed, if wondrously cluttered, in the Victorian style. How odd it felt, upon crossing that threshold, to have awakened in the dusty, shadow-choked old house on Harrington Lane and then, in a matter of hours, to find oneself in the lap of gilded luxury! I practically skipped to the window and pulled aside the heavy damask curtains to ogle the landscape from my vertiginous perch. The westering sun glittered off the pond nestled in its verdant bower, where toy sailboats bobbed in the gold-tipped swells. Lovers strolled arm in arm along West Fifty-ninth Street, the women with their brightly colored parasols, their beaus with their walking sticks. *Oh,* thought I, *could there be a more pleasurable place than this? Why couldn't we live here, in this city of wonders?*

"Will Henry," called the doctor. I turned to find him shirtless, holding a burgundy cravat. "Where is my cravat?"

"You're— It's in your hand, sir."

"Not *this* cravat. My *black* cravat. I specifically asked if you packed it before we left. My memory is quite clear on that."

"I did pack it, sir."

"It isn't in our luggage."

"It must be, sir."

I found it right away, and he snatched it out of my hand as if I'd pulled it from my back pocket.

"Why aren't you changing, Will Henry?" he asked querulously. "You know we have less than an hour."

"I'm sorry, sir. I didn't know, sir. Less than an hour to what?"

"And for goodness' sake run a comb through that mop of yours." With black-rimmed eye and unkempt hair tortured into cyclonic waves by his restless fingers, he added, "You look terrible."

On the eve of every congress, a reception was held in the grand ballroom at Charles Delmonico's restaurant on Fourteenth Street. Attendance was not mandatory, but few members failed to make an appearance. Food and libation were provided in abundance, and it was the rare monstrumologist who could resist free provender. A band was always hired to play the latest in popular music ("Over the Waves" and "Where Did You Get That Hat?"), and it was the sole function—formal or informal—in which women were allowed to participate. (The first female monstrumologist, Mary Whiton Calkins, would not be admitted to the Society until 1907.) Fewer than half of the men brought their wives, only because most monstrumologists were committed bachelors, like my master. This is not to say they were indifferent to the fairer sex or misogynistic in their perceptions—rather, monstrumology attracted men who were solitary by nature, risk-takers for whom the thought of hearth and home and the unending demands of domesticated bliss were anathema. Most, like Pellinore Warthrop, had fallen in love long ago with an enchantress whose face they were doomed to never clearly see.

Hardly had we been relieved of our hats and overcoats when a little man materialized out of the milling crowd. He wore a black swallowtail coat over a vest of the same color, black trousers, a white shirt with a high, stiff collar, and patent leather pumps that added an inch or so to his diminutive height. His mustaches were waxed, twirled into points that curved upward toward his cheeks.

He greeted the monstrumologist in the typical continental fashion—*faisant la bise*, a peck on either cheek—and said, "Pellinore, *mon cher ami*, you do not look well." His dancing dark eyes fell upon me.

"Damien, this is my assistant, Will Henry," the doctor said, ignoring his colleague's observation. "Will Henry, Dr. Damien Gravois."

"Delighted," said Gravois. He squeezed my hand. "*Comment vas-tu?*"

"Sir?"

"He is saying 'How are you?'" Warthrop informed me.

Gravois added, "And you say '*Ça va bien*'—'I'm doing well.' Or '*Pas mal*'—'Not bad.' Or to show what a polite boy you are—'*Bien, et vous?*'"

I struggled to form the last suggestion, and either the awkwardness of my attempt or the futility of the attempt itself amused him, for he chuckled and gave my shoulder a consoling, if slightly patronizing, pat.

"*Pas de quoi*, Monsieur Henry. *La chose est sans remède.* You are an American, after all."

He turned back to Warthrop. "Have you heard the latest?" He was grinning wickedly. "Oh, it is terrible, *mon ami*. Scandalous!"

"If it involves scandal, I'm sure you will share it, Gravois," replied the doctor.

"I have it upon good authority that our esteemed president intends to shock us at the conclusion of this congress."

"Really?" Warthrop raised an eyebrow, feigning surprise. "In what way?"

"He intends to introduce the *mythological* into the lexicon!"

Gravois smiled smugly, anticipating, no doubt, Warthrop's dismay at this "news."

"Well," said my master after a weighty pause. "We will have to do something about that, won't we? Excuse me, Damien, but I haven't eaten anything all day."

We loaded our plates from a long buffet table groaning with food. Never before I had seen so much gathered in one place—smoked salmon and raw oysters, chicken gumbo and sweet pea puree, soft-shelled crab and broiled bluefish, stuffed shoulder of lamb and braised beef with noodles, broiled quail and blue-winged teal duck served in a *sauce espagnole*, mushrooms on toast and pigeon with peas, stuffed eggplant, stewed tomatoes, parsnip cakes sautéed in butter, hash brown potatoes baked in cream.... I wondered if the doctor, tipping back his head to slip the oyster into his mouth, was thinking like me of hickory bark and bitter wolf's claw and the pungent taste of toothwort. One might think my recent intimacy with starvation might have made me appreciate this cornucopia all the more, but it produced the opposite effect. The display appalled and offended me. It made me angry. As I looked about the richly appointed ballroom—the enormous crystal chandelier from England, the rich velvet curtains from Italy, the priceless artwork from France—and looked at the women glittering in their finest jewels, the silk trains of their imported gowns skimming the floor as they danced in the arms of their well-dressed escorts—and saw the waiters in their morning suits gliding through it all with groaning trays held high—I felt slightly sick to my stomach. In a tree that raised its boughs high in the trackless wilderness, a man crucified himself, his belly engorged with ice—his eyeless sockets seeing more than I, and I more than these ignorant fools who drank and danced and chattered drunkenly about the latest cause célèbre. I could not put it into words; I was but a child then. What I *felt*, though, was this: Jonathan Hawk's frozen entrails came closer to the ultimate reality than this beautiful spectacle.

A familiar voice shook me from my melancholic reverie. I looked up and stared with slightly opened mouth into the most luminous eyes I have ever seen.

"William James Henry, imagine finding you here among all these old fuddy-duddies!" Muriel Chanler exclaimed, flashing a smile briefer than a wink toward the doctor. "Hello, Pellinore." Then to me: "What's the matter, aren't you hungry?"

I looked down at my untouched plate. "I guess not, ma'am."

"Then you must do me the honor of this dance—unless your card is full?"

The band had taken up a waltz. I turned a desperate eye to the doctor, who seemed to have discovered some riveting aspect of his crab.

"Mrs. Chanler, I don't know how to dance . . . ," I began.

"Neither does any other male here, I'm sorry to say. You'll be in excellent company, Will. They can dissect a *Monstrum horribilis* but they can't master the two-step!"

She seized my sweaty hand and, without pausing for a reply, said, "May I, Pellinore?"

She pulled me to the floor, whereupon I immediately stepped on her toe.

"Put your right hand here," she said, gently placing it upon the small of her back. "And hold out your left like this. Now, to lead me, just a tiny pressure with your right—No need to crush my spine or shove me around like a rusty-wheeled cart. . . . Oh, you are a natural, Will. Are you sure you've never danced before?"

I assured her I had not. I did not look at her, but kept

my head turned discreetly to one side, for my eyes were level with the bodice of her gown. I smelled her perfume; I moved in an atmosphere suffused in lilac.

My waltz with the lovely Muriel Chanler was clumsy— and infused with grace. Self-conscious—and self-effacing. All eyes were upon us; we danced in perfect solitude. As she gently turned me—I cannot in honesty claim I did much leading—I caught glimpses of the doctor through the shifting bodies, standing where we'd left him by the buffet table, watching us . . . or her, rather. I do not think he was watching me.

Never before had I desired that a moment end as much as I desired that it go on. She extended her hand, curtsied, and thanked me for the dance. I turned away abruptly, anxious to return to the familiar orbit of one who was not quite so heavenly. She stopped me.

"A proper gentleman escorts his partner from the floor, Master Henry," she informed me, smiling. "Otherwise she is set adrift to effect a most embarrassing exit. Lift your arm, elbow bent, like this."

She laid her hand upon my raised forearm, and we paraded from the floor. I tell myself now it was my imagination—the slight favoring of her right foot as we negotiated our way back to the table.

"Will Henry, you do not look well," the doctor observed. "Are you going to be sick?"

"He is naturally graceful, Pellinore," Muriel said. "You should be proud."

"Why would I be proud of that?"

"Aren't you his surrogate father now?"

"I am nothing of the sort."

"Then I feel sorry for him."

"You shouldn't. I understand from a highly respected expert in the field that his *atca'k* flies like the hawk." He smiled tightly and abruptly changed the subject. "Where is your husband?"

"John did not feel up to attending."

"So you came alone?"

"Would that disappoint you, Pellinore?"

"Actually, I am pleased to find you here."

"I sense a thinly veiled insult coming."

"It must mean he's much improved—for you to abandon his bedside to dance the night away with other men."

"Do you know it isn't your lack of humor that makes you so boring, Pellinore. It's your predictability."

She was smiling, but her banter was forced, the lines delivered from an actress who could not identify with her character. The doctor, of course, detected her discomfiture at once.

"Muriel," he said, "what is it?"

"It's nothing. Really." She looked directly into his dark eyes and said beseechingly, "Tell me what happened. John says he doesn't remember, but I don't know whether I can . . ."

"I can speak only of the aftermath," the doctor answered.

"The rest—the part I suppose you'd like to know—is speculation, Muriel."

She waited for him to go on. A few feet away the dance went on, a confusion of whirling color, black and white, red and gold.

"And I do not speculate," he added.

"He's changed," she said.

"I'm aware of that."

"I don't mean physically. Though that, too. . . . He hasn't eaten a decent meal since we returned. He tries . . . and gags to the point of choking. And he won't . . . He doesn't want to keep himself properly groomed. You know what a stickler he was about hygiene, Pellinore. I have to bathe him after he falls asleep. But the worst . . . I don't know how to describe it . . . The *vacancy*, Pellinore . . . He is there . . . and he is not there."

"Patience, Muriel. It's been less than three weeks."

She shook her head. "That is not what I mean. I am his wife. I knew the man who went into the wilderness. I do not know the man who came out of it."

At that moment Damien Gravois appeared at her side. "There you are," he cried softly. "I thought I had lost you."

Muriel smiled down upon his glowing countenance; he was a good two inches shorter.

"Monsieur Henry asked me for a dance," she teased. "*S'il vous plait, pardonnez-moi.*"

"*Bien sûr*, but if Monsieur Henry persists in these outrageous attempts to steal my date away, I shall challenge him to a duel."

He turned to the doctor. "Now, Pellinore, I am taking the wagers for this year." He pulled a slip of paper from his waistcoat. "I still have nine twenty, ten fifteen, and eleven thirty open if you'd care to—"

"Gravois, you know I do not gamble."

He shrugged. Muriel laughed lightly at my bewildered expression. "For the fight, Will. It happens every year."

"The later times book up quickly," put in Gravois. "The alcohol."

"Who fights?" I asked.

"Practically everyone. The Germans always start it," Gravois said with a sniff.

"It was the Swiss contingent last year," Muriel said.

"You realize how utterly absurd that is," Gravois said. "The Swiss!"

"There are few things more hopelessly ridiculous, Will Henry," said the doctor, "than an all-out brawl among scientists."

The brawl began a little after ten o'clock—at ten twenty-three precisely, according to Gravois's watch (he was the designated timekeeper for that year)—when an Italian monstrumologist named Giuseppe Giovanni accidentally (or so claimed Dr. Giovanni later) bumped into the date of a Greek colleague, causing her to spill her champagne down the front of her silk gown. The Greek rewarded the Italian's clumsiness with a roundhouse blow to the side of Giovanni's head, which sent his pince-nez flying across the room and into the back of the head of a Dutchman named Vander Zanden, who perceived that the man dancing behind him— a French colleague of Gravois's—had reached out and flicked him with his forefinger. The ensuing melee cleared the dance floor. Chairs smashed. Glasses and bottles shattered. Men shuffled across the floor with their arms wrapped around each other, impotently pounding their new partners on the back. The band played a rather rollicking ditty for a few minutes until the musicians were forced to flee after two men jumped onto the little stage and grabbed the music stands to hurl at each other's heads. The police were called to break it up—the duty falling, again, to Gravois, the self-designated master of ceremonies—but it was all but over by the time the police arrived.

"Who won the pool?" asked the doctor afterward.

"You will not believe this, Pellinore," answered Gravois.

"You did."

"It is a miracle, is it not?"

"Pity John couldn't be here," Warthrop said, taking in the devastation. "This was always his favorite part of the colloquium."

He did not speak to me until we returned to the Plaza.

"Don't do it now, but when we get to the door, take a

look behind us, Will Henry. I believe we are being followed."

I followed his instructions, turning at the entrance to the hotel, whereupon I saw hurrying across Fifth Avenue a tall, gangly man of around twenty, a bowler hat pulled low over his ears. He was dressed in a shabby black jacket and threadbare trousers, the knees of which were worn nearly clear through.

"Who is it?" I asked the doctor.

"My erstwhile New York shadow," he answered, and said no more.

SEVENTEEN

"Ich Habe Dich Auch Vermisst"

In those days the Society for the Advancement of the Science of Monstrumology—or "the Society," as it was informally known—was headquartered on the corner of Twenty-second and Broadway, in an imposing structure designed in the neo-Gothic tradition, with narrow arched windows and doorways, soaring turrets, and snarling gargoyles hunkered at the cornices. Originally it had been an opera house, but the company had gone bankrupt in 1842 and had sold the building to the Society, which had refurbished the structure to fit its own peculiar needs.

The main auditorium had been converted to a lecture hall and general assembly, where monstrumologists from around the world gathered for their annual congress. The second and third stories contained meeting rooms and administrative offices. The entire fourth floor had been gutted and remodeled into an extensive library that housed more than sixteen thousand volumes, including original manuscripts rescued from the Royal Library of Alexandria after Julius Caesar accidentally torched it in 48 B.C.

I did not know what to expect at my first congress. All I knew was that my mentor looked forward to the annual event the way a child anticipates Christmas morn. Once each year the crème de la crème of this odd and most esoteric of professions gathered to share their latest discoveries, to expound upon the cutting-edge research and methods, and to gather what comfort they could in a convivial gathering of like-minded souls who, for whatever reason, felt compelled to spend their lives studying creatures the majority of humankind would rather see extinct.

If I shared, by means of that peculiar osmosis of a keeper with his child, any of my master's enthusiasm, it was soon squelched at the commencement of the congress. I passed the hours of that first day in the main auditorium, with only a thirty-minute respite for lunch, in a stultifying atmosphere of interminable speeches delivered in dry monotones by men who possessed no oratorical gifts whatsoever (some with accents so thick as to render the mother tongue unrecognizable) on topics equally dull and arcane.

The congress formally began with a kind of roll call. The president pro tempore, the same Dr. Giovanni whose clumsiness had started the brawl the night before—he was sporting an impressive shiner and a large patch over his nose—stood at the lectern lugubriously reading aloud names from a long piece of foolscap, to which some in the hall responded with an "Aye!" and to which others made no reply at all.

I watched—or rather *endured*—the proceedings from a vantage point high above the stage. We were seated upon a dilapidated divan inside the doctor's private box, bestowed upon the family Warthrop by the Society in recognition of three generations of familial dedication to the cause. By ten o'clock, we had finally reached the *F*'s, and the doctor was nearly beside himself with boredom. I suggested this would be an excellent time to catch up on his sleep—he had tossed and turned the night before—but my gentle proposition was met with withering disdain.

The sole bit of excitement came with the announcement that the president of the Society, Dr. Abram von Helrung, would not be in attendance until the following day, with no explanation given for his absence. Rumors had been rife that something earthshaking was on the horizon—that von Helrung intended to drop a scientific bombshell at week's end, a proposition that would shake the world of natural history to its foundation. To those few colleagues who had the temerity to sound out Warthrop on the matter, the doctor gave a curt response, refusing to validate the *other* rumor that followed the first on eagle's wings—that upon the conclusion of von Helrung's presentation, his former pupil, the renowned Pellinore Warthrop, intended to rise in reply.

✳

We were back in our rooms by six, which gave us more than an hour to dress for our dinner date with Dr. von Helrung. In any other circumstance this would have been more than enough time to change (the doctor, as I have noted elsewhere, was heedless to the point of disdain about his appearance). On this evening, however, Warthrop became as punctilious as the fussiest quaintrelle. I, as his impromptu valet, bore the brunt of his anxiety. His waistcoat was wrinkled. His shoes were scuffed. His cravat was crooked. After my third unsuccessful attempt to tie a proper knot, he pushed my hands away roughly and cried, "Never mind. I'll do it!"

His lecture on proper etiquette—"Sit up straight, say 'please' and 'thank you' and 'may I', speak only when spoken to.'"The purpose and function of a finger bowl . . . ," et cetera, et cetera—was mercifully interrupted by the arrival of Skala promptly at a quarter past. He grunted a good evening to the doctor and swept out through the doors without a backward glance, one hand buried in the bulging pocket of his peacoat—perhaps, I thought, he was caressing the butt end of a truncheon.

As we exited the building, the doctor moaned under his breath. I looked around for the source of his distress and spied the same ragamuffin character from the night before loitering near the Fifty-ninth Street entrance to the park.

The rig bounced as the huge Bohemian took his seat; the whip snapped and cracked; and then we were off at breakneck speed, whipping south onto Fifth Avenue, while our driver yelled curses and epithets at anything that dared get in his way, including pedestrians for whom, but a moment before, the act of crossing the street had not seemed a life-threatening proposition.

Our journey was mercifully short—von Helrung's four-story brownstone occupied the corner of Fifth and Fifty-first Street. Still, by its end, I was battered and bruised and my pounding heart strained the buttons of my shirt.

We were met at the door by a person of color, a burly man whose girth rivaled that of Augustin Skala. He introduced himself as Bartholomew Gray, placed himself entirely at the doctor's service, and then, with dignified and deliberate ambulation, escorted us into the well-appointed parlor.

Our host fairly bounded across the room upon our entrance. He was a stocky barrel-chested man with short thick legs and small quick feet. His enormous square-shaped head was topped by an explosion of cottony white hair, and he had sparkling sapphire-colored eyes set deep beneath his bushy brows. His ruddy cheeks glowed with veritable delight at seeing his old friend and former pupil, and I watched dumbfounded as he gathered my aloof and undemonstrative master into a bear hug, pressing his face into the doctor's stiffly starched waistcoat. My astonishment was compounded when Warthrop returned the gesture, stooping a bit to wrap his leaner, longer arms around the shorter man's back.

With tears shining in his eyes, von Helrung cried softly, "Pellinore, Pellinore, *mein lieber Freund.* It has been too long, *ich habe dich vermisst!*"

"*Meister* Abram," murmured the monstrumologist with genuine affection. "*Ich habe dich auch vermisst. Du siehst gut aus.*"

"Oh, no, no," remonstrated the thickset Austrian. "*Es ist nicht wahr*—I am old, dear Pellinore, and near the end of my days, but *danke*, thank you!"

His flashing eyes fell upon me, and his joyful grin returned.

"And this must be the illustrious William Henry, conqueror of the wilderness, of whom I've heard so much!"

I bowed, extended my hand to him, and carefully repeated the greeting the doctor had taught me: "It is a pleasure and honor to meet you, Herr Doctor von Helrung."

"Oh, no, that will not do!" cried von Helrung. He brushed aside my proffered hand, pulled me into his arms, and proceeded to crush the air from my lungs. "The honor is mine, young Master Henry!"

He released me; I took a long, shuddering breath; and he looked long and deeply into my eyes, his gaiety giving way to gravity. "I knew your father, a brave and loyal man who died too young, but alas such is the fate of many a brave and loyal man! A grievous loss. A tragic end. I wept when I heard the news, for I knew what he meant to *mein Freund* Pellinore, *unsere Herzen sind eins*—his tears, mine; his heartbreak, ours! You have his eyes; I see that. And his spirit; I have heard that. Remain faithful to his memory, *mein Junge*. Serve your master as your father served him, and your father will smile down at you from paradise!"

As if "paradise" were a cue, a rumble and a clatter erupted from the hall behind us; it sounded like an entire regiment was thundering down the stairs. Bursting into our midst in a storm of white lace and verdant velvet, her raven ringlets pulled back from her round face and gathered into a crimson bow, was a young girl, perhaps a year or two older than me, with eyes the same remarkable shade of blue as our host.

She froze when she saw us, an abrupt halt nearly as violent as her charge. She recovered quickly, however, turned upon von Helrung, and, in a ringing, unaccented voice, made clear her indignation.

"They're *here*! Why didn't you tell me?"

"They've only just arrived, *mein kleiner Liebling*," replied von Helrung reasonably. "Dr. Warthrop, may I present my niece, Miss—"

"Bates," interrupted the girl, thrusting her hand, palm down, toward the monstrumologist, who accepted it graciously, bowed low, and waved his lips in its general vicinity. "Lillian Trumbul Bates, Dr. Pellinore Warthrop. I know who *you* are."

"Evidently," returned the doctor. He nodded toward me. "Miss Bates, may I present—"

"William James Henry," she finished for him, and turned

upon me those eyes saturated in blue. "'Will' for short. You are Dr. Warthrop's apprentice."

"Hello," I said shyly. Her stare was all too frank. From the first, it unnerved me.

"Uncle says you are my age, but if you are, you are quite undersized. How old are you? I'm thirteen. In two weeks I shall be fourteen, and Mother says I may go on dates. I like older boys, but Mother says I shan't be allowed to date them."

She paused, waiting for my response, but I was completely at a loss.

"Do you go to school, or does Dr. Warthrop instruct you?"

"Neither," I replied in a kind of squeak that sounded embarrassingly birdlike to my ears.

"Really? Why? Are you thickheaded?"

"Now, Lilly," remonstrated her uncle. "Will Henry is our guest." He patted her shoulder gently and said warmly to my master, "Come, Pellinore, sit with me; there are fresh cigars from Havana in the humidor. We will talk about the old days, and the new and exciting ones to come!" Then, turning back to his niece, he said, "Lilly, *mein kleiner Liebling*, why don't you take William to your room and show him your birthday present? We'll ring up when dinner is served."

Before either the doctor (who did not smoke cigars) or I (who did not wish to see Lillian Trumbul Bates's bedroom) could protest, I was yanked from the room, hauled up the stairs, and flung into her room. She slammed the door, threw the bolt, and then sailed past me to belly flop upon the canopy bed. Rolling onto her side, she rested her round dollish face upon her palm and studied me frankly from beneath her delicate brows, with an expression not unlike the doctor's upon ripping out the heart of Pierre Larose.

"So you are studying to be a monstrumologist," she said.

"I suppose I am."

"You *suppose* you are? Don't you know?"

"I haven't decided. I—I did not ask to serve the doctor."

"Your father asked?"

"My father is dead. *He* served the doctor, and when he died—"

"What about your mother? Is she dead too? Are you an orphan? Oh, you're Oliver Twist! And that would make Dr. Warthrop Fagi'n!"

"I like to think of him as Mr. Brownlow," I said.

"*I* have read everything that Mr. Dickens has written," Lilly averred. "Have you read *Great Expectations*? That's my favorite. I read all the time; it's practically all I do, except bicycling. Do you like to bicycle, Will? I bicycle practically every Sunday, and do you know I've seen Lillian Russell *seven* times on her gold-plated bicycle riding with her beau, Diamond Jim Brady? Do you know who Diamond Jim Brady is? He's very famous, you know. He eats everything. Once at breakfast I saw him eat four eggs, six pancakes, three pork chops, five muffins, and a beefsteak, washing it all down with a gallon of orange juice, which he called 'golden nectar.'

"Uncle Abram knows him. Uncle knows everybody who is anybody. He knows Buffalo Bill Cody. Two summers ago I saw his Wild West show in London when it played before the queen. I know her, too—Victoria. Uncle introduced us. He knows everyone. He knows President Cleveland. I met President Cleveland at the White House. We had tea. He has a love child because he's married and couldn't be with his true love; her name is Maria."

"Whose name?" I asked. I was having some trouble keeping up. "The love child's?"

"No, his true love's name. I don't know his daughter's name. I think it's a daughter, anyway. Are you an only child, Will?"

"Yes."

"So you have no one."

"I have the doctor."

"And *he* has no one. I know that. John Chanler married *his* true love."

"I don't think— He's never said— I can't imagine the doctor ever being in love," I said. I remembered his remark to Sergeant Hawk in the wilderness. "He says women should be classified as a different species."

"I'm not surprised he said that," Lilly said, and sniffed. "After what happened."

"What?"

"Oh, you must know. He *must* have told you. Aren't you his apprentice?"

"I know they were engaged, and he somehow fell off a bridge and got sick, and that's how she met Dr. Chanler—"

She threw back her head and laughed with abandon.

"I'm just repeating what he said," I protested, ashamed and angry at myself for the indiscretion. It was not a story the doctor was particularly proud of, and I knew he would be mortified if he knew I had shared it.

"I thought you were going to show me your birthday present," I continued, hoping to change the subject.

"Oh! My present! I forgot." She hopped from the mattress and scurried halfway under the bed to retrieve it, a weighty tome that she plunked down on the floor between us. Its leather cover was stamped with the title, in ornate script, *Compendia ex Horrenda Maleficii*.

"You know what this is?" she demanded. It sounded like a challenge.

With a sigh and a sinking heart, I answered, "I think so."

"Mother would kill Uncle if she knew he gave it to me. She *hates* monstrumology."

She flipped rapidly through the book's flimsy pages. I glimpsed gruesome depictions of human bodies flayed open; dismembered torsos and decapitated heads; the ironic leering grin of a skull whose frontal and parietal bones had been smashed to pieces; a tangle of rotting entrails in which squirmed what appeared to be gigantic larvae or maggots;

anterior and posterior views of a woman's corpse, her flesh ripped free from the underlying muscles and tendons and hanging like strips of peeling paint from the abandoned cathedral of her mortal temple. Page after page of macabre lifelike illustrations of human havoc wreaked, over which Lilly bent low with nostrils wide and cheeks flushed, eyes aflame with voyeuristic delight. Her hair smelled like jasmine, and it was a dizzying juxtaposition, the sweet odor of her hair against the backdrop of those disgusting drawings.

"Here it is," she breathed. "Here's my favorite."

She tapped her finger on the page, where the nude corpse of a young man was displayed in an obscene parody of Leonardo da Vinci's *Vitruvian Man*, arms and legs outstretched, head throw back in a silent howl, with what appeared to be a tentacle or perhaps a snake (though it may have been some of his intestines) issuing from his abdomen. Mercifully, Lilly did not elaborate on why she liked this drawing so much. She stared at it for a few seconds in silence, her eyes shining with macabre wonder, before looking up. A sound from downstairs had captured her attention.

"They're fighting," she said. "Hear it?"

I could—the doctor's strident voice, von Helrung's insistent response.

"Let's go listen." She slapped the book closed. Without thinking I grabbed her arm.

"No!" I protested. "We shouldn't spy."

"Do you hate him?"

"Who?"

"Dr. Warthrop! Is he your enemy?"

"Of course not!"

"Well, then, you can't spy on him. It's only spying when they're your enemies."

"I don't need to spy on him," I said, trying to think quickly. "I know what they're fighting about."

She stared intently at me for a moment with narrowed eyes. "What?"

I could not meet her gaze. I dropped my eyes and said softly, "The Old One."

There was literally no holding her back after that unfortunate admission. She ignored my frantic protests and crept down the hall, stopping at the top of the stairs to lean over the banister, her curls falling to one side as she cocked an ear to eavesdrop. It was a dramatic gesture. The two monstrumologists were arguing loud enough to be heard in Queens.

"... ashamed of yourself, *Meister* Abram," the doctor was saying. "To indulge that ... that ... *theater person.*"

"You judge before you know all the facts, *mein Freund.*"

"*Facts?* Facts, you say! And what facts might those be? Creatures neither alive nor dead who live off the blood of the living, who transform themselves into mist and bats and wolves. Chickens and pigs, too, I suppose—why not? Who sleep in coffins and rise each night with the moon? Are *those* the 'facts' to which you refer, *Meister* Abram?"

"Pellinore, tales of the vampire stretch back hundreds of years—"

"So do tales of leprechauns, and we do not study those—or are they next? Are we to include magical sprites in the canon? We might as well! Henceforth let us devote ourselves to determining how many fairies can dance upon the head of a pin—or perhaps in the vacuum that exists between your ears!"

"You wound me grievously, *mein Freund.*"

"And you insult me, *mein Meister.* If I had proposed such a thing when I was your pupil, you would have boxed my ears! What is it? Have you gone daft? Are you drunk? What in the name of God would compel you to pursue this madness?"

"You credit me too much power, Pellinore. I can only suggest—it is up to the Society to decide."

"I credit you with the death of two innocent men—and the attempted homicide of another. I do not count Will Henry and myself; we took that risk with no compunction from you."

"I did not tell John to go. He offered."

"You didn't have to tell him, you wicked old fool. You knew he would go if he thought it would please you."

"He said the case had never fully been explored. He insisted—"

The doctor cursed loudly, and I heard the hard thud of something being slammed to the thick carpet. Instinctively I started down the stairs, and Lilly pulled me back.

"Wait," she whispered.

"It is nothing," I heard von Helrung say. "It can be replaced."

"I hold you fully responsible for what happens to him," returned the doctor, refusing to be mollified.

"And I freely accept that responsibility. I shall do all within my power, though I fear it is too late."

"'Too late'? What do you mean?"

"He is in the state of becoming."

"Oh, for the love of— Has the whole world gone mad? Am I the sole sane person left in the cosmos? The state of becoming . . . what? No! Don't you dare say it. If you say it, I shall break the other one. *Over your thick Austrian head.*"

"You are understandably distressed."

"So, what is your plan? Keep him alive long enough to present him as a *Lepto lurconis* specimen, then shove a silver dagger through his heart? Burn his body upon a bloody pyre? I shall turn you over to the police. I shall see you prosecuted for cold-blooded murder and watch you hang."

"You must come to terms with certain facts—"

"*Facts!* Oh, wonderful. We are back to the *facts.*" Warthrop laughed harshly.

"The first of which is—regardless what you think of my proposal—that John will die, probably well before I can present my paper."

"And why do you say that?"

"Because he is starving to death."

For a moment there was no reply. I could well imagine, though, the expression on the doctor's face.

"He cannot eat?"

"He will not eat. Because what is offered is not what satisfies."

Lilly hissed between her teeth and yanked me backward, for the doctor had appeared below, practically running toward the front door.

"*Will Henreeeeeeeee!*" he bellowed.

"Pellinore! Pellinore, *mein lieber Freund,* where are you going? Please, I beg you. . . ." The stocky Austrian scurried after him on his thickset legs.

"Where I'm going is none of your damn business, von Helrung—but I'll tell you anyway: to John. I'm going to see John." He sidestepped his old master, and stopped short when he saw me standing above.

"Snap to, Will Henry," he snarled. "Visiting hours for the asylum are over."

"You should not go, Pellinore," von Helrung said.

"And why not?"

Von Helrung sighed. "Because he is here."

The doctor stiffened. He stepped toward von Helrung and said in a tone he had used often with me—stern, uncompromising, and intolerant of dispute—"Take me to him."

He was being kept in a bedroom at the far end of the second floor, four doors from Lilly's room. Von Helrung, noting the lateness of the hour and expressing concern for our appetites, instructed Lilly to escort me to the dining room so we might begin without them. Warthrop would have none of it. "Will Henry stays with me," he told our host. Lilly protested too, saying if I stayed, she should stay; it was entirely *unfair*. Von Helrung would have none of *that*; he had no say-so over me, but he did over her, and he ordered her downstairs. She shot me a hateful look as if it were all my fault, and traipsed down the stairs, her arms flopping loosely at her sides, lifting her knees high to slam her feet upon each step.

Von Helrung knocked on the door twice, paused, and then twice again. I heard the heavy tread of a large man crossing the floorboards, and then the sound of several bolts being drawn back. The door creaked open. Standing on the other side was Augustin Skala, a massive paw stuffed into the pocket of the old peacoat. He nodded silently to his employer and stepped to one side so we could slip past his mountainous bulk.

The room was small—a bed, a dresser and washstand, a single window, and a fireplace, in which a few damp sticks smoldered. A lamp sat on the mantel, begetting spastic shadows that jerked upon the dark carpeting and jittered across the muted wallpaper; I felt as if I had stepped into a cave.

Chanler reclined in the bed beneath a heavy quilted coverlet, eyes hidden under quivering lids, the lashes fluttering at the speed of a hummingbird's wings. His swollen blood-red lips were slightly parted, and I could hear his deep, wheezing breath from my spot on the other side of the room.

"Why have you moved him here?" asked the doctor softly.

"We thought it best," answered von Helrung.

"'We'?"

"The family and I."

"And what did his physician think?"

"I am his physician."

"When did you become a medical doctor, von Helrung?"

"In the sense that he's been entrusted to me, Pellinore."

"And Muriel agreed to this?"

The old Austrian nodded, and added somberly, "There is nothing more she can do for him."

"I can hear you, you know."

The subject of their discussion seemed to have not moved a muscle, but his eyes were now open, blood-red like his lips, shining with an overabundance of tears.

"Is that you, Pellinore?" he asked, with a swipe of his tongue over his suppurating lower lip.

"It is I," said my master, approaching the bed.

"And who is that with you? Not little Philly."

"Will. Will Henry," the doctor corrected him, motioning for me to come closer.

"Bittle filly," Chanler said, with a flick of his glowing eyes in my direction. "Congratulations, Willy Billy; he caught you but hasn't killed you yet. You know that's the plan, don't you? Same as your father, he'll see you die. Then donate your remains to the Society—put you on display in the Beastie Bin, where he puts all the nasty creatures he catches." He coughed. "It's where all you nasty things belong."

"I am disappointed in you, John," Warthrop said, ignoring the delirious tirade. "I expected you to be on your feet by now. You missed an excellent scrimmage last night."

"Who won the pool?"

"Gravois."

"That squirrelly frog. Don't tell me—he played bookie, too."

"I won't tell you, then."

"Do you remember the time he hid behind the band, and the tuba player vomited on him?"

"Which in turn made him sick."

"And he threw up all over his date—that dancer . . ."

"Ballerina," Warthrop said.

"Yes, that's the one. With the skinny legs."

"You called her 'the stork.'"

"No, that was you."

"No. I called her Katarina."

"Why did you call her that?"

"It was her name."

With some effort Chanler managed to laugh. "Damned literalist! 'Stork' is better."

The doctor nodded absently. "I fully expected to see you there, John. But it seems you've taken a turn for the worse . . ."

"I can't shake it, Pellinore," his friend admitted. "I felt a little better for a while, and then I fall back again—like Sisyphus and the rock."

"How do you expect to get better, though, if you refuse to eat?"

A look of anger flashed across Chanler's face. "Who told you that?"

Warthrop glanced at von Helrung, who was studying his patient with an expression of intense concern.

"Why can't you eat, John?" persisted the doctor.

"I would eat; I'm hungry enough, so hungry I can hardly stand it, but they won't *give* me anything!"

"Now, John," von Helrung scolded him. "You know that isn't true."

"Tell you me true!" shouted Chanler. "Tell me you true!" He closed his eyes and grunted in frustration. He spoke with great deliberateness, plucking each word clean from the tangled undergrowth of his thoughts before allowing it past his lips: "Don't . . . tell . . . me . . . what's . . . true."

"Anything you'd like—anything. Only name it, and I will see that you get it within the hour," said Warthrop.

Chanler was trembling. Fluid dripped from the corners of his eyes. The doctor reached down to wipe away the tear, and his friend jerked violently beneath the covers. "Don't! . . . *touch* me . . . Pellinore."

"Name it, John," the doctor insisted.

Chanler's head rocked from side to side. His eyes continued to leak tears; the pillowcase was stained with them. "I can't."

✳

The monstrumologist and von Helrung withdrew to the fireplace to confer out of earshot.

"This is unconscionable," Warthrop told von Helrung. "The man needs a doctor. The only question is, shall you summon one, or shall I?"

"I heard that!" Chanler called.

"His condition is beyond the scope of—," began von Helrung, but his former pupil would have none of it.

"He should be in Bellevue right now, not wasting away here with this baboon in a peacoat!"

"Shit!"

The two men started at the expletive.

"Worse than the hunger, Pellinore!" John Chanler called. "The shit! Every hour on the hour, buckets and buckets of shit!"

Warthrop glanced at von Helrung.

"He has been incontinent," explained the Austrian apologetically.

"So dysentery, too—and you still don't think he needs a doctor? It will kill him in a week."

"Do you know what that's like, Pellinore?" shouted Chanler. "To lie wallowing in your own shit?"

"We change the sheets immediately," protested von Helrung. "And you could use the pan, John. It's right there beside you." He turned to Warthrop and said beseechingly, "I try to make him as comfortable as possible. Understand, *mein Freund*, there are things that—"

The doctor brushed him aside and returned to the bed.

"The wrong metaphor," gasped Chanler. "The wrong hell. Not Sisyphus. Not Greek. Christian. Dante's rivers of shit. That's what it is."

"I'm taking you to the hospital, John," Warthrop told him.

"If you try, I'll shit on you."

"No doubt you will, but I'm taking you anyway."

"That's all is it—it is—Pell, but we forget."

"I don't understand, John. What do we forget?"

Chanler lowered his voice, pronouncing the word with great solemnity, as if he were sharing a profound truth: "Shit." He giggled. "It's all shit. I am shit. You are shit." His eye fell upon the simian features of Augustin Skala. "He is definitely shit. . . . Life is shit. Love . . . love is shit."

Warthrop started to speak, and von Helrung cut him off.

"Don't, Pellinore. It is not John who speaks now. It is the beast."

"You don't believe me," said Chanler. "You haven't bathed in it yet, that's all. The minute it sullies your unadulterated ass, you jump into a river, don't you?"

He coughed, and thick green bile broiled in his mouth and bubbled over his lips. His Adam's apple bobbed as he swallowed it back down.

"You disgust me," Chanler said. "Everything about you is repulsive—nauseating—you sickening mealy-mouthed piece of snot."

The doctor said nothing. If he remembered that he himself had spoken these words before, he did not show it. But I remembered.

"*Pellinore, Pellinore, being perfect is such a chore!* Do you remember that one?" Chanler asked.

"Yes," answered the doctor. "One of the kinder ones, as I recall."

"I should have let you drown."

Warthrop smiled. "Why didn't you?"

"Who would I have played my jokes on, then? It was all for show anyway. You didn't really mean to drown yourself."

"How do you know?"

"Because I was *with* you, you stupid bugger. If you'd really meant it, you would have waited till you were alone."

"An error owing to inexperience."

"Oh, don't worry, Pell. You'll get there. One of these days . . . all of us . . . suffocating in shit . . ."

His eyes rolled toward the ceiling. The lids fluttered. The doctor looked at me and nodded. He'd heard enough. He pointed toward the door. We'd crossed halfway to the exit when Chanler called out in a loud voice, "It won't do any good, Pellinore! He'll finish me before the ambulance leaves the gates!"

The doctor turned. He looked at von Helrung, and then swung his eyes in Skala's direction.

"What do you think he's got in his pocket, hmm?" Chanler said. "He'll have it in my heart the minute you close that door. He pulls it out when nobody's around and cleans his nails with it—picks his teeth—scrapes the crud off his crusty bunghole." Chanler was grinning ghoulishly. "Amateur!" he sneered at the stoic Bohemian. "Don't you know anything? That's a job for the *ogimaa*. Are you *ogimaa*, you stinking immigrant monkey?"

At the use of the *Iyiniwok* word, Warthrop stiffened. "How do you know that word, John?"

Chanler's head lolled upon the pillow. The eyes rolled back in their sockets. "Heard it from the man old, the old man in the woods."

"Jack Fiddler?" asked the doctor.

"Old Jack Fiddler pulled on his pipe, stuck it up his arse, and gave it a light!"

"Pellinore." Von Helrung touched the doctor's arm and whispered urgently, "No more. Call the ambulance if you like, but do not push—"

Warthrop shrugged off the hand and strode back to John Chanler's side.

"You remember Fiddler," he said to him.

Grinning, Chanler answered, "His eyes see very far—much farther than yours."

"And Larose? Do you remember Pierre Larose?"

I heard a snatch of the same nonsense he'd spouted in the wilderness, "*Gudsnuth nesht! Gebgung grojpech chrishunct.*" In a loud voice Warthrop repeated the question, adding, "John, what happened to Pierre Larose?"

Chanler's demeanor abruptly changed. A look of pro-found dismay—eyes welling with tears, the fat lower lip quivering like a child's when confronted by inexpressible loss—transformed his vaguely bestial appearance into one of heart-wrenching pathos.

"'You don't go doin' it, Mr. John,' he told me. 'You don't go peekin' up the Grand Lady's skirts. You don't look in them woods for the things that're lookin' for *you*.'"

"And he was right, wasn't he, John?" asked von Helrung, for Warthrop's benefit more than his own. My master shot him a withering look.

"*He left me!*" Chanler wailed. "He *knew*—and he left me!" Blood-flecked tears trailed down his hollow cheeks. "Why did he leave me? Pellinore, you've seen them—the eyes that do not look away. The mouth that cries on the high wind. My feet are on fire! Oh, good Christ, I am on *fire*."

"It called your name," murmured von Helrung encour-agingly. "Larose abandoned you to the desolation—and the desolation called to you."

Chanler did not reply. His mouth, its sores ripped open by the contortions of his despair, glistened with fresh blood. He stared vacantly at the ceiling, and I remembered Muriel's remark, *He is there . . . and he is not there.*

"*Gudsnuth nesht.* It's *cold. Gebgung grojpech.* It *burns.* Slow down . . . For the love of Christ, *slow down*. The light is gold. The light is black. What have we given?"

His hand emerged from beneath the covers. His fingers

seemed grotesquely long, the nails ragged and encrusted with his own filth. He reached desperately for the doctor, who gathered the withered claw into both his hands—and it was with utter astonishment that I saw tears shining in my master's eyes.

"*What have we given?*" Chanler demanded. "The wind says it is nothing to say nothing. In the center, in the beating heart—the pit. The yellow eye unblinking. The golden light black."

The doctor rubbed his hand, murmured his name. Shaken by the melancholic scene, von Helrung turned away. He crossed his arms over his thick chest and bowed his head as if praying.

"You must take me back," the broken man pleaded. "Mesnawetheno—he knows. Mesnawetheno—he will pull me out of the shit." He glared at the doctor with unalloyed animosity. "*You* stopped him. You stole me from Mesnawetheno. Why did you? *What have* you *given?*"

With that question lingering in the air, John Chanler fell back to the fevered dream of the desolation—that gray land where none can save us from the crush of the soundless depths.

Warthrop did not take him back to Mesnawetheno; he took him by ambulance to Bellevue Hospital, leaving me in the care of von Helrung, with instructions—as if he were boarding his horse—that I should be fed and given a proper bath before being put to bed.

"I will come by for him later tonight—or in the morning, if not."

"I want to stay with you, sir," I protested.

"I won't hear of it."

"Then, I'll wait for you at the hotel."

"I'd rather you not be alone," he said with a perfectly straight face, the man who left me alone for hours—sometimes days—at a stretch.

EIGHTEEN

"What Have I to Live For?"

I supped on warmed-over lentil soup and cold roasted lamb that night, sitting in the von Helrung kitchen with the butler, Bartholomew Gray, who was as kind as he was dignified, and who thoughtfully distracted me from my distress with a hundred questions about my home in New England, and with stories about his family's progress from slavery in the Deep South to the great "shining city on a hill," New York. His son, he proudly informed me, was abroad, studying to be a doctor. During my dessert of custard and fresh strawberries, Lilly appeared to rather officiously announce I would be sleeping in the room next to hers and she hoped I didn't snore because the walls were quite thin and she was a *very* light sleeper. She still seemed miffed that she had been banished, whereas I had enjoyed an audience with the stricken

John Chanler. I thought of her uncle's gift and the glow in her eye at its macabre contents. I suspected she would gladly have traded places with me.

At a little past one the following morning, my fate caught up with me—the doom that demanded I be disturbed at precisely the moment I was drifting off to sleep. The door to my room opened, revealing the fitful dance of a candle's flame, followed by Lilly in her dressing gown. Her voluptuous curls had been freed from their ribbons and cascaded down her back.

I pulled the covers up to my chin. I was self-conscious of my appearance, for I was wearing one of von Helrung's nightshirts and, though he was a small man, he was much larger than me.

We regarded each other for a moment by the flickering candlelight, and then she said without preamble, "He's going to die."

"Maybe he won't," I answered.

"Oh, no. He's going to die. You can smell it."

"Smell what?"

"That's why Mr. Skala is keeping watch. Uncle says we have to be ready."

"Ready for what?"

"You have to be quick, very quick, and you can't just use anything. It has to be silver. So that's why he carries the knife. It's silver plated."

"What's silver plated?"

"The knife! The pearl-handled Mikov switchblade knife. So when it happens—" She made a slicing motion over her heart.

"The doctor won't let that happen."

"That is very odd, Will—the way you talk about him. 'The doctor.' All whispery and fearful—like you're talking about God."

"I just meant if there's any way he can help it, he won't just let him die." I confided to her the most striking thing about that most striking scene in the sickroom—the tears in the monstrumologist's eyes.

"I've never seen him cry—ever. He's come close before"—*I am a mote of dust*—"but it was always for himself. I think he loves Dr. Chanler very much."

"Do you? I don't. I don't think he loves him at all."

"Well, I don't think you know him at all." I was becoming angry.

"And I don't think you know *anything* at all," she shot back. Her eyes sparkled with delight. "Fell into the Danube by accident! He jumped off and nearly drowned."

"I know that," I said. "And Dr. Chanler saved him."

"But do you know *why* he jumped? And do you know what happened *after* he jumped?"

"He got very sick, and that's when Muriel and John met, over his sickbed," I said with a note of triumph. I would show her who didn't know anything!

"That isn't everything. It's hardly nothing. They were engaged to be married and—"

"I know that, too."

"All right, but do you know why they didn't?"

"The doctor is not constitutionally suited for marriage," said I, echoing Warthrop's explanation.

"Then why did he propose in the first place?"

"I—I don't know."

"See? You don't know anything." She smiled broadly; her cheeks dimpled.

"Okay," I sighed. "Why did he propose?"

"I don't know. But he did, and then the next day he jumped off the Kronprinz-Rudolph Bridge. He swallowed a gallon of the Danube and got pneumonia and a case of putrid sore throat, coughing up blood and vomiting *buckets* of black bile. He nearly died, Uncle said.

"They were madly, desperately in love. They were *the* item, here *and* on the Continent. He *is* quite handsome, when he cleans himself up, and *she* is lovelier than Helen, so everybody thought it was a *perfect* match. After Dr. Chanler fished him out of the river, she came and sat by his bed day and night. She called to him, and he called to her, though they sat right beside each other!"

She ran her fingers through her thick fall of curls and stared dreamily into the distance.

"Uncle introduced Pellinore to Muriel, so he blamed himself for what happened. When your doctor didn't get any better after two weeks in Vienna, Uncle shipped him off to a balneologist in Teplice, and that's when things got *really* bad."

She paused for dramatic effect. I found myself fighting the urge to grab her by the shoulders and physically shake the rest of the tale out of her. How often does our desire spring upon us unawares—and from what unexpected hiding places! There was so much about the man that was hidden from me—hidden to this day, I will confess. To now have even the smallest of peeks behind the heavy curtain . . . !

"He stopped eating," she continued. "He stopped sleeping. He stopped *talking*. Uncle was desperate with worry. For a whole month this went on—Pellinore in silence wasting away—until one day Uncle said to him, 'You must decide. Will you live or will you die?' And Pellinore said, 'What have I to live for?' And Uncle answered, 'That, only you can decide.' And then . . . he decided."

"What?" I whispered. "What did he decide?"

"He decided to live, of course! Oh, I'm beginning to think you *are* thickheaded, William Henry. Of *course* he decided to live, or you wouldn't be here, would you? It wasn't the perfect ending. The perfect ending would have been him deciding the opposite, because it's the best kind of love that kills. Love isn't worth anything unless it's tragic— look at Romeo and Juliet, or Hamlet and Ophelia. It's all there for anyone who isn't so thickheaded he can't see it."

The doctor returned shortly after ten that morning, his morning suit slightly rumpled, the black cravat that had to be tied *just so* now hanging limply over his collar and dotted with a dark greenish stain—most likely the regurgitations of his friend. When I asked how Dr. Chanler was faring, he replied tersely, "He is alive," and said no more.

The day had dawned overcast with a blustery wind from the north that brought a plethora of bad memories with it. Von Helrung and Lilly walked us to the curb. Warthrop turned to his old mentor upon seeing Bartholomew Gray in the driver's seat of the hansom.

"Where is Skala?" he demanded.

Von Helrung muttered a vague reply, and the doctor's face darkened in anger. "If you've sent him over there like some apish angel of death, *Meister* Abram, I shall have him picked up by the police."

I did not hear von Helrung's response; Lilly had collared me.

"Are you going to be at the congress today?" she asked.

"I suppose," I said.

"Good! Uncle has promised to take me, too. I will look for you, Will."

Before I could extend my hearty thanksgiving at this piece of wonderful news, the doctor pulled me into the cab.

"Straight to the Society, Mr. Gray!" he called, knocking sharply against the roof with the heel of his walking stick. He sat back and closed his eyes. He didn't look much healthier than his dying charge at Bellevue. Thus we are entwined with each another in a fateful dance, until one falls and we must let go, lest we both go down.

✳

I spent the majority of that rainy day on the third floor of the old opera house, in a cavernous room that may have once been a dance studio, while Warthrop attended a meeting of the editorial board of the *Encyclopedia Bestia,* the Society's exhaustive compendium of all malevolent creatures great and small, to which he was a contributing member. The gathering was chaired by a lanky Missourian by the name of Pelt, who possessed the most impressive handlebar mustache I had ever seen. Throughout the meeting Pelt munched on salt crackers, and I marveled at his ability to keep the crumbs from lodging in his mustache's complicated tangles. It was this same Dr. Pelt who would later admit that he was the author of the anonymous letter that had launched our latest foray into the singular wilds of monstrumology.

Having hardly slept the night before, I dozed off in my chair to the droning of the learned men, while the latest treatises were discussed, debated, and dissected, against the pleasant background music of the drumming rain upon the high arched windows. It was in this state of sweet semi-stupor that I received a sharp jab to my shoulder. Jerking awake, I looked up to see Lilly Bates beaming down at me.

"Here you are!" she whispered. "I've been looking everywhere for you. You might have told me where you'd be."

"I didn't know where I'd be," I said honestly.

She plopped onto the chair beside me and watched glumly as a phlegmatic little Argentinean with the rather remarkable name of Santiago Luis Moreno Acosta-Rojas droned on about the poor composition skills of monstrumologists in general. "I understand they are not men of letters, but how can they be such unlettered men?"

"This is dreadfully boring." Lillian stood abruptly and held out her hand.

"I can't leave the doctor," I protested.

"Why? He might need a footstool?" she asked sardonically. She pulled me to my feet and dragged me toward the door. I glanced back at my master, but he was oblivious, as was usual, to my plight.

"Quiet now," she whispered, leading me to a door across the hall, over which a sign had been posted: ABSOLUTELY NO ADMITTANCE. NOT AN EXIT.

The door opened to a flight of stairs that dove downward, the darkness beneath swallowing the pitifully small light of the jets that burned on each landing.

"I don't think we should be going down there," I said. "The sign . . ."

She ignored me, pulling me behind her as she descended this little-used shaft, hardly concerning herself with the narrow treads or the fact that there was no railing. The walls—moist and festooned with long strips of peeling black paint—pressed close on either side. Another door confronted us at the bottom landing, two stories beneath the street, and another sign:

MEMBERS ONLY—NO UNAUTHORIZED ADMITTANCE

"Lilly . . . ," I began.

"It's all right, Will," she assured me. "He falls asleep every afternoon around this time. We just have to be very quiet."

Before I could ask why it was all right, despite the signs that gave every indication it was not, or ask *who* fell asleep every afternoon around that time, she forced open the door with her shoulder and flapped her hand impatiently at me to follow, which, for reasons still inexplicable to me, I did.

The door clanged shut, plunging us into absolute darkness. We stood at the threshold of a forgotten hallway that led directly to the holy of holies of natural history's abhorrent darker side.

Its official title was the Monstrumarium (literally, "the house of monsters"), for it housed thousands of specimens collected from the four corners of the globe, from *Gigantopithecus*'s malevolent cousin *Kangchenjunga rachyyas* of the Himalayas to the microscopic but no less terrifying *Vastarus hominis* (its name literally means "to lay waste to humans") of the Belgian Congo. In 1875 a wag had nicknamed the Monstrumarium, in a fit of sottish wit, "the Beastie Bin," and the name had stuck.

The so-called Lower Monstrumarium into which Lilly and I now made our shuffling way—trailing our fingertips along the damp subterranean walls to keep our bearings in the dark—had been added to the original structure in 1867. A warren of winding passageways and claustrophobic low-ceilinged rooms, some no larger than a closet, the Lower

Monstrumarium was the repository for thousands of yet-to-be catalogued specimens and macabre curiosities. In room after room, shelves groaned under the weight of thousands of jars wherein unidentified bits of biomass floated in preserving solution, where for all I know they still sit to this day. A tiny percentage carried labels, and those contained only the name of the contributor (if known) and the date of the donation; the rest were innominate reminders of the vast constituents making up the monstrumological universe, the seemingly inexhaustible panoply of creatures designed by an inscrutable God to do us harm.

We entered a small antechamber, where Lilly grabbed a lamp that was hung upon an iron pike embedded in the concrete wall. The atmosphere was cool and musty. Our breaths pooled in the lamplight.

"Where are we going?" I asked.

"Quiet, Will!" she said, raising her voice slightly. "Or you'll wake up Adolphus."

"Who is Adolphus?" Immediately I was convinced that the dungeon was guarded by some gargantuan man-eating creature.

"Hush! Just follow me and be *quiet*."

Adolphus, as it turned out, was not in the Lower Monstrumarium that day. His business rarely brought him down there, for he wasn't a monstrumologist and didn't consider himself a zookeeper. He was, rather, the curator of the Monstrumarium proper.

Adolphus Ainsworth was a very old man who walked with a cane, the head of which was fashioned from the skull of the extinct *Ocelli carpendi*, a nocturnal predator about the size of a capuchin monkey, possessing six-inch razor-sharp fangs protruding from its upper jaw and a partiality for the human eyeball (if that of other primates was not available), particularly the eyes of children, which the *Ocelli* would rip from their sockets while they slept. Adolphus had named the skull Oedipus and thought himself quite clever, despite the inconvenient detail that Oedipus had plucked out his *own* eyes.

Adolphus Ainsworth was well into his fortieth year underground in that fall of '88, and the sunless years had taken their toll upon his complexion. His eyes were weak and rheumy, magnified threefold by his thick spectacles, and his coat was threadbare, the sleeves an inch too short and tattered. He trudged about the narrow corridors in a pair of old open-toed slippers, his toenails glimmering like polished bronze in the dim light.

A maxim emerged during his tenure as curator of the Monstrumarium, "You can smell Adolphus coming," referring to a development or event easily predictable, along the lines of "as surely as night follows day." The aroma of those subterranean floors—a foul mixture of formaldehyde, mildew, and decomposition—seemed to seep from his very pores. A certain monstrumologist who was close to him politely suggested the smell was being absorbed by his profusive muttonchops, and perhaps he should shave. Adolphus rebuked the man, protesting that, since he was as bald as a billiard ball, he intended to maintain what hair he could, and, moreover, he cared not how badly he smelled.

Though he was well into his eighth decade, his memory was prodigious. A researcher, after hours of wandering through the labyrinthine corridors and claustrophobic dusty chambers housing thousands of samples, his patience tried by the seemingly inchoate system of unmarked drawers and unlabeled crates stacked floor-to-ceiling, would find his complaints answered by a simple question: "Have you asked Adolphus?" Suppose you wished to examine the phalanges of the rare Ice Man of the Svalbard Archipelago. Adolphus would lead you right to its little compartment, indistinguishable from all the others in the cabinet, and would hover about you as you examined it, lest you return it to the wrong place and thus throw off his entire catalogue.

His office was located a floor above us, where he napped behind a desk buried in papers and books and pieces of calcified material that may or may not once have been living. The office itself was as disheveled as he—stacks and stacks of materials occupying every available surface, including most of the floor. A small, winding pathway though the mélange afforded the sole artery into his roost.

One floor beneath where he snoozed that rainy November afternoon, Lilly's lamp supplied what little light there was to navigate the forbidding snarl of dusty narrow halls of the Lower Monstrumarium, with their faint odor of formaldehyde, their patina of dust, and the occasional fitfully waving cobweb.

We came to a juncture of two corridors, and Lilly hesitated, swinging the lamp this way and that, chewing on her bottom lip.

"We're lost," I said.

"I thought I told you to be quiet!"

She took the passage to the left and, with little choice in the matter, I followed. She had the only light, after all, and I might have wandered those acheronian halls until I collapsed of exhaustion and died of slow starvation. Presently we came to a door labeled—ominously, I thought—UNCLASSIFIED 101.

"This is it. This is it, Will! Are you ready?"

"Ready for what?"

"I asked for *this* for my birthday, and instead I got a stupid old book."

She pushed opened the door, and a very familiar smell charged into the narrow hall. I'd been assaulted by it many times in my service to the monstrumologist—the unmistakable evidence of biological functions—the smell of animal waste and rotting meat.

Lining three walls of the small chamber were steel cages stacked on top of one another, most of which were empty—but for a bit of damp straw and a dry watering dish in each—but a few had occupants that scurried to the comforting shadows of their prisons or pressed their snouts hard against the mesh, slobbering and snarling with bestial rage at our intrusion. What manner of organisms they were, I could not say; the cages were not labeled and I did not possess the entirety of the monstrumological canon inside my head. I saw the flame reflected in furious eyes here, a snatch of fur or scaly hide there, a talon yanking at the steel wire, the tip of a serpentine tongue exploring the latch as if for weakness.

Lilly ignored the clamor and made straight for a table placed against the far wall, upon which sat a rectangular container made of thick glass. She set the lamp down beside it and motioned for me to come closer.

Within the terrarium I spied a three-inch layer of fine sand, a saucer filled with a viscous fluid that resembled blood, and several large rocks—a desert landscape in miniature. I could not see, however, anything living, even after she removed the heavy lid and instructed me to look closely.

"It's just a baby," she said, forced by the din to bring her lips to within an inch of my ear. "They grow as big as five feet, Uncle says. That's it there, that big lump. He likes to do that—bury himself in the sand—if it *is* a he. Uncle says they're very rare and worth a great deal of money, especially alive. They don't do well in captivity. There! Did you see him move? He hears us." The hidden thing undulated under its blanket of ochre grains.

"What is it?" I breathed.

"Silly, you're the monstrumologist-in-training. I've given

you enough clues. It lives in the desert; grows to five feet; very rare; and very valuable. I'll give you another clue: It's from the Gobi Desert."

I shook my head. Her mouth dropped open in astonishment at my ignorance, and she said, "I knew right away what it was, with fewer hints than that, William Henry. You haven't learned very much under Dr. Warthrop, have you? Either he's a very bad teacher or you're a very poor pupil. I know more than you, I'm beginning to think. Uncle says women aren't allowed into the Society, but *I* will be. *I* will be the very first female monstrumologist. What do you think of that? . . . Look! I think he's poking his snout out."

Indeed something was emerging from the undulating sand—a quarter-size puckered ring with a pitch-black center, crowding into which appeared to be tiny triangular teeth. It was undoubtedly the creature's mouth, but that is all I could identify; it had no eyes or nose or any other distinguishing feature, only the little mouth opening and closing like a sucker fish.

"The Mongolians are so frightened of them that even saying their name brings bad luck," Lilly said. "Since you don't know, I'll tell you. It's an *Allghoi khorkhoi*."

She watched my face, waiting for it to light up with the shock of recognition. *Ah, of course! The* Allghoi khorkhoi. Without thinking it through, still smarting from her disdainful disparagement of the quality of my training, in one of those moments we are doomed to regret, I slapped my forehead hard, as I'd seen the doctor do a thousand times, and cried, "Ah, of course! The *Allghoi khorkhoi*! I didn't think of that. They *are* very rare, so it never occurred to me you might actually have a *living* specimen! This is really something!"

Her eyes narrowed suspiciously. "So you *have* heard of it?"

"Yes, I have. Didn't I just say so?" I could not meet her gaze, though.

"Would you like to hold it?"

"Hold it?"

"Yes. So we may sex it."

"Sex it?"

"Why are you repeating everything I say? We have to know if it's a boy or girl so we can name it. You *do* know how to sex a *khorkhoi*, don't you?"

"Of course I do." I waved my hand dismissively—again, as I'd observed the doctor do innumerable times—and snorted. "It's like eating pie."

"Good!" she cried. "I've decided 'Mildred' if it's a girl and 'Howard' if it's a boy. Pick it up, Will, and let's see."

There was no escape now. What excuse was available to me? I might have claimed to have a severe allergy to the things, but she would have seen through that instantly. I might have feigned expertise in sexing a *khorkhoi* by the shape of its mouth, and thereby negate the need to touch it, but that, too, could backfire, confirming her original suspicion that I didn't know a *khorkhoi* from a hole in the ground.

Thus, having chosen the iron chains of deceit—bound, as it were, by my own buffoonery—I reached into the terrarium and gently slid my hand beneath the undulating worm, careful to keep my fingers far from its contracting mouth. It was heavier than I thought it would be, and thicker, about the circumference of my wrist, making it difficult to grasp with one hand. The task was made more problematic by the immediately apparent fact that the *khorkhoi* did not like to be held. It writhed in my palsied hand, twisting and turning the end with the mouth. (I could not call it its "head," for there was no delineation between its forefront and hindquarters but for the orifice.) Its body was reddish-brown and reminded me in its appearance and texture of cow intestine.

"Use both hands, Will," she whispered. So intent was I in maintaining my hold upon the creature that I did not notice she had scooted away, putting distance between herself and me and my charge.

It seemed a prudent suggestion. The creature must have been more than six inches long. I had picked it up toward the tail end, and the little puckering mouth bobbed and weaved freely in the air. Carefully I reached with my left hand to grab it. How the thing sensed, without eyes or nostrils, my approach, I do not know, but sense it the *khorkhoi* did.

Faster than I could blink, it struck, more like a rattlesnake than a worm. (Only later would I discover it was indeed a member of the reptile family.) It coiled and then snapped whiplike directly at my face, the diminutive mouth expanding to twice its original size, revealing row upon row of tiny teeth marching backward into the lightless tunnel of its gullet. Instinctively my head snapped back, which saved my face but exposed my neck. The last thing I saw before it attached itself were the teeth emerging from the recesses of the yawning pit of its mouth.

I did not feel the bite at first. Instead, I felt an enormous pressure as, by means of its rubbery lips, it affixed itself with leechlike determination, and then there was the slap of its body against my chest, for it had pulled free from my hand. It coiled itself partway around my neck and immediately began to squeeze, cutting off my air as simultaneously something fire-hot scorched the spot beneath its anchored mouth. A *khorkhoi*, I would later learn, does not eat the flesh of its victims, nor does it, in the strictest sense, drink their blood. More like the spider, it uses its toxic saliva to liquefy the flesh of its prey; its teeth are vestigial relics from its evolutionary past. The choking behavior is used, like the web of the arachnid, to immobilize. It goes without saying that it is very difficult to defend oneself while unconscious.

Mad with panic, I clawed at the monster. Lilly recoiled in horror. Her little game had spun out of control, and now she seemed paralyzed by its denouement. I stumbled against the table . . . lost my balance . . . fell. Dark flowers blossomed in my field of vision.

She screamed, her cries coming to me as if from a great

distance, and it was through the veil of that spinning, ever growing garden of raven blooms that I watched her run from the chamber, taking the light with her, leaving the darkness and the crazed residents of Unclassified 101 of the Lower Monstrumarium with me.

NINETEEN

"Whom Did I Betray?"

I was in that darkness for quite some time.

And when the darkness went away, the monstrumologist was with me.

"Are you awake now?" he asked.

I tried to speak. My effort was rewarded with searing pain, from my throat to my lungs, which felt as if a great stone had been laid upon them. At first my mind was completely blank; then I remembered where I was, and for that I was glad, because the pillow under my head was very soft—much softer than my pillow at Harrington Lane. The hotel bed was much larger than the one in the little loft—and for that I was glad too. There was even a warm rush of what I hesitate to call—but having no better word to describe it—pleasure, when his lean face swam into focus.

"Hello, sir," I croaked.

"Tell me, Will Henry, do you think you are in a little trouble or a great deal of trouble?"

"A great deal, sir."

"And you're fortunate that your luck is not commensurate with the amount of trouble. By all accounts, you should be dead."

"It would not be the first time, sir."

I touched the thick bandage wrapped around my neck. That small touch, like my first attempt at speech, was rewarded with agonizing pain.

"I wouldn't touch that if I were you," he said.

"Yes, sir," I managed to gasp.

"Why is it that every time I leave you to your own devices, you end up seriously injured? I am beginning to think I shall have to cart you around with me like an Indian babe in a papoose."

"It wasn't my idea, sir."

"No? Miss Bates placed the *khorkhoi* around your neck?"

"No, sir, she didn't touch it. I picked it up."

"And can you tell me why in the world you would pick up a Mongolian Death Worm?"

"To . . . sex it, sir."

"Dear Lord, Will Henry. Don't you know *khorkhoi* are hermaphroditic? They are both male and female."

"No, sir," I choked out. "I didn't know that."

"By now I'm sure it's occurred to you that the price of

ignorance in monstrumology can be quite steep."

"Oh, yes, sir."

"Ignorance could cost your life. Did you weigh that cost against the exigency of sexing the worm?" He did not wait for my answer. "I think not. Why *did* you do it, Will Henry? Why did you go somewhere you clearly had no business being?"

"Lilly . . ."

"Lilly! What—did she bop you over the head with a chair and carry you down to the Monstrumarium?"

"She said she wanted to show me something."

"A word of advice, Will Henry. When a person of the female gender says she wants to show you something, run the other way. The odds are it is not something you wish to see."

"Thank you, sir. I didn't know that."

He nodded gravely, but through my tears of pain, did I see his eyes dancing merrily in the lamplight?

"There is still much you do not," he said. "About science— and more esoteric phenomena."

"Esoteric phenomena?"

"Females. In this instance the same girl who brought you to the edge of death also yanked you back. If not for her quick thinking, your indispensable services would have been quite dispensed with. She ran straight to Professor Ainsworth and roused him, with no small amount of effort, and to his subsequent annoyance for missing his nap on account of two silly children playing where no child should ever play. It was Adolphus who saved your life, Will Henry, and to whom you owe all gratitude, which I suggest you express to him at your earliest convenience—at a safe distance, for I believe it is his intention to wrap his cane around your neck if you step foot in his dominion again."

I nodded, and winced, for the motion caused a hot bolt of pain.

The doctor fished a cloth from the washbasin on the bed stand. He wrung out the excess water and began bathing me, starting with my sweating forehead and working his way down. He bent to the task with his usual level of intense concentration, as if there existed the absolute ideal of giving a recalcitrant apprentice a sponge bath, a precise procedure he was determined to follow to the letter.

"The next few days are critical," he began in that lecturing tone I'd heard a hundred times before. "Your good fortune includes the fortuitous fact that Adolphus keeps a supply of *khorkhoi* anti-venom on hand in the *heretofore* unlikely event of two children sneaking into the Lower Monstrumarium for the purpose of sexing something that by its nature cannot be sexed. *However*, the extent of that good fortune is mitigated by the nature of the venom. It is extremely slow-acting. In the wild the Death Worm may go for months without eating, so it relies on its venom to keep its prey more or less immobile while it feasts—for days— upon its living flesh.

"The venom is a narcotic, Will Henry, known for its hallucinogenic attributes. Native tribesmen harvest it and ingest it in small doses for its opium-like effects, sometimes by diluting it in distilled liquor or, which is more common, by smoking rabbit weed that has been treated with it. You must tell me immediately if you start to see things that by all reason should not be there, and I will have to keep a close eye on you for indications of paranoia and delusional thinking. The latter poses the greater threat, since one might argue it's your *normal* mode of operation. You'll be fine one moment, and the next you may be convinced you can fly or that you've sprouted a second head, which in your case would not be a particularly bad thing. Another brain could not hurt."

He was examining the earlier wound, the spot on my chest where John Chanler's teeth had bored into me.

"What else?" he asked rhetorically. "Well, you may experience an intense burning sensation when you urinate. In particularly sensitive individuals, circulation is lost to the extremities, gangrene sets in, and the appendage must be amputated. You may lose your hair. Your testicles might swell. There have been cases of spontaneous hemorrhagic bleeding from the orifices, particularly the anus. Your kidneys could shut down, your lungs could fill with fluid, and you could literally drown in your own mucus. Am I leaving anything out?"

"I hope not, sir."

He wrung out the cloth, pulled down my nightshirt, and arranged the covers around me.

"Now, are you hungry?"

"No, sir."

"Do you think you can manage to stay out of trouble while I check on my other patient?"

"Lilly?" For some reason my heart fluttered with dread.

"As is so often the case, the instigator of the misdeed has escaped unscathed. I was speaking of Dr. Chanler."

"Oh! No, sir, I'll be fine."

"If you do get hungry later, ring the front desk and have them send something up. Soft foods, Will Henry, and nothing too spicy."

The phone in the outer room rang, startling him. He was not expecting a call. He left to answer it and returned a moment later, running his fingers through his hair.

"I'm closing the door, Will Henry. Try to sleep now."

I promised I would try. I closed my eyes dutifully. Presently I heard voices coming from the sitting room. Were they real? I wondered. Or was this the venom talking? One was low-pitched, a man's, the other's register higher—clearly a woman's. *Muriel*, I thought. *Muriel has come to see the doctor. Why?* Had something happened to Dr. Chanler? Had he finally succumbed? I fancied I heard the sound of her crying. *The end has come*, I thought, my heart going out first to her and then, with a stabbing rush of grief, to my master. I saw him in my mind's eye trudging for mile after mile in the unforgiving wilderness, cradling her husband in his arms. I heard the desperate existential cry shouted in the sound-crushing atmosphere: *Why did you come here? What did you think you would find?*

Why *had* he gone into the wilderness? In Rat Portage he had seemed to mock von Helrung's proposal and the man he'd claimed was responsible for it. Why, then, had he gone in search of something he did not believe existed? Had it been, as the doctor had theorized, a sycophantic act or an overly zealous show of filial devotion to a beloved teacher? What had driven Chanler to risk his life for something he himself admitted was a chimera, a fairy tale?

The voices without rose and fell, like the currents of a spring-fed mountain stream. Yes, I decided, it was their voices, the doctor's and Muriel's, most definitely. After a while I convinced myself of their verity. They did not exist solely between my ears, but outside them.

I am not proud of what I did next.

A short hall led from our rooms to the living quarters. Thankfully, the jets here were not lit, and I navigated the distance in semidarkness. Slowly—oh, so slowly—lying upon the floor on my belly like an advancing marine, I slid forward until, while comfortably reclining on my stomach, I could observe unseen from the shadows.

She was sitting on the divan, wearing a fashionable riding cloak over a lavender gown of taffeta and velvet. Though from my vantage point her lovely emerald eyes appeared dry, she worried with a handkerchief in her lap. I could not see the doctor, but following her gaze, I determined he must have been near the fireplace—standing, if I knew Warthrop. In moments of stress the doctor either stood or paced about like a caged lion. And this was definitely a stressful moment.

"... confess that I am having some difficulty understanding why you've come," he was saying.

"They're insisting upon discharging him," she said.

"That's ridiculous. Why wouldn't they want him there? Do they wish for him to die?"

"It's Archibald—his father. He's furious at you for taking him there without his permission. And he's terrified the papers will get wind of it. That's why we didn't commit him in the first place. Archibald would hear none of it."

"Yes, how foolish of me," the doctor said sarcastically, "not to consult the great Archibald Chanler before saving his son's life!"

"You know how he's always felt about John's . . . profession. It embarrasses him, brings shame to the family. He is very proud—not a man who takes ridicule easily. You should be able to understand that at least."

"It would be prudent of you, Muriel, to avoid insulting me while on a mission to enlist my aid."

She forced a smile. "But you make it so easy to do."

"No. You *find* it too easy to do."

"If I retract it, will you help me?"

"I will do, as I have always done, everything within my power to help my friend."

"That's all I can ask."

"Is it?" His voice dropped. "Is that all you can ask?"

"Perhaps not. But it is all that I will for now."

His long shadow stretched over her, falling across her face—the downcast eye, the slightly lowered chin, the broken look of loss. She rose. Shadow met the man, and I saw him approach her, stop; with his back to me, he obliterated her from my sight.

"Are you prepared, Muriel? They may not be able to save him."

"I have been prepared since Rat Portage. I do not say 'since he came back,' because he never came back, Pellinore. John never came back."

She fell into him. He rocked back on his heels, not expecting it, and his long arms enfolded her instinctively. He looked down at her. He could see her upturned face, of course; I could not—and wished that I could.

"Where is he?" she asked. "Where is John?"

"Muriel, you know I—"

"Oh, I do. I know exactly what you're going to say. You're going to say I'm being hysterical, that I'm a hysterical female and I shouldn't worry my pretty little head, that I should let the strong and capable man take care of things. You're going to tell me there is a perfectly rational, scientific explanation for why my husband has become a monster."

"Your husband is suffering from a well-documented form of psychosis, Muriel, named for the mythical creature he was foolish enough to go hunting after. It has been exacerbated by physical hardship and deprivation—perhaps even torture—"

She pulled from his arms, straightened her hat, and said with a laugh, "See? I knew you would say that. You're so damned predictable that I wonder how I ever thought I loved you."

"Millions love the sun. The sun is predictable."

"Was that an attempt at humor?"

"I was merely being logical."

"You should take care with that, Pellinore. Your logic may kill someone one day."

She was pressed between the divan and Warthrop. As she stepped to one side to make her escape, he shifted with her, blocking the way.

"What are you doing?" she demanded.

"Acting unpredictably."

She laughed nervously. "I can think of only one other time when you did that."

"John accuses me of putting on a show. That I jumped in order to be rescued."

"Still, it surprised me. I was shocked when I heard the news."

"Which part? My jumping or his saving me?"

"I never understood why, Pellinore."

"We share in that, Muriel. I still don't understand why."

He stepped to one side, and I could see her again. Though her exit had been unblocked, she remained.

"Should I leave?" she asked. I could not tell if she was asking him—or herself. She was looking toward the door as if it stood at the end of a thousand-mile journey.

"It probably would be best," he answered softly.

"It's something you would do," she said with a note of wistfulness. "Entirely predictable."

"And perfectly logical."

I missed who moved first. Whether a trick of the light or the result of my poisoned anatomy, it seemed that neither moved first; their hands did not touch . . . and then their hands touched. She remained half-turned toward the door, Warthrop half-turned toward the window opposite, and her hand lightly brushed the back of his.

"I hate you, Pellinore Warthrop," she said without looking at him. "You are selfish. And you are vain. Even rescuing him was an act of vanity. He was . . . *is* twice the man you are. He risked his life because he loved you. You risked yours merely to prove him wrong."

The doctor did not respond. He stood ramrod straight, head slightly bowed, in an attitude of prayer.

"I pray every night that there is a God—that there is judgment for our sins," she went on in a level voice, now running her fingers, feather light, up and down his arm. "So you might spend an eternity in the deepest pit of hell with all the other betrayers."

"Whom did I betray?" he wondered aloud. He did not sound angry, only curious. "I brought him out."

Her hand fell away. He stiffened as if the loss of her touch were a blow.

"*You sent him there.* If not for you, he never would have gone."

"That's ridiculous. I didn't even know about it until you told me—"

"He always knew there would be a reckoning. He wouldn't admit it to himself—he was not an introspective man like you—but in his heart he knew there would be a price and that he would be the one to pay it."

"A price, you say. A price for what?"

"For love. For you loving me and—" Her voice faltered. "And for my loving you."

"But you hate me. You just said so."

She laughed. "Oh, Pellinore. How can a man so intelligent be so utterly dense? Why is John Chanler my husband?"

He did not answer. She moved closer; he still would not look at her.

"John knew the answer to that question," she said. "And John is not half as bright as you."

"I can think of a better question. Why are you his wife?"

She struck him across the cheek. He received it with more stoicism than he had when she'd withdrawn her touch. He barely moved.

"I wish you had died there," she said matter-of-factly.

"You nearly got your wish."

"Not in Canada. In Vienna. If you had died in Vienna,

I could have played the grieving fiancée and prostrated myself upon your premature grave. John would now be happily married to some bird-witted New York socialite, and I would have fallen in love again. I would not be in this hell of loving a man whom I despise, for as long as you walk this earth, I shall love you, Pellinore. As long as you draw breath anywhere—here or ten thousands miles from here—I will love you. I can't help loving you, so I choose to hate you . . . to make my love bearable."

"You— You should not— Muriel, there are certain things we should never . . ." For the first time in my memory, the monstrumologist struggled for words. "You should not tell me these things."

"No, I want you to hear them. I want you to know I still love you. I want you to think about it for the rest of your pitiable life. You abandoned me for a cold and heartless mistress, and on the day Will Henry finally leaves you for good, I want you to think about it, and each day thereafter until you are old and dying alone on your deathbed, until the debt is repaid, unto the final reparation for your cruelty."

Like a falling man who grabs whatever might be nearby, no matter how flimsy, he said, "Will Henry will never leave me."

I was back in bed when he opened the bedroom door. Through slitted lids I watched him watch me. The door eased closed. Then it opened again. He said my name. I did not answer. He shut the door.

I heard their voices pick up again. Or thought I did. I was terribly hot suddenly, and my breath was quick. I wondered if I was coming down with a fever. Perhaps it was not voices I heard at all but the echoes of them, the memory made tangible by the Death Worm's venom. I had retreated to my bedroom when he'd walked her to the door—surely Muriel had gone. I began to sweat. Paranoia . . . delusions . . . burning urine. I ticked them off one by one. Gangrene . . . bleeding. I reached under my nightshirt and gingerly touched my testicles. Had they grown any? How would I know if they had? It was not as if I measured them every morning.

In the outer room the murmuring gently swelled, receded. Closing my eyes, I had the sensation of something slipping, a loosening, like a poorly tied knot unraveling, and the voices undulated in what had been loosed in me, a sensuous undercurrent beneath the surface of the vast sea in which I found myself floating.

The latter poses the greater threat. . . . You'll be fine one moment, and the next you may be convinced you can fly.

I cannot attest to things my eyes have not seen.

And I do not mean to disparage them.

I know I was not myself; I know in my blood swam the poison.

But in the outer room there were voices and then there were none; there was no closing of the door or the bidding of good night.

In the outer room the voices fall and do not rise again. In the empty space where they had been, a woman lifts her emerald eyes. In them the mirror that defines him, that gives him shape and substance. Without their light his shadow has more substance than he.

What have we given?

He stumbles alone through a broken landscape; the wind whistles in the dry bones; there is no water.

In her eyes, the spring.

What have we given?

He has seen what the yellow eye sees; he has prayed in the abandoned cathedral among the dry bones, kneeling in the ruins; he has heard his name spoken by the high wind, by the dry limbs strumming the sterile air.

He has known these things. He is the monstrumologist. Too long he has been in the desolation.

Now, in her eyes, the abundance.

Some would judge them. I do not. If it was a sin, it was sanctified—the trespass consecrated by the act itself. He met himself in the purity of her eyes and obtained absolution upon her altar.

In the outer room their shadows meet and become one. The starving man eats; he drinks his fill from the pure waters overflowing. Her sweet breath. Her skin golden in the firelight.

For a moment, at least, he tastes what his enigmatic mistress, the one for whom he rejected this love, cannot provide. In the abundance of her emerald eyes, Pellinore Warthrop found himself in another human being at last.

FOLIO VI
Reparation

"IN THIS METROPOLIS, LET IT BE UNDERSTOOD, THERE IS NO PUBLIC STREET WHERE THE STRANGER MAY NOT GO SAFELY BY DAY AND BY NIGHT."
—JACOB RIIS

TWENTY

"A Beautiful Day"

He burst into my room early the next morning bearing a tray burdened with eggs, toast, pancakes, sausages, cranberry muffins, apple cobbler, and orange juice. My startled expression upon this completely unexpected and uncharacteristic display of largess did not go unnoticed. He laughed aloud and placed the tray before me with a flourish; he even snapped the napkin open and arranged it with great formality around my bandaged neck.

"Well, Master Henry," he cried in a disconcertingly joyful voice. "You look terrible!" He strode to the window and threw back the curtains. Brilliant sunlight flooded the room. "But it is a beautiful day—a beautiful day! Truly, the kind of day that stirs the slumbering poet in a man. We've been much too long in the doldrums, you and I, and we must work

to remedy our dour outlook. Without hope a man is no better than a draft horse pulling the heavy dray of his woes."

He laid a hand upon my forehead. He measured my
pulse. He examined my eyes. He chuckled when I stared
with near incomprehension at the feast laid before me.

"No, you are not suffering from a hallucination. Eat up!
I have decided to skip this morning's colloquia and explore a
bit of this marvelous city. Do you know I have been coming
here for fifteen years and have barely seen it? I wear a path
from the hotel to the Society and back again, blinders firmly
in place like the dray horse of my metaphor, never venturing
off the beaten path . . . too much in love with routine—and
routine is a kind of death too. What? Why are you looking
at me like that? Does your throat hurt too much to speak?"

"No, sir."

"How is your stomach? Do you think you can eat?"

I picked up the fork. "I think so, sir."

"Marvelous! I've been thinking . . . first we should take
the ferry over to Liberty Island to have a look at Monsieur
Bartholdi's statue. You know, he is a friend of mine—not
Bartholdi. The builder, Eiffel. Well, not precisely a friend,
more of an acquaintance. An interesting little story about
Eiffel. As you know, the International Exhibit is next year in
Paris, and the government wants to commission a suitable
monument to commemorate the centennial of the revolu-
tion. Well! Eiffel wrote to me about his plans to—"

The ringing of the telephone interrupted him. He

dashed from the room. I sipped my orange juice—"golden nectar," Lilly had called it—and heard him say, "Yes, yes, of course. I shall be right down."

He appeared in the doorway, his entire being transformed. Gone were the uncharacteristic sparkle in his eye and the rare spring in his step.

"I must go," he said.

"Why?" I asked. "What's happened?"

"It is . . . You should stay here, Will Henry. I don't know how long I'll be."

I placed the tray to one side and threw back the covers. He watched impassively as I struggled out of bed and stood swaying in my stocking feet.

"I feel fine, sir. Really, I do. Please take me with you."

A young officer of the Metropolitan Police Department came forward as we stepped off the elevator. Short of stature, dressed in a freshly starched uniform, with a shock of red hair and a round baby face sprinkled with freckles, he looked much too young for the role, like a child playing dress-up. He saluted Dr. Warthrop smartly and introduced himself as Sergeant Andrew Connolly. We followed him to a brougham carriage waiting at the curb.

Warthrop had been right. It *was* a beautiful day, chilly but cloudless, the bright morning sun etching sharp shadows and chiseling the buildings into exquisite relief. As we rattled south within sight of the choppy waters of the East River, I glanced at the doctor, wondering if I should risk asking him again what had happened—though I was certain it could be only one thing: John Chanler was dead.

Our carriage drew up before a block-length structure on the banks of the river—Bellevue, the nation's oldest public hospital. We followed Sergeant Connolly through a side door, up the dimly lit stairs to the fourth floor, and then down a long, narrow corridor whose walls had been painted a ghastly institutional pale green. Connolly knocked once upon the door at the terminus of this depressing passageway.

We were admitted at once by another uniformed officer who, with Connolly, stood at rigid attention by the door throughout the tense scene that followed.

The room was icy cold; the autumnal wind whistled through the broken window over the bed. A knot of plain-clothes detectives were gathered around the foot of it, watching two of their colleagues crouching over something on the floor. One of the men—an imposing figure with an impressive chest and an equally impressive mustache—turned when we entered. He scowled, his full lips clamped tightly around an unlit cigar.

"Warthrop. Good. Thank you for coming," he said in a thick Irish brogue. His gratitude was expressed gruffly, a formality to be promptly dispensed with.

"Chief Inspector Byrnes," the doctor returned tightly.

"But what's this?" asked Byrnes, glowering at me. "Who is this child and why is he here?"

"He is not a child; he is my assistant," returned the monstrumologist.

I was a child, of course, in most men's eyes, but the doctor saw things differently from most men.

Byrnes grunted noncommittally, studying me from beneath his bushy eyebrows, the right side of his prodigious mustache twitching. Then he shrugged.

"He's over here," the chief detective of the Metropolitan Police said. "Watch your step; it's slippery."

The men at the foot of the bed moved aside, like a human curtain pulling back. Lying on his back in a pool of coagulating blood was Augustin Skala—or what was left of him. I might not have recognized him if not for the size of the man and the tattered peacoat, for Augustin Skala had no face and no eyes. The empty sockets sought out the blank canvas of the off-white ceiling tiles.

His shirt had been torn open, exposing his hairy torso, in the middle of which yawned a hole the size of a pie plate. Protruding from the hole's jagged lip was a portion of his dislodged heart, partially ripped from its moorings and missing large bite-size chunks.

It was the heart that drew Warthrop's attention. He knelt beside the body, heedless of the tacky blood, to examine it.

"The nurse found him around seven o'clock this morning," said Byrnes.

"Where have you taken Chanler?" the doctor asked, not turning from his task.

"I haven't taken him anywhere. Dr. Chanler is gone."

"Gone?" Warthrop looked up at him sharply. "What do you mean—gone where?"

"I was hoping you could help with the answer to that question."

The door flew open, and von Helrung hurried into the room, his wide face flushed, hair flying willy-nilly around his square head.

"Pellinore! Thank God, you are here. Oh, this is terrible. Terrible!"

The doctor rose, his pants now soaked in Skala's blood. "Von Helrung, where is John?"

"Dr. Chanler has disappeared," said Byrnes before von Helrung could answer. He nodded toward the shattered window. "We think through there."

Warthrop stepped over to the window and looked down four stories to the ground below. "Impossible," he murmured.

"The door was locked from the inside," Byrnes rumbled. "Chanler is gone. There is no other explanation."

"The laws of nature demand another, Inspector," snapped the doctor. "Unless you propose that he sprouted wings and flew away."

Byrnes glanced at von Helrung, and then curtly told his men to wait outside, leaving the four of us alone with the remains of Augustin Skala.

"Dr. von Helrung has informed me of the particulars of Dr. Chanler's case."

Warthrop threw up his hands and said, "John Chanler is suffering from the mental and physical effects of a particular dementia, Inspector, called the Wendigo Psychosis. It has a well-documented history in the literature—"

"Yes, he mentioned this Wendigo business."

"It is finished," von Helrung put in gravely. "He has gone fully to *Outiko* now."

Warthrop groaned. "Inspector, I beg you not to listen to this man. I appeal to your reason. What man—much less a man in John Chanler's condition—could withstand a fall from a four-story window without suffering such injuries as to make escape impossible?"

"I'm not a doctor. All I know is that he's missing and that window was the only way out."

"He rides the high wind now," pronounced von Helrung.

"Shut *up!*" cried Warthrop, jabbing his index finger in the older man's face. "You may have enlisted Byrnes in this madness, but I will have no part of it." He turned to Byrnes. "I wish to speak with the nurse."

"She has gone home for the day," answered Byrnes. "She is quite shaken, as you might imagine."

"He *must* have walked out. . . ."

"Then he made himself invisible," countered the chief inspector. "There's always a nurse on this floor, and doctors and orderlies going about besides. He would have been seen."

"There have been some eyewitness accounts of—," von Helrung began.

"*Not . . .* another . . . word," Warthrop growled at his old master. He turned back to Byrnes. "Very well. I will allow for the moment that he somehow managed to endure the fall without losing the ability to ambulate. I assume you have men searching for him; he could not have gotten far in his condition."

A man came into the room at that moment—around von Helrung's age but taller and more athletic of build, well-dressed in a tailcoat and top hat, with piercing eyes and a thrust-forward chin.

"Warthrop!" he cried, marching straight to the doctor and striking him with the back of his hand.

The doctor touched the corner of his mouth and found blood. The blow had opened up his bottom lip.

"Archibald," he said. "Delighted to see you again too."

"*You* brought him here!" John Chanler's father shouted. The sole policeman in the room did not try to intervene; he seemed to be enjoying the show.

"This is a hospital," replied the doctor. "The usual spot for the sick and injured."

"And your spot as well when I'm finished with you! How dare you, sir! You had no right!"

"Don't speak to me of rights," Warthrop shot back. "Your son had the right to live."

The elder Chanler snorted angrily and whirled on Inspector Byrnes. "I want him found posthaste, with as little fuss and bother as possible, Detective. The quicker this matter is resolved, the better. And under no circumstances are you or anyone in your department to speak to the press. I will not have the Chanler name dragged through the muckraking penny dailies!"

Byrnes concurred with a brief nod, his lips curling around the dead stogie with disgust. "I'll shoot any man who even whispers the name, sir."

Chanler confronted the doctor again, saying, "I am holding you fully responsible, Warthrop. I've already spoken to my attorneys about your unconscionable negligence in regard to my son's treatment, and I can assure you, sir, there will be a reckoning. There will be reparations paid!"

He turned on his heel and stormed from the room. Warthrop gave an exaggerated sigh. "His concern is touching."

He turned to von Helrung. "Does Muriel know yet?"

"I sent word through Bartholomew," answered von Helrung. "He's bringing her to my house. She should be safe there."

"Safe?" the monstrumologist echoed. "Safe from what?" He didn't wait for an answer. "Detective, I shall for the moment accept the ludicrous proposition that John walked away from a fall out that window—and suggest you confine your dragnet to the immediate vicinity. He could not have gotten very far."

"There are certain other measures we should discuss first," von Helrung put in urgently. "For the well-being of your men."

"Abram, this is not the time—," began Warthrop.

"It cannot be brought down by ordinary bullets," von Helrung said, speaking over him. "They must be silver, and then only by a shot to the heart. You may fill its skull with twenty rounds and still fail to drop it. It has gone into hiding till nightfall. Look to a high place well away from human traffic, but don't confine your search to the immediate vicinity. It could be miles away by now. Spare no man; enlist every able-bodied officer in the hunt. I would suggest you contact the state militia as well."

Byrnes grunted. "I cannot very well mobilize the entire state of New York, Dr. von Helrung. You heard Mr. Chanler. I'm to keep this as quiet as possible."

"Oh, for God's sake!" Warthrop cried. "You can find him in five minutes with a single policeman and a bloodhound!"

"I defer to your judgment, Inspector," said von Helrung as if Warthrop hadn't spoken. "But you must prosecute the matter with all alacrity. These hours are critical. It must be found before night comes."

Byrnes's eyes widened at the injunction. "Why? What happens when night comes?"

"It will begin to hunt. And it will not stop hunting. It *cannot* stop, for now the hunger drives it. It will kill and feed until someone kills *it.*"

The doctor shook his head vehemently and spoke to Byrnes. "But before you do any of that, Detective, I suggest you speak with his attending physician and enlighten yourself as to John's physical condition—"

"Not so frail he couldn't overcome Augustin Skala," von Helrung noted triumphantly. "And how with such speed? Skala was alive and well when the night nurse checked on John at the end of her shift. Seven minutes later her relief walked in to *this*."

"It proves nothing, von Helrung."

"Does it not? Mortally wound a man twice his size, cut free the heart, remove the eyes and the face . . . all in seven minutes! I could not do it. Could you?"

"I most certainly could."

"That's very interesting," Byrnes put in, smiling dangerously around his cigar. "Quite talented, you monstrumologists, aren't you?"

Von Helrung urged the doctor to accompany him to his house. "Muriel is there; she needs you now, Pellinore," he said, but Warthrop refused to leave before he examined the alley from where Byrnes insisted Chanler must have made his getaway. He found nothing to sustain his objections to the absurd suggestion that this was the mode of escape. It was as if Chanler had somehow sprouted wings and flown into the blue. Warthrop did note a drainpipe that passed within a foot of the window.

"Perhaps he climbed up to the roof," he mused.

"By your own logic, impossible," pointed out von Helrung. "If he was as impaired as you say, Pellinore."

The monstrumologist sighed. "You examined him, von

Helrung. You know as well as I the extent of his impairment. It is confounding to me why you insist upon choosing the outrageous explanation over the rational one. What has happened to you? Have you suffered some kind of brain injury? Are you under the influence of a narcotic? Why do you persist, *Meister* Abram, in this bizarre and wholly disconcerting behavior? It's quite embarrassing to hear you prattle on to the authorities about silver bullets and men riding the wind like swallows."

"As the times change, so must we, Pellinore, or face certain extinction."

"Science is about progress, von Helrung. The things you are talking about belong to our superstitious past. It is a step backward."

"Let us just say there are more things in heaven and earth than are dreamt of in your philosophy."

The monstrumologist snorted. He scrubbed the bottom of his shoe upon the pavement; the broken glass from the shattered window crunched beneath his foot.

"My philosophy does not extend that far, *Meister* Abram. Heaven I leave to the theologians."

"If so, I do pity you, *mein lieber Freund.* If the theologians are right—and if I am, in this—you will live to regret it."

Warthrop looked at him sharply, but he smiled ruefully. "I already live with that," he said.

TWENTY-ONE
"I Do Not Think We Will Find Him"

Muriel Chanler was waiting for us in the von Helrung parlor. She rushed to Warthrop, threw her arms around him, and pressed her face into his chest. Warthrop murmured her name. He stroked her auburn hair. Von Helrung turned his head and coughed politely, ending the moment. The two withdrew quickly from each other's arms.

"Have they found him yet?" she asked.

"If not, it will be soon," the doctor said firmly. "In his condition he could not have gotten far."

"Muriel, *liebchen*, perhaps you would like to find little Will something to eat?" suggested von Helrung. "He is looking very pale to me."

"I'm not hungry," I said. I was, I will admit, deeply concerned about the doctor's mental state. I'd not witnessed him this close to breaking since those awful days in the wilderness.

"I hope you're right," Muriel was saying to him now. "And I hope *Meister* Abram is wrong. I hope it was someone else who murdered Skala."

"He is in the wrong about practically everything," the doctor allowed. "Except that."

She turned her lovely face away. Warthrop raised his hand as if to console her, then allowed it to fall.

"I'll see to it he has the best defense possible, Muriel," he promised. "And of course I will testify on his behalf. I'll see to it a proper place is found for him."

"An asylum," she whispered.

"Please, please, you must be strong, Muriel; you must be strong for John," said von Helrung, taking her by the elbow and guiding her to a chair. "Here. Sit. You will listen to your uncle Abram now, yes? There is a time to grieve, but that time is not yet! What shall Bartholomew bring you? Would you like some brandy? A glass of sherry, perhaps?"

She looked past him to Warthrop. "I want my husband."

The doctor demanded a word alone with von Helrung. They retired to the older man's study and shut the door. After a moment I could hear their row; the doctor was upbraiding him for telling the police they were hunting a mythical beast when their quarry was nothing more than a terribly disturbed man.

I looked over and found Muriel smiling at me through her lingering tears.

"Whatever happened to your neck, Will?" she asked.

I avoided those penetratingly beautiful eyes, casting my own upon the Persian carpet and mumbling, "It was an accident, ma'am."

"Well, I didn't think it was something deliberate!" She laughed in spite of herself. "It isn't easy, is it? Serving a monstrumologist."

"No, ma'am. It is not."

"Especially if his name happens to be Pellinore Warthrop."

"Yes, ma'am."

"So why do you?"

"My father served him. And when he died, I had nowhere else to go."

"And now I shall guess you are *indispensable* to him."

She smiled at my startled expression.

"Oh, yes," she said. "I have little doubt he's told you that. He used to tell me the same thing, but that was a very long time ago. Do you love him, Will?"

The question rendered me speechless. Love—the monstrumologist?

"I shouldn't ask that," she went on. "It is none of my business. I know he is all that you have. He was once the same to me. But a house cannot be built upon sand, Will. Does that make any sense to you? Do you know what I mean?"

I shook my head slowly. I did not.

"It used to comfort me to think he was incapable of love—that in no way should I take what happened between us personally. But I think I understand now. It isn't love he lacks—he loves more fiercely than any other man I have ever known—it is courage."

"Dr. Warthrop is the bravest man in the world," I said. "He's a monstrumologist. He's not afraid of anything."

"I understand," she replied gently. "You're just a boy and you see him through different eyes."

I had nothing to say to that. For some reason I heard his voice, echoing in a snowbound clearing, *You disgust me.* I lowered my head, and felt the memory of his arms pulling me close, his warm breath on my neck.

She sensed my distress, and her heart was moved with pity. "He is quite fond of you, you know," she said.

I searched out her expression. Was she teasing me?

"Oh, yes," she continued, smiling. "Worries about you like a mother hen. It's quite sweet—and quite unlike him. Just last night he was saying—"

She stopped herself. She looked away. I saw that she was blushing.

By the time the two monstrumologists had suspended their debate, she was ready to leave. Though von Helrung pleaded, there was nothing he could say that would change her mind.

"I will not hole up here like a frightened kitten," she said.

"If they don't catch him first, he'll find his way home, and I want to be there when he does."

"I will come with you," the doctor said.

She avoided his eyes. "No," she said simply. But Warthrop would not let it go; he followed her to the door, pressing his case urgently while he helped her with her wrap.

"You should not go alone," he said.

"Don't be silly, Pellinore. I am not afraid of him. He is my husband."

"He is not in his right mind."

"A defect not uncommon among you monstrumologists," she teased him. She spoke to his reflection. She was adjusting her hat in the hall mirror.

"Can we be serious for a moment?"

"Describe a moment when you were not."

"You'll be safe here."

"My place is at home, Pellinore. *Our* home."

He was taken aback by this; he did not attempt to hide it. He said, "Then I am coming with you."

"To what purpose?" she demanded. She turned from the mirror, the color high in her cheeks. "To protect me from my own husband? If he is as sick as you say, why should you feel the need?"

He had no ready answer. She smiled, and lightly touched his wrist with her gloved hand.

"I am not afraid," she repeated. "Besides, it would not do, a married lady in my position entertaining a gentlemen without my husband present. What would people think?"

"I don't care what they think. I care about . . ."

He would not—or could not—finish the thought. He raised his hand as if to touch her cheek, quickly dropping it again when he saw me out of the corner of his eye.

"Will Henry," he snapped. "Why are you constantly hovering about me like Banquo's ghost?" He turned back to her. "Very well. Your blasted stubbornness has worn me down, madam. But surely you can't protest to Bartholomew staying with you."

Von Helrung thought it was a capital idea, and Muriel relented to mollify them. She seemed amused by their concern.

"And you will ring me when you've arrived. Don't make me worry, *liebchen!*" von Helrung called to her from the doorway. He waited until the hansom had melted into the traffic, before closing the door. With a heavy sigh he ran a pudgy hand through his hair.

"My heart is troubled for her, Pellinore. Dear Muriel is in shock. The truth has not yet sunk in that John is lost to us forever."

"I do wish you'd stop with that melodramatic drivel," my master said. "It grates on my nerves. He may be lost, as you say, but it will be for considerably shorter than forever. I expect Inspector Byrnes will be calling within the hour to notify us of his death or capture."

The call did not come that hour or the next or the next. Shadows crept across Fifth Avenue. Von Helrung smoked cigar after cigar, filling the room with the noxious fumes, while the doctor paced, obsessively flipping open his pocket watch. Warthrop would occasionally pause before the window to scan the street for the chief inspector's brougham. At a quarter past four, with the sun slipping toward the Hudson, the maid poked her head into the room to inquire if the doctor and his ward would be staying for supper.

Warthrop shuddered at the question; it seemed to break inertia's hold upon him.

"I think Will Henry and I will head over to Mulberry Street," he said. "We can wait for word at police headquarters as well as here. Ring for us there if you hear anything, *Meister* Abram."

The cigar fell from the old man's mouth and rolled across the expensive carpet. "What?" he cried, leaping out of his chair. "*Lieber Gott*, what is the matter with me? How could I be so stupid?"

He rushed to the front door, calling for the maid to have Timmy—the livery boy—bring around the calash. He patted his pockets frantically, finally withdrawing from some inner recess of his jacket a pearl-handled derringer.

"What is it?" Warthrop demanded.

"It may be nothing—or it may be everything, Pellinore. In my distracted state I completely forgot, and now I pray it means nothing—I do pray so! Here." He pulled a long-bladed knife sheathed in leather from another pocket and pressed it into the doctor's hands. "Remember, aim for the heart! And never—*never!*—look into its eyes!"

He flung open the door and raced to the curb, where a boy not much older than me sat holding the reigns to a low-slung calash. We hurried after him. "Tell me what you forgot, von Helrung!" Warthrop demanded.

"Muriel, *mein Freund*. Muriel! She never called."

Situated a few blocks north of the Plaza Hotel at Central Park, the Chanler residence sat squarely in the middle of Millionaires' Row, palatial abodes lining Fifth Avenue above Fiftieth Street, mansions of such staggering size and architectural extravagance that they perfectly reflected the ethos of their owners. Here lived the titans of American capitalism and avatars of the Gilded Age—families with names such as Gould and Vanderbilt, Carnegie and Astor, to whom Muriel was now, by marriage, distantly related.

The Chanler House was not the largest of these estates by any means; still, compared to the housing in which "the other half" of the city lived—the crowded and filthy tenement buildings—it was a castle in the style of a fifteenth-century French château.

With surprising agility for a man of his years, von Helrung jumped from the calash, and he dashed through the front gates, attacking the steps two at a time.

He pounded his pudgy fist against the door for several seconds, shouting, "Muriel! Bartholomew! Open up! It is I, von Helrung!"

He turned to the doctor. "Quickly, Pellinore! We must break it down."

The doctor responded reasonably, "Perhaps they are upstairs and simply don't—"

"Ack!" the old monstrumologist groaned. He shoved Warthrop roughly to one side, stepped back to give himself a running start, and threw himself against the door. It bowed, but did not give way. "Dear God in heaven!" he shouted, gathering himself for the next blow. "Give." *Slam!* "Me." *Slam!* "Strength!"

The door gave way with a final desperate wallop of his shoulder, the splintered remains crashing into the wall inside with the force of a thunderclap. Von Helrung's momentum carried him into the entryway, but he maintained his balance, lunging several steps into the cavernous space, where the crystal chandelier splintered the light of the setting sun into a thousand glittering pieces.

I smelled it the moment I stepped inside—the sickly sweet odor of death, the unmistakable perfume of decay. The doctor reacted to it immediately. He pushed past his winded companion and strode to the grand staircase. Von Helrung, now holding the derringer, grabbed Warthrop's cloak with his free hand and pulled him back.

"We stay together," he whispered harshly. "Where is the knife?"

Warthrop clucked impatiently, but took out the knife and handed it to me. "I have my revolver," he said.

"Good, but you will need these." Von Helrung held out several shining silver bullets. They clinked softly in the eerie silence. Warthrop pushed the offering away.

"I think my ordinary ones will do, thank you."

We followed Warthrop up the grand staircase, past portraits of the Chanler clan's progenitors, the occasional marble statue of a Greek god, and the bust of some anonymous personage glaring down from its perch upon the pedestal.

Upon the first turning of the stair, we found the body of a young girl in a chambermaid's uniform, lying faceup—but she was upon her stomach. Someone had twisted her head completely around. Her eyes and face were gone. Her skirt was pushed up around her waist, exposing her naked backside. There was nothing but a gaping wound where her buttocks should have been, and the air was saturated with the smell of excrement.

Von Helrung recoiled in shock, but Warthrop hardly took note of the gruesome find. He hopped over the pitiful creature and continued up the stairs, shouting Muriel's name at the top of his lungs, his eyes wide with panic. Von Helrung and I took more care in our ascent, carefully squeezing around her before continuing after him. I told myself not to look down, but I did, and I nearly swooned with disgust, for what I saw exceeded everything I'd ever witnessed in my tenure as a foot soldier in the service of Warthrop's exacting mistress.

Someone—or some*thing*—had carefully arranged her facial mask, including her bright brown eyes, inside her evacuated bowels, so she appeared to stare up at me from the violated depths.

"Stay back, Will!" whispered von Helrung.

I nearly ran into the doctor upon the second turning of the stairs. Another body lay in our path, lying on its back with legs together and arms spread wide, the same position in which we'd discovered Sergeant Hawk. He had been eviscerated. His organs, still shimmering with bodily fluid, lay in disarray, as if they had been rummaged through to find a special prize—which might have been the heart (I could see its half-eaten remains), or perhaps the intestines, which had been cleaved from his abdomen and wound about his faceless head like a crown.

It was Bartholomew Gray.

The monstrumologist barely paused. He barreled onto the second floor, bellowing her name, kicking open doors with such force that their hinges splintered. Von Helrung caught up with him, touched his shoulder, and cried out when Warthrop swung around and jammed the end of his revolver against his forehead. The older scientist pointed to a door at the end of the hall, over which someone had scrawled this, perhaps with blood, perhaps with the contents of the poor girl's bowels:

LIFE IS

Von Helrung called softly, "No, Pellinore!" but the doctor was already at the door, which stood slightly ajar, his revolver held at the level of his ear.

He pushed open the door, and something fell from its hiding place above—a chamber pot brimming over with a sludgy mass. The pot had been balanced between the top of the door and the wall, a trap my master had fallen for years before, only this time the joke wasn't a pail filled with a Tanzanian *Ngoloko*'s blood. It was a chamber pot filled with human feces.

LIFE IS

Warthrop stumbled backward, gagging and spitting (his mouth had been slightly open), his cloak and hair saturated in stinking excrement. He recovered himself quickly, however, and rushed into the room. Von Helrung and I followed close behind.

Reposed upon the bed was a third body, wearing the same green dress she had worn when I'd danced with her, legs obscenely spread, arms folded over her head. On the headboard had been scrawled the words "Good Job!"

Warthrop rushed toward the bed with a strangled cry of despair, and abruptly stopped, a look of nearly comical bewilderment upon his haggard features.

"Oh, no," he murmured.

I peered over his shoulder—and into the face of Bartholomew Gray.

The beast had stripped it off and laid it over *her* face.

Beside me von Helrung gave a small, horrified sob. The doctor took a deep breath, set his jaw, and pulled the makeshift mask away.

The beast had left the face beneath intact.

"Regina," whispered von Helrung. "It is Regina, the cook."

Warthrop turned, and his eyes were flint-hard. He pushed past us and strode to the opposite side of the room to the remains of a window; the frame still held a few wickedly gleaming broken shards. He gazed past them, down to the small courtyard below.

"We'll search the rest of the house," he said, "but I do not think we will find him."

He turned around to face us. I looked away. The expression in his eyes was unendurable.

"His business here, I think, is done."

TWENTY-TWO

"The Story of a Lifetime"

The doctor's prediction proved to be correct. We did not find John Chanler—or the thing that once had been John Chanler. Neither did we find Muriel. Either she had escaped or he had taken her. We searched every room from the damp cellar to the dusty attic. While von Helrung remained inside to call the police, Warthrop and I explored the grounds, focusing our attention on the small courtyard beneath the broken window. We found nothing out of the ordinary. It was as if John Chanler had taken to the high wind.

The arrival of the black-and-white police wagons drew the attention of the neighborhood almost immediately. The small crowd outside quickly swelled until two detectives had to be pulled from their grisly work to keep the human tide from flooding the front lawn.

The chief inspector appeared shortly thereafter. He commandeered the library to question the two monstrumologists. Von Helrung was deferential, even apologetic; knowing to what lengths Byrnes would go to make an arrest for the crime—his brutal methods were legendary—the older monstrumologist understood his interrogator better than Warthrop, who was surly and combative, asking more questions than he answered.

"Have you found John Chanler?" Warthrop demanded.

"You and I wouldn't be having this conversation if we had," answered Byrnes.

"Did you use dogs?"

"Of course, Doctor."

"Witnesses? His appearance is certainly something that would draw attention—even in New York."

Byrnes shook his head. "None we've turned up."

"Flyers!" barked the doctor. "Plaster every corner. And the newspapers. Who is that muckraker with the huge following? Riis. Jacob Riis. Within the hour he can have something in the evening edition."

Byrnes was slowly shaking his massive head, smiling a small enigmatic smile.

"And put John Chanler at the top of that list of yours," Warthrop feverishly continued. "What do you call it—the rogues' gallery? Within twenty-four hours we can make him the most famous man in Manhattan. Even the little old ladies' *dogs* will know what he looks like."

"Those are all wonderful ideas, Dr. Warthrop, but I'm afraid I can't do that."

Before the doctor could ask why, the door behind him flew open and the answer to that question barged into the room.

"Where is Warthrop? Where is that—"

Archibald Chanler's hand flew to cover his nose.

"Good God, man, what is that *smell*?" He eyed with disgust the doctor's filthy cloak.

"Life," answered the doctor.

Scowling, John Chanler's father turned to Byrnes. "Inspector, isn't it the usual procedure to handcuff persons under arrest?"

"Dr. Warthrop is not under arrest."

"I think the mayor may have something to say about that."

"He may indeed, Mr. Chanler, but until he does . . ." Byrnes shrugged.

"Oh, he will. I assure you he will!" He whirled on Warthrop. "This is entirely your fault. I shall do everything in my power to see you prosecuted to the full extent of the law."

"What is my crime?" asked the monstrumologist.

"That question is better put to my daughter-in-law."

"Then I shall put it to her—the moment she is found."

Chanler stared at him, and then looked quizzically at Byrnes.

"Mrs. Chanler is missing," the chief inspector informed him.

"John has taken her," Warthrop opined, "but I have hope that he will not harm her. If that was his intention, he would have done it here." He addressed Byrnes urgently. "Time is of the essence, Inspector. We must get the word out immediately."

"The word, as you say, will most certainly *not* 'get out,'" snapped Chanler. "And if I see a single mention of the Chanler name in the obscurest fish wrapper, I shall sue you for everything you have, do you understand? I will *not* have the name of Chanler besmirched or sullied in any way!"

"It isn't a name," answered my master. "It is a human being. Would you have her suffer the same fate as those we found in this house?"

Chanler brought his face close to Warthrop's and snarled, "I don't care what she suffers."

The monstrumologist exploded. He seized the larger man by the lapels and slammed him into a bookcase. A vase toppled off and shattered on the floor.

The object of my master's wrath did not fight back. His cheeks glowed, his eyes danced wickedly. "What are you going to do? Kill me? That's what you so-called monster hunters do, isn't it? Kill what frightens you?"

"You mistake disgust for fear," said Warthrop to Chanler.

"Pellinore," von Helrung pleaded. "Please. It solves nothing."

"She deserves it, Warthrop," growled Chanler. "Whatever she receives she has earned. If not for her, my son never would have gone on that hunt."

"What are you talking about?" the doctor demanded. He gave Chanler a violent shake. *"What is her fault?"*

"Ask *him*," said Chanler, with a jerk of his head toward von Helrung.

"All right now, boys. Let's play nice," rumbled Byrnes. "I don't want to shoot either of you—much. Dr. Warthrop, if you please . . ."

Warthrop released his captive with a frustrated groan. He whipped away, took a few steps, then turned back. He punched his finger in the direction of Chanler's nose.

"I am not frightened, but *you* have every reason to be! If there is any credence to our notions of heaven and hell, it will not be *me* who spends all eternity wallowing in shit! May God damn you for loving the precious name of Chanler more than the life of your own son! Explain *that* upon the Day of Judgment—which may come sooner than you expect."

"Are you threatening me, sir?"

"I am no threat to you. What visited this house is the threat, and it *remembers*, Chanler. If I understand what drives him at all, *you are next*."

We returned to the von Helrung brownstone, where the doctor washed the filth from his face and hair and disposed of his ruined riding cloak. Von Helrung was clearly shaken to his marrow, burdened with guilt—if only we had made our expedition earlier when Muriel had failed to call—and with grief—Bartholomew had been with him for years.

Warthrop was nearing the end of his considerable endurance. Several times he literally stormed the door, vowing to search every avenue and street, backyard and alleyway, until he found her. Each time he made as if to flee, von Helrung pulled him back.

"The police are her best hope now, Pellinore. They will spare no man to find her; you know this, *mein Freund.*"

The doctor nodded. Despite—even because of—Archibald Chanler's influence, no man would remain idle while John was loose. And Chief Inspector Byrnes had a reputation for ruthlessness. It was Byrnes, after all, who had invented that special form of interrogation called "the third degree," which some critics rightfully characterized as torture.

"What was Chanler talking about?" the doctor asked von Helrung. "That nonsense about this being her fault?"

Von Helrung smiled weakly. "He was never very fond of Muriel, you know," he offered. "He wishes to blame anyone else but John."

"It brought to mind something Muriel said," the doctor continued, his bloodshot eyes narrowing at his old mentor. "She told me it was *my* fault. That *I* sent him into the wilderness. It is exceedingly odd to me, *Meister* Abram, how everyone involved in this matter blames someone *other* than the person who actually *did* send him there."

"I did not tell John to go."

"It was entirely his idea? He volunteered to risk his life

in search of something that he had no faith existed?"

"I showed him my paper, but I never suggested . . ."

"Good God, von Helrung, can we quit these silly semantic games and speak frankly to each other? Is our friendship unworthy of the truth? Why would Muriel blame me and why would Archibald blame Muriel? What do either of us have to do with John's madness?"

Von Helrung folded his arms over his thick chest and bowed his head. He swayed on his feet. For a moment I feared he might keel over.

"All seeds must take root in something," he murmured.

"What the devil does *that* mean?"

"Pellinore, my old friend . . . you know I love you as my own son. I should not speak of these things."

"Why?"

"It serves no purpose but to cause pain."

"That's better than no purpose at all."

Von Helrung nodded. Tears glistened in his eyes. "He knew, Pellinore. John knew."

Warthrop waited for him to go on, every muscle tense, every sinew taut, steeling himself for the blow.

"I do not know all the particulars," his old master went on. "On the day he left for Rat Portage, I asked him the same question you now ask me: 'Why? Why, John, if you do not believe?'"

Tears now coursed down the old monstrumologist's cheeks—tears for John, for the doctor, for the woman between them. He held out his hands beseechingly. Warthrop did not accept them; his own hands remained clenched at his sides.

"It is a terrible thing, *mein Freund*, to love one who loves another. Unbearable, to know you are not the beloved, to know the heart of your beloved can never be free from the prison of her love. This is what John knew."

In a rare moment of disingenuousness, Pellinore Warthrop feigned ignorance. "I am surrounded by madmen," he said in a tone of wonder. "The whole world has gone mad, and I am the last sane man alive."

"Muriel came to me before he left. She said, 'Do not allow him to go. It is spite that drives him. He would humiliate Pellinore, make him the fool.' And then she confessed that she had burdened him with the truth."

"The truth," echoed Warthrop. "What truth?"

"That she loves you still. That she loves you always. That she married him to punish you for what happened in Vienna."

"Vienna was not my fault!" Warthrop cried, his voice shaking with fury. Von Helrung flinched and drew back, as if he feared the doctor would strike him. "You were there; you know this to be the truth. She demanded that I choose—marriage or my work—when she knew, she *knew*, my work was *everything* to me! And then, in the ultimate act of treachery, she ran to the arms of my best friend, demanding that he sacrifice *nothing*."

"It was not treachery, Pellinore. Do not say that of her.

She chose the one who loved her more than he loved himself. How can you judge her for this? She had been scorned by the one she loved, for a rival against whom she could never prevail. You are not a stupid man. You know *Outiko* is not the only thing that consumes us, Pellinore. It is not the only spirit that devours all mankind. Her broken heart drove her to John, and John's drove him into the wilderness. I think now he went never meaning to come back. I think he sought out the Yellow Eye. I think he called to it before it called to him!"

He fell into his chair, giving way to his sorrow. Warthrop made no move to console him.

Though von Helrung begged him not to leave, the doctor insisted on returning to our hotel. His logic was brutally efficient. "If he is in fact exacting some kind of twisted reparation for the past, he will look for me next. Better to be in the place he expects to find me."

"I will come with you," von Helrung said.

"No, but if you're concerned about your own safety—"

"*Nein!* I am an old man; I have lived to the fullness of my days. I am not afraid to die. But you cannot be both bait and hunter, Pellinore. And Will Henry! He should stay here."

"I can think of no worse idea," shot back my master.

He would brook no more arguments or entreaties. Timmy brought the calash around, and in short order we were disembarking at the Plaza.

Warthrop stopped abruptly outside the lobby doors, his head down and cocked slightly to one side, as if he were listening to something. Then, without a word, he took off, leaping over a hedge and tearing down the lawn toward the Fifty-ninth Street entrance to the park, running as fast as his long legs could carry him, which was very fast indeed. I raced after him, convinced he had spotted his quarry lurking along the low stone wall. I fell farther and farther behind. He was simply too fast for me. By the time I entered the park, he was a hundred yards ahead. I could see his lanky silhouette darting between the arc lights.

Warthrop's prey veered off the path and into the woods. The doctor followed, and I lost sight of both for a moment. The racket of their scuffle led me to where they rolled on the ground locked in each other's arms, first the doctor on top, then his opponent. I stopped a few feet from the tussle and drew the silver knife von Helrung had given me. I did not know if I would be able to actually use it, but it gave me comfort to hold it.

I would not need it for anything other than comfort, for I quickly discerned the man was not John Chanler but the same raggedy figure who had been stalking us since our arrival in New York. He fought bravely enough, but he was no match for the monstrumologist, who had by this point managed to straddle him, one hand clutching his scrawny neck, the other pushing down on his narrow chest.

"Don't hurt me!" the man squealed in a high-pitched English accent. "Please, Dr. Warthrop!"

"I'm not going to hurt you, you fool," gasped the doctor.

He released the man's neck and sat back upon his chest with his legs thrown on either side of his torso. The doctor's catch turned his light gray eyes beseechingly in my direction.

"I can't breathe," he wheezed.

"Good! I should squeeze the life out of you, Blackwood," said the doctor. "What in the devil do you think you're doing?"

"Trying to breathe."

The doctor heaved an exaggerated sigh and pushed himself to his feet. The man clutched his stomach, sat up, cheeks ablaze, sweat shining on his high forehead. His nose was extraordinarily large; it dominated his pinched face.

"You've been following me," the doctor accused him.

Blackwood was staring at me—or rather at the deadly object in my hand.

"Could you ask the young man to put away the knife?"

"He will," said the doctor. "*After* he runs you through with it."

The monstrumologist held out his hand to Blackwood, who accepted it, and Warthrop hoisted him to his feet. Then the thin man's face split open into a wide unabashed grin, as if they had dispensed with some kind of bizarre preliminaries. He thrust his hand toward the doctor's chest.

"How have you been, Dr. Warthrop?"

Warthrop ignored the gesture. "Will Henry, may I

introduce Mr. Algernon Henry Blackwood, a reporter who masquerades as a spy when he isn't a spy masquerading as a reporter."

"Not much of either, really."

"Is that so? Then, why have you been lurking outside my hotel since I got here?"

Blackwood grinned sheepishly and lowered his eyes. "I was hoping for the same thing I always hope for, Dr. Warthrop."

The doctor was nodding slowly. "That's what I suspected— and what I hoped. Blackwood, you look terrible. When was the last time you had something decent to eat?"

The monstrumologist had an idea.

And so it was that I found myself, a half hour later, sitting on a sofa of rich velvet in the lavishly adorned sitting room of a private "gentlemen's club," as such organizations were called in that day, situated within sight of the more famous Knickerbocker Club.

Like the Knickerbocker, the club to which Warthrop belonged prided itself on its exclusiveness. The membership was limited (exactly one hundred, not one more, not one less), and the identities of its members were a closely guarded secret. No man in my memory ever publicly acknowledged his membership in the Zeno Club, and its existence, as far as I know, was never exposed or advertised.

Normally guests were not allowed within the rarified

atmosphere of the club, but certain members, Warthrop among them, were a bit more equal than others. His knock was answered by the doorman, who glared down his nose at us through the small trapdoor situated beneath the brass plaque with the initials ZC. He took in Blackwood's ill-fitting suit, and it was clear he was not pleased, but without a word he turned and escorted us into the deserted sitting room, where Blackwood seemed to shrink before my eyes, intimated, perhaps, by the Victorian excess of the décor. Our orders were taken by another member of the staff with the same moribund attitude as the doorman—a gin and bitters for Blackwood, and a pot of Darjeeling tea for the doctor.

Our waiter turned to me, and my mind went blank. I was thirsty, and a glass of water would have been most welcome, but, like Blackwood, I was somewhat intimidated by the surroundings and the barely disguised disdain of the staff. Warthrop rescued me, whispering something into the waiter's ear. The man glided silently away with a tread as measured and sedate as an undertaker's.

A few moments later he returned with our drinks, setting before me a tall, clear glass in which a caramel-colored liquid bubbled. I eyed my drink doubtfully—why would someone serve a boiling beverage in a glass?—and the doctor, who missed nothing, smiled slightly and said, "Try it, Will Henry."

I took a tentative sip. My attendant delight must have been evident, for Warthrop's smile broadened, and he said,

"I thought you might like it. It's called Coca-Cola. Invented by an acquaintance of mine, a gentleman by the name of Pemberton. Not to my taste, really. Too sweet, and the inclusion of carbon dioxide is an inexplicable and not altogether pleasant addition."

"Carbon dioxide, did you say?" asked Blackwood. "Is it safe to drink?"

Warthrop shrugged. "We shall observe Will Henry carefully for any negative effects. How do you feel, Will Henry?"

I told him I felt very good, for I, with half of the fizzy concoction already in me, was feeling very good indeed.

Blackwood's gray eyes darted about; his hands moved restlessly in his lap. He was waiting for Warthrop to take the lead. The great scientist had never so much as granted him the time of day, and now here he sat across from him at the most exclusive club in New York. It was a wonder—and a riddle.

"Blackwood, I need your help," the monstrumologist said.

The Englishman's eyes widened at this confession. It was clearly the last thing he'd expected Warthrop to say.

"Dr. Warthrop—sir—you know I have only the deepest admiration and respect for you and your important work—"

"Spare me the sycophantic drivel, Blackwood. For the past two years you've been hounding my every step, to what purpose I can only guess, though I suspect it has more to do with scandal and gossip than admiration and respect."

"Oh, you wound me, Doctor. You cut me to the quick!

My interest goes far beyond the necessities of my employment. Your work comes so close to my true passion: the universe that lies beneath—or *within*, I should say—the hidden universe of human consciousness, the metaphorical equivalent, if you will, of your Society's Monstrumarium."

"Henry, I care not for your theories of consciousness or the 'universe within.' My concern is far more practical."

"But it is only by extending ourselves past the ordinary that we journey to the undiscovered countries of our boundless potential."

"You'll forgive my lack of enthusiasm," replied the doctor. "I have had my fill lately of undiscovered countries."

"'The ultimate truth does not lie in science," insisted the amateur philosopher. "It lies in the unplumbed depths of human consciousness—not the natural but, for lack of a better word, the *super*natural."

Warthrop laughed. "I really must introduce you to von Helrung. I think the two of you would hit it off splendidly."

Then the monstrumologist got down to business. He leaned forward, crooked his finger at his flushed-faced companion, and whispered conspiratorially, "Henry, I have a proposition for you. I need someone to break a story for me in tomorrow's papers. It is scandalous, it is sordid, and it involves one of the city's most prominent families. It is certain to make you a pretty penny—at least enough for you to buy yourself a decent suit. It may even earn you steady employment—a good thing, because it is obvious to me you have too much time on your hands."

Blackwood nodded eagerly. The gray eyes sparkled; the magnificent proboscis flared with excitement.

"With this proviso," Warthrop went on. "You are not to reveal your source to anyone, even to your editors."

"Of course not, Doctor," whispered Blackwood. "Oh, I must tell you I am intrigued! What is it?"

"What you've been waiting for, Blackwood. The story of a lifetime."

On the way back to the Plaza, the doctor confided, "I may live to regret my bargain with Blackwood, but we must trust what aid fate puts in our path. His story in tomorrow's papers will set the city ablaze, mobilizing millions to our cause—and the good name of Chanler be damned."

He looked utterly exhausted. His face was a ghastly yellow by the light of the streetlamps, and he was more tired and careworn than I had ever seen him, even worse than those terrible days in the wilderness, borne down by the weight of his burden. That burden he had set down in Rat Portage, but now he carried another, far greater one.

"I should have gone with her, Will Henry," he confessed. "I should have listened to my instincts."

"It isn't your fault, sir," I tried to console him.

"Don't be stupid," he snapped at me. "Of course it's my fault. Did you not hear a word that *Meister* Abram said? The entire affair is my fault. I told you we should be honest with each other. More important by far is that one be honest with oneself. I have always been, and it has cost me dearly," he added bitterly. "Nothing matters but the truth. I have dedicated my life to the pursuit of it, no matter where it hides. That is the heart of science, Will Henry, the true monster we pursue. I gave up everything to know it, and there is nothing I will not do—no place I will not go—to find out the truth."

I did not have to wait long for proof of this vow. Hardly had we stepped foot into our digs when the doctor directed me to fetch his instrument case.

"We've one small matter to resolve before the night is out," he informed me. "It involves a modicum of risk and could lead to certain difficulties with the law. You may wait for me here, if you wish."

The thought of being alone after the day's gruesome events rendered the suggestion intolerable. The burden of accompanying him on whatever dark errand now beckoned was far more preferable than the burden of a solitary vigil while the high wind sang outside the windows. Upon that final terrifying flight through the malefic wilderness, he had shouldered the burden he'd inherited, but he was not the only one so borne down. I declined the offer.

In short order we were disembarking our taxicab at the Twenty-third Street entrance of the Society's headquarters. A diminutive figure stepped out of the shadows to greet us.

"You are late, *mon ami*," murmured Damien Gravois.

His eyes widened at the sight of the bandage around my neck. "There has been an accident?"

"No," answered the doctor. "Why do you ask?"

The Frenchman shrugged, removed a snuffbox from the pocket of his fashionable short-tailed jacket, and partook of the powdered tobacco with a noisy snort.

"It is all arranged," Gravois said. "Except the portage charge. I would have paid it myself, but such was my haste to comply with your request that I completely forgot my purse."

The monstrumologist scowled. He had just completed a lengthy negotiation with our driver over the fare.

"Did you agree upon a price?"

Gravois shook his head. "I merely told him we would make it worth his while. You might know, Pellinore, but I do not know the going rate for body snatching."

The doctor sighed heavily. "And the weapon? Or did you forget that too?"

Gravois responded with a wry smile. He reached into the inner pocket of his jacket and removed a pearl-handled switchblade. He pressed the button with his thumb, and the six-inch blade sprang out with a wicked *click*.

"A Mikov," he said. "Identical to the one wielded by our Bohemian bodyguard."

On the second floor of the old opera house, the Society had constructed an operating theater where lectures, demonstrations, and the occasional dissection were conducted upon a small stage specially built for the latter purpose: the floor was concrete and slightly concave, with a drain installed in the center for the conveyance of blood and other bodily fluids. The room itself was bowl-shaped, the seats arranged on steep risers that surrounded the stage on three sides in order to provide the participants unobstructed views of the gruesome proceedings.

Two large metal rolling tables occupied center stage, and upon each lay a body. The two cadavers were of nearly identical proportions, both were male, and both were as naked as the day they were born. I recognized immediately one of the corpses. It was the eyeless, faceless remains of Augustin Skala.

A burly man heaved himself from a seat in the front row upon our entrance, nervously patting his pockets as if searching for a bit of change. Gravois made the introductions.

"Fredrico, this is my colleague Dr. Warthrop. Warthrop, this is Fredrico—"

"Just Fredrico, please," the man interrupted. His eyes darted about the theater; he was clearly suffering from a bad case of the jitters. "I brung 'em." He jerked his head unnecessarily at the stage. "You brung the money?"

Had time not been a crucial factor in his investigation, I am sure the doctor would have indulged in a lengthy negotiation over the orderly's fee for the illicit removal of two bodies from the Bellevue morgue. Still, Warthrop expressed outrage over the man's asking price, deeming it exorbitant past all reason; the man had not delivered the crown jewels, after all, but a couple of bodies—and on loan, to boot! It wasn't as if we expected to keep them. But time was of the essence, so the monstrumologist relented, and the man, once the money was counted and safely ensconced in his pocket, effected his retreat, informing us he had no interest in observing the proceedings; he would wait for us in the hall outside.

We began with Skala. Under the harsh glare of the electrified lighting, the doctor examined first the hollowed-out eye sockets, then the remnants of the face, and then the wound in the chest and the mutilated heart.

"Hmm, as I initially thought, Will Henry," the doctor murmured. "Nearly identical to the wounds of our friend Monsieur Larose. Note the scoring of the ocular bone and the appearance of denticulated trauma to the heart."

"Except the face," I said. "Larose's face hadn't been stripped off."

Warthrop nodded. "The skinning is reversed—with Larose it was the body, with Skala the face, but that could be owing to the factors of location and time. He had to work quickly with this one."

"But not with Larose," observed Gravois, who stood a bit to one side, looking somewhat sick to his stomach. "So why leave his face?"

The doctor shook his head. "There may be a pathological

factor involved here. A reason that makes sense only to the author."

"Or Larose was mutilated by someone else and Chanler employs his own interpretation upon the theme," Gravois replied.

"A possibility," Warthrop allowed. "But one that raises more questions than it answers. If not John, then who?"

"You know what von Helrung would say," teased Gravois.

Warthrop snorted. His lip curled up into a derisive snarl. I spoke up to snuff out the fuse of his temper.

"It couldn't have been Dr. Chanler, sir. Larose left him— that's what Dr. Chanler said—left him with Jack Fiddler. He couldn't have been the one who killed Larose."

"John did say he was abandoned," admitted my master. "But we do not know if Fiddler had him when Larose was murdered. He may have wandered into the Sucker encampment *after* the crime."

He sighed and ran his gore-flecked fingers through his hair. "Well. We can speculate till dawn and still be no closer to the truth. Some answers only John can provide. Let us keep to our purpose, gentlemen!" He stepped over to the other body procured from the Bellevue morgue. "I'll take that knife now, Gravois." He pressed the button. The blade whipped from its compartment and glittered wickedly under the bright lights. "How long did von Helrung say that John had? Seven minutes? Damien, keep the time, please. Upon my mark."

Warthrop plunged the blade into the middle of the dead man's chest.

"The blow strikes true," the monstrumologist said. "Puncturing the right ventricle. Thirty to sixty seconds for the victim to lose consciousness, and Skala collapses to the floor." He pulled the blade free and thrust it in my direction. "Here! You must do the rest, Will Henry. We should approximate John's weakened condition."

"Me, sir?" I was appalled.

"Quickly; the clock is ticking!" He pressed the switchblade into my hand and forced me to the table.

"Six minutes," Gravois announced.

"The eyes first," Warthrop instructed. "Based on the amount of blood in the ocular cavities, Skala's heart was most likely still beating when John removed them."

"You want me to cut out his eyes?" I was having some difficulty grasping it. Surely the doctor didn't expect me, of all people, to do such a thing.

The doctor misread my horror at the prospect as a question over procedure.

"Well, he didn't gouge or pry them out with his bare hands. You saw the scoring as well as I did, Will Henry. He must have used the knife. Snap to now!"

"May I point out that a two-year-old could remove someone's eyes?" asked Gravois. "Strength has very little to do with it, Warthrop."

"Very well," the doctor snapped. He grabbed the knife

from my hand, pulled back the upper lid, and inserted the knife into the spot above the corpse's right eye. He rotated the blade around, severing the optical nerve, and unceremoniously pulled the eye free with his bare fingers. He turned to me and I instinctively raised my cupped hands to catch the prize, which he dropped into them. I looked around desperately for somewhere to put it. The doctor stood between me and the table, and dropping it onto the floor seemed disrespectful, even sacrilegious. Warthrop leaned over the table and removed the left eye in the same manner. That one too he dropped into my hands. I willed myself not to look, lest I find those lifeless eyes looking back at me.

"Time!" called Warthrop.

"Five minutes, forty-five seconds," answered Gravois.

The monstrumologist grimly proceeded to hack open the alabaster chest, widening the initial wound with quick, savage strokes, mimicking the viciousness of the attack. He flung the knife upon the table and turned back to me.

"Now, this part you *must* do, Will Henry."

"Which part?" I squeaked.

"His hands are full," Gravois pointed out.

Warthrop scooped up the eyes and absently dropped them into his coat pocket. He pushed me toward the table. "Reach inside and grab the heart."

My stomach rolled. I burned and shivered as if with fever.

I blinked back hot tears, and stared beseechingly at him.

"Quickly, Will Henry! These two ribs, here and here, were broken from the sternum. Can you do it?"

I nodded. I shook my head.

"Four minutes!"

"This is monstrumology, Will Henry," the doctor whispered fiercely. "This is what we do."

I nodded a second time, took a deep breath, and, willing my eyes to remain open, plunged my hands into the chest. The cavity was surprisingly cold—colder than the surrounding air of the auditorium. The ribs were slippery with their covering of periosteum, but once I had a good grip, they broke off easily; it required no more effort than snapping a stick in two.

"Do you see the heart?"

"Yes, sir."

"Good. Now, with both hands. It's slippery. Pull it straight toward you. That's it! Stop. Here, take the knife now. No, no. Keep your left hand beneath the heart to support it; John is right-handed. Now chop—carefully for God's sake! Don't bring the blade so high or you will slice open your wrist! Vary the angle . . . more. Deeper! What, are you afraid of *hurting* him?"

"Three minutes!"

"Enough!" cried Warthrop. He pushed me back and snapped his fingers at me. "The knife! Stand back. If you're going to be sick, kindly use the drain, Will Henry."

The monstrumologist then proceeded to remove the face—an incision just below the hairline, then sliding the thin blade between the dermis and the underlying musculature. It was not easy work. There are many delicate muscles in our faces, the authors of a myriad different expressions—joy, sorrow, anger, love. Removing the facial mask while leaving what lay beneath unmolested required the fine touch of an accomplished student of anatomy—a monstrumologist, in other words.

"One minute!" cried Gravois. "The nurse is coming down the hall!"

Warthrop cursed softly. He had only cut down to the mandible. He twisted the loosed slick flesh of the face into his fist and ripped the rest free.

"Done!" he cried. "Now out the window and up—or down—the drainpipe! He doesn't have to make it to the ally or the rooftop—as long as he is out of sight when she opens the door."

He was gasping for breath, the skin of the anonymous corpse protruding from his clenched fist, congealed blood quivering on his stained knuckles like the morning dew upon rose petals.

"What about the face?" wondered Gravois. "And the eyes? They were not found in the room. What did he do with them?"

"He took them, obviously."

"Took them? How? He was dressed in a hospital gown."

"He dropped them outside and retrieved them once he had descended."

"This scenario leaves very little room for error," Gravois observed. "And you weren't able to finish the job properly. John was."

"He was always better with the knife than I," countered Warthrop.

"But in a maddened, weakened state?"

Warthrop waved the objection away. He was completely satisfied with the demonstration.

"The wounds approximate Skala's," he insisted. "The scoring of the eye sockets, the triangular cuts of the heart resembling those made by fangs or teeth . . . all proving superhuman strength and speed aren't required to inflict the damage suffered. Von Helrung is wrong."

"There is one obvious objection to your little demonstration, Pellinore," Gravois said. "The knife. How did a man in Chanler's condition manage to wrest it from a man twice his size?"

"He merely had to wait for him to fall asleep."

"But Skala was awake when the night nurse looked in at the end of her shift."

"Then he took it earlier in the evening while he slept, *before* she checked on him!" barked Warthrop. "Or he lured Skala to his bedside under some pretense and picked his pocket. He knew where it was kept."

Gravois looked dubious but did not press the issue. He simply said, "Perhaps so, but do you think this is enough to disprove von Helrung's theory?"

The monstrumologist sighed and slowly shook his head. "Do you know why I think he clings to it with all his heart and soul, Gravois? For the same reason our race clings to the irrational belief in Wendigos and the vampires and all their supernatural cousins. It is very difficult to accept that the world is righteous, ruled by a just and loving God, when mere mortals are capable of such unthinkable crimes." He nodded toward the desecrated corpse upon the gleaming stainless steel table. "The monstrous act by definition demands a monster."

It was well past midnight when we returned to our rooms at the Plaza. The doctor seemed on the verge of collapse, and I urged him to rest. He resisted at first, and then saw the reasonableness of it, relenting only after he barricaded us inside. He pushed the divan against the bedroom door and, after contemplating the eight stories between us and the ground, pulled the large dresser over to block the window.

He laughed mirthlessly. "Madness . . . madness!" he muttered.

"Dr. Warthrop, may I ask a question, sir? In the wilderness you told me perhaps there might be some creature like the Wendigo. . . . Could it be that Dr. Chanler was attacked by one and . . . perhaps infected with something like I am? Something that gives him great strength and speed and—"

He surprised me by taking the suggestion seriously. "It

has occurred to me, of course. Certainly some rather mundane organisms can cause madness and homicidal rage—jungle fever and other maladies that fall well outside the purview of monstrumology. But I reject von Helrung's interpretation for a simple reason, Will Henry. It *spits* in the face of everything to which I have dedicated my life, the reason I turned my back upon ..." He let the thought die unfinished. "We are doomed, Will Henry, if we do not set the past aside. Superstition is not science. And science will save us in the end. Though some might say it damned John—and not only John." The words caught in his throat. He looked away and added softly, "My faith in it has cost much, but true faith always does."

I waited for him to go on. There seemed to be something he was leaving unsaid. I can only guess what it was, but with great age comes perspective and, if we are lucky, a dollop of wisdom. The monstrumologist would not—could not—would *never* have admitted to the transformation of his friend into a supernatural beast. To do so would have been an acknowledgment that the woman he loved was doomed. He *had* to believe John Chanler was human, for if he wasn't, the woman they both loved was already dead.

TWENTY-THREE

"I Should Have Known"

The venom of the *khorkhoi*, the doctor had warned me, was slow-acting. A victim might feel perfectly fine one day—and plunge into complete delirium the next. It may have been the Death Worm's poison. It may have been that I had not slept more than four hours in total that night—or that those hours had been devoted to a twilight sleep adrift in a horizonless sea. Whatever the cause, I must confess my memory of the next few hours is vague—perhaps mercifully so.

I remember the bell ringing just before dawn and the doctor stumbling around in the dark. *Snap to, Will Henry, snap to!*

I remember Connolly standing in the lobby, and the dizzying sense of déjà vu at seeing him. *Dr. Warthrop, you must come with me.*

The cold predawn air . . . the stars fading in the indigo sky . . . the black brougham . . . the blur of darkened storefronts along Fifth Avenue . . . the shoveling of the white-coated sanitation workers calf-deep in the sidewalk filth, a noxious mixture of human and animal excrement deposited daily on the streets of the greatest city on earth.

Indeed, this was the hour of filth, when thousands upon thousands of chamber pots were emptied of their "night soil" directly onto the street from the brownstone and tenement windows, when the two million pounds of manure, produced the day before by a hundred thousand horses, lay piled in stinking four-foot-high drifts—high enough in some neighborhoods that a man might enter his second-floor walk-up without using the stairs. The hour when carts slid along ruts cut into muddy refuse, carrying the remains of the horses that had decayed enough to be broken apart and transported to the rendering house. The average horse weighed fifteen hundred pounds, too cumbersome to remove while whole, and so it would be left to rot on the street where it had died, a bloated, reeking feast for the "queen of the dung heap," the typhoid fly, until the horse could be dismembered easily and carted away.

It was the hour of filth. The average workhorse produced twenty-four pounds of manure and several quarts of urine every day. The sheer enormity of that waste threatened the human population with extinction, as the waste bore the poisoned fruits of cholera, typhoid, yellow fever, typhus, and malaria. People literally dropped like flies—twenty thousand each year, most of them children—while the flies themselves prospered.

Each morning the manure was collected and hauled to special staging areas, called "manure blocks," to await transport over the Brooklyn Bridge. The largest manure block was located on Forty-second Street, one block away from where a hundred thousand people got their drinking water, the Croton Reservoir.

The doctor's haggard profile . . . the cold wind off the river . . . "I should have known. . . . I should have guessed."

In spring the rains turned the streets into quagmires of mud and manure, and "crossing sweepers" cleared paths for the well-to-do ladies in their sweeping skirts, lest their finery be soiled. In dry weather, dust storms of pulverized manure blew through the broad avenues or floated like the volcanic ash of Pompeii, piling half an inch deep upon windowsills and the stalls of the fruit vendors and sausage sellers, particles fine enough to be inhaled. In this, the proudest city in America, you literally breathed shit.

The cries of the teamsters. The curses of the dray drivers. The harsh call of crows. And the doctor beside me: "I should have known. . . . I should have guessed."

The dizzying stench of the six-foot-high city-block-long banks of spilth, a foul miasma of garbage, excrement, and animal parts—and the maddening hum of a million blowflies. . . .

A burly black-clad figure appeared against the backdrop of that worm-infested replica of Dante's hell, the largest manure block, on Forty-second Street. The monstrumologist leapt from the carriage and accosted Chief Inspector Byrnes.

"Where?" Warthrop demanded.

Byrnes pointed to the top of the hill, and Warthrop started up the slick slope to the top. It was a hard climb; he sunk to his calves in the muck.

"No! Stay here," he called to me when I started to follow.

Byrnes must have concurred, for he laid a huge hand upon my shaking shoulder, his full lips working the expired stump of his cigar. I saw the doctor's head disappear over the horizon of waste. Only a moment must have passed, but it seemed an eternity before I heard his cry—a sound unlike anything else I have ever heard. It was difficult to imagine a human being producing such a sound. It did not belong to our race, but to the poor beast in the slaughterhouse. That anguished scream was more powerful than the big man's hold upon me; it pulled me toward it, but Byrnes caught me by the back of the coat before I could get very far, and hauled me back.

"Don't worry, boy. He'll come down. There's nowhere else for him to go."

And he did come down. Not the same man who had gone up that hill, but a man who looked like him. Not unlike the way John Chanler had retained the vestiges of his humanity, my master's facade was intact. But my master's eyes were empty, as empty and soulless as Pierre Larose's or Sergeant Hawk's eye sockets, considering the end of the desolation he would never reach.

"Pellinore Warthrop," Byrnes formally intoned, "I am placing you under arrest for suspicion of murder."

Though I wailed and screamed, kicked and punched, they separated us, throwing me into the brougham carriage, which took off at once for police headquarters. I turned around and saw them leading the doctor away in handcuffs. I did not see him again for some time.

The city was coming to life, albeit a life wholly foreign to a young boy from a small New England town. Tramps lingered in doorways or loitered around the smoking ash barrels, eyes glowering beneath ratty hats, and hands tucked inside the fraying sleeves of their secondhand coats. Ragpickers pushed wooden carts along the sidewalks, scavenging in the narrow recesses of dark alleys and in the piles of trash that seemed to gather like autumn leaves against stoop and storefront.

Here the slouching tenements, with acres of laundry fluttering on lines strung from rooftop to rooftop. Here the stale-beer saloons, drunks passed out in their basement doorways, while urchins knelt beside them, picking their pockets for change. Here the gambling house, eerily quiet at this hour; there the concert hall with posters plastered on its blackened windows, advertising the latest burlesque. And at Mulberry and Bleecker, the disorderly house, where young women, their faces heavily painted, leaned out the open windows calling down to anonymous passersby and uniformed policemen alike.

At the station house Connolly took me to a small, windowless room furnished with a table and two rickety chairs. He was not unkind; he offered to find me something to eat, but I declined—food was the farthest thing from my mind. He left me alone. I heard a bolt being thrown, and I noticed the door had no handle on my side. An hour passed. I wept until I was too weak to weep. I swooned at one point and smacked my forehead on the tabletop. *It might not be true*, I thought. *It might not have been her.* But I could think of no other explanation for that inhuman cry.

At last I heard the bolt being thrown back with a loud screech. Chief Inspector Byrnes came into the room, threatening to overwhelm the space with his prodigious bulk, followed by another large man wearing a bowler hat and an overcoat a size too small for him.

"Where's the doctor?" I asked.

"No need to worry," said Byrnes with a patronizing wave. "Your doctor's resting very comfortably." He nodded to the man beside him. "This is Detective O'Brien. He has a boy about your age, I believe; don't you, O'Brien?"

"Yes, sir, I do," answered his subordinate. "His name is William too, only we call him Billy."

"You see?" Byrnes beamed at me as if a significant point had been made.

"I want to see the doctor," I said.

"Oh, now, we don't want to rush things, do we? All in good time, all in good time. Will you be wanting anything, Will? We'll bring you anything you like. Anything at all."

"What can we bring you, Will?" echoed O'Brien.

"The doctor," I answered.

Byrnes glanced at his cohort, and then turned to me. "We can do that. We can bring you to the doctor. We just need you to be honest with us and answer some questions."

"I want to see the doctor first."

Byrnes's smile faded. "Your doctor is in a bad way, Will. He needs your help now, and the way you can help him is by helping us."

"He didn't do anything wrong."

O'Brien snorted. "Didn't he now?"

Byrnes laid a hand on his forearm. He kept his small piggish eyes on me, though.

"You know who was up on that manure block, don't you, boy? You know what your doctor found."

I shook my head. I willed my quivering bottom lip to be still.

"And now we've got a problem, Will—and so does he. We've got a problem, and your doctor's got a bigger problem. This is serious business, boy. This is murder."

"Dr. Warthrop didn't murder anyone!"

Byrnes dropped a paper sack upon the tabletop. "Go on. Look in there, Will."

Trembling with dread, I peeked inside the sack, then pushed it away with a soft cry. He had forgotten about them, had dropped them into his pocket in the operating theater and forgotten completely.

"It's interesting, don't you think, Will? What a man keeps in his pockets. I carry my wallet and a comb, some matches . . . but it's a rare man who carries eyeballs about!"

"They aren't hers," I gasped.

"Oh, we know. Wrong color, for one." Byrnes jerked his head toward the door, and O'Brien opened it, admitting the man I knew as Fredrico. His face was deathly pale; clearly he was terrified.

"Is this him?" demanded Byrnes, pointing at me.

The big orderly nodded violently. "That's him. He was there."

Byrnes said, "You see, Will, we know the doctor's been brushing up on his technique—"

"That isn't what he was doing! That isn't it at all!"

He held up his hand to silence me. "And one other thing you should know. There's another crime besides murder. It's called being an accessory. That's just a fancy way of saying you *have* to talk to us, Will, if you don't want to see yourself behind bars till you're as old as me, and I'm pretty old."

I sank into the chair. My thoughts refused to be still long

enough to form a coherent sentence. *You know who was up on that manure block, don't you, boy?*

"It was Mrs. Chanler, wasn't it?" I asked when my tongue could fashion the words.

O'Brien was grinning ghoulishly down at me.

"Take all the time you need, O'Brien," Byrnes said on his way out with his quaking witness. "Get it out of him in the usual way, only leave the face clean."

The "usual way"—before it was abolished by a charismatic young reformer named Theodore Roosevelt—began with verbal abuse. Name-calling, cursing, threatening. This then progressed to the physical—spitting, punching, slapping, pinching, hair pulling. A typical suspect could be expected to break somewhere near the middle of the method's continuum. Rarely did he last till the third and final degree, which might include the breaking of his thumbs or the rupturing of a kidney. There were rumors that some subjects had to be carried from the interrogation room in a body bag, their premature demise carefully covered up with a ludicrous explanation—*Had a heart attack and dropped over dead, the poor bastard!*—for a poor bastard whose face resembled hamburger meat.

O'Brien followed orders. He did not mar my face. But in every other way, he applied the tried-and-true formula for wresting confessions from recalcitrant witnesses.

He screamed into my face, "Your precious doctor's going

to hang. It's over for him—and for *you* unless you talk!"

He bellowed, "Do you think we're fools, boy? Is that what you think? You think we don't know about the Mountie and that French Canuck? How he killed one to hide the fact that he'd killed the other? You think we're ignorant, boy? And that fat Bohemian at Bellevue—you really believe some ninety-pound weakling stole his knife and gutted him like a pig? What fools do you take us for? Your doctor knows his way around the body, don't he? He's cut up his fair share of 'specimens,' ain't he? Knows how to cut 'em up good, just like he cut off that black butler's face and hung it on the old lady, right?"

Graduating next to hard slaps to my cheeks, delivered as a kind of exclamation point. "Don't you think we know his game?" *Slap!* "'Oh, it ain't *me*; it's some *monster* that's doin' it!'" *Slap!* "Then he takes his knife to his ladylove, don't he? *Don't he?*"

Then towering behind me, yanking my head back by a fistful of hair and shoving his flushed pockmarked face into mine. "You want to see him before he hangs? Huh?" Pulling so hard I could hear the roots ripping free from my scalp.

"You start talkin', you miserable pup. You was with him; you saw it. Say you saw it. Say it!"

He slammed his fist into my solar plexus. I folded over in the chair and fell into a miserable ball on the concrete floor. O'Brien leisurely stepped over my writhing body and knocked once upon the door.

Two strong arms lifted me from the cold floor. I found

myself enfolded in Byrnes's arm, pulled tightly to his chest. His large hands caressed me and wiped the tears from my cheeks.

"There, there, boy," murmured the chief inspector. "It'll all be over soon."

I could not speak. I brought my hand to my mouth and sucked on my knuckles like a squalling babe.

"It ain't fair what that man's put you through. Why, it just makes me sick, thinking how much hurt he's done. And not just to you, Will. . . . I should've showed you. I should've showed you what he did to that poor lady—that poor, beautiful lady, Will! Do you want to know what he did, Will? You want to know what your doctor's done?"

I shook my head fiercely.

He told me anyway.

And then: "All's you got to do is say it, Will," he said. "Say you saw it. You saw him do it."

"No."

"You want to see him, don't you? You can. All's you got to do is tell me you were with him and you saw it."

"I—I was with him."

"Good boy."

"I'm always with him."

"That's the lad."

"I—I am with him."

"And you saw . . ."

"And I saw..."

I was shaking uncontrollably in the warmth of his embrace. I had seen ... but what had I seen? A dead man straining toward the indifferent sky. The ruins of God's temple impaled upon a tree. I had seen the yellow eye and the emerald eye, the desolation and the abundance ... what had been given and what was still owing. There was the heart cradled in the monstrumologist's hands. There was the brilliant smile of the one who had danced with me, and there was the jagged teeth of the one who had ferried me into the golden light.

"What did you see, William Henry?"

TWENTY-FOUR

"He Wanted Me to See"

I was taken to a holding room—not precisely a cell, since there were no bars anywhere, but close enough. There was a cot, a washstand, and a very narrow window of frosted glass that filtered the weakened autumn sun into a kind of mockery of light, light's emaciated cousin. I threw myself upon the cot and fell almost immediately into a deep sleep—so deep, in fact, that it took Connolly several hard shakes to wake me.

"You have a visitor, Will."

I must have been staring uncomprehendingly at him, for he said it again, smiling reassuringly all the while, a friendly hand upon my shoulder.

"Take your hands off him!" I heard a familiar voice cry. "He's had quite enough of your department's hospitality, my good sir!"

Von Helrung jostled Connolly out of the way and crouched beside me. He cupped my face in his pudgy hands and stared intently into my eyes.

"Will . . . Will," he murmured. "What have these animals done to you?"

He swept me up into his arms with surprising vigor and swung round, kicking open the door with his foot and marching out, a panicky Connolly trailing behind us like an abandoned puppy.

"Doctor von Helrung, sir, I don't think you're allowed to do this," huffed Connolly.

"Watch, and you will see what I am allowed to do!" von Helrung roared over his shoulder.

"Inspector Byrnes left strict orders—"

"And you may take the orders of Herr Inspector Byrnes and stick them up your wide Irish arse!"

He had reached the front doors. I could see the glare of the bawdy houses glimmering across Mulberry Street. He might have made good his escape then—his bluster had frozen the half dozen or so personnel in their tracks—but he could not resist a final parting shot across the bow.

"Shame on you! Shame on all of you! The most vicious of the predators I study cannot hold a candle to you! To treat a man like this is one thing, but to torture a child! And a child who has already endured more than any of you could possibly imagine. *Diese Scheißpolizisten. So eine Schweinerei! Pah!*"

He spat contemptuously, then carried me straight to the curb and heaved me into the back of the calash. He jumped into the seat beside me and shouted for Timmy to take us home.

"The doctor?" I gasped.

"Safe, Will," answered my rescuer. "Safe. Not well, but safe—and I beg you to forgive me for not extricating you sooner from the clutches of those oafish brutes."

"I want to see the doctor," I said.

"And you shall, Will. I am taking you to him now."

Von Helrung's personal physician, a young man by the name of Seward, had given the doctor a thorough examination and had found no serious injuries except a painful—and painfully obvious—fracturing of the lower jaw. Seward was concerned about the condition of Warthrop's kidneys; already ugly bruises had formed along his lower back where the truncheons had been vigorously applied, but there was nothing he could do but wait. The symptoms of renal failure were hard to miss.

I found my master propped up in the bed, dressed in one of von Helrung's nightshirts, which was much too small for him and, to my allegiant eye, added insult to injury. A bag containing ice had been wrapped in a cloth and the cloth then tied around his head to keep the compress tight against his jaw. He opened his eyes when I stepped inside the room.

"Will Henry," he said, wincing from the effort. "Is that you?"

"Yes, sir," I said.

"Will Henry." He sighed. "Where have you been, Will Henry?"

"At the police station, sir."

"That cannot be," he said. "My memory is not altogether clear, but I distinctly remember you were *not* at the police station with me."

"I was in another room, sir."

"Ah. Well, you could have been a little more precise."

I took a hesitant step forward, reached for his hand, and stopped myself.

"I'm sorry, sir."

I could hold it in no longer. It was too much, to see him like that. And if it was too much for me, what was it like for him? He motioned for me to come closer, and reached for my hand.

"You should not be sorry," he said. "You should be glad. You were spared. You did not see what I saw upon that hill." He spoke fiercely through gritted teeth. "What I still see— what I am doomed to see—until I can see no more!" He closed his eyes. "He wanted me to see . . . what he had done to her. . . . More than mutilation—an act of desecration. I think I disappointed him. I think he waited for me last night. I think she was alive when he took her to the summit, and he waited awhile for me before he exacted his deranged vengeance."

"No," I cried. "Don't say that, sir! Please don't—"

"He left enough clues for me, but I was blind to them.

I think that's why he took her face but left her eyes, as if to say, 'Even *she* sees more than you!' The serving girl butchered on the stairs, the phrase scrawled over the door, the trick of the chamber pot, and the words 'Good Job!' on the headboard. Not 'job' as in a task or accomplishment, but Job from the Bible, Job crying for justice upon the dung heap. He did everything but draw me a map."

I struggled for something to say, but what might be said in such dolorous circumstances? What balm existed to soothe his torment? I had nothing to offer but my own tears, which he tenderly wiped away—a measure of his distress, perhaps his concern for my anguish.

"She had not been dead long, Will Henry. No more than an hour, I would guess. He gave up on me and then he—he consummated the transaction."

Von Helrung had arranged a hearty repast for my supper, and though I managed to force down but a few sips of soup and a crust of pumpernickel, I felt renewed. I could not recall the last time I had eaten. I was still dreadfully tired, desiring nothing more than another taste of the dreamless sleep I'd feasted on in the holding room on Mulberry Street. My desire was destined to be thwarted. The kitchen door flew open and Lilly Bates skipped into the room, her cheeks aglow with delight.

"There you are! I've been looking all over for you, William James Henry. How is your neck? Can I see it? Your Dr.

Warthrop wouldn't let me see it, even though I assured him I had seen worse things than the bite of a Mongolian Death Worm, much, *much* worse. Did it liquefy your flesh? That's what happens, you know. Their spit melts your flesh like butter."

I confessed I hadn't examined the wound myself, an admission she found shocking. Why wouldn't I want to look at it?

"Perhaps you're ashamed to look at it, because you are a liar and that's what happens to liars—liquefied flesh. Don't you think that's funny, Will? It's so perfectly *metaphorical*."

She was sitting quite close to me, resting her elbows on the table and cupping her chin in her hands, studying me with her disconcertingly wide sapphire-blue eyes.

"Muriel Chanler is dead," she stated matter-of-factly.

"I know."

"Did you see her? Uncle said you were there."

"I did not."

"Uncle said the police beat and tortured you."

"They tried to make me confess—or, not confess, but say that the doctor did it."

"But you didn't."

"It wasn't the truth."

She would not stop staring at me. I stirred my cold soup.

"They're going to hunt him down now," she said.

"Who is?"

"The monstrumologists. Well, not all of them; just the ones Uncle has picked specially for the job. They're coming over tonight to draw up their battle plans. I told Mother I'm staying. She thinks it's to keep *you* company. 'That lonely little Henry boy,' she calls you. 'That poor little orphan stuck with that horrible man.' 'That horrible man' is your doctor."

For some reason the wound beneath the bandage began to itch terribly. It took everything in me not to dig into it with my nails.

"It's not altogether a lie," said Lilly. "For here I am—keeping you company! You're not angry at me, are you? I didn't mean for it to happen, you know. I'm not wicked. I honestly didn't know until Adolphus told me they couldn't be sexed. He killed it, you know. Not Adolphus—your doctor. Adolphus got it off you and Dr. Warthrop tore it to pieces with his bare hands—as if he were angry at it, as if it had attacked *him*. I don't think that's right, do you? I mean, it wasn't the Death Worm's fault. It was just being what it was."

"What?" I asked. As usual with Lilly Bates, I was having some trouble keeping up.

"A Death Worm! All he had to do was put it back into its crate, but instead he killed it. It's not like Dr. Chanler. They have to kill him, because if they don't, he'll just keep feeding. Uncle says there's no prison on earth that can hold a Wendigo."

"He's not a Wendigo," I countered, ever Warthrop's loyal servant. "Wendigos aren't real."

"Tell that to Muriel Chanler."

My cheeks burned. I had a sudden, nearly overwhelming urge to strike her.

"She never stopped loving him," she went on. "That's something you don't understand, Will, because you are a boy. Dr. Chanler knew it and he couldn't stand it, and so he went off to Canada, and I don't think he ever really believed he was coming back. His heart was broken. The woman he loved had never stopped loving his best friend. Can you imagine anything more tragic than that? And then his best friend rescues him and brings him back to her, only now he's not even human anymore—"

"Stop it!" I cried. "Please stop it!"

I pushed away from the table and stumbled toward the door. She followed, saying, "What's the matter, Will? Where are you going?"

"Leave me alone!"

"Some apprentice monstrumologist you are!" she called after me. "What did you suppose it was all about when he accepted you, William James Henry? What did you suppose it was all *about?*"

I remained in the room beside the doctor's, restlessly turning this way and that upon the bed, until the clock struck ten and the monstrumologists began to arrive. I heard their voices below, low-pitched and somber like mourners in a death house, and that made me angry, for them to behave as if the doctor were already lost. My distress motivated me to abandon my desperate need for rest. I peeked into his room on the way downstairs and found him fast asleep. I decided not to wake him. I would risk another encounter with Lilly and join their strategy session, if for no other reason than to represent the doctor. He would want to know what was being plotted in his absence.

I found them in the library—von Helrung, the diminutive Frenchman Damien Gravois, Dr. Pelt, and two other monstrumologists whom I had not met, whose names I came to learn were Torrance and Dobrogeanu. The library had been converted to their budding operation's command center. A large map of the island had been plastered to one wall. Bright red pins dotted its surface, marking the places where Chanler's victims had fallen; I counted eight in all, three more than I knew of. The beast had been busier than I'd realized. *It will not stop hunting,* von Helrung had said. *It will kill and feed until someone kills it.*

Beside the map were newspaper clippings with blaring headlines: MADMAN STALKS CITY. MASSIVE MANHUNT UNDERWAY FOR AMERICAN "RIPPER." And this poignant one, from an early edition: POLICE DENY RUMORS OF MISSING WOMAN/WHERE IS MRS. JOHN CHANLER?

"Where is Warthrop?" asked Dr. Pelt. "We shouldn't decide anything without him."

"He rests from his ordeal at the hands of our esteemed Inspector Byrnes," answered von Helrung. "May God in his mercy grant Pellinore succor from his woes—and may God in his divine justice send a plague upon the Metropolitan Police!"

"We can always apprise him of our plans later," said Gravois. "Or Monsieur Henry, who lurks in the shadows over there by the door. Come, come. *Veuillez entrer*, Monsieur Henry. You may serve as scribe for our proceedings!"

Von Helrung thought it an excellent idea. He seated me at the table and procured some paper and a pen for me to record, in his words, the minutes of the first official inquiry into the species *Lepto lurconis* in the history of monstrumology.

"It is a seminal moment, *mein Freund*, Will. We are like the first explorers stepping onto the shores of a new continent. This shall ever be remembered as the hour when our science met the grandest mystery of all—the intersection of ignorance and knowledge, light and dark. Ah, if only Pellinore were well enough to be here!"

"If he were, I think he'd pop you in the nose for what you just said," opined Pelt dryly.

"He can deny it for only so long," huffed von Helrung with a wave of his pudgy hand. "For seven thousand years the wise believed the earth was flat, and men were murdered for claiming otherwise. Change is always resisted, even by— or especially by!—men of Pellinore's caliber. It is the way of things."

He clapped his hands and said, "So we begin, *ja*? Herr Doctor Pelt has read my paper, so he knows already much of what I am about to tell you. He will forgive me, I pray, for plowing familiar ground, but it must be broken, else no seed may germinate that will yield the fruit of success in this, our most grave undertaking.

"John Chanler is dead. What has arisen in his place—what animates his lifeless form—is a spirit older than the oldest bedrock. It has many names in many cultures. Wendigo or *Outiko* are just two of them; there are more—hundreds more. For the sake of clarity I shall refer to it simply as the beast, for that word describes its nature best. There is no humanity in the thing that was John Chanler."

The monstrumologist Dobrogeanu raised his hand and said, "I would dispute that claim, Herr Doctor. While his actions have been abhorrent, there is a method to them, a diabolical method—to be sure, but certainly some humanity remains, if we include the darker angels of our nature. No beast plays pranks or acts out motives of jealousy and revenge. If so, then we all are beasts."

"Some vestiges of his personality linger," acknowledged von Helrung. "That is undeniable. But these we may think of as distant echoes of his evolutionary past. It is no more human than a display in Madame Tussauds museum. It is the hunger that drives it. The rest is like ripples upon the water or the aftershocks of an earthquake. You will note I do not refer to it as 'John.' I purposely do not, and I suggest you do not, for if we wish to destroy it, we must first destroy any impressions we have of its humanity. I could not exterminate the man—nor could any of us, I think—but I can—and I will, if God allows—destroy *it*. I will repeat, gentlemen: John Chanler is dead. It is the beast that remains."

"I think we're all agreed upon that goal, Dr. von Helrung," said Torrance. He was the youngest of von Helrung's recruits, possessing a powerful physique and a commanding baritone. "I am not altogether convinced that we are dealing with a creature of supernatural origin, but I concur that where the police have failed to capture him, it is our duty as Chanler's friends and colleagues to bring the matter to a satisfactory conclusion."

"I pray the police do not try to apprehend him, Dr. Torrance," replied von Helrung. "For success in that regard would ultimately be a tragic failure. They do not understand that which they hunt. It cannot be captured, and it cannot be killed. Although I have told them how to destroy it, they do not listen."

"Well, *I'm* listening," said Pelt. "How do we destroy it?"

"Silver—by bullet or knife—to the heart. Only the heart! Then it must be cut from its chest and burned. The head we must remove and inter in running water. Though it is not absolutely required, the rest should be dismembered and scattered, a portion entrusted to each one of us, and none may tell the others where he has buried that portion."

Pelt squinted at him dubiously. "You understand this is quite a mouthful to swallow, Dr. von Helrung."

"Will Henry was there," von Helrung replied. "He saw the Yellow Eye. Did you not, Will?"

All eyes turned to me. I squirmed uncomfortably in my chair.

"What did you see?" demanded Gravois.

It was the same question Byrnes had asked. I had an answer, but it was no answer, really. I cleared my throat.

Torrance snorted. "Well, I might still go along with it— sort of like hedging a bet—though we could be prosecuted for desecrating a corpse."

"Desecration!" cried Gravois. "Gentlemen, we are conspiring tonight to commit murder."

"No, no!" von Helrung insisted heatedly. "No, not murder, Damien. It is an act of mercy."

"Only if you're right, Abram," said Dobrogeanu. He was von Helrung's age, but, like the stocky Austrian, in excellent physical condition for a man of advanced years. "If you're not, may God grant us more mercy than we show John!"

"Assuming we are even given an opportunity," put in Torrance. "Murder or mercy killing—it's an interesting philosophical argument but wholly academic if we can't find him—Sorry, *it*."

"Yes," agreed Dr. Pelt. He nodded to the clippings on the wall. "The entire city has been alerted—I won't say 'panicked.' Every able-bodied man on the force is searching every back alleyway and beating down every door. Four million pairs of eyes are looking for it. Where do you suggest we direct ours?"

"Forgive me, dear Dr. Pelt, but you forget who you are," returned von Helrung. "We shall succeed where others fail because we are monstrumologists. We have devoted our lives to the study and eradication of aberrant species such as *Lepto lurconis*. Where do we look? Where do we begin? We begin with what it *is* to discern where it might *be*. So the question is not *where* is it, but *what* is it. And what is it?"

He paused, and then answered his own question. "It is a predator. More ruthless than any in our catalogue, and far more cunning. It is wounded in a way, in that it perpetually lingers on the edge of starvation, which forces it to keep moving in search of its prey. Thus the hunger that drives it is also its greatest weakness. The hunger governs everything it does. And like any other predator, it will go where its victims are most plentiful and most vulnerable. It will choose to attack those the herd is willing to sacrifice. The weak. The unprotected. The easily discarded."

He pointed out the locations of the pins on the map.

"Disregard for the moment the hospital and the Chanler residence, which are merely aberrations of the more general pattern. Where do we have verified victims of our quarry?"

His colleagues crowded around the map.

"Five Points," said Dobrogeanu, squinting through his pince-nez.

"Hell's Kitchen," read Torrance. "Blindman's Alley. Bandit's Roost."

"The slums," Dr. Pelt said. "The tenement neighborhoods."

Von Helrung was nodding. "I fear so. Thousands upon thousands crammed twelve to a room, the poorest of the poor, most of them recent immigrants who do not speak the language and who are distrustful of the police. And who, in turn, are despised even as they are exploited by the so-called genteel class. What does it matter if one or a hundred go missing or are found mutilated beyond recognition? There are so many, and so many thousands more arrive every day from every corner of the civilized world."

He had a sickened look on his florid face. "It is the perfect hunting ground."

"And quite large," said Dobrogeanu. "Even for five monstrumologists—six, counting Pellinore—two of which are well past their prime, if you'll forgive me for saying so, Abram. If this indeed is its chosen hunting ground, how do you propose we box in our prey?"

"We can't. But we can enlist the aid of someone who knows those grounds better than anyone else on this island. I have taken the liberty of inviting him to join us in our expedition—"

He was interrupted by the ringing of the front bell. Von Helrung glanced at his pocket watch. "Ah, and speak of the devil—right on time! Will, be a dear and escort Mr. Jacob Riis into our assemblage."

TWENTY-FIVE

"His Only Hope"

Jacob Riis was a short man on the cusp of middle age, and a study in geometry. Everything about his physique, from his small feet to his large head, suggested the rectangle, offset only by his round spectacles, through which he now glared at me.

"I am seeking a Dr. Abram von Helrung," he growled in a thick Scandinavian accent.

"Yes, sir, Mr. Riis. He's expecting you. Right this way, sir."

"Ah, Riis! Good, good, now you are here. Thank you!" Von Helrung pumped his guest's hand vigorously and quickly introduced the Dane to the rest of the hunting party. They knew Riis, of course, if only by reputation. For ten years Riis had been unrelenting in his demands for social reform, his calls heard but largely ignored until 1890, with the publication of his book, *How the Other Half Lives*, a scathing indictment in words and pictures of the evils of tenement life. The book exposed the open dirty secret of New York's slums in the midst of Gilded Age excess and rocked the city to its self-satisfied core. Like those whose wretched lives he'd immortalized in his work, Riis was an immigrant, a journalist by trade, who maintained an office for the *New-York Tribune* directly across the street from police headquarters on Mulberry Street, where I had just recently enjoyed—and still suffered from—Chief Inspector Byrnes's particular brand of hospitality.

Riis was immediately drawn to the clippings hanging on the wall.

"Blackwood!" he muttered, reading the byline. "Algernon Henry Blackwood. And now my editors are asking *me* to cover it. Do you know what I tell them? 'Ask Blackwood! Blackwood knows everything!' That's what I tell them."

Von Helrung smiled easily, placed a convivial hand upon his guest's arm, and turned to the others. "I have given Mr. Riis full confidence in our little trouble. He knows all that you know and can be trusted completely."

Riis grunted. "Well, I can't say I put much stock in this monstrumology business. Seems to me like an excuse for grown men to act like boys hunting frogs in the forest, but this latest business concerns me very much." He nodded at the map. "Von Helrung's theory makes good sense, regardless of *what* may be behind it, man or monster. I will do all that I can, but I am unclear as to what that might be. What do you wish me to do?"

"We need a man who knows the territory," explained von Helrung. "Better than anyone else, better even than the thing we hunt. You have been there. For years you have wandered every side street and alleyway; we have not. You've been in their homes, their churches and synagogues, their speakeasies and penny beer dives and opium dens. They will not speak to us—or to the police—but they will speak to you. They trust you. And it is that very trust that will save them from the beast."

Riis stared at him for a moment. Then he looked at the other monstrumologists, who were nodding gravely. For a moment I actually thought he might burst out laughing. But he did not. He turned back to von Helrung and said, "When do we start?"

"We must wait for tomorrow. Though my heart breaks for those who will surely perish this night, it would be foolhardy to hunt it now. We must attack in the daylight hours, for the night belongs to the beast."

I returned upstairs after the hunting party—or cabal, depending upon one's perspective—had left for the night. I crept past the doctor's room, lest I wake him and be forced to answer questions I'd rather not until absolutely necessary. The hour was late and I was more tired than I ever remembered being, even during that interminable march in the wilderness. My prayer for a peaceful night with only a downy pillow and feather mattress for companionship was to be denied, however. He called to me the moment I passed his door.

"Did you call, sir?" I asked, hovering, quite purposefully, with one foot remaining in the hall.

"I thought I heard voices downstairs."

I cocked my head, pretending to listen. "I don't hear anything, sir."

"Not *now*, Will Henry. *Earlier*. Why do you insist on treating me this way? I'm not entirely imbecilic, you know."

"No, sir. I was confused, sir. I'm sorry."

"Oh, *stop it*. Come in here and close that door. . . . Now tell me what von Helrung's been up to while I've been trapped in this room—the walls of which, by the way, close in by the minute."

I told him everything. He listened without comment or question, until I concluded with von Helrung's closing remarks: *We pray for the dead, but our duty is to the living. We are no match for it—no mortal man is—but with courage and fortitude, life may conquer death, and all this loss, this unbearable sorrow, will not have been in vain. We cannot bring peace to John. He is past all peace; he is beyond all redemption. Remember that when the test comes! It knows nothing but the hunger. But we know more. Nothing but the hunger drives it. But more than that drives us. We are more than what is reflected in the Yellow Eye. Remember that always! In the hours to come we may fall into temptation. We may come ourselves to envy the dead, for they are past all suffering, while our suffering, like Judas's in the pit, goes on and on. And if it should take you, if it should call your name upon the high wind, do not despair. Do not give in to fear as John did. His fate reflects the wages of fear! Have pity upon it as you rip out its heart. It is nothing less than the wreckage of God's temple, forlorn and abandoned, the final, fleeting echo of Adam's sin.*

Wearily the monstrumologist said, "Well, there you have it. He is nothing but marvelously consistent in his madness. 'The wreckage of God's temple!' I'm not surprised about Gravois—he's always been a little bootlicker. Von Helrung could tell him that the sun rose in the west and that little men lived like monkeys in the hairs of his nose, and Gravois would believe him, or say that he did. Dobrogeanu is no surprise either. He and von Helrung cut their monstrumological teeth together; they are quite close. Torrance is somewhat of a surprise. He always struck me as levelheaded, a fine scientist when he wasn't chasing skirts, but he did study under von Helrung for a time. It could be he's giving his old master the benefit of the doubt. But the presence of Pelt is a bit of a shock. It was Pelt, after all, who alerted me to von Helrung's ridiculous proposal in the first place."

He sighed. "We shall see, won't we, Will Henry? God bless Henry Blackwood anyway! You must remind me to thank him when all this is finished. I still owe him the tale of our journey through the wilderness."

"Are you going to join them in the hunt?" I asked.

"What choice do I have? I am his only hope now. If the police find him, I'm not so sure they'll be interested in holding him over for trial. If von Helrung— Well, he's made it clear what he intends to do, hasn't he? The irony of the situation is not lost upon you, I hope."

No, I assured him. It was not.

I walked slowly to my room, wondering what sort of man was this monstrumologist, who saw his mission as one to save a friend—not to bring to justice a brutal killer who had slaughtered ("desecrated" had been his word for it) the woman he loved. Ah, the human heart is darker than the darkest pit, with more winding paths and confusing turns than a Monstrumarium! The more I learned about him, the less I knew. The more I knew, the less I understood.

I started when I opened my bedroom door, for sitting on the bed was Lilly Bates, wearing a pink dressing gown, an open book lying on the bed next to her.

"I'm sorry." I started to back out of the room.

"Where are you going?" she demanded.

"I am in the wrong room. . . ."

"Don't be silly. This is your room. You should sleep with me tonight." She patted the spot next to her. "Unless you're afraid," she teased.

"I'm not afraid," I said with as much firmness as I could muster. "I'm just used to sleeping alone."

"So am I, but you are my guest. At least you are my uncle's guest, which makes you my guest, once removed. I promise I do not snore and I do not bite, and I only drool a little bit." She smiled gaily at me and patted the covers again. "Don't you want to be close to the doctor's room, in case he needs you?"

That argument I had difficulty refuting, and for a moment I considered returning to him and asking if I could share his bed. But then I would have had to explain why, and the cost of *that* answer would have been very high. He might have never shut up and let me sleep. With a sigh I dragged myself over to the bed and sat upon the very edge.

"You're not on," she pointed out.

"I am on."

"You're barely on."

"Barely on is still on."

"How are you going to sleep like that? And you haven't even put on your nightshirt."

"I'm going to sleep in my clothes. In case of an emergency."

"What kind of an emergency?"

"The kind of emergency where you can't be wearing a nightshirt."

"You could curl up on the rug there and sleep at my feet like a faithful dog."

"But I'm not a dog."

"But you're very faithful like a dog."

Inwardly I groaned. What god had I offended to deserve this?

"I think you will make a fine husband one day, William Henry," she decided. "For a woman who likes husbands fearful but faithful. You're not the kind at all I am going to marry. My husband will be brave and very strong and tall, and he will be *musically inclined*. He will write poetry, and he will be smarter than my uncle or even your doctor. He will be smarter than Mr. Thomas Alva Edison."

"Too bad he already has a wife."

"You may make jokes, but don't you ever think about what sort of person you will marry?"

"I'm twelve."

"And I am thirteen—nearly fourteen. What has age to do with it? Juliet found her Romeo when she was my age."

"And look what happened to her."

"Well, you *are* his little apprentice, aren't you? What, you don't believe in love?"

"I don't know enough about it to believe or disbelieve."

She scooted across the bed and brought her face very close to mine. I dared not turn my head to face her.

"What would you do right now, this very moment, if I kissed you?"

I answered with a shake of my head.

"I believe you would fall over in a dead faint. You've never kissed a girl, have you?"

"No."

"Should we test my hypothesis?"

"I would rather we didn't."

"Why not?" I could feel her warm breath on my cheek. "Aren't you studying to be a scientist?"

"I think I'd rather have a Mongolian Death Worm liquefy my flesh."

I should not have said that. I think she had forgotten up to that point. Before I could protest she pulled down the bandage to expose my wound. I remained frozen to the spot as her breath traveled down to the sore.

"I don't think I've ever seen a scab that big," she whispered. She ran the tip of her finger over the spot. "Does that hurt?"

"No. Yes."

"Which is it?"

I didn't answer. I was shivering. I felt very warm, but I shivered.

The mattress squeaked softly. Her weight compressed the springs, tipping me in her direction. Her moist lips pressed against my violated flesh.

"There. Now you've been kissed."

I quickly discovered that, among other things, Lillian Trumbul Bates was a terrible liar. Though she did not bite and did drool only a little bit, she was a terrific snorer. By one a.m. I was actually considering placing a pillow over her face to muffle the sound.

I was thankful, though, for my clothing. The room became very cold during the night; I lost feeling in the tip of my nose. I think Lilly got cold too, for she rolled over in her sleep and pressed herself against me. The moment was both disconcerting and comforting.

We are more than what is reflected in the Yellow Eye, von Helrung had said.

With Lilly curled against me, I stared at the golden splay of light coming from a streetlamp on the avenue below. I rose toward it. I came into it. There was nothing but the golden light.

Then I heard the wind high above. There was the light and there was the wind. There was nothing else. I could hear the wind, but I could not feel it. I floated, incorporeal in the golden light.

There was a voice there in the wind. It was beautiful. It called my name. The voice was in the wind and the wind was in the voice and they were one. The wind and the voice were one.

In the empty room my mother sits, combing out her hair. I am there with her and she is alone. Her face is turned away from me. Her bare arms are golden in the light. It is not her voice that calls me. It is the wind's voice.

The wind has a current like a river rushing to the sea.

It pulls me to her. I do not fight against the current of the wind. I want to be with her in the empty room of golden light.

There, my mother turns to look at me. She has no eyes.

Her face has been stripped of its skin. Her empty sockets are black holes where the golden light is sucked down and cannot escape. There is no escape.

The high wind howls. There is no difference between the wind and my name, and my name has no beginning and no ending.

I fall into the lightless pit of my mother's eyes.

Out of the nothingness a hand reached out, grabbed my collar, and yanked me backward, away from the open window. I fought against my rescuer, but he had wrapped his long arms around me, and now I could hear his voice, not the wind's voice, calling my name.

"Will Henry! Will Henry . . ."

The doctor grunted softly as I strained to free myself, kicking impotently against the smooth floorboards, trying to answer the wind that sighed its cold breath upon our faces. I heard Lilly asking again and again in a high-pitched, hysterical voice, "What is it? *What is it?*" And then I saw Dr. von Helrung kneeling beside me, holding a lamp close to my face. He was saying to the doctor, "*Nein, nein,* not his name, Pellinore. Do not say his name!" He slapped me lightly across the cheek.

"Look at me!" he shouted. "Listen to me! To *me*! It is passed—gone!"

He was right; it *was* gone. And I started to cry, for I felt so empty without it. I was overwhelmed with shame; I was mortified. *I was supposed to answer.* The wind wanted me, and I wanted the wind.

"Please, Pellinore, please," von Helrung urged the doctor. Warthrop's grip loosened, and the old man pulled me into his arms. He wrapped one around my shoulders and with his large hand pressed my ear to his chest; I could hear the beating of his heart. Like the wind upon which my name rode, an irresistible current runs deep in the hidden chambers of our hearts, "till human voices wake us, and we drown."

"A dream," the monstrumologist said. "A hallucination borne of *khorkhoi* venom and severe physical and psychological trauma."

"It is my fault," groaned von Helrung. "I should have barred the window."

"In all likelihood he would have survived the fall."

"He would not have fallen, *mein Freund*. Oh, if that were the only thing to fear! It has come for him. For him! This cannot be. We cannot allow it, Pellinore. He must be sent away immediately—"

"Don't be ridiculous," snapped the doctor.

"On the first train to Boston."

"Will Henry is not going anywhere."

"He is in grave danger, should he remain."

"And worse if he leaves, von Helrung. I am all the boy has, and I am not leaving."

"Please don't send me away, sir," I whispered. My throat hurt terribly, as if I had been screaming at the top of my lungs.

"I understand, Pellinore, but you must understand it will not stop. It *cannot* stop. It will call until it finds him—or he finds it, for it compels him now. As it compelled the others—Larose, Hawk, Skala, and Bartholomew—and Muriel, Pellinore. Think of Muriel! Would you have him suffer the same fate? In your stubbornness, will you stand idly by and let it take Will, too?"

"I am at the end of my patience with this lunacy. Nothing has 'called' Will Henry. Will Henry had a nightmare, completely understandable and even predictable, given what has transpired over the past twenty-four hours."

Von Helrung threw up his hands in a gesture of dismay.

"Eyes that do not see! Ears that do not hear! Ack! I thought I had trained you better than that, Pellinore Warthrop! Set it aside, then. Set it all aside! John is not dead—he is not *Outiko*. He is psychotic, driven to murder by the demons found in the desolation, a monster still, but a monster of human proportions. If it is not the hunger that drives him, what does? Why does he take Muriel, and why now does he try to take Will Henry? What do they share, Pellinore? What is the one thing they have in common? Please, for the love of God, at least admit that. Call it what you will. Call it lunacy. Call it madness. But within the madness there is method. You know this to be true."

"I won't make the same mistake twice, *Meister* Abram. Will Henry will be safe with me."

TWENTY-SIX
"He Is Not So Different"

Lilly took her leave early the next morning. Though shaken by the strange and disturbing events of the previous night, she was well aware of the plan to hunt down the remnants of Dr. John Chanler, and she was not happy to be excluded from the chase. Her dissatisfaction was made all the more unpalatable by the fact that I, in what she called my "deplorable condition," would be a full participant.

"It's because I'm a girl," she pouted. "Look at this!" She held up her index finger and flexed it rapidly in my face. "It can pull a trigger as well as yours, William Henry—better even, and probably faster. I wouldn't be afraid, either; I'd walk right up to him and blow his brains out. I don't care what sort of man-eating monster he's become."

I didn't argue with her. I completely agreed, actually, that she had it in her to walk up to almost anything and blow its brains out. She had the heart of a monstrumologist, that was certain; it just so happened that that heart belonged to a girl.

"You will see," she promised me. "One day I *will*. You can't keep us down forever; I don't care how hard you try. One day we'll even have the right to vote, and then see what happens to all you pompous men. We'll make a woman president! You'll see."

Then, moving with the lightning speed of an attacking Mongolian Death Worm, Lilly Bates grabbed my shoulders and planted a wet kiss upon my cheek.

"That is for luck," she said. "And good-bye. I may never see you again, Will."

Shortly thereafter the first pair of hunters arrived, the experienced Dobrogeanu and the young Torrance, followed a few minutes later by Pelt, his drooping mustache dotted with fine grains of snow. Bad weather was coming, he said, and Dobrogeanu agreed, averring that the aching in his knees invariably presaged that. Gravois was the last to arrive. He'd had trouble finding a cab, he explained as he brushed crumbs from his vest.

His face lit up at the sight of Warthrop, who winced when Gravois hugged him. The doctor begged off the traditional greeting of a kiss on either cheek. Despite the previous day's compress, Warthrop's jaw was horribly swollen.

"It is not so bad," opined the Frenchman of my master's

distorted features. "An improvement, in my opinion. What does the physician say? You will be able to join us, yes?"

"I am here, aren't I?" Warthrop answered testily.

Gravois's eyes grew misty. "Pellinore, words cannot express my grief. The loss, it is . . ."

"Inexplicable," said the doctor. "And avoidable."

"You must not blame yourself."

"Who do you propose? I am open to suggestions."

Von Helrung called the meeting to order and briefly, for him, welcomed Warthrop into their little band.

"Good to see you on your feet, Warthrop," Pelt said. "I must admit I had my reservations until von Helrung told me you were joining our party."

"You'll be hiring an attorney, I suppose," said Dobrogeanu. "*I* would. Demand a formal inquiry, force the city into bankruptcy, have that terrible man Byrnes arrested for assault and battery!"

"He is not so different from us," my master replied cryptically.

"Yes, thank you, Pellinore," said von Helrung quickly. "Now to the most recent development, which bears directly upon our task."

He related to the astonished men the events of the night before. A lively discussion ensued. What did it mean? Was it, as the doctor vehemently maintained, merely a nightmare—a hallucination induced by *khorkhoi* venom and exacerbated by the day's horrific events? Or was it, as von Helrung claimed with equal fervor, exactly what it appeared to be—an attempt by their quarry to snatch me? Torrance proposed the latter possibility should be put aside for now, suggesting that if we failed in locating the beast by any other means, we might turn its desire against it.

"Let it come to us," he said.

"So your plan is to use the boy as bait," said the doctor. "Because he has heard voices inside his head."

"Only as the last, desperate measure," Torrance replied, his face turning red. Warthrop clearly intimidated him.

"There is a flavor of desperation about it," Warthrop returned.

"For myself," intoned Pelt in his sonorous voice, "I am heartened by the news of this attack—*if* it was an attack; I do not say that it was, Pellinore—for it's the only news that I've heard from last night. Have any of you seen the papers this morning? I'm happy to report there's nothing that fits our subject's modus operandi."

Von Helrung waved his hand. "That means nothing. The city will suppress all that it can now to avoid panic and political embarrassment. I doubt a reporter can get within a hundred yards of police headquarters."

"If any representative of the third estate can, though, it is Riis," said Dobrogeanu.

"Speaking of Riis, where the devil is he?" wondered Torrance.

"It would be terrible, would it not," Gravois said with a

sparkle in his dark eyes, "if he, the one indispensable cog in our machine, should have fallen victim to the one we seek?"

"That is a horrible thought," huffed Pelt.

"I am a monstrumologist," returned Gravois easily. "It is my business to think horrible thoughts."

Riis had survived the night, of course. He appeared near midmorning, when the discussion had petered out to an errant comment here and there with long pauses in between. The day, as if in spite, grew darker. The buildings across Fifth Avenue brooded in semidarkness; the snow, now half an inch deep, shone gray on the sidewalk. Von Helrung smoked two puffs from his Havana and then put it out. When the bell rang, he jumped from his chair, knocking over the ashtray and sending the extinguished stogie rolling across the Persian carpet. Gravois picked it up and slipped it into his pocket.

"Warthrop," the Danish journalist said, shaking the doctor's hand. "You look terrible."

"It's a pleasure to see you again too, Riis."

"I meant no offense. If it's any comfort, I have seen much worse coming out of Mulberry Street, the kind that is carted away in a hearse."

"Thank you, Riis; I feel much better now."

Riis smiled. That smile quickly faded. "Well, von Helrung, you had better break out your box of red pins. Your beast has been quite busy. There have been three, perhaps four, more," he informed the monstrumologists. He pointed out the spots on the map, whereupon von Helrung stabbed it with his symbolically colored pins. "I say 'perhaps' because one is a disappearance, from the Bohemian quarter. No body has turned up, but the circumstances seemed to fit the disturbing criteria you described. Witnesses report a terrible smell, glimpses of a wraithlike figure with enormous glowing eyes, and, in one remarkable report from a none-too-reliable source, the appearance of a large gray wolf upon a nearby rooftop."

"A wolf?" echoed Torrance.

"It is a shape-changer," von Helrung said. "Fully supported by the literature."

"Yes, catalogued under *fiction*," Warthrop responded contemptuously.

Riis shrugged. "The others are clearly the work of our man—or whatever it is. Remains—and I do mean *remains*—were discovered high above the street. Two upon tenement roofs, the third impaled upon a stovepipe above a restaurant there"—he nodded toward the pin—"in Chinatown. That one is particularly striking, I thought, if for no other reason but the sheer *force* it would take to drive such an object through a human body."

I glanced at the doctor. Was he thinking the same thing as I? Did he see in his mind's eye, as I did, the jagged trunk of a shattered tree rising from Pierre Larose's desecrated corpse?

"All were missing their eyes and the skin on their faces,"

Riis continued. "It had been stripped from the underlying musculature with surgical precision. All were found nude." He swallowed, for the first time a bit overcome. He pulled a handkerchief from his pocket and dabbed his brow.

"And all three were young. The oldest was the only son of a Chinaman who immigrated here last August. The boy was fifteen and quite small for his age."

"The weakest," murmured von Helrung. "The most vulnerable."

"The youngest was found at Mulberry Bend, only a few blocks from my office. A girl. She was seven. She suffered by far the worst mutilations. I will spare you the details."

No one spoke for a moment. Then von Helrung asked softly, "Their hearts."

"Yes, yes," Riis nodded. "Ripped from their chests—and when I say 'ripped,' I do mean *ripped*. Flesh flayed open, ribs snapped in two, and the hearts themselves . . ."

He did not finish. Von Helrung placed a consoling hand on his shoulder, a hand that Riis immediately shrugged off.

"I thought I had seen every horror imaginable in the slums of this metropolis. Starvation, drunkenness, depravity. Deprivation and despair that rivals the worst of the most wretched European ghetto. But this. *This.*"

"It is only the beginning," von Helrung said somberly. "And only the part of the beginning we know of. More victims will be found this day, I fear."

"Then we haven't a moment to lose," said Torrance. Riis's

report had gotten his blood up. "Let's do what we're trained to do, gentlemen. Let's hunt down this thing and kill it."

Warthrop's reaction was immediate. He whirled upon the younger man and slammed his cane onto the tabletop, causing Torrance to jerk in his chair.

"Any man who harms John Chanler will answer to me!" the doctor snarled. "I will not truck with cold-blooded murder, sir."

"Nor I," agreed Pelt. "Unless we've no choice."

"Of course, of course," von Helrung said hurriedly. He avoided Warthrop's icy glare. "The line between what we are and what we pursue is razor thin. We will remember our humanity."

Von Helrung proposed the division of the group into three teams, each to investigate the crimes reported by Riis. Warthrop did not like the idea; he insisted the party should stay together; division only weakened us and diminished our chances for success. He was overruled, but he retreated by inches, not yards, disagreeing next with the composition of the teams as devised by von Helrung. He had paired Warthrop with Pelt, himself with Dobrogeanu, and Torrance with Gravois.

"Experience should be paired with youth," he argued. "I should go with you, *Meister* Abram. Pelt with Torrance, Gravois with Dobrogeanu."

"Pellinore is correct," agreed Pelt. "It would not do if you and Dobrogeanu were faced with it—if it is as strong and fast as you say."

Dobrogeanu stiffened. He was offended. "I resent the implication that I can't handle myself in a pinch. Need I remind you, sir, who it was that single-handedly captured— *alive*, I might add—the only specimen of *Malus cerebrum comedo* in the history of monstrumology?"

"That was quite a few years ago," Pelt said dryly. "I meant no offense. I am not much younger than you, and I think Pellinore's idea makes capital sense."

That—and the urgency of the hour—put an end to the debate. Riis took his leave, promising he would return at nightfall with an update and, hopefully, to congratulate us on a successful prosecution.

It fell to me to escort Riis to the door. He tucked his muffler into his coat and tugged the collar high, squinting through his round spectacles at the gray landscape. The snow brought back disquieting memories; we had left the gray land, and now it seemed the gray land had come back for us.

"I would like to give you a piece of advice, young man," he said. "Would you like to hear it?"

I nodded dutifully. "Yes, sir."

He leaned toward me, bringing to bear the entire force of his formidable presence. "*Leave*. Run away! At once, without delay. Run as if the devil himself were after you. There is something altogether unnerving about this business. Unfit for children." He shuddered in the cold air. "He seems to like children."

✳

Back in the war room von Helrung had laid out six boxes and several long silver-plated knives. All, with the exception of Warthrop, were checking their weapons, testing the firing mechanisms and examining with frank curiosity the contents of the boxes, holding the gleaming silver projectiles up to the light.

"There is nothing in the literature to suggest that *Lepto lurconis* requires sleep," the Austrian monstrumologist was saying. "And it is my inclination that we will not find it in such a felicitous state.

"Legend *does* tell us with what tremendous speed it attacks and what frightful power is employed in that attack. The *Outiko* uses its eyes to mesmerize its prey. To look into the Yellow Eye is to perish; do not forget!

"Do not waste your ammunition; it is precious. Only by piercing the heart can you destroy *Lepto lurconis*."

"And only as a last resort," put in Warthrop.

Von Helrung cut his eyes away and said, "More powerful than its eyes is its voice. Little Will heard it last night and nearly succumbed. If it calls your name, resist! Do not answer! Do not think you can deceive it by pretending to fall under its spell. It will consume you."

He looked at each man in turn. The gravity of the moment settled over our little assemblage. Even Gravois seemed subdued, lost in his own dark thoughts.

"What we seek, gentlemen, is as old as life itself," von

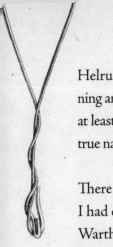

Helrung said. "And as constant as death. It is ruthless and cunning and ever hungry. It may be as devious as Lucifer, but in this at least it has been honest with us. It has not hidden from us its true nature."

There remained but one small matter—what to do with me. I had expected, naturally, to accompany the doctor, but even Warthrop didn't seem keen on the idea. He worried with some justification that I might be in danger of falling into a venom-induced delirium at any moment, rendering me an unwanted and potentially fatal hindrance. Equally unattractive was leaving me behind. Von Helrung was particularly opposed to this alternative; he was convinced that the beast had "marked" me the night before. Dobrogeanu suggested they drop me off at the Society.

"If he isn't safe among a hundred monstrumologists, where will he be?" he wondered.

"I think he should come with us," Torrance said. Apparently he had not given up on the idea of somehow using me as bait. "Other than Warthrop, he's the only one among us who's come face-to-face with one of these things."

Warthrop winced. "John Chanler is not a 'thing,' Torrance."

"Well, whatever he is."

"But I do agree that his experience could prove indispensable," Warthrop continued. "Therefore, he should come, but not with me. Gravois, you and Dobrogeanu shall take him."

"But I don't want them to take me!" I cried out, forgetting

myself at the intolerable notion of being separated from him. "I want to go with you, Doctor."

He ignored my entreaty. His eyes had taken on that familiar backlit glow. He seemed both with us and very far away.

He pulled me aside as the men loaded their weapons with silver bullets and strapped the silver blades to their belts.

"Understand, Will Henry—my chief concern is protecting John from these madmen. I cannot be all places at once. I've spoken with Pelt, who has agreed to keep the overeager Torrance on a tight leash. I must rely on you to be my eyes with Gravois and Dobrogeanu. Gravois I have little concern about—the man hasn't fired a weapon in his life and couldn't hit the broad side of a barn if he did. And Dobrogeanu can't see four inches past his own nose. But he is fierce, even if he is old. Do you still have the knife?"

I nodded. "Yes, sir."

"It is nonsense, you know that."

"Yes, sir."

"John Chanler is a very sick man, Will Henry. I do not pretend to understand everything about his illness, but he himself would not argue that you have every right to defend yourself."

I told him I understood. The monstrumologist was giving me permission to kill his best friend.

TWENTY-SEVEN
"The Water"

They were not so different in the end, the place where he was lost and the place where he was found. They differed only in their topography.

The wilderness and the slum were but two faces of the same desolation. The gray land of soul-crushing nothingness in the slum was as bereft of hope as the burned-out snow-packed *brûlé* of the forest. The denizens of the slums were stalked by the same hunger, preyed upon by predators no less savage than their woodland counterparts. The immigrants lived in squalid tenements, crowded into rooms not much larger than a closet, and their lives were mean and short. Only two of five children born into the ghetto could expect to see their eighteenth year. The rest succumbed to the ravenous hunger of typhoid and cholera, the insatiable appetites of malaria and diphtheria.

It was little wonder that the beast had chosen this for its hunting ground. Here was prey numbering in the hundreds of thousands, packed into a radius measured in blocks, not miles, prey more anonymous and powerless than the most isolated of *Iyiniwok* villagers, but just as familiar with the call that rode on the high wind, beckoning them in the universal language of desire.

By coming here, the beast had come home.

By lot my group had drawn the Bohemian ghetto, where a young girl named Anezka Nováková had vanished the day before, her disappearance not reported to the police but to the local priest, who in turn had told Riis.

Anezka, we learned, was not the sort of girl who would simply take off. She was extremely shy, and small for her age, a dutiful elder daughter who helped her parents roll cigars for $1.20 a day (to feed, clothe, and house a family of six). She was shut up in their tiny two-room flat for eighteen grueling hours each day, just one of the thousands of indentured slaves of the tobacco lords. Her family had discovered her missing that morning. Sometime in the night, while the family had slept, Anezka Nováková had vanished.

Dobrogeanu, who spoke passable Czech, obtained the address from the priest, who seemed to have some trouble understanding our interest in the case, but the name of Riis held great currency in his parish. The reformer's involvement granted legitimacy to our cause, though the cleric retained his native distrust of outsiders.

"You are not detectives?" he asked Gravois. He seemed particularly suspicious of a Frenchman poking his Gallic snout into the neighborhood.

"We are scientists," Gravois answered smoothly.

"Scientists?"

"Like detectives, Father, only better dressed."

Anezka's flat was within walking distance of the church, though the walk was more like a hike in the premature twilight of billowing snow. On every corner the fires of the ash barrels burned like beacons marking our descent into the teaming tenement, the smoke from which thickened the curtain of snow and obscured the landscape. We moved in a world of few contrasts, a purgatory of gray.

Midway down the block, Dobrogeanu slipped into a narrow space (it could hardly be called an alley) between two decrepit buildings, a passage so narrow we were forced to turn sideways and shuffle along, our backs to one wall, our noses only an inch or so from the other. We emerged into an open space no larger than von Helrung's parlor.

We had arrived in the warren of the rear-houses—so called because of their location off the main thoroughfare. There were perhaps thirty to forty hastily constructed tenement buildings crammed three or four to a single lot, separated by winding passages as narrow as jungle footpaths, amid a labyrinth of weathered fences and clotheslines strung from posts and rickety stair rails, the lifeless ground packed as hard as concrete by the tread of a thousand ill-shod feet. I heard the bleating of goats and smelled the reek of the outdoor privies that sat astride shallow trenches brimming with human waste.

"Which one is it?" wondered Gravois nervously. His hand had vanished into his overcoat pocket, where he carried the gun loaded with silver bullets.

Dobrogeanu scowled. "I can't see three feet in this hellish soup."

A group of four ragamuffins materialized out of that soup—the oldest no more than ten—dressed alike in the filthiest of hand-me-downs, their baggy trousers held up with belts fashioned from rags. They crowded around the two monstrumologists, tugging on their coats and extending their palms, piping in a cacophonous chorus, "*Dolar? Dolar, pane? Dolar, dolar?*"

"Yes, yes," Gravois said testily. "*Ano, ano.*"

He distributed the begged-for coins into the clawing hands, and then withdrew a five-dollar note from his purse, holding it before their startled faces. Suddenly they were as quiet as church mice.

"*Znáš Nováková?*" asked Dobrogeanu. "*Kde žije Naváková?*"

At the mention of the name the little group grew very grave, their avariciousness replaced by trepidation. They quickly crossed themselves, and two made a sign to ward off the evil eye, muttering, "*Upír. Upír!*"

"*Kdo je statečný?*" Dobrogeanu asked in a stern voice. "*Kdo mě vezme domů?*"

While three of the boys shuffled their feet and cast their eyes upon the ground, a lad—by no means the oldest or the largest of the lot—stepped forward. His face was drawn, the cheekbones large, the eyes dominant. He tried his best to speak bravely, but the tremor in his voice betrayed him.

"*Nebojím se,*" he said. "*Vezmu vás.*"

He snatched the note from Gravois's hand. It disappeared into some secret pocket in his filthy attire. His comrades melted back into the shadows, leaving the four of us stranded on that little island of bald earth, ringed on all sides by the crumbling edifices of the rear-houses.

Our newfound guide navigated the serpentine course through the bewildering snarl of clotheslines and fences with unerring step. This was his universe, and no doubt, if every particle of light had been sucked from our atmosphere, he could have found his way through the utter blackness left behind.

He stopped at the rear of a building indistinguishable from the rest—the same sagging stairs masquerading as a fire escape, zigzagging four stories up to the roof; the same warped platforms that passed for balconies, framed in by broken rails.

"*Nováková,*" the boy whispered, pointing at the tenement.

"Which floor?" Dobrogeanu asked. "*Jaký patro?* What flat? *Který byt?*"

The urchin's reply was silent. He merely presented his palm. Gravois sighed heavily and gave him another five-dollar note.

"*Ve čtvrtém patře. Poslední dveře vlevo.*" His expression became very serious. "*Nikdo tam není.*"

Dobrogeanu frowned. "*Nikdo tam není?* What do you mean?"

"What does he mean?" echoed Gravois.

The boy jabbed his finger at the brooding tenement. "*Upír.*" He clawed the air and bared his teeth. "*To mu ted' patří.*"

"He says it belongs to the *upír* now."

The urchin nodded vigorously. "*Upír! Upír!*"

"'*Upír*'?" asked Gravois. "What is this *upír* he's talking about?"

"Vampire," answered Dobrogeanu.

"Ah! Well, now we are getting somewhere!"

"The building is empty," the other monstrumologist said. "He says it belongs to *upír* now."

"Does he? Then, we are wasting our time. I suggest we return to von Helrung and make a full report—*tout de suite*, before night falls."

Dobrogeanu turned to ask the boy another question and was astonished to find him gone. He had disappeared into the icy mist as abruptly as he had appeared. For a moment no one spoke. Gravois's mind was already made up, but the elderly monstrumologist teetered between charging forward and sounding the retreat. It was a tantalizing lead—an abandoned building that now belonged to the *upír*, the closest the lexicon could come to *Lepto lurconis*. Yet he suspected our guide may have been merely giving us our money's worth. For five dollars more he might have gladly informed us that in the basement we might find a stairway to hell.

"He could be lying," he mused. "It may not be abandoned at all."

"Do you see any lights inside?" asked Gravois. "I do not see any. Monsieur Henry, your eyes are young. Do you see lights?"

I did not. Only dark panes dimly reflecting the glow from the ash barrels in the courtyard.

"And we have none," pointed out Gravois. "What good will it do, stumbling about in the dark?"

"It isn't dark yet," countered Dobrogeanu. "We have a few hours still."

"Perhaps our definitions of 'dark' differ. I say we let Monsieur Henry break the tie. What is your opinion, Will?"

So rarely was I asked for one, I did not realize I even had an opinion until it came out of my mouth. "We should go in. We have to know."

Up the rickety back stairs we climbed, Dobrogeanu leading the way, one hand hidden in his cloak, no doubt gripping his revolver. I followed next, fingering the hilt of the knife to steady my nerves. Gravois brought up the rear, muttering in

French what sounded like curses. Once or twice I caught the word 'Pellinore.'

The stairs were alarmingly insubstantial, swaying with each step of our slow ascent, the old boards crying tremulant squeaks and protesting groans. We reached the fourth-story landing, whereupon our leader pulled the revolver from his pocket and pushed open the door, and we followed him.

A narrow, poorly lit hallway ran the length of the building, its walls coated with decades of accumulated grime, the floor speckled with water stains and darker blemishes of unknown origin, perhaps urine or excrement, for the passage reeked of both—and of boiled cabbage, tobacco, wood smoke, and that peculiar funk of human desperation.

It was very cold and deathly quiet. We stood for a moment without moving, hardly breathing, straining our ears for any sound that might give proof of life. There was nothing. Dobrogeanu whispered, "End of the hall, last door on the left."

"Will Henry should investigate," urged Gravois. "He is the smallest and the lightest of tread. We'll stay here and cover his advance."

Dobrogeanu stared at him from beneath his thick gray eyebrows.

"How did you ever become a monstrumologist, Gravois?"

"A combination of familial pressure and social retardation."

Dobrogeanu grunted softly. "Come along, Will; Gravois, stay here if you like, but watch those stairs!"

We proceeded carefully down the hall, passing midway down a central staircase on the right. The sole source of light came from the fire escape door, and that light faded as we went.

Dobrogeanu stepped over a bundle of rags, pointing it out lest I trip over it in the gloom. To my surprise I saw the bundle was *moving*—and then I realized the rags were wrapped around an infant, no more than a few months old, its toothless mouth stretched wide in a pitifully silent cry. Its dark eyes moved restlessly in their sockets; its stick-thin arms flailed the air.

I tugged at the old man's sleeve and pointed at the child. His eyebrows rose in astonishment.

"Is it alive?" he whispered.

I squatted beside the abandoned child. Its little hand caught my finger and held it tight. The eyes, which appeared very large in the emaciated face, had fixed upon me. It considered me with frank curiosity, squeezing my finger.

"Its parents must be somewhere," Dobrogeanu surmised. "Come, Will."

He urged me to my feet. The baby did not cry when I withdrew my finger. Perhaps it was too weak or too sick to cry.

Dobrogeanu started down the hall, but I did not move. I looked down at the baby by my feet. It was too much for me. How many times had I bemoaned my fate, the gross injustice of my parents' deaths, or my service to an eccentric genius whose dark pursuits demanded that I endure the most alarming of scenarios, unto the risk of my very life? Yet what was my experience compared to that hungry child's, forlorn in a filthy hall reeking of piss and cabbages? What did I understand of suffering?

"What is it?" asked Dobrogeanu. He had looked behind and discovered me frozen to the spot.

"We can't just leave it here," I said.

"If we take it, what will happen when its parents return for it? Leave it alone, Will."

"We can take it to the priest," I said. "He'll know what to do with it."

I could see its dark eyes in the gathering night, seeking mine.

The line between what we are and what we pursue is razor thin. We will remember our humanity.

My soul writhed. I felt as if I were being ground between two great stones.

Dobrogeanu was now at the end of the hall. "Will!" he called softly. "Leave it!"

Biting my lip, I stepped over the child. What could I do? Its suffering had nothing to do with me. It would have been in that cold, stinking hall whether or not I'd been there. So I stepped over it. I turned my back upon it and left it there.

The baby did not cry after me; in its eyes I had recognized the same dull listlessness I'd seen in the wilderness, the way Sergeant Hawk's eyes had looked the night he'd disappeared, the vacant stare of hunger, the inexpressible ache of desire.

Dobrogeanu commenced banging on the door. The sound jumped and bounced between the close walls; it seemed very loud, as all sounds do in the near dark. We waited, but no one answered. He tried the knob next, and the door opened with a protesting screech.

"Hello?" the old monstrumologist called. *"Je někdo doma?"* He drew out his revolver.

The Nováková flat was typical of most dismal tenement roosts: walls of cracked and crumbling plaster; a ceiling pockmarked with water stains; a warped floor that groaned in protest with every step. The room was clean, though, and an effort had been made to brighten the dingy walls with cheap prints of bright sunlit landscapes. It was heartbreaking—almost cruel—those fields of daffodils and lilies mocking the squalor around them.

A table and bench ran the length of one wall. Large wicker baskets filled with cut tobacco leaf were lined end to end beneath the table. Here Anezka and her parents had hunched with cramping fingers, rolling cigars that would, by the great machinations of American commerce, end up in the mouths of men such as Chief Inspector Thomas Byrnes.

There was only one other room, separated from the first by a ratty sheet, a closet-size sleeping space that was a disaster of wadded clothing and rumpled bedsheets. I spied a doll propped up against the far corner, its bright eyes glittering in the washed-out light filtering through the window behind us.

"Where have they gone?" I whispered.

"To look for her," Dobrogeanu surmised, but it was as much a question as a statement.

"The rest of the building too?"

He shook his head and turned back. He tapped me on the shoulder and pointed to a lamp that sat upon the table. I understood at once. After I lit the lamp, he said, "We'll have to search the building. Knock on every door, top to bottom. . . . Either they have fled into this foul weather—and there is only one reason I can think of—or they huddle in terror inside their hovels. Only one way to find out, Will!"

We left the flat. I looked for the baby immediately, but it was gone. The significance of this was not lost on Dobrogeanu. "*Someone* is here, at least," he said. He turned toward the fire escape and caught his breath. "Filthy coward!" he softly snarled.

Gravois, like the child in the hall, had vanished.

Dobrogeanu pushed open the fire escape door and stepped outside. He leaned over the rickety railing and squinted down to the courtyard below.

"Useless," he muttered. "Completely useless!" He shook his head with frustration. "What to do," he muttered. "What to do?"

From the stairway down the hall came a resounding crash.

A moment later we heard the heavy *thump-thump-thump* of a large object tumbling down the wooden steps. Dobrogeanu yanked his gun from his pocket and hurried as fast as his old legs could carry him to the head of the stairs. I trailed a few steps behind, heartbeat thudding in my ears like a sympathetic echo of that unseen fall. Our light fought against the dark, failing to penetrate but a few feet in the deep gloom. Dobrogeanu laid a hand upon my shoulder.

"Stay here," he whispered. He pulled the lamp from my hand and proceeded downward toward the third-floor landing. He turned the corner, gun thrust in front of him, his shadow hard-edged as if etched upon the boards, and then I lost sight of him. The glow of the lamp faded.

"Oh, no." His disembodied voice floated up to me. "Oh, *no.*"

I followed the light down. Midway to the next landing I discovered Dobrogeanu sprawled on the stairs, his back pressed against the wall, and cradled in his arms the lifeless, broken body of Damien Gravois, his white shirtfront shining with fresh arterial blood, his sanguine face enshrouded by the same soiled swaddling clothes that had wrapped the baby in the hallway. His eyes had been pulled from their sockets; they dangled over his cheeks, still attached to the optic nerves.

"I found him," Dobrogeanu said. It was an absurdly obvious observation.

He eased the body onto the stairs and pushed himself

to his feet, using the wall behind him for support. I grabbed the lamp off the step.

"What do we do?" I whispered, though my voice seemed terribly loud.

"What we are trained to do," he answered grimly, echoing Torrance. His gray eyes sparked with fire. He yelled down the stairs, *"Chanler!"* and then he took off, descending with the speed of a man half his age. I caught up to him on the first-floor landing, where he had paused, listening.

"Do you hear that?" he asked.

I shook my head. I heard nothing but the sound of our ragged breath and the far-off *drip-drip* of a water pipe. And then I did hear it, the soft, plaintive crying of an infant. It seemed to be coming from everywhere—and nowhere.

"He has taken the child," Dobrogeanu whispered. He peered down the stairs leading to the cellar. He wet his lips nervously. He seemed torn. "Down there, do you think?"

We had only minutes to decide. If we chose wrong—if he had taken it instead to the first floor and we chose the other path—the child was doomed. My companion, with his years of experience, seemed paralyzed by indecision.

"We'll have to split up," I said. He did not reply. "Sir, are you listening?"

"Yes, yes," he muttered. "Here," he pressed Gravois's pearl-handled pistol into my hand. He nodded toward the blackness beneath us. "You keep the lamp, Will. I should have enough light up here."

And so I went down, to the very bottom, alone.

The steps narrowed. The suppurating walls closed in. A stench rose up to meet me, the smell of raw sewage. A pipe had burst and never been repaired, transforming the tenement cellar into a cesspool. The smell nearly overpowered me. Midway down I gagged; my throat burned and my stomach rolled in protest. I heard nothing at all now, and that emboldened me, for it must have meant he was not down there, but I knew I had to look to be sure.

The water at the bottom was more than two feet deep and was covered in a greenish-yellow slime. Broken boards—the remnants of storage barrels—floated in the stagnant stinking pool. I saw the body of an enormous rat floating near my feet, the skin of its bloated corpse peeling off as it rotted; something had already devoured its eyes. I could see its yellow fangs glimmering in its mouth, which was yawning open in a silent howl.

I stopped on the last step, upon the banks of this foul underground pond, holding my light high, but it could not drive back all the darkness. The far end remained swallowed in stygian shadow. What was that bobbing just on the edge of the light? A piece of broken wood? An old bottle? The scum-covered surface undulated; the boards seesawed in the reeking black water. I heard nothing except the steady *drip-drip* of the leaking pipe.

I turned to leave—clearly nothing was down here—and

a voice inside my head spoke up. It was the voice of my master:

Pay attention, Will Henry! What do you notice about the water?

I hesitated. I had to get out. I could not *breathe* in that nasty hole. Chanler was not there. The baby was not there. Dobrogeanu needed me.

And still the voice persisted: *The water, Will Henry, the water.*

I started back up the stairs. Should I call out for Dobrogeanu? Or had he already met the same fate as Gravois, and now it was my turn?

Will Henry, the water . . .

Shut up about the water! I shouted silently at the voice. *I have to find Dr. Dobrogeanu. . . .*

I froze about six feet above the pool. I turned back. The rat's empty eye socket stared back at me.

"The water is *moving*," I said to the dead rat. "Why would it be moving?"

The voice in my head fell silent. Finally I was using that indispensable appendage between my ears.

Hot tears stung my eyes, partly from the smell, but mostly from understanding. I knew why the water moved. And I knew why I'd heard no crying.

The lamp created a perfect sphere of light around me. I waded into the sewage, my feet slipping on the slimy brick bottom. I could feel the filthy water seep into my boots. The dead rat nudged my knee with its long nose as I passed.

It was not a bottle or an old board I had seen floating in the excremental soup. When I reached for it, my foot slipped and I fell with a soft cry, catching myself by dropping the gun and pushing against the bottom with my right hand. That allowed me to keep the lamp aloft in my left. Its light played along the upturned face that floated a foot away; that was all I could see—the baby's face. The rest was hidden beneath the mustard yellow scum. I pushed myself up. Now I kneeled before it—coughing, gagging, sobbing. I didn't care anymore if the beast heard me. All I could see was that face, smeared in jellylike feces, the blank eyes sightlessly staring into the abyss above.

I could not leave it there, not in this place. I reached out for it.

My knuckles brushed across the cheek. The face dipped down, bobbed up again. It turned leisurely like an unmoored boat.

I knew then. I had found him, but not all of him. I had found just his face.

"Oh, no," I whimpered, as Dobrogeanu had, as the doctor had when in the wilderness he'd realized we were lost—the timeless refrain, the ageless response. "No."

We can take it to the priest. He'll know what to do with it.

With those words I had abandoned him in a cold and dirty hallway. I had stepped over him, thinking there was nothing I could do. I had stepped over him, telling myself that his suffering had nothing to do with me.

In the wasteland of the gray light, where the black buteos rode on updrafts above the ruins of the forest, a man had heaved his burden over his shoulder. *This is mine!* he had cried in the cold, dead air. *Mine!* He had not sent him there; it had not been the doctor's choice that he go. But the doctor had claimed his friend after the fall. He had accepted his burden.

So overwhelmed was I by the enormity of my crime that I did not hear the beast. The water bubbled behind me, a board bumped against my back; I did not feel it. When the beast rose out of the filth and its shadow fell hard upon me, I did not see it. The sightless eyes of the child held me. The discarnate face gripped me.

Out of the corner of my eye, there was the blur of its arm rocketing around before the hard fist slammed into the side of my head. Something tore free in my mind, a violent upheaval like a volcano exploding. The lamp flew from my hand and shattered against the cellar wall with a loud pop before dropping into the sewage and sputtering out. I pitched forward, tumbling into the abyss.

TWENTY-EIGHT

"I Have Found Him"

My name was in the wind, and the wind was high above the snowbound city. There was no difference between the sound of my name and the sound of the wind. I was in the wind and the wind was in me, and beneath us were the crystalline haloes of golden light wrapped about the streetlamps, and the muffled plops of snow falling from eaves, and the dry rattles of the dead leaves clinging to the indifferent boughs.

It is beautiful here on the high wind. From here our suffering shrinks to insignificance; the wind drowns out the human cry. The city in snow glitters like a diamond, its streets laid out in mathematical precision, the rooftops identical blank canvases. There is perfection in the emptiness. They say God looks down upon us, like the buteos that soar above the blasted landscape of the gray land. There is God in the distance. Humanity's stench cannot waft this high. Our betrayals, our jealousies, our fears, they rise no higher than the tops of our heads.

In a lightless cellar flooded with human waste, a starving infant is held under until it drowns, its tiny lungs filled with the effluvia of six hundred of its fellow human beings, and then its face is peeled off, as one takes off the skin of an apple, peeled off, and cast into Dante's river. . . .

In the name of all that's holy, tell me why God felt the need to make a hell. It seems so redundant.

I woke in the arms of the beast.

I smelled it first—the cloyingly sweet odor of putrefying flesh. Then the powerful arms locked around me, hugging me from behind, like Dobrogeanu had embraced Gravois on the tenement stairs. The floor upon which we sprawled was hard and cold; the air was musty and basement-damp. I had a sense of gaping space, like a subterranean cave deep in the belly of the earth.

Ambient light surrounded us; I could not discern its source. Then I thought, *Its eyes. The light is coming from its eyes.* I could hear my breath and I could hear its breath, and its breath was as foul as the grave. Its mouth must have been very close to my ear; I could hear every swipe of its tongue across its chapped and bleeding lips. When it spoke, thick spittle dripped from its swollen, blubbery tongue, landed on my exposed neck and soaked into my collar. The tongue fumbled clumsily the simplest words, as if the thinking part of its brain had atrophied from disuse.

"What is our name?"

"You're . . . you're Dr. Chanler."

"*What . . . is . . . our . . . name?*"

My legs were jerking uncontrollably. In a moment my bladder would let go. My bowels would empty.

"I don't know . . . I don't know your name."

"*Gudsnuth neshk. . . .* That's a good boy."

Something very cold and very sharp pressed into the soft flesh beneath my ear. I felt my skin split open and the heat of my blood as it welled over the lip of the wound.

"It won't hurt much," it blubbered. "Not very muh-uch. But the blood; there'll be a lot of bluh-duh. . . . We have been inter-eshted in the eyes. . . ." It paused, hiccupping for breath. Talking taxed it. A starving animal has no energy to waste.

"You are study-aying to be a shy-ent-tish, Will. Do you want to purr-form a shy-ent-tish-ist experiment-ed? Here ish our idea. We will pull your eye-shh out and turn them round so you can look at yourself. We never see ourselves the way we truly are, do we, Will? The mirror *lies* to us."

Its arm was like an iron bar across my chest. My eyes had adjusted to the light, and now I could see its spindly naked legs splayed on either side of mine. The skin was jet black, as black as charcoal, the skin peeling off in thin curling sheets.

"Hold out your hah-and."

"Please." I started to sob. "Please."

I held out my hand. Its gift to me was small—it fit perfectly in my palm—around the size of a plum, the surface rubbery and slightly sticky.

"Thish one's yours . . ."

My body convulsed with revulsion—it was the heart of the baby I'd left in the tenement hall. I flung it away with a strangled cry.

"Repul . . . repuh-puh . . . repushiv child. Wayshful."

It pressed its drooling mouth against my ear. "*What have we given?*" Its arm tightened around my chest, constricting my lungs; I could not breathe. "*What have we given?*"

I couldn't speak. I had no air with which to speak. I could no nothing but rock my head an inch from side to side.

"What . . . what ish . . ." It seemed to be having as much trouble breathing as I. "What ish the greatesh love? What dush it look like?"

The arm relaxed a bit. I gulped air choked in the swill of the beast's decay. My head lolled forward. The beast yanked it back by a fistful of my hair; its sharp, jagged nails cut into my scalp.

"Do you want to shee its faysh, Will? Then, look at ush. *Look at ush.*"

It dug its claw into my chin and rotated my face around until my neck popped. The proximity of its face skewed my perspective; there was a moment before my mind could absorb what I was seeing. I perceived it in fragmented strobe-like images. The first image was of the huge eyes burning a sickly amber, then the slobbering mouth, the bloodstained chin. Most striking was the *flatness* of its features, as if all underlying bone had receded into its head. It was the lack of contours that kept me from recognizing it at first; so much of our looks are ordained by our bones.

But I had seen this face many times—by the gentle caresses of a fire's glow, by the cool winter light of a November afternoon, by the shimmering brightness of a chandelier in a ballroom where she had danced with me, her emerald eyes—now smoldering fiendish orange—filled with promise, overflowing with abundance.

The beast had taken her face. On top of the steaming pile of human and animal wreckage, he had shaved it off and had somehow affixed it over the decimated remnants of his own.

"See ush, Will? Thish is the faysh of love."

I whipped my head from its grasp; its nails tore open the soft flesh beneath my chin. I heard it sucking my blood from its fingers.

"You have promish, Will. Good, good apprentish. We think we'll make you ours. Would you like to be our apprentish? Such a good start with that baby . . ."

Something was tugging on my shirtfront. I felt a button pop loose, then another, and then the cold of steel against my bare skin—or *was* it steel? Did the beast press a knife into the scar that had been made by its teeth in the wilderness, or was it its nails, grown as sharp as a hawk's talon? I could not bring myself to look.

"Ish so indesh-sker-ibal," it whimpered. "You wayshful lil' shit, you threw it away, our gift. You don't know. But ish delyshful. You bite it when ish still *beating*, and it pumpsh the blood, woosh, woosh, into your mouth. . . ."

I could feel the skin parting, the warm trickle of blood, and then a fingertip worming its way into the wound. My heart thundered inches away from its probing digit.

"Indesh-sker-ibal . . . ," it blubbered hungrily into my ear. "Like sucking on your per-esh-sish muf-ther's teat—"

It stopped. Its breath huffed in my ear. Its body became stock still. It had heard him calling to me: "Will Henry! Will Henreeeee!"

It was the doctor.

The beast flung me away as if I weighed no more than a ragdoll, and it fled the chamber with inconceivable speed. I slammed into a wall and crumpled to the floor, where I lay for a moment, too stunned from the force of the impact to move. I sobbed aloud, unable to speak above a tiny choking whisper.

"Dr. . . . Dr. Warthrop . . . it's coming. . . . *It's coming.*"

I crawled across the floor, groping blindly in the dark. I found a wall and used it to push myself up. I stumbled forward, but it was as if the tenebrous air pushed back; I moved with all the speed of a bather wading in heavy surf. A feeble glow had appeared before me, enough that I could see the outline of the chamber doorway. I lunged through it. I found myself in a narrow hall. Lining the walls were stacks of boxes and wooden crates embossed with the words "SASM—New York."

It had carried me to the spiritual home of Warthrop's mistress. It had brought me to the Monstrumarium.

The glow came from the lamps of my would-be rescuers, beacons that beckoned me out of the darkness, and now I ran, if a lurching stagger could be called that, careening off the slick walls and slamming into the listing towers of boxes, which toppled to the floor behind me. I could raise my voice only to the level of a hoarse whisper. "It's coming. . . . It's coming. . . ."

My toe caught on the edge of a crate. I pitched forward, meeting the concrete with my forehead. The ground seemed to open up beneath me and I was falling, falling, crying his name, or perhaps only screaming it in my head.

It's coming. It's coming!

I felt someone's hand upon my shoulder. Brilliant light brighter than a thousand suns rushed up to blind me, and I wasn't falling anymore. The doctor was pulling me up.

He gathered me into his arms and whispered my name fiercely. I tried to warn him. I tried. I knew the words. I heard them in my head. *It's coming.* But the ability to speak was lost.

"Where is he, Will Henry? Where is John?"

When I didn't answer, he raised his head and called out, "Here! I have found him! Over here!"

He turned back to me. "Is he here, Will Henry? Is John here?"

I looked over his shoulder and saw, through the face of his beloved, the yellow eye looking back down at me. The beast towered behind the doctor; the top of its head brushed the ceiling. Like an angry child flinging a broken toy, it reached down with its enormous claw, seized my master by the nape of the neck, and hurled him down the corridor.

Warthrop landed on his back with a startled grunt. He brought up his revolver, but did not fire. As to why he didn't, I can only conjecture. Out of the wilderness he had borne his friend; through unimaginable suffering and sacrifice he had carried John Chanler home. How could he now end that life he had given so much to save? Would not pulling that trigger negate everything the doctor believed in? Indeed, would it not prove von Helrung correct in the most fundamental sense— prove that love itself is the beast that devours all mankind?

The blackened wreckage that was John Chanler smacked the gun from the doctor's hand with such velocity that the act painted an afterimage upon my eyes. It yanked him close so that he might see clearly what both Muriel and John had given him and what he had given them in return. *This is the face of love.*

Then it pressed their mouths to his.

In the next second I was upon it, the silver-plated knife in my hand. I thrust the blade to the hilt into the thin neck. The beast shrugged me off its back as easily as a man flicks off a bit of lint from his coat. The doctor thrashed beneath it; one ebony claw was clamped over the doctor's nose and eyes while it pressed its mouth tightly against the doctor's mouth. The beast was smothering him with its kiss.

I leapt again onto the thing's back, von Helrung's words echoing in my ears: *Silver—by bullet or knife—to the heart. Only the heart!*

I swung my arms around in a ludicrous parody of its earlier embrace of me, and plunged the silver blade again and again into its heaving chest.

Its skeletal form jerked; behind Muriel's lips the bloody mouth came open in an animal squeal of pain. The beast rose, throwing me free, and then fell away. It rose again, collapsed, and curled into a mewling fetal ball.

Welling with pain and yearning, the yellow eyes sought out mine. I brought the blade high over my head, and beneath the human mask something inside the beast remembered, and John Chanler smiled. His heart rose up to meet the orgasmic thrust.

"God damn it!" The doctor's voice thundered in my ears. "God damn it, *why?*"

He shoved me aside and gathered his attacker into his lap, and now the thing appeared pitifully small and frail, nothing like the giant wraith of just a moment before. With one hand the monstrumologist compressed the wound; the blood, as black as tar in the weak light, pulsed between his fingers with each beat of the dying man's heart. Then Warthrop gently peeled off the overlaid face of the one they both had loved, and stared into the unseeing eyes of the one he thought he had brought out of the desolation. But he hadn't brought him out. The desolation was within him.

"No, no, no," Pellinore Warthrop protested, the impotent human cry.

TWENTY-NINE

"The Gift Was Mine to Give"

On the last Friday of the colloquium, my master rose from his chair, the chamber became still, and a hundred of his colleagues leaned forward in their seats, waiting with bated breath to hear his reply to von Helrung, upon which the future of their discipline hung in the balance. If he should fail, monstrumology would be doomed. It would never be accepted as a legitimate line of inquiry; its practitioners would henceforward and forever be perceived as laughing-stocks, eccentric pseudoscientists on the fringes of "real" science.

Von Helrung had presented a compelling case, rework-ing his original paper to incorporate his star witness, the "indispensable proof," as he called it—one William James Henry, special assistant to the chief spokesman for the oppos-ing side!

I had expected the doctor's presentation to be as awkward as his practice of it had been, tortured in its logic, inconsistent in its arguments—and I was not disappointed. It was painful to listen to, but everyone listened politely. The real show was to follow, the question and answer period, during which Warthrop would have to yield the floor.

Von Helrung posed the first question immediately upon the conclusion of Warthrop's reply.

"I thank my dear friend and former pupil, the honorable Dr. Warthrop, for his cogent and entirely earnest response. I am flattered—indeed, I am humbled—to be the recipient of such an impassioned—may I say, even *passionate*—reply. I have taught him well, have I not?"

He joined in their nervous laughter.

"But I do have one or two questions before I yield the floor, if that suits the honorable doctor? Thank you. I know the hour grows late; we have trains to catch; we long for our homes and families and, of course, our work . . . and we have friends to bury. Alas! Such is our lot. Such is the price we pay for the advancement of human knowledge. Dr. Gravois understood this, and accepted it. We all accept it. Even John . . ." His voice broke. "Even John accepted it.

"But I digress. To my question, then, Dr. Warthrop, *mein Freund*. If your hypothesis is correct in this most strange and pathetic episode, how do you explain the testimony of your own apprentice regarding the nature of the beast?"

"I have explained it already," replied the doctor tightly.

Though the swelling of his jaw had receded somewhat, it still pained him to speak. "The evidence is as plain as the wound on his neck."

"Ah, by that you mean the bite of the *Allghoi khorkhoi*, which he suffered prior to the events to which he has this day testified?"

"I mean precisely that. The effects of the creature's venom have been well documented, by some of the very people who now sit in this room."

"But it is my understanding that the good Adolphus Ainsworth administered to him the anti-venom within minutes of the exposure."

"Equally supported in the literature," said the doctor through gritted teeth, "is the tendency of the victim to suffer lingering, intermittent aftereffects, even *after* the administration of the antidote."

"So your explanation for Herr William Henry's testimony is that it was all a dream?" He was chuckling warmly.

"A hallucination would be more accurate."

"He did not hear the *Outiko* calling him upon the wind?"

"Of course not."

"And the *Outiko* did not remove him to the Monstrumarium by riding with him upon that wind?"

"I would ask you, and all members present, to close your eyes and imagine such a scenario."

There was a smattering of applause. A point scored by Warthrop.

"Then, how do you propose he brought him there from that tenement cellar? Did he hail a taxi?"

Now laughter, much louder than the tepid applause. A point for von Helrung.

"I propose he carried him there."

"On foot."

"Yes, of course. Under the cover of darkness."

"I see." Von Helrung was nodding with mock gravity. "Now turning your attention to the first incident, Dr. Warthrop. It is your contention that the creature—"

"John. His name was John."

"Yes, it did used to be John."

"It was *always* John."

"It is your contention that he jumped through a fourth-story hospital window—"

"It is my contention that he escaped through that window. Whether he went up a drainpipe or down it, he escaped. He did not 'take to the high wind' as you suggest, unless he sprouted wings, which I suppose you will say he did."

"And as to the other eyewitness accounts—what do you say to them?" The old Austrian held up the stack of sworn affidavits. "Are they also unfortunate victims of the Death Worm?"

Warthrop grimaced through the attendant laughter, waiting for it to die away before saying, "I can't say what they suffer from except perhaps a form of mass hysteria exacerbated by an overzealous press eager to sell newspapers."

"So you would have this august assembly reject the sworn testimony of seventy-three eyewitnesses based upon . . . what? What, Dr. Warthrop? Based upon the fact that since *you* say it can't be so, it can't be so? Is this not the very thing of which you accuse me? Assuming facts not in evidence?"

"I don't accuse you of assuming facts not in evidence. I accuse you of making them up out of whole cloth."

"Very well, then!" von Helrung cried, throwing the papers down with a dramatic flourish. "Tell me—enlighten all of us, good doctor—what killed Pierre Larose? What stripped him of his skin and fed upon his heart and impaled him upon a pole? What dragged Sergeant Jonathan Hawk forty feet into the sky and crucified him upon the highest tree? What did our beloved colleague find in the desolation that did *this* to him?" He flung his hand toward the autopsy table, where the body lay exposed under the harsh glare of the stage lights.

"I don't think," said the doctor deliberately, "that he found anything at all." He rose from his chair. I fought the instinct to rush to his side. He looked on the verge of collapse.

"I don't know who killed Pierre Larose. It may have been the natives in an act of superstitious dread. It may have been a disgruntled creditor or someone to whom he owed a gambling debt. Perhaps John himself did it after he had succumbed to whatever demon possessed him. I doubt anyone will ever know. As for Hawk . . . clearly a case of bush fever. I ask what is a better explanation—that something dropped him from above or that he climbed that tree? A boy half his size climbed it. Why couldn't he?"

He turned his head toward the body of his friend, and then turned away again.

"And John . . . I suppose that is the crux of it, isn't it? What happened to John Chanler? You would make a monster of him, and I suppose one could call him that. I do not deny his crimes. I do not say he suffered horribly from something I little understand. The key being . . . Well, I suppose I am the sole gardener on earth who is ignorant of the seeds he plants. But I will say"—and here the monstrumologist's voice became hard—"I will say he did his best to meet all our expectations. You wanted him to be a monster, and he obliged you, didn't he, *Meister* Abram? He exceeded your wildest dreams. We do strive to become what others see in us, don't we?

"I tried to save him. From the beginning I was willing to lay down my life for him, for there is no love greater than this . . ."

He stopped, overwhelmed. I rose to go to him. He waved me back.

"He asked me 'What have we given?' I do not pretend to know all that he meant by that, but I know this much: It shall not stand. I will not allow it to stand. You will *not* desecrate his body as you desecrated his memory. *That* is what I can give him. That is all I can give him. I will bury my friend, and I swear I will kill the man who tries to stop me."

He swung his eyes to the crowd, and the crowd could not return his righteous glare.

"Take your vote now. I will answer no more of your questions."

The doctor and I retired to our private box while the vote was taken. It would be, at von Helrung's request, by secret ballot. Warthrop lay across the divan, arms folded over his chest, head upon the armrest. He stared up at the ornate ceiling and refused to watch the vote.

The silence between us was not of the comfortable variety. Since the death of Chanler, he'd barely spoken to me. When he looked at me, I detected that he was more confounded than angry. The affair had begun with his firm conviction that his friend had been past all salvation—and had ended with the equally steadfast belief that he would save him. That the doctor's faith had been shattered by me, the last soul on earth bound to him in any way, seemed beyond his ability to comprehend.

So it was with no small amount of courage that I decided to breach the wall he had erected between us.

"Dr. Warthrop, sir?"

He took a deep breath. He closed his eyes. "Yes, Will Henry, what is it?"

"How did—I'm sorry, sir, but I've been wondering—how did you know to look for me in the Monstrumarium?"

"How do you think?"

"Someone must have seen us?"

He shook his head; his eyes remained closed. "Try again."

"Dr. Dobrogeanu—he followed us there?"

"No. He returned straightaway to von Helrung's after he discovered you missing."

"Then you must have guessed," I concluded. It was the only explanation.

"No, I did not guess. I applied the lesson from the Chanler house massacre. What was that lesson, Will Henry?"

Though I gave it my best effort, I could think of nothing instructional in that horrific scene, except the sickening macabre stab at humor scrawled above the bedroom door: *Life is.*

"John himself told me where to find you," the monstrumologist explained. "Just as he tried to tell me where to find Muriel. After Dobrogeanu brought us the news, I realized at once where he had taken you. Don't you remember what he said? 'He'll put you on display in the Beastie Bin, where all you nasty things belong.'" He opened his eyes and, raising his head a bit, peeked over the railing. "Hmm. They're taking their time. I wonder if that's good or bad." He lay down again. "They found the Nováková girl, by the way, at the bottom of the sludge, once they drained the cellar."

I knew she was not the only victim who'd been found in that cellar. He noted my troubled expression and said, "There was nothing you could have done, Will Henry."

And I answered, "That is what I did, sir. Nothing."

"Your guilt serves no purpose. Will it resurrect the child or change the past? You did exactly what I would have done—what anyone would have done in the circumstance. Suppose you had picked up the child and left. How many more victims might have fallen that night because of your misplaced altruism? There are hard choices to be made in life, Will Henry, and monstrumology has more than its fair share of them."

He waited for me to respond. He knew I would agree; I always agreed with him. *If the house were on fire and I told you to throw gasoline upon it to quench the flames, you would cry, 'Yes, sir! Yes, sir!' and blow us both to kingdom come!*

"I should have saved him," I said.

"Saved him? Saved him from what? You had no idea at the time if John was in that building."

"I should have saved him," I repeated.

"Very well. Assume for a moment you did. And assume you managed to find to whom he belonged. And now you may assume he would not live to see his first birthday regardless, for those are the odds, Will Henry; that is the grim fact of the ghetto. You would have saved him from one monster only to deliver him to another no less murderous."

I shook my head. "I should have saved him," I said a third time.

His face grew red; his dark eyes flashed. He was not prepared, perhaps, for my obsequious response to his demand that I become less obsequious!

"*Why?*" he demanded.

"Because I could have," I answered.

They were laid to rest side by side, my master's two loves, in the Chanler family plot, for the father of the most wayward son is a father still. The elder Chanler did not speak to Warthrop, except for a few threatening words upon the conclusion of the graveside service, to the effect that he intended to strip him down to his last piece of silver. Warthrop's reply: "Seems only just, but I beg you to leave me at least my microscope."

Von Helrung was in attendance, as well as several other monstrumologists, including the survivors of the hunting party. Dobrogeanu shook my hand gravely and pronounced the doctor fortunate to have found a most resourceful and brave assistant.

Lilly had come along too. I was never sure how she'd managed to arrange it, but she hopped out of the hansom wearing a black dress with a matching black ribbon in her curls, and during the service she sat next to me, at one point pulling my hand into hers. I did not try to pull it away.

"So you are leaving," she said. "Was it your plan to leave without saying good-bye?"

"I serve the doctor," I answered. "I have no plans of my own."

"I think that is the most pitifully tragic thing I've ever heard anyone say. Will you miss me?"

"Yes."

"You're just saying that. You won't really miss me."

"I will miss you."

"Are you planning to kiss me good-bye? Oh, sorry. Is your doctor planning for you to kiss me good-bye?"

I smiled. "I shall ask him."

She wanted to know when she would see me again. Would she have to wait a whole year? "Unless the doctor's business brings us here sooner," I answered.

"Well, I can't promise you anything, Will," she said. "I may be entirely too busy to fit you in. I will be dating in a year, and I expect my calendar will be quite *full*." Her eyes danced merrily. "*Are* you coming back for the next congress? Or will your doctor leave the Society now that he's lost his little vote?"

It was true. The doctor had failed. Von Helrung's resolution had passed by the narrowest of margins, sounding, to Warthrop's mind at least, the death knell of monstrumology. He might soldier on in exile, a solitary vessel of reason in a sea of superstition—but what would be his reward? What meager solace could he take in his principles when the one thing he'd lived for had been snatched away in the space of an hour?

He took the news as hard as I'd expected—though his reaction took me completely by surprise.

"I have committed a grievous error, Will Henry," the doctor confessed on the eve of our departure for home. "But unlike yours in the tenement, mine can be rectified. It is not too late."

His face glowed beneficently in the eldritch autumn light eking through the window that overlooked the park. He spoke with the firmness of one who had perceived his way with untarnished clarity.

"John asked a question of me before he died, a question to which I had no answer: *What have we given?* I must admit, I am not the kind of man to whom a question like that makes sense. To me, it was just another bit of his gibberish. Your father understood, though, and paid the highest price for his gift. You see, Will Henry, it is not *what* we give but what we are *willing* to give. What we can give.

"You abandoned that child in the hall. The gift was within your power, and you withheld your hand. You cannot take that back now, any more than your father can take back his gift to me. But I am not so helpless. I have a choice still—to answer John's question."

He drew close to me. "I have lost—everything. John. Muriel. Even my work, the one thing that has given me solace through the lonely years—even that I have lost. You are all that's left for me, Will Henry, and I fear I will lose you, too."

"I'll never leave you, sir," I said. And I believed it. "Never."

"You do not understand. Tell me again why you should have saved that child in the hallway."

"Because I could have."

He nodded. "And I will save you, Will Henry. Because I can. *That* is the answer to John's question."

I understood then. I backed away on unsteady legs. The room began to spin around me.

"You're sending me away," I said.

"You nearly died," he reminded me. "Three times by my count. If you remain with me, eventually your luck will run out, just like your father's did. I cannot allow that to happen."

"No!" I shouted. My voice shook with rage. "That isn't why you're doing it. You're sending me away because I killed him!"

"Don't raise your voice to me, Will Henry," he cautioned in a level voice.

"You're angry and you want to punish me for it! For saving your life! I saved your life!" I could hardly contain my fury. "She was right about you—they were both right! You're a terrible man. You're nothing but a . . . You're full of nothing but yourself, and you don't know anything! You don't know anything about . . . about *anything!*"

"I know this," he roared back at me, no longer able to contain his temper. "She would be alive now if not for me. The gift was mine to give, and I withheld it—I withheld it!" His face was contorted with self-loathing. He struck his breast like a penitent before the sacrificial altar. "I allowed her to go home—when I knew, I *knew* she was in danger. I turned away just as *you* turned away, Will Henry, and what happened? Tell me what happens when we turn away!"

He fell backward onto the sofa, the place where he had

tasted, for the briefest of moments, the love he had denied himself by that plunge into the Danube years before.

"Oh, Will Henry," he cried. "Aren't we the pitiful pair? What did Fiddler say? 'What he loves does not know him, and what he knows cannot love.' He was talking about you, but he might as well have been talking about both of us." He raised his eyes to me. He seemed so lost, so hopelessly bereft that I stepped toward him in spite of myself.

"Don't send me away, sir. Please."

He raised his hand. He let it fall. "Life is," he murmured. "John filled in that blank, didn't he? John gave his answer— but is it *the* answer, Will Henry? *Meister* Abram claims we are more than what's reflected in the Yellow Eye, but are we? I carried him the entire way—we almost died, you and I, to bring him out of the wilderness—so he might kill the only woman I have ever loved."

I sat beside him. "That isn't why you brought him out."

He gave a little wave of his hand, dismissing my effort to comfort him. "And the baby died. That isn't the reason you turned aside. My question remains, Will Henry. Is John's answer *the* answer?"

I shook my head. I don't think he expected me to decipher a riddle that had plagued humankind from its infancy. I am not sure to this day what he expected of me.

Or what I expected of him. We were indeed a pitiful pair, the monstrumologist and I, bound to each other in ways inexplicable to both of us. In the Monstrumarium the beast had forced me to turn and behold "the true face" of love. But love has more than one face, and the Yellow Eye is not the only eye. There can be no desolation without abundance. And the voice of the beast is not the only voice that rides upon the high wind. It was there in every weary step the doctor took in the wilderness. It was there the night he gathered me into his arms to keep me from freezing to death. It was there in Muriel's eyes the night their shadows met and became one. It is always there, like the hunger that can't be satisfied, though the tiniest sip is more satisfying than the most sumptuous of feasts.

I reached across the space that separated us—no farther than a foot and wider than the universe—and gathered the monstrumologist's hand into mine.

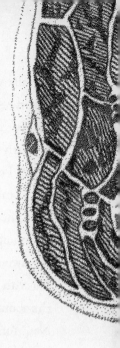

EPILOGUE

November 2009

None of the famous personages mentioned in the journals (Thomas Edison, Algernon Blackwood, Bram Stoker, Henry Irving, John Pemberton, Alexandre-Gustave Eiffel, Thomas Byrnes, and Jacob Riis) ever wrote or spoke publicly of anyone named Pellinore Warthrop or anything remotely resembling the science of monstrumology. This fact, of course, doesn't prove that these real people from the era did not know Warthrop; however, if they did, it is very odd that they never mentioned him or his esoteric "philosophy." For example, nowhere have I found any indication that Stoker based his Van Helsing character upon a "real" doctor named von Helrung.

It was Blackwood's story, published in 1910, that put the Wendigo on the map and established Blackwood as a popular writer of the horror genre. I have found no evidence that the story was inspired or in any way derived from Will Henry's account in the fourth folio, but that interpretation is clearly intended, based on the meeting at the Zeno Club, which I could find no record of having existed either.

A careful search of newspaper archives yielded nothing from the time period beyond the articles reproduced at the beginning of this book. I was unable to find any mention, under Blackwood's byline or anyone else's, of the murders described in the sixth folio. No mention of the name Chanler and no stories about an American Ripper running amok on the streets of New York. This part of Will Henry's story—the scene where he mentions the newspaper clippings in the von Helrung library—is undeniably fictional. A scandal involving a prominent New York family certainly would have been covered by the newspapers of the day. And if *that* isn't true, the entire record must be called into question ... but did I ever really have any doubt the journals were a work of fiction?

Frustrated in my efforts to corroborate their contents, I turned to the journals themselves. I contacted an expert in handwriting analysis based in Gainesville at the University of Florida, who was kind enough to take a look at the material. His report contained the following observations:

> Author has received formal schooling, at least
> through secondary schools, perhaps some
> college ...

Author is extremely meticulous, with anal-
retentive tendencies. Would probably be
extremely neat in appearance, fastidious to a
fault, particular about the way he looks and is
perceived by others . . .

Author may be suffering from certain personality
disorders, but it is highly doubtful, given the
coherence of the text, that he is afflicted with
schizophrenia or any other serious mental
disease. Unlikely he was delusional.

Author loves habit, routine, predictability.
Would be extremely uncomfortable in alien
surroundings. Shy, introverted, a "feeler and
thinker," not a "doer."

The report went on to speculate that Will Henry suffered from arthritis, may have been bipolar, and may have
been alone or without companionship for long periods of
time. The part about his being meticulous in his appearance
I found particularly poignant, given his condition when he
was discovered in the drainage ditch, covered in filth, dressed
in ratty clothes, with a matted beard and long, knotted hair.
What had happened to bring a man like him to that point?
The other striking thing about the report, to my mind, was
the assertion that it was "unlikely he was delusional."

Wendigos. Mongolian Death Worms. An organism that
secretes some kind of enzyme that gives its host unnaturally long

life. And it is unlikely this person was delusional? Hand-writing analysis is as much art as it is science; still, at first I found that statement confounding, to put it mildly.

On further reflection, though, it makes sense under the theory that Will Henry (or whoever he was) was a writer of fiction. One can write fiction—it is possible, I hear—and not be delusional. Fiction itself could be characterized as highly organized delusional thinking. Simply because the author *wrote* about the life of someone named Will Henry doesn't make the story *his* life.

My hope is that the publication of these journals, as with the first three, may generate a lead. As the director of the nursing home told me in the beginning, everyone has someone. Someone out there knows who this person was. Perhaps not under the name William James Henry, but someone knows him. One day I hope to open up an e-mail or get a phone call from that person, and at last I'll have some answers. After I finished reading this latest set of diaries, it occurred to me that Will Henry had found himself at the end of his life's journey in that desolation he—and his enigmatic master—had found so terrifying. Perhaps my quest, if one could call it that, is more about *bringing* him out than *finding* him out. Perhaps by discovering who he was and to whom he belongs, I can bring Will Henry home.

Here's a glimpse of **THE ISLE OF BLOOD,**
the next adventure of the monstrumologist.

An old friend of Dr. Warthrop's comes asking him for
help to track down Warthrop's colleague, the
sociopathic Dr. John Kearns. At first, Warthrop is
reluctant—but soon, evidence suggests that Kearns
may be in possession of information leading to a
creature widely regarded as the "Holy Grail of
monstrumology," an organism so rare and elusive
that it has never been killed or captured or even
observed in the wild.

Dr. Warthrop can't resist, and soon he and Will
Henry are off on another hellish quest, this time
to the bizarre island of Socotra, home to some of
the strangest flora and fauna in the world. On
Socotra, Will Henry will come face-to-face with
the most horrific creature yet and just may pay the
ultimate price for his master's ambition.

"A Very Dangerous Poison"

It began on a freezing February night in 1889 with the arrival of a package to the house on Harrington Lane. The delivery was unexpected but not unusual. Having been an apprentice to the monstrumologist for almost three years, I was accustomed to the midnight knock upon the back door, the furtive exchange of the portage charge, and the doctor like a boy on Christmas morn, his cheeks ablaze with feverish anticipation as he bore his present to the basement laboratory, where the box was unwrapped and its foul contents revealed in all their macabre glory. What was unusual about this particular delivery was the man who brought it. In the course of my service to the monstrumologist, I had seen my fair share of unsavory characters, men who for a dollar and a dram of whiskey would sell their own mothers, willing mercenaries in service to the natural science of aberrant biology.

But this was not the sort who stood shivering in the alleyway that night. Though bedraggled from a journey of many miles, he wore an expensive fur-lined coat that hung open to reveal a tailored suit. A diamond ring glittered on the little finger of his left hand. More striking than his regalia was his manner; the poor fellow seemed nearly mad with panic. He abandoned his cargo on the back stoop, pushed his way into the room, seized the doctor by his lapels and demanded to know if he had found number 425 and if he— the doctor—was Pellinore Warthrop.

"I am Dr. Warthrop," said my master.

"Oh, thank God! Thank God!" the tormented man cried in a hoarse voice. "Now I've done it—it's right out there— take it, take it—I've brought you the blasted thing, now give it to me! He said you would—he said you had it—quickly, before it's too late!"

"My good man," replied the doctor calmly. "I would gladly pay the charge, if the price is reasonable." Though he was a man of substantial means, the monstrumologist's parsimony soared to near operatic heights.

"The price? The price!" The man laughed hysterically. "It isn't you who'll pay, Warthrop! He said you had it—he promised you would give it to me if I brought it—now keep his promise!"

"Whose promise?"

Our uninvited guest let loose a banshee howl and doubled over, clutching his chest. His eyes rolled back into his head. The doctor caught him before he hit the floor and eased him into a chair.

"Damn him to hell—too late!" the man whimpered. "I am too late!" He wrung his hands in supplication. "Am I too late, Dr. Warthrop?"

"I cannot answer that question," replied the doctor. "For I have no idea what you're talking about."

"He told me you would give me the antidote if I brought it, but I was delayed in New York—I missed the train and had to wait for the next one— more than two hours I had to wait— oh, God! To come all this way only to die at the end of it!"

"The antidote? The antidote to what?"

"To the poison! 'Bring my little gift to Warthrop in America if you wish to live,' he told me, the devil, the fiend! So I have and so you *must*. Ah, but it is hopeless. I feel it now—my heart—my heart—"

The doctor shook his head sharply and with a snap of his fingers directed me to fetch his instrument case.

"I will do all within my power," I heard him say to the poor man as I scampered off. "But you must get a grip on yourself and tell me simply and plainly . . ."

Our tormented courier had fallen into a swoon by the time I returned, eyes rolling in his head, hands twitching in his lap. His face had drained of all color. The doctor removed the stethoscope from the case and listened to the man's heart, bending low over his quivering form, his legs spread wide for balance.

"Galloping like a runaway horse, Will Henry," the monstrumologist murmured. "But no abnormalities or irregularities that I can detect. Quickly, a glass of water."

I expected him to offer the distressed man a drink; instead Warthrop dumped the entire contents of the glass over his head. The eyes snapped open. The mouth formed a startled *O*.

"What sort of poison did he give you?" demanded my master in a stern voice. "Did he say? Answer!"

"Tip . . . tipota . . . from the pyrite tree . . ."

"Tipota?" The doctor frowned. "From what kind of tree?"

"Pyrite! Tipota, from the pyrite tree of the Isle of Demons!"

"The Isle of Demons! But that is . . . extraordinary. Are you quite certain?"

"Bloody hell, I think I would remember what he poisoned me with!" the man sputtered vehemently. "And he said *you* had the antidote! Oh! Oh! This is it!" His hands clawed at his chest. "My heart is exploding!"

"I don't think so," said the doctor slowly. He stepped back, studying the man carefully, dark eyes dancing with that eerie backlit fire. "We still have a few moments . . . but only a few! Will Henry, stay with our guest while I mix up the antidote."

"Then I am not too late?" the man inquired incredulously, as if he could not dare to allow himself to hope.

"When was the poison administered?"

"On the evening of the second."

"Of this month?"

"Yes, yes—of course this month! I would be dead as a doornail if it was last month, now wouldn't I!"

"Yes, forgive me. Tipota is slow acting, but not quite *that* slow acting! I shall be back momentarily. Will Henry, call me at once should our friend's condition change."

The doctor flew down the stairs to the basement, leaving the door slightly ajar. We could hear jars knocking against each other, the clink and clang of metal, the hiss of a Bunsen burner.

"What if he's wrong?" the man moaned. "What if it is too late? My eyesight is failing—that's what goes just before the end! You go blind and your heart blows apart—blows completely apart inside your chest. Your face, child—I cannot see your face! It is lost to the darkness. The darkness comes! Oh, may he burn for all eternity in the lowest circle of the pit—the devil—the fiend!"

The doctor bounded back into the room, carrying a syringe loaded with an olive-green colored liquid. The dying man jerked in the chair upon his entrance and cried out, "Who is that?"

"It is I, Warthrop," answered the doctor. "Let's get that coat off. Will Henry, help him please."

"You have the antidote?" the man asked.

The doctor nodded curtly, pulled up the man's sleeve and jabbed the needle home.

"There, now!" Warthrop said. "The stethoscope, Will Henry. Thank you." He listened to the man's heart for a few seconds, and I thought it must be a trick of the light, for I spied what appeared to be a smile playing on the doctor's lips. "Yes. Slowing considerably. How do you feel?"

A bit of color had returned to his cheeks and his breathing had slowed. Whatever the doctor had given him was having a salutary effect. He spoke hesitantly, as if he could hardly believe his good fortune. "Better—I think. My eyesight is clearing a bit."

"Good! You may be relieved to know that . . . ," the monstrumologist began, and then stopped himself. It had occurred to him, perhaps, that the man had already suffered enough distress. "It is a very dangerous poison. Always fatal, slow-acting and symptom-free until the end, but its effects are entirely reversible if the antidote is administered in time."

"He said you would know what to do . . ."

"I'm quite certain he did. Tell me, however did you come by the acquaintance of Dr. John Kearns?"

Our guest's eyes widened in astonishment. "However did you know his name?"

"There is only one man I know—and who knows me—who would play such a fiendish prank."

"*Prank?* Poisoning a man, hurling him to the threshold of death's doorway for the purpose of delivering a *package*—that's a prank to you?"

"Yes!" the doctor cried, forgetting himself—and what this suffering soul had been through—for a moment. "The package! Will Henry, carry it down to the basement and put on a pot for tea. I'm sure Mister—"

"Kendall. Wymond Kendall."

"Mr. Kendall could do with a cup, I think. Snap to now, Will Henry, I suspect we're in for a long night."

The package, a wooden box wrapped in plain brown paper, was not particularly heavy or cumbersome. I toted it quickly to the laboratory, placed it on the doctor's worktable and returned upstairs to find the kitchen empty. I could hear the rise and fall of their voices coming from the parlor down the hall while I made the tea, my thoughts a confusion of dreadful anticipation and disquieted memory. It hadn't been quite a year since my first encounter with the man named Jack Kearns—if that was his name; he seemed to have more than one. Cory he had called himself, and Schmidt. There was one other name, the one he gave himself in the fall of the previous year, the one by which history would remember him, the one that best described his true nature. He was not a monstrumologist like my master. It was not clear to me then *what* he was, except an expert in the darker regions of the natural world—and of the human heart.

"He was renting a flat from me on Dorset Street in Whitechapel," I heard Kendall say. "He was not the usual kind of tenant one finds on the East End, and clearly he could afford better, but he told me he liked to be close to his work at the Royal London Hospital. He seemed very dedicated to his work. He told me he lived for nothing else. Do you know the funny thing is I liked him; I liked Dr. Kearns very much. He was quite the conversationalist . . . a marvelous, if slightly skewed, sense of humor . . . very well-read, and always on time with his rent—so when he came up two months' late I thought something must have happened to him. This is Whitechapel, after all. Dr. Kearns kept very late hours and I was afraid he might have been waylaid by ruffians—or worse. So more out concern for his welfare than the arrears, I decided to check up on him."

"I take it you found him well," offered the doctor.

"Oh, he was the picture of soundness and good cheer! The same old Kearns. Invited me in for a spot of tea as if nothing were remiss, told me he had been distracted lately by a particularly troublesome case, a yeoman with the British Navy who was suffering from some mysterious tropical fever, and seemed completely taken aback—though touched by—my concern for his welfare. When I brought up the matter of the rent, he expressed his mortification, blaming it on this case of his and assuring me I would have it, plus interest, by the end of the week. So soothed was I by his silver-tongued rationale and also a bit embarrassed to intrude upon his important work, I actually apologized for coming to collect what was rightfully mine. Oh, he is the devil's own progeny, this Dr. John Kearns!"

"He has a way with words," the doctor allowed. "Among other things. Ah, but here is Will Henry with the tea."

The monstrumologist was standing by the mantel when I entered, running a finger contemplatively up and down the nose of the bust of the ancient Greek philosopher Zeno. Our guest reclined on the divan, his lean face still flushed from his ordeal. He reached for his cup with a quivering hand.

"The tea," he murmured. "It must have been the tea."

"The medium for the poison?" asked the doctor.

"No! That he injected once I had come to my senses."

"Ah, you mean he slipped you some sort of sleeping draught...."

"That must have been the case. There can be no other explanation. I thanked him for tea—oh, how he must have relished my appreciation!—and was no more than two steps from the door when the room began to spin and all went black. When I awoke, many hours had passed—night had fully come on—and there he was beside me, smiling ghoulishly.

"'You've had a bit of a spell,' he said.

"'I fear so,' said I. I felt utterly drained and entirely helpless, emptied of all vitality. Just turning my head to look at him required every ounce of strength in my body.

"'Lucky for you it struck in the presence of a doctor!' he observed with a perfectly straight face. 'I thought something was the matter when I first saw you, Kendall. A bit green around the gills. Of course, you've probably been working too hard exploiting the poor and downtrodden, collecting rents on hovels a rat would be ashamed to call home—a case of slumlord exhaustion is my guess. I would suggest you consider a holiday in the countryside. Get some fresh air. The atmosphere of these neighborhoods is absolutely putrid, infused as it is with the funk of human suffering and despair. Take a trip. A change of scenery would work wonders.'

"I protested vehemently these offensive remarks. I am no

slumlord, Dr. Warthrop. I provide a necessary service and only once or twice have I put someone out for not paying the rent. So complete was my outrage, I would have struck him for these repugnant jibes upon my character, but I could not raise my hand even an inch from the bed.

"'I am exceedingly glad you dropped by,' he went on in that maddeningly chipper tone of his. 'God himself must have sent you—God, or something very much like him. You see, I can't trust it to the mails and I can't go myself—I must take my leave of this blessed isle tomorrow—and finding a reliable courier in this milieu has proved more difficult than I anticipated. You simply cannot rely upon anyone from the ghetto , but I don't have to tell *you* that. And now here you are, Kendall! Delivered unto me like the best of presents—wholly satisfactory and completely unexpected. The answer to a prayer of a man who never prays! It is serendipitous to say the least, don't you think?'"

Kendall paused, sipped his tea, and stared silently for a moment into space. He possessed the haunted look of a man who had barely escaped a brush with Death's angel, which, literally, he had.

"Well, I will confess I didn't know what to think, Dr. Warthrop. What was I to think? In an instant and without warning, all my faculties had been stripped from me, and now I lay dizzy, my thoughts a blur, paralyzed upon his bed, with him leering down at me—what was a man to think?

"'It is a small matter,' he went on. 'A trifle, really. But it should be delivered sooner rather than later. If it is what I suspect it is and represents what I think it represents, he'll want it quickly. Delay might cost him the entire game and he would never forgive me.'

"'Who?' I asked. Understand, I was quite beside myself at this point, for it had at last dawned on me that *he* was the cause of my sudden and mysterious affliction. 'Who would never forgive you?'

"'Warthrop! Warthrop, of course. The monstrumologist. Now don't tell me you've never heard of him. He's a very dear friend of mine—you might call us brothers, in a spiritual sense of course, though we couldn't be more different from each other. He's entirely too serious, for one, and he possesses a curious romantic streak for someone who fancies himself a scientist. Has a savoir-complex, if you want my opinion. Wants to save the whole bloody world from itself, while my motto has always been "live-and-let-live." Why, the other day I killed a large spider, quite without thinking it through—and afterward I was consumed with remorse, for what had that spider ever done to me? What makes me, by virtue of my superior intellect and size, any better than my eight-legged flat-mate? I did not choose to be a man anymore than he chose to be a spider. Are we both not equal players in the grand design, each fulfilling the role given to us—until I violated the sacred covenant between us and the one who made us? It's enough to tear a man's soul in twain.'

"'You're mad,' I told him; I could not help myself.

"'To the contrary, my dear Kendall,' the monster replied. 'It is your great good fortune to be in the company of the sanest man alive. It has taken me years to rid myself of all delusion and pretense, the cloak of self-righteous superiority with which we humans drape ourselves. In this sense, the spider is *our* superior. He does not question his nature. He is not burdened by the sense of self. The mirror is nothing to him but a pane of glass. He is pure, as sinless as Adam before the fall—even Warthrop, that incorrigible moralist, would agree with me. I've no more right to kill the spider than you've to judge me. *You*, sir, are the Hare at this tea party; *I* am Alice.'

"He withdrew for a moment while I lay as if a two-ton boulder pressed down upon me, barely able to draw the next breath. When he returned, he was holding the syringe in his hand. I will confess, Dr. Warthrop, I'd never known fear like that—the room began to spin again, but not from any sleeping draught—from sheer terror. Helplessly I watched as he tapped the glass and pressed upon the plunger. A single drop clung to the needle's tip, glistening like the finest crystal in the lamplight.

"'Do you know what this is, Kendall?' he asked softly, and then he chuckled long and low. 'Of course you don't! I wax rhetorical. It's a very rare toxin distilled from the sap of the pyrite tree, an interesting example of one of the Creator's more maleficent flora, indigenous to a single island forty nautical miles from the Galapagos Archipelago, called the

Isle of Demons. I love that name, don't you? It's so . . . evocative. But now I wax poetical.'

"He drew close—so close I could see my own reflection in the dark, blank pools that were his eyes. Oh, those eyes! If I ever should see them again in a thousand years, it would be too soon! Blacker than the blackest pit, empty—*so* empty of . . . of *everything*, Dr. Warthrop. Not human. Not animal. Not *anything*.

"'It's called *tipota*,' he whispered. 'Remember that, Kendall! When Warthrop asks you what I've stuck you with, tell him that. Tell him, "It is tipota. He poisoned me with tipota!"'

My master was nodding gravely, but did I detect a hint of amusement in his eyes? I wondered what in this horrible tale the monstrumologist could find the least bit comical.

"He slipped a piece of paper into my pocket. Yes! Here it is; I still have it."

He held it up for the doctor to see.

"'Your address and the name of the poison, lest I forget it.' Forget it! As if I will ever forget that accursed name! He told me I had ten days. 'More or less, my dear Kendall.' More or less! He proceeded to lecture me—hovering there with that horrid needle glistening an inch from my nose—on how prized this poison was; how the Czar of Russia kept a stash of it in the royal safe; how it was valued by the ancients ('They say it was what *really* killed Cleopatra'); how it was the method of choice of assassins, preferred because it was so slow-acting, allowing the perpetrator to be miles away by the time the victim's heart exploded in his chest. That ghastly address was followed with an extended description of the poison's effects: loss of appetite, insomnia, restlessness, racing thoughts, palpitations, paranoid delusions, excessive perspiration, constipated bowel—in some cases— or diarrhea—in others. . . ."

The doctor nodded curtly. He had grown impatient. I knew what it was: the box. The package was pulling on him, beckoning him. Whatever Kearns had entrusted to this loquacious Englishman, it was valuable enough (at least in the monstrumological sense) to risk killing a man over its successful delivery.

"Yes, yes," Warthrop said. "I am familiar with the effects of tipota. As acquainted, if not as intimately, as—"

Now it was Kendall who interrupted, for he was more *there* than *here*, and ever would be, lying helpless upon Kearns's bed while the lunatic leaned over him, leering in the lamplight. I doubt the poor man ever fully escaped that dingy flat on London's East End, not in the truest sense. To his death, he remained a prisoner of that memory, a thrall in service to Dr. John Kearns.

"'Please,' I begged him. 'Please, for the love of God . . .!

"Ill-chosen words, Dr. Warthrop! At the mention of the Deity's name, his entire manner was transformed, as if I had profaned the Virgin herself. His ghoulish grin disappeared; the mouth drew down; the eyes narrowed.

"'For what, did you say?' he asked in a dangerous whisper. 'For God? Do you believe in God, Kendall? Are you praying to him now? How odd. Shouldn't you rather pray to me, since I now hold death literally an inch from your nose? Who has more power now—me or God? Before you answer, "God," think carefully, Kendall. If you are right, and I stab you with my needle, does that prove you right or wrong—and which answer would be worse? If right, then God surely favors me over you—in fact, he must despise you for your sin and I am merely his instrument. If wrong, then you pray to nothing.' He shook the needle in my face. '*Nothing!*' And then he laughed."

As if in counterpoint, he paused in his narration and cried bitter tears.

"And then he said, the foul beast, 'Why do men pray to God, Kendall? I've never understood it. God loves us. We are his creation, like my spider; we are his beloved . . . yet when faced with mortal danger we pray to him to spare us! Shouldn't we pray instead to the one who *would* destroy us, who has sought our destruction from the very beginning? What I mean to say is . . . aren't we praying to the wrong person? We should beseech the Devil, not God. Don't mistake me; I'm not telling you where to direct your supplications. I'm merely pointing out the fallacy of them—and perhaps hinting at the reason behind prayer's curious inefficaciousness.'

Kendall paused to angrily wipe clean his face, and said, "Well, I suppose you can guess what he did next."

"He injected you with tipota," tried my master. "And within a matter of seconds, you lost consciousness. When you awoke, Kearns was gone."

Our tormented guest was nodding. "And in his stead, the package."

"And you made straightaway to book your passage to America."

"I considered going to the police, of course . . ."

"But doubted they would believe such an extravagant tale."

"Or admitting myself into hospital . . ."

"Risking that they would not know the antidote for so rare a toxin."

"I had no choice but to do his bidding and hope he was telling the truth, which it seems he was, for I am feeling myself again. Oh, I cannot tell you what agony these last eight days have been, Dr. Warthrop! What if you were away? What if those two hours delayed in New York were two hours too much? What if he was wrong and you knew not the antidote?"